I0763335

Bonded Chaos

Book One of the Twisted Fates Duology

K.J. JOHNSON

K.J. Johnson Books

First published by K.J. Johnson Books 2025

Copyright © 2025 by K.J. Johnson

All rights reserved. No part of this publication may be reproduced, stored or transmitted in any form or by any means, electronic, mechanical, photocopying, recording, scanning, or otherwise without written permission from the publisher. It is illegal to copy this book, post it to a website, or distribute it by any other means without permission.

This novel is entirely a work of fiction. The names, characters, and incidents portrayed in it are the work of the author's imagination. Any resemblance to actual persons, living or dead, events or localities is entirely coincidental.

K.J. Johnson asserts the moral right to be identified as the author of this work.

Cover art: GhostDx

Cover design: K.J. Johnson

Dedication art: GhostDx

Character art: GhostDx

Chapter art: Creations by Kade

Map: T.K.J. Designs

Edited by: Reneé Black

ISBN: 978-1-7636825-7-3

Contents

Dedication

To all my Fire & Flame readers who thought they could fix Kieran, this one's for you.

Content Warning

Please be advised that Bonded Chaos is a dark fantasy romance and is intended for mature audiences only. It contains material that may be triggering or distressing for some readers.

The main male character is morally grey and he makes deeply questionable and at times, outright cruel choices, especially where the female main character is concerned.

You may love him, hate him, or find yourself frequently oscillating between the two. He is not a hero. He is an unapologetic villain and his actions may be disturbing, unsettling, and/or difficult to read. If you are looking for an easily redeemable love interest, a bad guy turned good, this may not be the book for you.

A full list of trigger warnings is included on the following page but please note, some do contain spoilers.

Reader discretion is strongly advised.

Your mental health matters.

TRIGGER WARNINGS

- Drugging
- Kidnapping
- Coercive control
- Extremely possessive/(OTT) jealous MMC
- Profanity
- Mentions of genocide
- Sexual assault
- Interference with birth control involving deception and lack of consent regarding reproductive choices
- Explicit sexual content including but not limited to:
- Degradation kink
- Primal play

- Breath play (choking)
- Impact play
- BDSM elements
- Rough sex
- Anal sex
- Dubious consent
- Blood and gore
- Depictions of violence
- Violence against a pregnant character (not between the main couple)

If you have any questions or concerns, or believe further trigger warnings are required, please feel free to reach out to me on any of my social media accounts or via my website.

If you have made it this far, thank you for reading and I hope you enjoy Ryker and Cadence's story.

Pronunciation Guide

- Cadence: Cay – dance
- Ryker: Ry – ker
- Riordan: Reer – dun
- Malesh: May – lesh
- Eamon: Ay – mun
- Callum: Cal – um
- Seelie: Seel – ee
- Unseelie: Un – seel – ee

Map of the Fae Isle

Chapter One

RYKER

I stepped into the wide street of the marketplace, and the smell of piss assaulted my nostrils. As my boots connected with the cobblestone, a loud splash met my ears, and something wet seeped into the fabric of my trousers. My upper lip curled, and I had to force myself to contain my snarl.

That better not have been piss.

While I loathed the Seelie Court at all times, it was the fact that they insisted on pretending their kingdom was more elegant, more pristine, more superior, that truly irked me. Once you ventured outside of the palace walls, their streets reeked of piss and other filth, the same as everywhere else.

"Ryker," Malesh called, jutting his chin toward a man lounging against the wall of an alley.

He hid in the shadows, pulling the hood of his cloak low over his face, obscuring his features from anyone passing by. He was a bulky man, easily six feet tall and almost as wide. The broad span of his shoulders and the thick limbs masquerading as arms made him appear vicious and lethal.

The nervous glances over his shoulder and the unsettled way he shuffled his feet told me he was the man we had come to meet.

I tilted my head toward the man, signaling for Malesh and Eamon to follow me as I strode toward him.

The market buzzed with activity, its air heavy with the aroma of spices and something sweet. Animated conversations surrounded me, but the moment they glimpsed our trio, they moved as though they were fleeing the Wild Hunt.

They could sense the danger lurking in their midst. Their primal instincts flared to life, urging them to seek safety... far away from me.

I pulled my hood lower over my head to avoid being recognized. Being the Crown Prince of the Unseelie Fae, my presence in the Seelie Kingdom wouldn't go unnoticed. I needed to be quick, cautious, and, most importantly, invisible. My eyes scanned every face for any sign of recognition as I moved with purposeful strides toward the alley.

Ahead of us, a young boy, maybe twelve years old, pulled a cart full of vegetables. He peered over his shoulder and jumped when he saw the three of us following him.

I supposed we didn't exactly give off welcoming vibes with all three of us dressed in black and our faces hidden beneath our cloaks. Not to mention the array of weapons we each carried. I had my longsword sheathed at my waist, my hand resting on the pommel as if expecting a need to draw it. There were also a dozen daggers concealed beneath my cloak, not that the boy could see those.

On my right, Malesh wore twin blades across his back, a battle axe hung from his hip, and he was casually using one of his daggers to clean beneath his fingernails. Eamon, who was on my left, had a lethal-looking crossbow hanging over his shoulder, already pulled taut with a bolt just waiting to be unleashed. He too had a longsword strapped to his hip and, unlike me, he wore his daggers proudly, sheathed in his thigh holsters and within reach, should the need arise.

So it was little surprise when the boy darted to the side, leaving the path in front of us clear.

When we reached the man awaiting our arrival, we took three steps past him, moving further into the shadows, and gestured for him to follow us.

"Your Highness," he said, his voice low and rough. "I have news of the Crimson Enclave."

"Lower your voice," Malesh hissed.

"Apologies, Your Highness," the man whispered.

I gave him a curt nod, encouraging him to continue.

The man wiped his meaty fingers on his tunic, the only sign he was nervous about what he had to say.

"Word is, they are no longer focusing their efforts on the King." His gaze darted to me, and I caught the hint of green eyes peeking out beneath his hood.

It had been damn near impossible to get any solid information on the remaining faction of the Wraith Borne. Those who survived the Cleansing had disappeared, staying hidden for years. The Crimson Enclave, as they now referred to themselves, had only started to retaliate in the last decade or so.

Their sole purpose was to bring about the death of our King, my father, and it was my duty to ensure they never succeeded.

They had first attacked our outermost villages in an attempt to draw out my father. Initially, it was only minor incidents: raids on food supplies and livestock, and the destruction of roads and bridges. When those tactics failed, they slowly escalated until they were slaughtering entire villages.

The attacks had become more frequent and more gruesome in recent months. The people were terrified, but my father and the council ignored the problem. Instead, they made me responsible for suppressing any unrest.

It didn't help that my father continued to host extravagant events at the palace, a demonstration of exorbitant wealth and gluttony while others starved and were forced to flee their homes.

"It appears you have garnered their attention, my Prince," the man said, drawing me back to the present.

"What does that mean?" Eamon pressed.

"My source didn't have all the details, but it seems the Crimson Enclave is seeking a way to weaken your power. They know you are the strongest member of the royal family and the greatest threat they need to overcome to unseat your father."

"Can you provide evidence beyond mere speculation?" Malesh gritted out.

"I'm afraid that's all my source could tell me. I know it isn't much, but I thought it prudent to alert you nonetheless."

"Thank you," I said and nodded to Eamon. "Pay the man."

Turning on my heel, I started back toward where we had tethered our horses. While there was little to go on, I wasn't foolish enough to ignore the warning. I would remain vigilant.

It was no secret that I was more powerful than my father. It was why he trusted me to quash any resistance to his rule, but that wasn't the only reason he used me as a shield. My father was paranoid about any potential threat to his power. Keeping me away from the council and out among the people served two functions. My absence from the palace made it less likely that I would earn the council's favor. Sending me out to disperse any unrest from the starving and victimized within our kingdom also made me the villain.

I was pulled from my ruminations when I caught the most delicious scent, a mixture of vanilla and wildflowers, and something... unique. Whatever it was, it was intoxicating, euphoric, even.

The marketplace faded into the background, and my attention narrowed as I tried to locate its source.

A strange feeling stirred to life within me, foreign yet insistent. Then something tightened in my chest, and a tugging sensation pulled at my ribcage. It wasn't painful, exactly, but uncomfortable. Almost as if my skin was too tight.

I scanned the crowded marketplace and inhaled deeply. That same enticing scent filled my nostrils, and a low growl escaped me without warning.

What the fuck was happening to me?

My every instinct was suddenly alert, and my muscles were coiled tight with tension as if preparing to spring into action at any moment. The feeling grew stronger, more potent, as the seconds ticked by, and I felt as though there was a caged beast inside me, prowling endlessly, just waiting to be set free.

Then I saw her.

It was almost by accident. A glimpse of something — no, someone — I may have missed, if not for the hulking man who stepped to the side.

She had long brown hair, which she wore in a braid, and a radiant smile that captivated all of my attention. My throat thickened, and I swallowed roughly as I watched her, transfixed, too afraid to even blink in case she disappeared.

She was talking excitedly with another man, and the sight had me clenching my hands into fists. The sudden surge of jealousy that ravaged me caught me by surprise, and I had to stop myself from marching over to them and snatching her away.

The woman had a petite frame, and she possessed the type of figure that would have men falling to their knees if only she would let them worship at her feet. Her rounded hips would be perfect for gripping tightly while I pounded into her from behind, and her breasts were just the right size to fill my palm. The slender column of her neck would look exquisite with my hand wrapped around it, cutting off her oxygen until she came so violently that she saw stars.

Fuck. Now I was hard.

When a breathy laugh escaped her lips, the tugging sensation in my chest started up again, and my feet moved of their own accord. When I realized what was happening, I dug my heels into the ground to stop myself.

As if sensing my presence, the woman turned, her gaze meeting mine, her eyes a rich brown. She was stunning, breathtaking, ethereal even, and I couldn't look away despite my best efforts.

She held me imprisoned with her gaze, and I smirked at her as I stepped closer, if only to relieve some of the suffocating tension threatening to choke me. When her eyes darted away, breaking our connection, I inhaled a shaky breath.

My heart pounded, and sweat coated my brow as I realized what was happening.

The woman was my mate.

And she had her delicate little fingers wrapped around the forearm of another man.

I clenched my jaw so hard that I was surprised I didn't crack a tooth.

"What's wrong?" Malesh asked, sensing the shift.

"You see that woman over there?" I said, nodding in her direction.

"Yes."

"She's coming with us."

Malesh's eyebrows disappeared into his hairline before he and Eamon shared a look.

However, they both knew better than to question my orders.

"And be quick about it before her companion loses his head."

Without another look in her direction, I stalked away, eager for the moment I could lay my hands on my little mate.

Chapter Two

CADENCE

The sun warmed my face as I soaked in the beauty of the day. Inhaling a deep breath, I let the smell of freshly baked bread mix with the floral scents of the nearby flower display and made a mental note to collect a bouquet for the apothecary before leaving the marketplace.

"Cadence, are you even listening to me?"

I turned toward my brother and rolled my eyes. "Callum, as your sister, I have absolutely no interest in your sexual exploits."

Callum's lips twitched, and a smirk pulled up the corner of his mouth. "Even if said exploits were with Teal?"

"You did not!" I gasped as I clutched his forearm.

"I most certainly did," Callum grinned.

"You know that if Roarke finds out you were fooling around with his sister, he *will* murder you without a moment's hesitation," I teased.

"Are you going to tattle on me, Cadence?" Callum asked with a raised brow.

"Of course not," I scoffed. "But don't say I didn't warn you."

"You know, one night with Teal might just be worth the risk."

I narrowed my gaze at him, and he winked.

"You're a pig," I chastised, but I couldn't keep the laughter out of my tone. If the wide grin on Callum's face was any indication, he'd heard it, too.

A sudden sense of awareness prickled up my spine, and I resisted the full-body shiver that fought to break free. The surrounding air felt suddenly stifling, and my next inhale of breath was filled with suffocating tension.

I scanned the marketplace, searching for the unseen eyes that I knew were watching me. The feeling of awareness grew stronger before morphing into something far more unsettling as it crept along my skin.

A short distance behind me, I spotted a man dressed entirely in black. He had his hood pulled low over his head, concealing most of his face.

He just stood there, in the middle of the street, staring at me.

Despite not being able to see all of his face, I could make out his grey eyes boring into me from beneath the hood.

His unblinking gaze remained fixed on me with a disturbing intensity. I sucked in a sharp breath, unsure why I suddenly felt cold all over. Even though I stood in a wide, open marketplace, the man's gaze made me feel trapped, cornered... like prey.

My heart thundered inside my chest, and my palms grew clammy. As if the man could sense my mounting discomfort and was enjoying it, he took a step closer, and a small smile spread across his lips, visible from beneath his cloak.

"Cadence?" my brother asked. "Are you all right?"

I pulled my gaze from the hooded man and faced my brother. "I... I'm fine," I said, forcing a smile.

Callum's eyebrows furrowed in concern, unconvinced by my faltering grin, and he glanced around the marketplace, trying to identify the source of my unease.

I looked back toward the man, but he was gone.

"What errand were you running for Mama, anyway?" I asked, changing the subject.

Callum cast another worried look in my direction before he shrugged. "She wanted to make Papa's favorite pie, and I stopped by at the wrong time."

"Good. You're always leaving their chores for me. It wouldn't kill you to help out more," I grumbled.

"Ah, but you are the responsible one," he said, raising a finger. "Not to mention a healer. Isn't it part of your role to be caring and compassionate?"

"I have a business to run, Callum," I replied incredulously. "Yet still I make time to ensure our parents have everything they need."

"Exactly! You own the apothecary and, therefore, can work when it suits you. Meanwhile, I must labor under the tyranny of old man Reynolds and his construction projects."

"You are an Earth Fae, Callum. All you have to do is wave your hands, and the forest bends to your will."

"It's very hard work," Callum deadpanned.

"You're unbelievable."

Callum grinned and nudged my shoulder with his. "You coming out tonight?"

I pursed my lips. Callum was the outgoing, sociable one of our family, while I preferred late nights brewing elixirs and perfecting my craft.

"Come on," he teased. "You'll never find a mate if you don't venture beyond your apartment occasionally."

"One," I said as I rounded on him. "I neither want nor need a mate. And two, I have orders to fill. I know it may be a foreign concept to you, but people rely on me."

"Ah! You wound me, Little Sister," Callum said as he placed a hand over his heart. "At least think about it."

"No promises," I mumbled. Standing on my toes, I kissed my brother on the cheek. "I have to go. Try to stay out of trouble."

"No promises," he repeated with a smirk.

I shook my head and turned away from my brother, my basket clutched in my hands, as I headed back toward my store.

I'd barely rounded the corner when the feeling of being watched returned, stronger than ever. A tingling sensation crawled up my nape, and cold sweat beaded on my forehead. I glanced around, but couldn't see anything amiss.

I quickened my pace as I hurried along the cobblestone street. Movement in my periphery caught my attention, and I turned abruptly, tightening my grip on the handle of my basket, ready to confront my pursuer.

But there was no one there.

"Get a hold of yourself, Cadence," I admonished as I released a shaky breath.

I forced my feet to keep moving, and I almost sagged in relief when I saw the apothecary up ahead. The moment I crossed the threshold into my store, the tension drained from my body, and I let out a small chuckle at how unnerved I had been.

I placed my supplies on the counter and headed toward the staircase at the back of my shop, which led to my apartment upstairs. Exhaustion tugged at my limbs. The endless late nights spent filling orders were catching up to me.

I climbed the stairs absentmindedly, my fingers gliding over the smooth railing.

My thoughts drifted to the elixirs I still had to make before morning, and despite my exhaustion, a grin turned up the corners of my mouth. I wouldn't be able to join Callum at the tavern after all.

I loved my brother, and I enjoyed spending time with him, but I preferred to do so in the quiet of my apartment, away from prying eyes and interested glances.

I was halfway up the staircase when a shadow moved at the base of the stairs, just at the edge of my vision. My heart thumped against my chest as I glanced down, but there was no one there.

Great. Now my exhaustion was making me see things.

I hurried up the remaining steps, wanting to be inside my apartment.

As I reached the top of the stairs, I leaned forward and gripped the door handle that would lead me into the safety of my home. The air shifted behind me, and a cold sensation raised the hair on the back of my neck.

Before I could scream, a rough hand clamped over my mouth, muffling my cries. My heart lurched as someone dragged me backward. I stumbled down a few steps before my attacker's arm locked around my waist, pulling me flush against a hard chest. I clawed at the arm covering my mouth, my nails scraping across exposed flesh, but their grip was ironclad.

Something was pressed against my mouth and nose, and my vision blurred. My arms and legs flailed as I struggled to fight off my attacker, but a foul, potent smell overpowered me, and my limbs grew heavy.

The room grew darker with each step, and every instinct screamed at me to run, to break free. But my body had already conceded the fight.

Panic clawed at my throat, and I called upon my magic, the familiar tingling sensation bursting to life at my fingertips. Just as quickly as it came, however, my magic drained away, and my arms fell slack at my sides.

"Shh," a low, masculine voice whispered from behind me, right before the darkness pulled me under.

Chapter Three

CADENCE

The first thing I noticed when I woke, was the dull throbbing sensation that erupted at my temples. Light pulsed across my eyelids, sending little bursts of pain deep into my skull with each pass, and I groaned.

I tried to roll onto my side, but quickly realized my limbs were not cooperating. My body felt heavy and numb as I struggled to force it to move. I could make out distant noises somewhere nearby, but they sounded muffled, like I was hearing them from underwater.

I fought against the heaviness of my eyelids as I forced them to open, only to be assaulted by a blur of bright lights. My vision swam as a mass of indistinct shapes spun around me.

The entire room seemed to be moving, and my stomach roiled in response.

Where the hell was I?

A thick fog clouded my mind, and no matter how hard I tried, I couldn't shake it.

When my vision finally cleared, I blinked several times as I struggled to make sense of what I was seeing. An unfamiliar ceiling glared down at me, with its gilded beams and intricately carved cornices.

Panic pricked at the edges of my mind, and I forced myself to inhale deep, calming breaths as I studied my surroundings.

I was lying on a four-poster bed, the dark mahogany wood reminding me of congealed blood. A sea of finely embroidered pillows surrounded me, and I was enveloped in the most luxurious blankets I had ever felt.

I swallowed thickly as I pulled myself into a sitting position, allowing the blankets to pool around my waist. My limbs protested under the strain, but eventually surrendered to my demands.

The heavy, leaden feeling that had been holding my body captive began to slowly ebb away, and I forced myself to stand on unsteady feet. When I peered over my shoulder, I took in the black silk sheets that were now crumpled, and I ignored the fastidious side of me that wanted to smooth them out.

I had bigger issues to contend with.

My gaze darted to a large arched window that dominated one wall. I took slow, tentative steps towards it until I was close enough to peer through the stained glass that depicted some kind of crest.

In the center was a pair of black, feathered wings with twin blades that poked out between them. Tendrils of black smoke danced around the wings, and, as I leaned in closer, I realized the wings were not feathered at all. Rather, the black tendrils of smoke appeared to be emanating *from* them.

Unease washed over me at the realization.

I stared down at the courtyard below, where people bustled about. The vast open space spanned in every direction and was abuzz with activity. Towering stone walls enclosed the area, but the trellises of ivy growing along the stone softened the harsh exterior.

A magnificent chestnut tree stood in the center of the courtyard, its branches offering shade to those resting on the benches beneath its sprawling limbs. Birds flitted from limb to limb as they serenaded those below with the occasional burst of song.

The sound of steel grating against steel caught my attention, and I turned toward the noise. Practice areas littered the far edge of the courtyard, and two men with swords sparred in the center of one square, while others watched from the sidelines.

Next to them, straw targets were set up as soldiers perused the offerings of bows that sat alongside the weapon racks filled with arrows, swords, shields, lances, and a variety of other deadly looking instruments.

The soft laughter of children pulled my attention in the opposite direction. I glimpsed a large, ornate fountain sculpted from a pearlescent marble. The cascading water shimmered in the sunlight, which made the structure appear ethereal. Children jumped in and out of the water, squealing in delight as the cool liquid soaked their clothes.

The people below appeared unconcerned, going about their day as if nothing was amiss.

And I recognized none of it.

As I turned back toward the room, I studied my surroundings more closely as I tried desperately to recall how I had ended up here. My eyes narrowed on a desk in the corner, and my feet carried me over to it without conscious thought.

The desk held an assortment of objects — scattered parchment, a wax seal with the same crest that appeared on the window, a quill and an inkpot, a bejeweled dagger, and a half-empty goblet of wine.

I brushed my fingers over the parchment, shifting it aside to reveal a map. I pulled it free from the pile and studied it closely. A small gasp escaped me when I realized it was a map of the Unseelie Kingdom. The map noted strategic trading posts and highlighted weak spots along the border shared with the Seelie Kingdom.

Only someone high-ranking in the Seelie Court would possess such a thing.

As I glanced around the room once more, it dawned on me that I must be in the capital, where the Seelie King and Queen held court.

But I was no closer to discovering who brought me here or why.

A faint memory drifted to the forefront of my mind.

A strong aroma.

The sound of a male voice.

My failing magic.

Fear crept up my throat, making it hard to breathe as understanding settled over me.

Someone had taken me from the apothecary.

Sinister grey eyes flashed in my mind, and something stirred inside my chest, tightening and squeezing as my pulse quickened. The thrum of my heartbeat rang out loudly in my ears, each beat heavy and insistent. A cold sweat broke out all over my body, and I raced toward the door as the primal need to escape gripped me.

My feet skidded against the floor as the chamber door swung open. A commanding figure crossed the threshold, and I sucked in a ragged breath.

A man stood before me, tall and broad. His white-blond hair, which was dark at the roots, was tied in a loose bun with a few strands falling around his face.

His strong jawline and perfectly sculpted facial features were accentuated by the rough stubble that lined his cheeks, and his sun-kissed skin was smooth, highlighting the muscular contours of his shoulders peeking out from beneath his tunic.

He looked wild, yet controlled, and he was absolutely breathtaking.

But it was his intense grey eyes that bore into me, piercing me all the way to the inner depths of my soul that held me frozen in place.

His full, sensual lips pulled up into a smirk as he stepped closer to me.

Gods, the man was so beautiful that it was almost painful to look at him.

He took another step toward me, and his smirk grew wider.

My body moved on instinct, and I stepped back, trying to create distance between myself and this... predator.

Because that's what he was. A predator. It was clear in the way he moved. The way his muscles coiled tight as if he was readying himself to strike.

I had no idea what a man like him would want with someone like me. Or more importantly, why he had brought me back to the Seelie Palace of all places.

Whatever his intentions, they weren't good. You didn't kidnap someone and steal them away from their home just to chat.

"My name is Ryker," the man said.

The deep resonance of his voice caressed me like the softest velvet. The low, rumbling tone was sensual, as if he had whispered each word against the shell of my ear. My nipples puckered under the fabric of my dress, and heat crawled its way up my neck, coloring my cheeks.

"But you may know me by another name."

He prowled closer, and I held my breath as I waited for his next words. The sinking feeling in the pit of my stomach warned me that I was in trouble. That I needed to escape this beautiful Adonis before it was too late.

"Many call me the Night Cursed Prince."

All the blood drained from my face. It was much worse than I had imagined.

The man before me was solely responsible for the most painful moments of my life.

The Prince of the Unseelie Fae.

I'd been brought to the Unseelie Kingdom, where the streets were lawless and the leaders ruthless.

And their prince was the worst of them all.

Known for his cunning brutality, and his inability to show the slightest ounce of compassion, it was rumored that even his own father, the King of the Unseelie, was wary of him.

And now I was at his mercy.

As if he could sense my thoughts, the prince's smirk grew into a wide grin.

"I see my reputation precedes me."

Chapter Four

RYKER

I was a cruel bastard.

I knew this because I couldn't help but revel in the fear shining from within the chocolate depths of my mate's eyes as she took me in.

It wrapped around her, squeezing her tight until her breaths became labored and her body trembled.

It was intoxicating.

I stepped into her space, and her breathing hitched. Her hands shook violently as she tried to steady them in the fabric of her skirts. Despite her obvious terror, however, she lifted her chin and looked me straight in the eye.

A feral grin spread across my face at her defiance. It was an expression that had made seasoned warriors cower at my feet plenty of times before.

Not her, though.

Not *my* mate.

Something akin to pride welled inside me as I stared her down.

She was strong, resilient, and perhaps a little unhinged.

And I couldn't wait to tear her down and reshape her into my darkest desire.

"What is your name?" I murmured as I reached out and tucked a lock of her silky chestnut hair behind her ear.

My fingers lingered on her skin, and I traced the column of her throat before she swatted my hand away.

I chuckled at her defiance, and she narrowed her eyes at me.

My mate was a little spitfire.

"Shouldn't you already know my name? You abducted me from my home! Or do you make a habit of stealing women from the streets?"

Her voice was a melodic symphony to my ears. Soft, yet firm, with a sultry undertone that I wasn't sure she was aware of.

"Not often, no. Women fall all over themselves for the chance to land at my feet."

"How fortunate you must be," she bit out. "Now that we have cleared that up, if you wouldn't mind returning me to my home, I'd be grateful. I'd hate to keep you from your harem, so I'll just be on my way."

She was adorable.

"That won't be happening."

"Why the hell not?" she demanded as she crossed her arms over her chest.

The movement drew my attention to her breasts, which were now pushed up and on display for my perusal. If I hadn't already been certain that she did not know the effect she had on me, I'd say my little mate was a temptress.

"Because," I drawled. "As my mate, your life belongs to me now."

Her eyes widened in shock, and she inhaled sharply as she staggered away from me. When her thighs collided with the edge of my desk, I pushed forward, caging her in with my arms on either side of her petite body.

"No," she said in a hoarse whisper. "I cannot be your mate."

She stumbled over the word as though she'd never heard it before.

I ran my nose along her throat and inhaled a deep breath. Satisfaction washed over me when I felt her body tremble beneath mine.

"Oh, but you are," I purred. "The moment I saw you in that marketplace, I sensed the pull. You beckoned me to you like a godsdamned siren."

Her breathing stalled, and I pressed my body further into hers.

"No," she repeated. "You're Unseelie."

I barked out a laugh, and she jumped in surprise.

"How very observant of you. Now, why don't you tell me your name, Temptress?"

She paled at the moniker but quickly schooled her features.

"I owe you nothing," she said with renewed bitterness. "My name, least of all."

"You can tell me your name of your own free will, or," — I quirked a brow in challenge — "I'll summon a truth teller right now and force it from you."

Her eyes snapped to mine, and the fear I saw there had all my blood pooling below my waistband.

She seemed to weigh her options for a moment. Then she realized I'd have her name, regardless.

"Cadence," she hissed. "Cadence Tiernan."

"Cadence," I repeated.

The word rolled off my tongue effortlessly, as though I had known it all my life.

Hearing her name from my mouth seemed to stoke Cadence's ire, and she pushed against my chest, forcing me to retreat a step. She darted behind my desk as if it would protect her from me.

Her fight had returned, and that only made me more determined to break her.

"Even if I were your... mate." Cadence winced as she forced the word between her lips.

"Even if I were, which I don't believe for a second, it doesn't excuse taking me from my home and turning my life upside down."

I merely shrugged and folded my arms across my chest.

Her eyes narrowed with her barely contained fury as she growled, "I want to go home. I have responsibilities and people who depend on me."

"No."

"You can't just keep me as your prisoner!" she shouted as she threw her hands into the air.

"I am the Prince of the Unseelie," I said with a smirk. "I think you'll find I can."

"I know exactly who you are," Cadence snarled, and I had to wonder which of my misdeeds had offended her to this extent.

Not that it mattered. I would keep her all the same.

"As my mate, you are the single greatest threat to me."

"Then let me go. Be rid of me," she pleaded.

A dark chuckle rumbled from my chest as I stalked closer to her. Cadence darted to the side, backing herself into a corner as she stood trapped between my bed and my armchair.

My hand moved toward her face, and I gripped her chin between my thumb and forefinger. I angled her head until she was facing me, refusing to let her escape my gaze, and her nostrils flared in anger.

"So my enemies can get their hands on you?" I tsked. "Do you even understand the power of the mate bond, Cadence?"

She clenched her jaw but didn't respond.

"As my mate, should any harm come to you, I would be left weakened."

"That's only if the bond is fully formed," she scowled. "And I have no intention of accepting anything that comes from you."

My gaze traveled the length of her, taking in the swell of her breasts and the way her hips flared, before settling back on her face.

"I guess we'll see, won't we?" I murmured. "Besides, acceptance brings its own rewards, which reminds me, what magic do you possess?"

"I... I'm a healer," she stuttered.

"A healer," I hummed. "I won't deny I'm a little disappointed."

Indignant rage flashed across Cadence's face, and she curled her palms into fists at her side.

"Since I'm worthless to you, there is no reason to keep me here."

An amused smile pulled up the corner of my mouth. Did she think she could escape me?

"You're smart enough to understand that fate doesn't work like that."

Cadence scoffed. "And how would you know anything about my intelligence, or lack thereof? You don't even know me."

"Your rapid quips for one," I replied as I lifted a single brow.

Cadence's cheeks flushed crimson, and a look of pure frustration contorted her beautiful face. She was doing all that she could to warn me away from her, and she'd only piqued my interest.

Cadence let out a resigned sigh. "Look," she said as she raked her fingers through her hair.

I was struck with the overwhelming desire to wrap her silky strands around my fist and yank her to me as I conquered her mouth with my tongue.

Mine, an insistent voice snarled inside of me.

"I have a family back in the Seelie Kingdom. They will be worried. I can't let them think I abandoned them or that something untoward has happened to me."

She eyed me up and down as if to say something untoward did, in fact, happen to her. I wouldn't argue the point. I was comfortable with the actions I had taken to secure her, no matter how unscrupulous she may find them.

"So, write them a letter. I'll ensure they receive it."

"Argh!" Cadence screeched. "I don't want to write them a letter. I want to go home!"

"And as I've already told you, that's not happening."

Cadence lunged for me, and I grabbed her wrists in one of my hands as I spun her around, pressing her back against my front.

"Listen closely, Cadence, as I'll only say this once."

Her breasts heaved under my forearm, which held her hands pinned against her chest.

"From this moment forward, every action you take, every word you utter, every place you go, will be at my discretion. You are mine. Obey me, prove that you can be a good girl, and perhaps I'll grant you more freedom. But make no mistake, Cadence. You cannot escape me. I can already feel the bond growing stronger, pulling me toward you with every passing moment we're apart. No matter where you run, I will find you. You'd do well to accept it."

I leaned down and placed a gentle kiss on the side of her neck. She recoiled and jerked her head away from me.

"I see you haven't quite accepted things yet," I chuckled. "In that case, you will remain locked in my chambers. I'll send a maid up to you to ensure you have everything you need."

Releasing her, I stepped back and spun on my feet as I headed toward the door.

I'd only taken a few steps when something whizzed past my head, barely missing me. I straightened and glanced over my shoulder to see Cadence's burning fury glaring back at me.

My gaze darted to the door. Buried deep in the wooden panes of the door frame was a dagger. The same one that had been sitting on my desk atop a wine goblet.

As I reached the door, I pulled the blade from the wood and toyed with the sharpened tip.

"I think I'll take this with me," I said with a wink.

Before Cadence could grab another projectile, I slipped through the door and locked it behind me.

Chapter Five

CADENCE

Part of me knew I should fear the man who held me captive. More so than others, considering my past. He was known to be ruthless and unforgiving, and no one in their right mind would challenge him, let alone try to attack him.

More importantly, he was the Prince of the Unseelie.

The two Fae courts despised one another. After the Gilded King's betrayal, the courts had gone to war. The feuding had lasted centuries before finally tapering off. But I'd be a fool to believe that the lack of active conflict meant I wasn't still standing on a battlefield. Every new generation had inherited that hatred, with few exceptions. He was just as likely to slit my throat for being Seelie as he was for my attempt to maim him.

Despite knowing this, however, I was beyond caring, and I had let my rage and desperation convince me it was a good idea to hurl a dagger at him.

And now I was locked inside his chambers, seething.

I paced the small area in front of the window and imagined a myriad of ways I could bring about the prince's bloody demise. It had been foolish of me to relinquish my only weapon. Still, his shocked expression had almost made it worth it.

"You need to think, Cadence. Smugness won't get you out of this situation," I murmured.

My gaze swept the room. There was no hidden door or concealed passageway, no servant's entrance, or even a small pet flap that I could use to slip free.

I was trapped, and that knowledge made my skin crawl.

My footsteps slowed as I considered the one thing that I had promised my mother I would never do again.

My magic stirred to life inside me as if in response to my thoughts. The familiar feeling of warmth spread across my chest, and for the briefest moment, I allowed myself to bask in it.

No. There was a reason I couldn't use my magic. The risk of exposure was too great.

I shuddered at what they'd do to me if anyone ever found out.

As I resumed my pacing, I tried to come up with an alternative plan of action. I went to the door and tested the handle again.

Locked. Just like the last three times I had checked.

The cold metal remained unmoving in my grasp, taunting me.

Even if it were unlocked, it wouldn't have helped. I'd never slip past the castle walls unnoticed.

"Don't think like that, Cadence. You've got to try," I reminded myself.

Now that I thought about it, I didn't even know if I was actually at the Unseelie Palace.

Didn't monarchs have a plethora of homes they frequented? This could be one of many.

I could feel the oppressive weight of the room closing in around me as my desperation grew stronger. I took a calming breath and forced myself to reassess the space with fresh eyes.

My gaze flicked to the window. Even if I could have pried it open, it was too high up for me to escape without breaking my neck.

I dismissed the window and surveyed the room once more. There had to be something else, some unnoticed weakness I had yet to find.

My thoughts were interrupted as a woman with long burgundy hair, twisted into an elegant braid, entered the chamber. She appeared youthful, although that meant very little considering that Fae were all but immortal and did not age beyond their first twenty years.

She dipped low to the ground in a curtsy, almost dropping the bundle of fabric she clutched in her arms.

I blinked, unsure if she was real or just a figment of my desperation.

"Forgive my interruption, My Lady."

My Lady.

I scanned the chamber, searching for another woman I might have overlooked. My brows furrowed in confusion when I confirmed I was alone.

"Are you talking to me?" I asked, jabbing a finger at my chest.

The woman gave me a puzzled look before she stood. "Yes. The prince instructed me to bring your garments to his chambers."

"My garments?"

"Yes, the Seamstress just dropped them off," she said as she walked over to a closet and started hanging the items inside.

"I don't understand."

"The prince commissioned a wardrobe for you," she answered.

"How would he even know my size?"

Of all the questions I should've asked — like how to escape — my indignation took hold, and the words slipped out before I could stop them.

I didn't expect the woman to answer, but she did anyway.

"He took your measurements while you were resting."

She cast a glance over her shoulder, and her eyes were awash with sympathy.

"Dreadful situation. I do hope you have recovered from the rough handling of the brutes who tried to kidnap you."

I was certain her prince had omitted the part about how *he* had been the brute in question.

Wait, did she just say he *measured* me?

Before I could dwell on it, the woman finished and turned to me. "I will be your chambermaid. If you need anything, just ring that bell over there."

I turned to where she pointed. Sure enough, a bell hung beside the bed.

"Thank you," I muttered, not knowing what else to say.

"You're very welcome, My Lady," she replied as she turned to leave.

Panic surged inside my chest. The woman's arrival was the perfect opportunity for escape, and it was already slipping between my fingers.

"Wait!" I called after her. "I don't know your name."

"Oh my!" she gasped as she placed her hand at the base of her throat. "Where are my manners? My name is Scarlette," she said and offered me her hand.

"Cadence."

"It's a pleasure to meet you, Cadence," she said, beaming.

"Likewise."

My mind raced for a way to get past her... unless I didn't have to. Perhaps this woman would be an ally. It would be a lot easier to escape if I had help. I needed to gauge how loyal she was to the prince. Maybe she despised Ryker like those in the Seelie Kingdom. I could turn her to my side. I just needed to...

A door clicking shut pulled me from my thoughts. As I scanned the chamber once more, I realized Scarlette had already left.

"Perfect!"

I sighed in defeat and made my way over to the closet where she had deposited my clothes.

I couldn't help the gasp that escaped me when I took in the garments. The closet was filled with the most beautiful dresses I'd ever seen. Made from the finest materials and embroidered with the most elegant designs, they were simply breathtaking. My fingers slid over the different fabrics, and I all but groaned when I touched a silk nightdress.

While he was a complete bastard, I had to admit, the prince had exceptional taste.

I plucked a nightdress from the offerings and pulled it flush against my body. It looked about right.

I quickly rid myself of my clothing and pulled the nightdress over my head.

It fit like a glove, and this knowledge only made my blood boil hotter.

That asshole.

It was bad enough that he kidnapped me, brought me to an unknown and deadly kingdom, kept me locked up like some godsdamned pet. You'd think he would draw a line somewhere.

But no.

He also thought it was acceptable to touch my body without my permission while I was unconscious and couldn't do anything about it.

I shouldn't have been surprised, knowing what I did about him, but I was.

Ryker may have been a prince and used to everyone dancing to his tune, but he had crossed a line.

The gods wouldn't be cruel enough to make that man my mate.

Would they?

My only comfort for the time was knowing that I didn't feel the same pull toward him that he seemed to feel towards me.

Are you sure? My inner voice taunted. *Didn't you feel him watching you in the marketplace?*

I shook my head to rid myself of the intrusive thoughts. I refused to accept the Unseelie Prince was my mate, no matter his claims.

Even if he hadn't taken me by force, he would always be my enemy.

That was not a healthy foundation for a bond.

That was bonded chaos.

I laughed bitterly at the thought.

The one man who would kill me without hesitation if he knew the truth about me, believed he was my mate.

Chapter Six

RYKER

The fire crackled, and light flickered across the polished wooden desk that dominated the room.

Ignoring the inviting ambiance, I headed straight for the wine cabinet. It had been a long day, and I needed a moment to myself before I faced the vixen locked inside my chambers.

The thought of Cadence's violent outburst brought an amused smirk to my lips. I had no idea she would be so bloodthirsty, but I had to admit, I didn't hate it.

My cock swelled inside my trousers as if in agreement.

Bringing Cadence to the palace with me had been an impulsive move. Necessary, but still impulsive.

Now I had to ensure that no one discovered who she was to me.

Especially my father.

That thought had my cock deflating.

He would use her to curtail my power. My strength had far surpassed his own and he no longer looked at me as the son he used to adore.

Now, he only saw another threat to his reign.

Still, I couldn't help but think the prize waiting in my chambers was worth the risk.

"What has you smiling like a fool?" an amused male voice called from the shadows near my desk.

A muttered curse escaped me as I faced the man lurking in the darkness. My failure to sense his presence earlier galled me.

"What are you doing in here?" I snapped.

My younger brother, Riordan, sat in the armchair beside my desk, his expression smug as he swirled the contents of his goblet.

"Does it involve the woman hidden in your chambers?" he asked, ignoring my question.

Anger tightened my features, and I crossed my arms over my chest. I had the sudden urge to punch something, but I refused to let my brother see that he was getting under my skin.

He'd enjoy it far too much.

"Where did you hear that?" I asked.

"The servants talk, Brother. You know this."

My brother's grin showed he knew exactly how much his words irritated me.

"They must wish to be separated from their tongues," I growled.

So much for keeping myself in check.

Riordan chuckled. "You didn't think you could keep her a secret forever, did you?"

I grunted in response, not willing to acknowledge that had indeed been my plan.

"So," Riordan pressed, raising an expectant brow.

When I didn't answer, he added, "Who is she?"

I sighed, running a hand over my face. There was no escaping this conversation.

I could delay it, though.

I grabbed a bottle of wine and a goblet from the cabinet. My gaze flicked to my brother, who watched me with keen interest as I poured.

Extending the bottle toward him, I topped up his goblet before replacing the cork and stowing the wine. I took a deep gulp, as if the answers I required lay at the bottom.

The cool liquid glided across my tongue, awakening my taste buds as bursts of ripe berries comforted me. Slowly, the more complex, earthy tones of the wine followed, making me think of the woods in the fall.

I wanted to savor the moment, but I could feel the penetrating gaze of my brother boring into me.

Lowering my goblet, I met my brother's gaze, and he took a sip of his wine as he watched me intently.

"She is my mate."

Warm liquid splashed across my face, followed by the sound of coughing and wheezing. Riordan hunched over his knees, his goblet abandoned on the table as he struggled to fill his lungs with oxygen.

I should have been concerned for my brother, but all I felt was disgust.

He had spat his wine all over my face upon my admission.

Warm wine.

Made so from being in his mouth.

Disgust seemed appropriate under the circumstances.

"Are you done?" I barked.

Riordan put his hand up, signaling for me to wait a moment. When he finally recovered, he stared at me as if I were a stranger.

"Did you say mate?" he eventually managed.

"Yes, and if you're wise, you won't speak those words inside these walls again."

Riordan's wide grin instantly dropped. "You can't let Father find out who she is to you," he warned.

"I know," I growled as I ran my hand through my hair.

"What's she like?"

"I don't know," I murmured. "She's never too thrilled when I'm in her company."

Harsh laughter cut through the silence of the night as I narrowed my eyes at my brother.

"A woman who isn't desperate to kneel before the Crown Prince. Impossible," he mocked.

"It's difficult to comprehend, I know."

Riordan snorted. "What will you do with her?"

"She's mine. I'm keeping her."

Riordan eyed me. "I'm not saying you should give her up, Brother. I'm only wondering how you intend to balance her arrival with Celeste —"

"That is none of your concern," I scowled, interrupting him.

Riordan raised his hands in a placating gesture. "All right, all right, forget I said anything. When do I get to meet her?"

"You don't," I said as I turned away from him. "Any interest in her must be kept to a minimum."

"I could pretend she was one of my consorts," Riordan offered.

I ground my teeth together to stop myself from stalking across the room and ripping my brother's head from his body.

"Oh, don't look at me like that, Ryker," he said as he rolled his eyes. "I don't intend to bed the woman."

The thought of them tangled in his sheets turned my vision red, and my hands itched to hit something.

"Oh no. Stop right there, Ryker. You know I was only trying to help you," he said as he darted away from me.

It was then that I realized I had moved across the room, closing the distance between us.

"If people believe her to be one of my conquests, they won't look twice at you."

"If you value your life, Little Brother, you will stop talking. Right. Now."

"Not another word," he agreed.

I took a moment to rein in my anger. My brother would never betray me. Yet, that knowledge did little to quiet the primal urge to eliminate anyone who even breathed in Cadence's direction.

As much as it pained me to admit, however, Riordan's idea was a good one.

"You make a valid point," I grunted.

My brother tried in vain to hide his grin, but he was smart enough to know when he should remain quiet.

"Once I allow her some more freedom, it wouldn't hurt to have her seen in your company around the palace."

"More freedom? You make it sound like she's a prisoner," Riordan scoffed.

When I didn't contradict him, Riordan's eyes widened in horror.

"Where exactly did you meet your mate, Ryker?"

"The Seelie Kingdom."

"The... the Seelie Kingdom," he repeated in disbelief. "Are you telling me that your mate is one of the Seelie Fae?"

I gave a curt nod in response.

"One," Riordan said, raising a finger. "Why the fuck were you in the Seelie Kingdom to begin with?"

I opened my mouth to respond, but Riordan cut me off. "Two, the fact that she is Seelie is a *huge* fucking problem!"

"I'm aware," I gritted out.

"How are you not seething right now?" he demanded, throwing his arms up. "You have a Seelie mate?"

"I do not care that she is Seelie, only that she is mine. And if you are wise, Little Brother, you will not question me again."

Riordan tilted his head toward the ceiling and blew out a breath before returning his gaze to me.

"And what, she just came with you?"

When I failed to answer, Riordan pressed, "She *did* come willingly?"

"Define willingly," I mused.

"For the love of the gods, Ryker, you cannot just steal your mate away like she's some kind of treasure."

"Of course I can," I sneered. "I am the Prince of the Unseelie Fae."

Riordan pinched the bridge of his nose. "That does not justify kidnapping," he muttered.

"I don't see the problem."

"You wouldn't, you oaf. You know nothing about charming women."

"I've charmed plenty of women," I countered.

"No, you have had plenty of women willing to look past your uncivilized nature for the chance to share space with true power."

"What's the difference?"

"See," Riordan said as he pointed a finger at me. "That right there is the problem. If you want this woman to enjoy being in your company, you're going to need to improve your courting skills."

"One minute you're acting like having a Seelie mate is the worst fate possible, and the next, you're worried about my courting efforts," I huffed, my irritation getting the best of me. "I don't need to court her, Riordan. She's my mate. She's already mine."

"We'll see," he taunted with a knowing smirk.

Without further discussion, I turned on my heels and marched towards the door.

"Where are you going?" Riordan called from behind me.

"To ensure my mate understands exactly who she belongs to."

"Fuck," Riordan muttered, but I was already out the door.

A slow grin worked its way across my face. Cadence wouldn't see me coming.

Chapter Seven

CADENCE

A low groaning sound filled the chamber, and I sat bolt upright as I watched the door swing open. The aged hinges protested under the strain, disturbing the quiet of the night.

True to his word, Ryker had left me locked inside the four walls of his chambers all day, and I would have gone stir-crazy if not for the occasional visits from Scarlette bringing me food. But just like her first visit, she escaped my probing questions before I could interrogate her.

One moment, she was there, and the next, nothing. Poof. Gone. She disappeared like a whisper in the wind.

My exhaustion eventually won out, and I climbed into the enormous bed that had no business being so damn comfortable. I could almost forget how I'd ended up here, lost in the luxury of silken sheets and pillows so soft they felt like clouds.

Almost.

The illusion came crashing down the moment Ryker's towering frame filled my vision.

"Where have you been all day?" I demanded.

Ryker lifted his head, and his piercing gaze struck me all the way to my core. His grey eyes held a magnetic intensity that was so powerful, I couldn't look away.

"Miss me, Cadence?"

His voice was smooth against my skin, the deep timbre a gentle caress that had my nipples puckering under the sheer fabric of my nightdress.

"Of course not," I scoffed.

Ryker's gaze dipped to my chest, and his tongue darted out as he swiped it across his bottom lip.

It was then that I realized I had failed to hold onto the sheet in my haste to confront him. My nipples were standing to attention, and Ryker had a front-row seat to my mortification.

My hands fumbled for the bedding as I yanked it up to my chin, shielding myself from further scrutiny.

Ryker chuckled darkly, and, godsdamn, the sound... *did something to me.*

Warmth flooded my core, and liquid fire pooled at the apex of my thighs.

My body was a lust-induced traitor. Clearly, she had forgotten that he was the enemy.

Ryker stalked toward the bed before settling on the edge opposite me. I watched as he removed his boots and tossed them to the side, not bothering to put them away.

The action irked me more than it should have.

Next, he reached over his head and gripped his tunic in his fist before dragging it over his body.

I bit my tongue to stifle a groan.

He obviously spent a lot of time training.

The muscles along his back rippled and strained with each movement, and I couldn't help but wonder what it would feel like to be pressed beneath his muscular frame.

My went dry, and I had to shake my head to break the trance I had fallen into.

No. Nope. Not happening.

Pull yourself together, Cadence!

Ryker stood abruptly, and I held my breath as the sound of his belt buckle being undone echoed around the space. He gripped the waistband of his trousers, and his forearms flexed with the motion.

"Wait! What are you doing?" I cried just as Ryker was about to pull his trousers down over what were undoubtedly thick, toned thighs.

I felt his smirk before I saw it.

Ryker peered over his shoulder at me, his gorgeous face framed by a wayward strand of his snowy hair, that knowing smirk pulling up the corner of his full lips.

"I'm getting ready for bed, Cadence." Without further warning, Ryker shoved his pants down his legs, and I was suddenly face to face with the toned globes of his bare ass.

"What is wrong with you?" I hissed, slapping a hand over my eyes.

Not that I didn't want to look. Rather, I wanted to look too much.

And if I allowed myself to be pulled into his intoxicating orbit, I knew I'd sink so deep I'd never be able to find my way back to the surface.

I needed to hold on to my rage.

I needed to remind myself who this man was to me.

The bed dipped next to me, and I tensed as I waited for Ryker to make his next move. A rough, calloused hand gripped mine, and Ryker pulled my palms away from my face.

"Don't be embarrassed, Cadence. It's just a body," he cooed. "Unless, of course, you're not acquainted with the male form."

I scoffed. "If you think I've been waiting around for you to grace me with your presence, Ryker, then you'll be disappointed."

Ryker's jaw tightened, and all hints of teasing fell away, leaving only menace in its wake.

"Who?" he demanded.

"That's none of your business."

Before I realized what was happening, Ryker was on top of me, his large body pressing me into the mattress as his hand circled my throat.

His grip was firm, but not tight enough to cut off my air.

I tried to hide the way my body trembled beneath him, but I was certain he could feel every shudder.

"You are my mate, Cadence. Mine!"

He tightened his grip slightly, as if to emphasize his words.

"Everything about you is my business. Now tell me who dared to touch what's mine, so I can show them why crossing me was a mistake."

Despite my unease, I couldn't contain the words that slipped from my tongue.

"Gods! What's wrong with you? I don't *belong* to you, Ryker. You didn't even know I existed before yesterday."

My chest heaved as I tried to get control of my anger.

"What did you imagine I was doing with my time? Just waiting idly for you to sweep me off my feet?"

I didn't know why I bothered defending myself. He was nothing to me and never would be. He had ruined my life, and I could never lose sight of that.

Ryker moved his hand up my throat, his fingers gripping my chin between his thumb and forefinger. His hold was harsher this time, and I fought the urge to wince.

He drew my face close to his, and his warm breath fanned across my lips. I struggled against the shiver that worked to break free, unsure why I was responding to him in this way.

"I don't care that you had a life before I found you, Cadence. You are *my* mate, and I will eradicate anyone who has ever touched this smooth skin, kissed these plump lips, or entered this tight body. And when I'm done, I'll sear every last one of them from your memory until the only touch you can recall is mine."

Ryker closed the distance between us and claimed my mouth with his.

It wasn't a sweet or gentle kiss.

It was brutal, an act of claiming.

Ryker thrust his tongue between my lips as he went to war on my mouth. His kiss was electric, all-consuming, and it sent goosebumps spreading across my skin.

Ryker's hand sank into my hair as he pulled me closer, deepening the kiss. My own hand shot up, and I sent my open palm sailing through the air to meet Ryker's cheek.

Ryker jerked back in shock, and it took him a moment to realize I'd slapped him.

"Don't you ever touch me without my permission again," I seethed.

Ryker's shock melted away, and a dangerous glint danced in his eyes. A wicked grin spread across his face, the searing red handprint on his cheek only making him look more dangerous.

"Oh, Cadence," Ryker purred. "You're a little temptress, aren't you? I *do* enjoy a challenge. Trust me when I say it won't be long before you're begging me to touch you."

"This is not a fucking game, Ryker. This is my life!"

"Oh, I'm well aware. It's you who haven't come to terms with it yet."

He leaned in close to me, his lips brushing against my neck as he pressed his mouth to the shell of my ear.

"You may think you're strong and resilient now, Cadence, but I will break you," he said huskily.

A foreign feeling settled in my stomach, and I couldn't decide how I felt about it. Choosing to ignore it instead, I pulled back as far as the mattress would allow and leveled Ryker with a bored expression.

"I'm tired, so if you wouldn't mind..." I eyed the door, then Ryker.

He grinned, as if he saw right through my feigned indifference.

"So go to sleep." He shrugged as he made himself comfortable.

"I'm not sharing a bed with you, Ryker."

"You don't have a choice, Cadence. This happens to be my chamber and therefore, my bed. I intend to sleep in it."

To prove his point, Ryker tucked his hands behind his head and closed his eyes.

My gaze traveled down his body, only to remember he was naked when my eyes landed on his very large and very erect cock.

"You can kiss it goodnight if you'd like," he said, without opening his eyes.

My cheeks heated, and I was thankful his eyes remained closed.

"You're. Naked."

"Again, very observant of you, Cadence."

"Why are you naked?"

"I sleep naked. You should try it sometime. It might relieve some of that self-righteousness you're carrying around."

Self-righteousness! From the asshole who'd never heard 'no' in his life.

My fingertips tingled with the familiar sensation of my magic, and it would be so, so easy to end his miserable existence here and now.

It won't seem worth it when you're just as dead, I reminded myself.

Taking a deep breath, I scooped up some pillows and yanked the cover off the bed, making Ryker tumble off the side.

Small victories.

"What are you doing now, Cadence?" he asked, having the audacity to sound exasperated.

"I refuse to share a bed with you, so I'm sleeping on the floor."

"Don't be ridiculous."

"I'm not being ridiculous," I snapped. "I'm keeping myself from smothering you in your sleep."

Ryker chuckled, unperturbed by my threat to his life.

"Not that you wouldn't deserve it," I muttered.

No matter how much I fluffed the pillows or adjusted the cover, the ground remained hard and uncomfortable.

"If the floor isn't to your liking, you can always return to the bed," Ryker taunted. "You'd have to ask nicely, of course," he added.

I inhaled a calming breath before I closed my eyes and resolved to come up with an escape plan in the morning.

One way or another, I was leaving the Unseelie Kingdom, and its prince, behind.

Chapter Eight

CADENCE

I was warm.

Too warm.

In fact, I was sweltering.

There was a chill in the air when I'd fallen asleep, but now it felt as though I was cocooned in the warm embrace of the sun.

I sank into the mattress as I stretched my limbs to ease the discomfort.

My eyes flew open when I remembered I was not supposed to be lying on a mattress. I had gone to sleep on the floor to escape the insufferable asshole who occupied the bed.

As I glanced down at my body, my gaze halted on the large, corded forearm thrown over my middle. A quick peek over my shoulder confirmed what I had hoped to avoid.

I was in bed with Ryker.

That bastard must have moved me once I'd fallen asleep.

He had touched me without my permission.

Again.

The man didn't understand boundaries.

As slowly as I could, I gently lifted Ryker's heavy arm and placed it atop his thigh. I let out a relieved sigh when the movement failed to rouse him.

I inched away from his sleeping form, careful not to disturb the blankets strewn across his naked waist. My heart raced inside my chest as I neared the edge of the mattress before swinging my legs over.

Maybe it was foolish, but I didn't want Ryker to see how much waking in his arms rattled me. He was the type of man who would identify your greatest weakness and exploit it to his advantage.

I eased myself out of the luxurious bed and winced as the floorboards creaked beneath my weight.

Ryker stirred, and he mumbled something incoherent as he flung his forearm over his eyes.

I waited a moment longer before taking a tentative step toward the door. When Ryker didn't wake, I took another, then another.

I closed the distance between me and the door before reaching out and twisting the handle.

Locked.

Of course.

I whirled around and scanned my surroundings, intent on finding the keys Ryker had undoubtedly discarded somewhere nearby.

A familiar bejeweled dagger lay haphazardly on the nightstand, catching my eye.

Did he truly see me as such an insignificant threat?

I wanted to laugh out loud at the absurdity, but refrained.

Determined to teach him a lesson, I tiptoed over to the nightstand. My hand darted out, and my fingertips brushed the precious gemstones that decorated the hilt.

I picked up the dagger, careful not to scrape it against the wood beneath, and rolled it over my palm. The steel was cool against my flesh, and I wrapped my fingers around the base as I adjusted to its weight.

Satisfied that I had a decent grip, I lifted the hem of my nightdress and climbed onto the bed.

I looked down at Ryker's sleeping form and then at the dagger gripped firmly in my hand. I lowered myself until I was straddling his waist, then I leaned forward and pressed the sharpened tip of the blade to the soft underside of Ryker's throat.

We were so close that our breaths mingled, and I wasn't prepared for the unwelcome shiver that raced down my spine.

"Is there something you need, Cadence?" Ryker murmured, his voice thick with sleep.

I pressed the dagger further into Ryker's flesh. Not enough to draw blood, but enough that the threat lingered unspoken between us.

Ryker chuckled, and the sound sent butterflies soaring inside my belly, my body forgetting once again that I hated this man.

Ryker shifted beneath me, his hips moving upward as he readjusted his position.

I could feel the hard outline of his erection pressed against my center, and I peered between us, despite knowing the lower half of his body was concealed beneath the sheets.

When I glanced back up again, steel-grey eyes met mine.

"Kinky," he rumbled.

I stiffened and mentally chastised myself for losing my advantage. Narrowing my eyes at him, I allowed the fury that had been building since he'd kidnapped me to course through my veins.

"I told you not to touch me without my permission," I growled.

"I don't need your permission, Cadence. You're mine, and I'll do as I please with what belongs to me."

As I studied his face, I realized Ryker believed what he was saying.

And that enraged me.

Leaning into him, I let my weight press against the blade. Crimson liquid beaded at the tip, and I watched transfixed as it slowly made its way down the column of his throat.

The room darkened, and before I could stop him, Ryker had gripped my waist and flipped me so that he was the one hovering above me.

I tightened my grip on the hilt of the dagger and willed my arm not to tremble as I held it in place against his neck.

A black mist-like substance appeared behind his broad frame, and my mouth dropped open as I gaped at the mass. Dark tendrils coiled around Ryker's arms, slithering up to his shoulders like a serpent.

"What are you?"

I was unaware I had voiced my question out loud until Ryker's answer cut through the haze clouding my mind and chilled me to the bone.

"I am one of a kind, Cadence," he murmured. "And I can be your strongest ally or your worst nightmare. That choice is up to you."

My gaze darted back to his beautifully lethal face. His stormy, grey eyes had been completely swallowed by darkness. It consumed the whites of his eyes until only endless night stared back at me.

My heart pounded against my ribcage. I was torn between fear and a thrilling excitement I didn't dare name.

"They're shadows," I gasped.

Suddenly, the moniker Ryker had donned for a century made sense.

The Night Cursed Prince.

Ryker's lips curled into a sinister grin as his hand snaked up to grip my wrist.

"Don't test me, Ryker," I said as I pressed the dagger further into his skin, making more blood well at the site.

If he was in pain, he showed no sign of it.

"Oh, but I will," he purred, just as his shadows wrapped themselves around my wrists, holding them in place.

Unbothered by the way the blade sliced through his tender flesh, Ryker leaned in close to whisper against my ear.

"Do you feel that, Cadence?" he murmured. "My magic is stirring, fighting my hold to reach you."

A jolt of electricity shot through me the moment the words left his mouth, and my grip on the dagger faltered.

"There have been no shadow wielders for eons," I said, struggling to grasp what I was seeing.

"I'm no ordinary shadow wielder," he purred.

That much was abundantly clear.

The thought of what Ryker might be capable of made me shudder. I'd heard the stories depicting the devastation shadow wielders had wrought during the War of Night.

"And just think, if you accept our bond, you'll share in the power that courses through my veins."

His words crashed into me like a bucket of ice-cold water.

"Get off me," I gritted out.

"So rude, Temptress," he crooned.

I refused to acknowledge how my body came to life at his use of the pet name.

"Let go of me, Ryker. Now!"

Ryker made an annoyed sound in the back of his throat as he rolled off me. His shadows followed in his wake, taking the dagger with them.

He leaned over the bed, grabbing his trousers from the floor. Panic welled inside me as I watched him dress.

"Where are you going?"

Ryker barked out a harsh laugh.

"You want me gone, or you want me to stay? Make up your mind, Cadence."

"Don't flatter yourself," I scoffed. "I'm not eager for more of your underwhelming company. I just don't want to be locked inside this chamber all day."

"You want your freedom, Cadence?" he asked, not bothering to look at me. "Earn it."

"Earn it?" I shrieked, before cringing.

This time, he did look at me. Ryker raked his eyes over my scantily clad form, and I moved to cover myself with the sheets, remembering I was only in my nightdress.

He chuckled and shook his head.

"You seem to still be entertaining the idea that you can escape me, Cadence."

The intensity of Ryker's gaze had me fighting the urge to squirm in place. He lifted his thumb to run the pad across his bottom lip, and I bit the inside of my cheek to keep myself from showing how much that simple action had affected me.

"You want out of this chamber, Cadence," Ryker said as he spread his arms out wide. "Submit to the bond, and I'll grant you your freedom."

Heat crept into my cheeks, but it wasn't from embarrassment.

It was rage.

I grabbed the closest object and launched it across the room toward him.

Unfortunately, I'd grabbed a pillow, and Ryker merely swatted it away.

"I will *never* accept any kind of bond with you," I hissed.

"Then get used to these four walls." Ryker shrugged before pivoting on his boots and marching toward the door.

By the time I disentangled myself from the sheets and chased after him, Ryker was gone.

I pulled on the door handle, already knowing what I would find.

Locked.

"Fuck!"

I slammed my palms against the cherry-colored wood, but he didn't respond.

"You can't keep me locked up like an animal, Ryker!" I bellowed.

For the first time since I had arrived at the Unseelie Court, a small pang of despair tugged at my heart.

I slid down the door and buried my head in my hands.

My thoughts drifted to my parents, and how worried they must be. Callum would try to assuage their fears, but I knew my brother would be just as concerned.

An idea sprang to life in my mind, and I pushed myself off the ground as I scurried toward the desk.

After finding everything I needed, I sat down and began to write.

Chapter Nine

RYKER

The sound of my boots pounding against the hard stone floor echoed around me, intensifying my blackening mood.

Cadence's refusal to acknowledge, let alone accept, our bond, had my blood boiling.

I wanted to claim her as mine, to own her body and ravish her in ways that would have my name falling from her lips like a prayer.

But more than that, accepting the bond promised greater power.

I hadn't lied to Cadence when I told her I was disappointed that the only magic she had to offer was healing. However, I had brushed my disappointment aside when I thought of how much my own power would grow.

If she wouldn't submit to me, I'd have to force her to accept my claim.

I let out a frustrated growl as I pulled my hair away from my face and tied it at my nape.

Gods, the woman was infuriating.

She looked upon me with a level of disdain that suggested I had slaughtered her nearest and dearest, which I knew was not the case, as Malesh had confirmed her parents and older brother were very much alive.

As if conjured by mere thought alone, Malesh fell into step beside me.

"Your father summoned you?" he asked, not one for small talk or idle pleasantries.

I made an affirmative sound, and Malesh nodded.

"Where's Eamon?"

Malesh and Eamon, my most trusted guards, were rarely apart.

"Preparing the men. There's been another attack."

The Crimson Enclave had returned with a vengeance. Despite their near eradication during the Cleansing, a small group had somehow survived. And they'd been biding their time, waiting for the perfect moment to strike.

Now they were out for blood.

Specifically, the blood that ran through my veins.

We continued in silence as we made our way toward the throne room. The guards stationed outside the door bowed their heads and moved aside to let us pass.

As expected, my father sat on the dais, his arm slung over the side as he waited for me to approach.

Malesh dropped back as I went to stand beside my brother.

"Brother, you look positively joyous," Riordan murmured from the corner of his mouth. "Who pissed in your milk this morning?"

I cast a glance in his direction, and whatever he saw in my expression silenced him.

"Ryker," my father called out in a sing-song tone. "How gracious of you to join us."

The men on my father's council snickered, but they quickly averted their eyes when I turned my lethal glare on them.

I wasn't late by any stretch of the imagination, but that didn't matter to my father. He took any opportunity he could to undermine me in the presence of those he deemed important.

"What is the urgency, Father?" I asked, not giving him the reaction he desired.

My father straightened on his throne. "There's been another attack on a village outskirt, less than half a day's ride away," he said.

"The Crimson Enclave?" I asked, the challenge clear in my tone.

My father scoffed. "Don't tell me you have fallen for this nonsense too, My Son."

If my father thought belittling me in front of his sycophants would deter me, he had grossly overestimated the weight I attributed to their perception of me.

"It's not nonsense if it's true," I said with a knowing smirk. "You may not know how a body looks after a Wraith Borne drains it, Father, since you took no active role in the Cleansing."

Red stained my father's cheeks. Had he possessed the power, I was certain he would have incinerated me on the spot.

"As you sent *me* to disperse the uprising," I continued, "I am very much acquainted with the signs, so believe me when I tell you that the Crimson Enclave is no fantasy. They are as real as you and me."

Uncomfortable murmurs broke out among the council, and my father raised his hand to silence the room.

"Then I trust you to do what is necessary to ensure the safety of our kingdom, Ryker."

"Always," I grinned, but it wasn't friendly.

Spinning on my heel, I marched from the throne room with Riordan and Malesh on my trail.

"This could be a trap," Malesh muttered as soon as we rounded the corner.

"Brother," Riordan said, his usual teasing tone noticeably absent. "Malesh has a point. Didn't that Seelie Fae tell you the Crimson Enclave had set their sights on you?"

"I'm still going."

Riordan made an irritated sound before he puffed out a breath. "I'm all for a dalliance with death, Ryker —"

"Actually," I said, cutting him off. "I have another assignment for you."

That piqued his interest.

"Oh," Riordan said, his teasing tone returning with full force. "Please tell me it involves the little mate you have locked up in your quarters."

I will not murder my brother, I chanted as I took a calming breath.

Malesh spluttered beside me, and he coughed as he choked on his surprise. "You don't have her locked in your chamber, do you, Ryker?"

"He does," Riordan said way too gleefully.

Malesh groaned. "She's your mate. You can't treat her like some kind of plaything. You have a lifetime together. Trust me when I tell you it's best to start things off on the right foot."

When Malesh had found his mate, he was nursing a bruised heart from the loss of a woman he thought he'd spend his life with. Then Melania crossed his path, and he was none too pleased to realize she was his mate. He made some poor decisions in the beginning, and Melania never let him forget it.

"I'm still uncertain how this will work, considering Celeste —" Riordan murmured.

I rounded on my brother, and he had to dig his boots into the ground to stop himself from colliding with my chest.

"I told you that was none of your concern," I bit out.

Riordan stepped back and rubbed his hand over the nape of his neck.

"I won't mention it again," he promised before casting a pointed look in Malesh's direction.

My friend knew better than to weigh in on the discussion, however.

I gestured toward Riordan. "I want you to stay with Cadence while I am away. You are not to let her out of my chambers or feed her tidbits that may aid her in her defiance of me."

Riordan grinned, and I growled.

"I'm serious, Brother. This is important. Cadence and I must settle a few things before she may leave my quarters."

Like her willing submission.

"Now promise me you will obey my command."

"You can be so boring when you put your mind to it. Has anyone ever told you that, Ryker?"

"Riordan," I snarled.

"Fine. I'll be as dull as you are while I entertain your mate."

I gave him a curt nod and strode away from him.

"Ryker, where are you going?" he called after me.

"There's something I have to do before I leave," I called back.

The thought brought a smirk to my lips.

This would be entertaining, if nothing else.

Chapter Ten

RYKER

As I passed through the curtain of beads that framed the doorway, they swayed gently, making a soft clicking noise as they brushed against one another. Each line was woven with care, and the beads were strung closely together to offer the interior some privacy.

I pushed the strands aside and entered the small space without waiting to be invited. The curtain settled at my back, its faint rustling slowly faded, restoring the quiet.

Unnatural darkness cloaked the room, and I waved my hand in front of me, parting the shadows with my own.

A woman stood behind a counter, her head bowed, grinding something with a mortar and pestle. She lifted her head as I approached, her crimson eyes narrowed and calculating as she tracked my movements.

"Eleanor," I rumbled, and a slow grin spread across the Blood Fae's features that were too sharp to be called warm.

Eleanor straightened and dusted her hands off before she smoothed her long, raven-colored hair, which was a stark contrast to her alabaster skin. Her fathomless, blood-stained eyes gleamed with intrigue, and she pursed her painted lips as she considered me.

"Your Majesty," she purred. Her voice was as smooth as silk but edged with danger. "To what do I owe the pleasure?"

She moved around her workstation. Her black gown, which was more suited to a ballroom than a workshop, clung to her every curve, accentuating her figure. I could feel the intensity of her magic radiating from her, and the way she held herself told me she was aware of the aura her presence cast.

Eleanor was among the last Blood Fae to serve the King. The Unseelie Fae were notorious for disposing of those they feared were stronger, and blood magic was one of the most potent.

I, however, had no such reservations.

Eleanor *was* powerful, but her magic was at my disposal.

Reaching into my pocket, I retrieved the rose gold collar and ran my fingers over the intricate design. The collar was made of thick, interconnected chain links, forming a smooth, continuous surface. The polished, reflective finish made it look luxurious, and I was sure it would be considered the height of elegance under different circumstances.

Eleanor's eyes dropped to the collar, and an unreadable expression crossed her features. Her fingers twitched at her sides, as though she wanted to reach for it, but she held herself back.

"I want you to enchant this so that the wearer cannot leave the palace grounds unless I have removed it."

Eleanor raised a perfectly manicured brow.

"What an odd thing to bring me, Your Highness," she mused. "A collar can symbolize so many things." She waited for me to elaborate, but I merely stared back at her. Relenting, she continued, "It symbolizes submission and control, but I'm guessing you already knew that?" she said, her tone bordering on mocking. "Who is it for?"

"That is none of your concern," I replied curtly.

Eleanor's eyes flashed with anger. She was not accustomed to being dismissed. Her considerable powers demanded respect, but not from me. She quickly concealed her fleeting outrage, knowing better than to stoke *my* ire.

"I can bind the object to you if that is what you are seeking?"

"Will that prevent her from crossing the wards unless I remove the collar first?"

"It will," Eleanor said cautiously.

Her gaze roved over me, and she didn't shy away from her assessment. More than I could say for others in the kingdom. Many recoiled from my nearness.

"May I?" Eleanor asked as she held out her hand for the collar.

My fingers brushed against her ice-cold skin as I passed it to her. Eleanor's eyes narrowed as she studied it, her long nails tracing the individual links almost reverently.

"You must name your intent," Eleanor declared.

"My intent?"

"Blood magic is drawn to intent. You seek control, or protection perhaps?"

Her gaze flicked to mine once again. "Or is it punishment? Whatever your reason for seeking my aid, you will need to state that purpose before I can perform the enchantment."

I weighed her words. Cadence needed to stay with me for her protection, yes, but I would be lying if I said I didn't seek to control her in every way possible.

She was mine.

Mine to command. Mine to keep. Mine to own.

"I seek her protection, her loyalty."

My tongue darted out to wet my lips, savoring my next words. "Her submission. I want her bound to me so completely that it can never be undone."

Silence fell between us as Eleanor contemplated my demands.

"I can bind her to you, ensuring she cannot leave as long as she wears this," she said, holding up the collar.

"I can even infuse it with tendrils of my magic to encourage her loyalty and submission. But you must understand, Your Highness, complete devotion is an act of free will. I can only take her so far. She will still need to cross the threshold herself."

I ground my teeth together, but nodded in acknowledgment. "Do it," I demanded.

Eleanor eyed me curiously once more before nodding.

"I'll enchant the collar so only your blood has the power to remove it, but you must offer a sacrifice first."

"What offering?" I asked, suspicion lacing my tone.

Eleanor chuckled. "It's nothing onerous, Your Majesty. A little blood will suffice."

"Good," I grunted as I rolled up my sleeve.

Eleanor disappeared beneath the counter and rummaged around her cupboards. When she reemerged, she held a bowl and a wicked-looking dagger.

She dropped the collar into the bowl and then lifted her gaze to meet mine as she waited expectantly. I placed my exposed forearm over the receptacle and nodded for Eleanor to proceed.

The sharp tip of the blade pierced my skin with a sudden jolt, leaving behind a burning sensation in its wake. I watched in fascination as crimson droplets of my blood welled to the surface before running down my arm and into the bowl. With each drop of my blood, the wound throbbed as if it had its own heartbeat.

Eleanor dipped her fingers into the metallic substance and coated the collar in my blood. Next, she used my blood to draw runes around the base of the bowl before marking the same symbols on her arms.

The candlelight flickered, and then darkness swallowed the room.

My shadows stirred to life inside me, feeling at home in the endless night.

Eleanor chanted in the ancient language of the Fae, and a bone-chilling cold seeped beneath my skin. Whispers surrounded me, as if the shadows were answering the Blood Fae's call.

A gust of wind tore through the space, and the whispers grew louder, swirling around us like an enchantress of dark promises. My shadows continued to writhe, eager to join the dance of power that Eleanor was weaving.

Eleanor's chanting intensified, and her commanding voice rose above the din. The runes Eleanor had painted with my blood ignited, casting a crimson glow across her face.

Concentration creased her brows, and beads of sweat lined her temples. I watched as Eleanor's lips moved in sync with the pulsing runes as her chanting reached a crescendo.

Then, one by one, the candles reignited, the darkness slowly retreated, and the glowing runes faded. Silence replaced the eerie whispers that had tried to tempt me, and the room settled once more.

I cast a glance towards the bowl, which now only held the collar; all traces of my blood had vanished. When I looked up at the Blood Fae, her head was bowed, and she pressed her arms against the counter to steady herself as she regained her breath. She was panting heavily, her chest rising and falling with each ragged inhale, and sweat slicked her forehead.

If I were a good man, I would offer her a seat and perhaps a glass of water as I waited for her to recover from the vast amount of power she had expended on my behalf.

I was no such man, however.

"Is it done?" I pressed, impatience coloring my tone.

"Y-yes," Eleanor wheezed.

I stalked towards the counter and plucked the collar from the bowl. It felt heavier than before, as though it carried more than mere magic — an unseen presence that demanded to be noticed.

"Good."

I slipped the collar beneath my tunic and narrowed my gaze at the Blood Fae. My shadows filled my eyes as I pinned her in place with my stare.

"I trust you understand the consequences should you speak of this to anyone?" I said in a lethal tone.

She swallowed thickly, a tendril of fear spiking in her blood before she let her anger get the best of her.

"I'm not in the business of spilling secrets," Eleanor bit out as though I had offended her. Then, remembering who she was talking to, she added, "Your Majesty."

I rapped my knuckles on the counter. "Make sure it stays that way."

I brushed past the beaded curtain. The sound of the beads clicking together followed me as I proceeded down the hall.

I might not have my mate's submission yet, but I couldn't deny the feeling of victory stirring inside my chest.

Oh, sweet Cadence, you never stood a chance.

Chapter Eleven

CADENCE

With my letter clutched tightly in my palm, I paced the length of the chamber in front of the door. I had to persuade Ryker to send it, which meant I would have to swallow my pride and be cordial with the asshole.

Just thinking about it made me shiver with revulsion.

The man had wronged me countless times, yet I had to play nice to get what I needed.

The injustice of it sent my blood simmering in my veins.

Ryker should be kneeling at *my* feet and begging for *my* forgiveness.

Of course, the gods knew I would never forgive him.

Ryker's transgressions were beyond forgiveness.

As if my wayward thoughts had summoned him, the door flew open, and Ryker strode into the room.

It never ceased to amaze me how big the man was. I had to crane my neck just to look him in the eye.

"Cadence," Ryker purred, and the sound of his rich, masculine voice washed over me, leaving me wanting.

Mentally shaking myself, I softened my features and ran my palms over my skirts.

"Ryker," I replied. "Just the man I needed."

Ryker raised an amused brow as he studied me.

"Oh."

The single word hung heavy between us, Ryker's skepticism deafening in the silence.

Clearing my throat, I continued. "I have reconsidered your offer to send word to my family. I don't want them to worry."

I lifted my hand, still clutching the letter, and thrust it into Ryker's chest. Too late, I realized I had been a little more aggressive than I had intended, and I winced as I waited for his response.

An ominous grin spread across Ryker's face, and I forced myself to swallow my unease.

The rough pads of his fingers brushed my own, and I jumped back when a small jolt of electricity raced through me at the point of contact.

Ryker studied the letter for a moment before he reached beneath his tunic and stowed it in his pocket.

"I'll send your letter, Cadence," he murmured.

I retreated another step, but Ryker wasn't having it. He prowled after me, a hunter closing in on his prey.

"There's something I want you to do for me in return."

It took everything in me not to scoff at him. I'd already exercised immense restraint by not murdering the man in his sleep, yet he had the audacity to ask for more. Maybe it'd be worth it just to wipe the smug look off his perfectly proportioned face.

Ryker moved behind me, and I stiffened. Every instinct screamed at me not to turn my back on this predator, and I was inclined to listen.

Think about your letter, I reminded myself.

I released a shaky breath, exhaling the tension that had locked me in place.

"See," Ryker whispered against the shell of my ear, "submitting to me wasn't so difficult after all."

Think of your family. Think about your letter.

Ryker chuckled darkly, as if he could hear the internal war I was waging, and he found great amusement in my struggle.

Large palms settled on my shoulders, and Ryker steered me toward the mirror attached to his closet.

"Close your eyes."

Reluctantly, I did as he instructed and allowed my eyes to close. I could hear the rustling of fabric as Ryker searched for something. Anxiety knotted my stomach. Was this all an elaborate attempt to harm me? He wouldn't have taken such drastic measures, only to end my life now. Would he?

Before my mind could spiral further, something cool brushed my throat, followed by a soft *snick* as it clicked into place.

My eyes flew open, and I stared into Ryker's triumphant grey ones, not comprehending what had passed between us but knowing it was significant all the same.

A small glint caught my attention, and my gaze was drawn to the rose gold necklace that now adorned my throat. The thick metal links were interconnected in a tight, continuous design, and the polished finish gave the impression that it was of the highest quality.

While beautiful, the necklace sat flush against my throat, and the longer I stared at it, the more I felt like the walls were closing in around me, suffocating me.

Instinctively, my hands went to the back of my neck as I tried to pry the clasp open, but it didn't budge.

Mirth twinkled in Ryker's eyes when I returned my gaze to my reflection. I angled my head to the side and studied the necklace. It almost looked like...

"Is this a..." I breathed, unable to finish my sentence for fear that the nausea raging inside my stomach would spill free if I uttered another word.

"A collar?" Ryker preened. "Yes, it is."

My fingers flew to the metal, and I clawed at it as I tried to rip it from my throat.

"That won't work," Ryker taunted.

"Take it off me now!"

"The only way to remove that collar, Cadence, is with my blessing."

"You fucking bastard!"

My fists pounded into Ryker's chest, over and over, but if he felt anything beneath the solid wall of muscle, he didn't show it.

"That's it, Cadence," he said in a low, mocking tone as he drew me close. "Let it all out."

I screamed in frustration as I intensified my efforts, slamming my fists against him with all the strength I possessed.

By the time I gave up my fight, I was a panting, sweaty mess. My hair was askew, and my chest rose and fell in rapid succession.

"You will be free to roam the castle and the exterior courtyard, but the collar will prevent you from crossing the outer wards surrounding the forest."

I tried to push Ryker away from me, but he cupped the back of my head as he pressed me against his broad chest.

"I'm going to kill you for this," I snarled.

"Don't threaten me with a good time, Temptress."

A sob tore its way free from my throat before I could stop it. I bit down on my tongue to prevent any more emotions from escaping without my permission.

"Shh, Cadence," Ryker said, almost adoringly.

Once I regained my composure, I lifted my head and glared at him, letting him see the unbridled hatred shimmering in my eyes.

"Careful, Cadence," Ryker purred. "I like a feisty woman."

"I promise you, you will regret this, Ryker."

This time, when I pushed against his chest, Ryker stepped back, allowing me to escape the warmth of his embrace.

"We shall see," he said with a smirk.

Ryker straightened his tunic. "I have to leave on an errand for my father. My brother Riordan will keep you company in my absence."

"I want nothing to do with you or your family," I spat.

Ryker ignored my outburst. "Be a good girl for him, won't you, Cadence?"

I. Was. Seething.

Ryker stalked toward me, and before I knew what was happening, he'd brushed his lips against my own.

Then he walked away, leaving me to stew in my rage.

Chapter Twelve

RYKER

The moment my boots met the damp earth, I knew something was wrong.

I flicked my head to the side, signaling Malesh to fan out, then repeated the gesture to Eamon. Both men acknowledged my silent orders with a barely perceptible nod before they disappeared into the darkness.

I inhaled a deep breath, allowing my senses to delve into the surrounding woods as I tried to locate the source of my unease. A twig snapping underfoot was all the confirmation I required.

"They're still here."

"The Wraith Borne?" one man asked, and I didn't miss the slight tremor in his tone.

Most of my men knew the power of the Wraith Borne first-hand, but a small contingent had been too young to serve during the Cleansing.

"Do not allow the Wraith Borne to get their hands on you," I warned. "Their toxic magic can drain the life from you with a single touch, should they choose."

Eight decades had passed since that blood-soaked day, which was now immortalized in the pages of our history books. My father had grown paranoid about the Wraith Borne over the years. Their ability to break a person from the inside out as their magic twisted and crushed their victim's organs with a mere touch, had already made most of their brethren wary of them.

They were some of the most lethal Fae the Unseelie Kingdom had ever produced, and when their numbers continued to rise, my father had judged them to be a significant threat to his position on the throne. It took little work to convince the council to gradually restrict their freedoms as he nudged the Unseelie Fae toward his ultimate end.

The eradication of the Wraith Borne.

His fears proved to be well-founded. The Wraith Borne had descended on the palace, wielding their deadly touch and killing anyone who stood in their way before my father even had the chance to go on the offensive.

What followed was a coordinated effort to hunt down and kill any Wraith Borne who survived the initial attack until my father had achieved his goal.

The cleansing of the Unseelie Kingdom from the disease that was the Wraith Borne.

No one had been spared. Men, women, and children had been sentenced to death by virtue of the magic that flowed in their veins.

Now, as I stood within the tree line of the darkened woods, I was reminded of the fact that the Cleansing had failed.

My father had only given the deadly Fae more reason to despise him and his rule.

The telltale signs of the Wraith Borne had marked the bodies scattered across the kingdom's outskirts in recent years.

Like the one we had just left.

My palms tightened on the pommel of my sword as I stepped further into the woods.

An unnatural stillness hung in the air, the silence wrapping around me like a shroud. It seemed as though even the trees held their breath, waiting and watching as we tracked our prey.

My shadows seeped from me, twisting and writhing as the dark tendrils scoured the path ahead. An icy chill settled in, and I saw mist form in front of me as I exhaled.

"Kane," I called, and the Earth Fae fell into step beside me. "Does the earth speak to you?"

The man dropped to his knees and pressed his palm flat against the ground. His magic pulsed around him as he sent it into the dirt beneath our feet, searching.

After a moment, Kane lifted his gaze to mine, his eyes full of dread as he shook his head. "It's as if everything inside these woods is dead."

"Dead? How is that possible?"

"I don't know," he murmured. "Something is wrong."

The Earth Fae rose from the ground and returned to his position. A moment later, Malesh emerged from the brush and took his place.

"I couldn't find any trace of them, Ryker. I don't like it. What if your father —"

Malesh's words were cut off as an arrow whistled through the air and struck his flank with a *thud.* Malesh grunted as he clutched his side, and blood coated his fingers in a torrent.

Then chaos erupted.

Arrows flew in every direction, and my men scrambled for cover, ducking behind tree trunks and diving to the ground.

I gripped Malesh by his bicep as I pulled my shadows around me and stepped through the inky mass. I closed the distance to a nearby tree, where I laid Malesh against the thick base.

"Wait here. I will return for you."

With a pained grunt, Malesh acknowledged my command.

I returned to the fray and saw Eamon fending off a blow from one of the Wraith Borne, who had finally given up their position. He raised his sword above his head before bringing it down in an arc toward his assailant. The Wraith Borne sidestepped the blow and lunged for Eamon.

Eamon lifted his muscular leg and landed his boot in the center of his attacker's chest. The man crumbled to the ground, a pained moan escaping him. The sound faded abruptly as Eamon swung his sword again, this time severing the man's head in one swift blow. A crimson fountain erupted from the man's neck, and Eamon stepped back to avoid the spray.

When he caught my eye, he gave me a curt nod to let me know he was unharmed before he lunged for his next opponent.

Another Wraith Borne leaped toward me, and I raised my sword to meet his.

I didn't even glance in his direction. I was acting on instinct as my shadows whirled inside me, warning me of the impending danger.

Power thrummed through my body, and I sent an inky-black tendril sailing through the air toward him. It wrapped around his throat, and I squeezed.

The man dropped his sword as he clawed at his neck.

That only made me squeeze harder.

A loud crack echoed between us as the man's head lolled to the side.

Fuck.

I hadn't meant to break his neck. I'd wanted to drag it out a little longer.

Tossing the man aside, I studied the battle unfolding before me.

I saw one of my men sprawled out on the ground, unmoving. His body lay twisted and contorted, as if drained of every ounce of life. His withered skin clung to his bones, resembling old parchment left to shrivel with time.

His vacant eyes had sunken deep into their sockets, and his lips had been pulled into a tight line, with only the barest gap visible, as if his last breath had been violently wrenched from him. His fingers were curled into skeletal claws, forcing his knuckles to protrude against the gaunt, withered skin.

All that remained was a fragile husk, ready to crumble at the slightest touch.

Rage flooded my body, and I clenched my jaw tight.

The Wraith Borne killed without mercy, stealing the very souls from their victims, leaving nothing for their families to mourn.

I returned my sword to its scabbard and held my hands out in front of me. My shadows responded to my call as they contorted and danced beneath my palms.

I directed them forward, and they slithered across the ground undetected by the combatants above them. My shadows snaked their way up the bodies of the men, rising and expanding until darkness encased the entire battlefield.

Frightened gasps and low curses cut through the air.

Fear permeated the woods, and my lips curved into a menacing grin.

I was at home in the darkness.

My men had long since grown accustomed to my shadows, and their silence allowed me to track the enemy with ease.

I reached beneath my tunic and retrieved the two daggers sheathed at my back. My shadows concealed the sound of my footfalls as I snuck up behind one man and ran my blade over his throat.

The smell of copper filled my nostrils, and I let the scent ground me. The man dying at my feet gurgled and spluttered as he tried and failed to take a breath.

At that moment, I embraced the name many whispered behind closed doors, fearing I might hear and come for them too.

I became the Night Cursed Prince.

Hidden in the darkness, they couldn't see me coming, and their fear grew potent. It swarmed my senses, and I let it wash over me as I savored the intoxicating aroma of their terror, letting it fuel my strength.

With each hushed whisper and panicked inhale, I drew closer, moving silently through my shadows undetected. The Wraith Borne thrashed wildly, turning in circles and stumbling over their own feet as they moved through the dark matter aimlessly, desperate to find an escape.

I cut, stabbed, and sliced my way through them, their horrified cries spurring me on.

All too soon, the killing ceased, and my shadows retreated, curling and twisting along my body until they were one with me once more.

I stood among a field of bodies, covered in the blood of my enemies, as I caught my breath.

A low whistle sounded beside me, and I turned to meet Eamon's gaze.

"You really outdid yourself this time, Ryker."

I grunted in response as I swiped at the blood trickling into my eyes.

"Where's Malesh?" Eamon asked, and I stiffened, remembering the dire state in which I had left my friend.

I darted behind the large tree and sucked in a sharp breath when I saw his unconscious form slumped against its base.

Eamon cursed behind me as I pressed my fingers against the pulse point at the base of Malesh's throat.

It was faint, but it was there.

"He needs help," I said as I lifted Malesh's body and pulled his arm around my shoulders to support his weight.

"Get the men home safely."

Eamon nodded at my command, and I pulled my shadows around me once more.

Malesh needed a healer.

Luckily for him, I knew exactly where to find one.

Chapter Thirteen

CADENCE

I was stewing in my fury, so fixated on my desire to end my newfound nemesis, no matter the consequences, that I didn't notice someone else had entered my space.

The sound of a throat clearing behind me had me jumping out of my skin. I spun around to berate the newcomer for their lack of manners, but my words died on my tongue.

The man standing before me was the spitting image of Ryker.

The same strong jawline accentuated by perfectly sculpted facial features. Same sun-kissed skin that radiated vitality, making him look impossibly more beautiful.

The only difference was that while Ryker's hair caressed his shoulders, this man's hair was cut short on the sides with longer strands on top.

The man smirked, amused by my appraisal of his form, and even that slight gesture reminded me of Ryker.

Hadn't Ryker said he was sending his brother to watch over me?

This had to be him. The resemblance was uncanny.

"Who are you?" I demanded as I crossed my arms over my chest.

"Did my brother not advise you of my impending arrival?"

He quirked a brow in challenge, and godsdamn, he even sounded like Ryker.

Why that comforted me, I had no idea.

"He might have mentioned it," I muttered.

The man chuckled. "Oh, Cadence. My brother sure has his work cut out for him with you, doesn't he?"

"I distinctly recall telling your brother that I did not want, nor need, a babysitter."

He clutched his palms over his heart and staggered backward until his back collided with the door.

"Cadence, you wound me!"

He slid down the wooden frame, landing in a heap on the floor.

"Please," he panted. "I need your help."

He stretched his arm out toward me, and for a moment, I thought he was truly having some kind of episode.

"I think I need mouth to mouth."

An undignified snort escaped me before I could contain it, and he grinned.

"Nice try."

"Wasn't it, though?"

The man pushed himself up from the floor and offered me his hand.

"My name is Riordan," he said. "The smarter, funnier, and more handsome of the Unseelie Princes," he added with a wink.

I chuckled at his antics despite myself and placed my palm in his.

"It's nice to meet you, Riordan. I'm Cadence, but you already knew that."

Riordan pulled my hand toward his lips and placed a soft kiss on my knuckles.

"For what it's worth, my brother most certainly does not deserve a mate as splendid as you."

"He's not my mate," I corrected him.

Riordan released my hand and chuckled to himself. Marching toward Ryker's bed, he picked up an apple off the fruit tray Scarlette had brought me earlier, before flopping down onto the mattress.

Making himself comfortable, Riordan rested his arm behind his head as he took a bite of the apple.

"So, what mischief should we get up to today?" he asked between bites.

The devious glint in Riordan's eyes hinted at his fondness for causing trouble. Perhaps he'd be good company after all.

Then I remembered the collar.

"Well, seeing as your brother collared me so that I cannot move beyond the wards, I'm guessing our choices are limited," I said with a scowl.

Riordan began choking, and his face flushed crimson as he fought to suck in a breath. I rushed toward him and thumped him on the back a few times, before a half-chewed chunk of apple flew across the room.

I turned to the nightstand and grabbed the empty tumbler and pitcher of water, then thrust a half-full cup at him, commanding him to drink. He grabbed it eagerly and gulped down the cool liquid until the entire glass was drained.

"Thank you," he croaked.

"Are you all right?"

I couldn't ignore the healer in me, even if I wanted to.

With shaky hands, Riordan placed the glass back on the nightstand.

"Did you say collared?" he asked, ignoring my question.

My fingers went to the rose gold chain that adorned my throat.

I refused to be embarrassed for something that was done to me, so I lifted my chin and met Riordan's gaze.

"Yes. The asshole you call a brother tethered me with a magical collar that prevents me from leaving his domain."

Riordan muttered under his breath, and I thought I heard him say, "That is not what I meant by charming, brother."

Riordan studied the collar as if it were a puzzle he could solve.

"May I?" he asked as he raised his hand.

I gave him a curt nod, and he directed me to turn around. His fingers grazed the skin of my nape as he reached for the clasp, and I inhaled sharply.

What if he could remove it?

My hopes shattered a moment later as Riordan flew across the room with a shrill cry. He collided with the armchair beside Ryker's bed, and I hurried over to check on him.

"By the gods, are you all right?"

Riordan groaned. "Ryker never did like sharing his things."

I bristled at Riordan's comment and straightened.

"I am not one of Ryker's *things*," I spat. "I am a person!"

Riordan dragged a hand down his face. "I didn't mean it like that," he mumbled.

He extended his arm to me and said, "Help me up, will you?"

Begrudgingly and with great effort, I helped the enormous Fae male to his feet.

"All I meant was that Ryker often bewitched his possessions when we were children, and if I ever tried to play with them, there was always some sort of trap waiting for me. I didn't mean to imply *you* were a possession."

He flashed me an apologetic smile, and I felt my anger fade. Why was that one expression so damn endearing?

"What happened when you touched it?" I asked, changing topics.

"It shocked me!"

I didn't miss the outraged indignation in Riordan's voice.

Riordan's face turned serious, and he placed a hand over his heart before dipping into a low bow.

"On behalf of my brother, I apologize for his unwavering stupidity."

A chuckle bubbled up my throat, and before I knew it, I was shaking with raucous laughter. Riordan lifted his head, and his features split into a wide grin.

"I'm sorry to interrupt whatever bonding session is going on here," a rough, masculine voice said from behind me.

I didn't need to turn to know exactly who it was.

Gooseflesh rose on my skin, and my heart thundered against my ribcage as if it were trying to reach him.

When I turned, grey eyes locked with mine.

I had no time to be swept away by Ryker's intense gaze, however, as he clutched an unconscious man in his arms, who was bleeding profusely.

Riordan swore under his breath before asking Ryker what had happened.

Ryker's gaze remained fixed on me.

"You will help him."

It wasn't a question. He was telling me what was about to unfold.

I opened my mouth to argue, but some emotion I couldn't quite detect flashed across Ryker's face, and it left me feeling unsettled.

I glanced away to break the hold Ryker had over me and inhaled a deep breath.

This was something I could control, and it brought me a certain level of comfort.

I rolled my sleeves up to my elbows and gave Ryker a curt nod. "Put him on the bed."

Chapter Fourteen

CADENCE

The scent of blood hung thick in the air, sharp and cloying.

"I need a bowl of water and some cloth," I called as I examined the man lying inert on Ryker's bed.

"I'll get it," Riordan answered before he sprinted from the room.

"What was he hit with?"

Careful not to jostle the injury, I peeled the crimson-stained fabric from the man's side.

"An arrow," Ryker rumbled.

"He should be healing by now," I muttered under my breath.

"Here," Riordan panted, startling me for the second time that day.

"Thank you."

I dipped the cloth into the clean water and set about clearing the blood away so that I could study the injury. An acrid odor hit my nostrils, and I leaned in closer to sniff the wound.

I turned to Ryker and Riordan. "I can smell iron," I said, ignoring their twin expressions of disgust.

Riordan's face paled, while Ryker's expression darkened as he struggled to contain his mounting fury.

"Since he's not healing as he should, I suspect a piece of shrapnel is still lodged in the wound. He's unconscious now, but the moment I start poking around in his side, he's going to wake up with one hell of an attitude. I need you both to hold him down while I work."

The brothers rose in unison, with Ryker securing the man's shoulders while Riordan held his legs.

"Do you have any brandy?"

I directed my question to Ryker, and he nodded toward a small cabinet I hadn't noticed before. I rushed over, unlatched the lock, and rifled through it until I found what I needed.

Aged fifty years. What a waste.

Returning to the bed, I crouched beside the man, positioning myself so I had the best view of his side. My teeth wrapped around the cork, and I pulled it free before pouring a healthy dose of liquor over the wound. Unable to resist, I lifted the bottle to my lips and drank deeply.

When I lowered the brandy, both brothers were staring at me in disbelief. Their mouths hung open, and their eyes were wide with surprise.

I wondered if they realized just how similar they were. It didn't seem like the opportune time to ask them, however.

"What?" I shrugged. "It's aged fifty years."

Riordan snorted, and a hint of amusement flashed across Ryker's usually stony face.

"Ready?"

Both men nodded.

I took a deep breath to steady my pounding heart and pulled my magic around me. The man's chest rose and fell with shallow, uneven breaths, each one more strained than the last.

He didn't have long.

When my fingers dipped inside the open wound, blood gushed from the site, and the man woke with a feral roar.

I could hear the brothers trying to soothe their friend, but it did nothing to quell his thrashing limbs. He bucked his hips off the bed as he tried to dislodge the arms holding him down. Riordan cursed when one of the man's feet broke free and struck his lip.

"Come on, come on," I murmured as I dug my fingers in deeper.

I let my magic guide me as I searched for the stray piece of iron that would be the death of this man if I couldn't remove it.

My fingertips grazed something sharp, and the man roared in agony.

"How much longer?" Ryker gritted out as he continued to hold his friend down.

"I'm working on it."

"Work faster."

I glared at the Fae prince, and he glared right back. If the wounded man still struggling in their grasp didn't require my attention, I'd have challenged him to do better.

Removing the iron was a delicate task as my fingers kept slipping off the metal from all the blood coating it. I swore under my breath when I failed to get a proper grip on the deadly tip for the third time.

The man on the bed ceased thrashing, and my gaze swung to him. His lips parted in a gasp, but no sound escaped. His eyes fluttered closed, and his breathing grew even shallower.

"No, no, no," I muttered. It was then that I realized I didn't know the man's name. "What's his name?"

"Malesh," Ryker supplied.

"Malesh, I need you to stay with me, all right?" I said, working hard to keep the panic from my voice.

Malesh didn't open his eyes, and Ryker cast a worried glance in my direction.

"Talk to him," I instructed. "Try to rouse him."

I doubled down on my efforts as I pressed my fingers against the iron tip. I slowly worked my way up the metal until I found a roughened groove.

Malesh jerked underneath me, and a pained groan sounded from his throat.

At least he was responding.

"You've got him?" I asked, and both men nodded in agreement.

I exhaled a shaky breath and apologized for what I had to do next, then I yanked on the tip, drawing on my magic for added strength.

The metal snagged on something, but I kept tugging until the resistance gave way.

Malesh, who had been writhing in agony, went still, losing consciousness as the pain overwhelmed him.

"He's out again," Riordan called, a note of hysteria infecting his tone.

"Ugh!"

The metal got caught again, and I cursed the gods for making things so difficult. A strand of hair fell onto my face, and I blew it out of my eyes as I worked. With one final pull, the iron tip came free, and I dumped it in the bloodied water bowl beside me.

"Put pressure on the wound," I instructed, as I turned to grab the brandy.

Pouring a generous amount over the gash, I placed my palm against it and allowed my magic to flow through my fingers. The brandy would stave off any infection, but my magic would knit the skin back together and stem the bleeding.

Once I'd finished, I collapsed against the bedpost, exhausted, and rubbed my temples.

"You've got a little..." Riordan said, as he gestured toward my forehead.

Then I remembered my hands were coated in blood. And now, so was my face. I groaned and then reached for a piece of clean cloth to scrub it away.

Once I caught my breath, I leaned forward and placed my fingers against the pulse point of Malesh's throat. It was weak, but steady. His chest rose and fell with effort, but his breathing had improved, and color had returned to his skin.

"He's going to be all right," I declared.

A collective sigh of relief filled the room.

I turned toward Ryker, truly taking him in for the first time since he had appeared. His hair was matted with blood, and the crimson substance was smeared all over his face and arms. There were several tears along the front of his tunic and a small gash on his forearm.

"What the hell happened to you?" I asked before I could stop myself.

Ryker smirked at me. "Worried about me, Cadence?"

I pressed my lips together and shrugged, refusing to give him the answer he wanted.

"Professional curiosity," I said as I took another sip of the brandy.

Ryker's large hand covered mine and tugged the amber liquid out of my grasp. He raised the bottle to his lips and drank greedily. And, gods help me, I couldn't pull my eyes away as I watched his throat bob with each swallow.

When he set the brandy down, Ryker looked at me with a knowing grin. Heat scorched my cheeks, and I turned away from him, focusing my attention on Riordan.

"He needs rest and plenty of fluids to help him regain his strength. I'd also recommend having someone stay with him while he's sleeping to monitor for any signs of complications."

Riordan nodded. "Help me get him back to Melania, will you, Ryker?"

Ryker grunted and moved to grab Malesh's upper body.

As the men left, I pressed a hand to my stomach, where tiny winged creatures fluttered wildly.

"Enemy, Cadence. He's the enemy," I reminded myself.

If only my traitorous body would accept it.

Chapter Fifteen

CADENCE

A week had passed since Ryker had uprooted my life and dragged me to the Unseelie Kingdom. I didn't even know if he had delivered my letter to Callum, but I chose to believe that he had.

Sunlight filtered through the dense canopy overhead, and I watched the tree branches sway in the breeze as I meandered through the surrounding woodland. Small patches of gold dappled the forest floor, reminding me of my last day in the market back home.

A sense of longing settled in my stomach, but I pushed the feeling away as quickly as I could, fearing I would succumb to it and break apart where I stood.

A masculine grunt came from behind me, drawing my attention to the six guards following me as I explored the palace grounds. Malesh's presence among the men gave me no small measure of relief. The man had glued himself to my side since I had saved him from certain death.

I had tried to convince him it was all in a day's work, but he refused to hear it. When I pleaded with his wife to get him to stop, she only encouraged him further, telling me he had a debt to repay and that anything short of kissing the ground I walked on wouldn't do.

The memory brought a smile to my lips.

If circumstances were different, I was certain I could have become fast friends with Melania. But I would never form connections in this kingdom, not with the band of gruff men stalking my every move.

They didn't exactly give off welcoming vibes.

They were all trained soldiers, muscular and tall, and each carried enough weaponry to start their own army. People took one look at them and scurried in the opposite direction.

I'd hoped to discreetly test the collar's limits, but my companions quickly dispelled that thought.

As I continued my stroll through the woodland, I relished the cool air that caressed my skin. It wasn't my intention to wander so far from the palace, but when the scent of damp earth and pine filled my lungs, I was pleased that I had.

The deeper I ventured, the quieter the world around me became. I hadn't realized how much I needed the silence until

I had left the palace walls. Gone were the sounds of the busy courtyard. Deep within the forest, only the rustling leaves and the distant call of birds remained.

It soothed my aching soul and revitalized my senses.

The sound of water trickling over stones, gentle and persistent, caught my attention, and I headed in the same direction.

A thick grove of trees came into view up ahead, and I imagined they were ancient beings standing sentinel over the woodlands. Their trunks were wide and draped in moss, and their low-hanging branches seemed to lean toward something unseen, as if they were guarding the forest's secrets.

As I parted the limbs, stepping through the natural barrier, a surprised gasp escaped me as I took in what lay before me. Beyond the trees was a small clearing, the bright sun lighting up the area and falling on a pool of shimmering water.

I couldn't contain my excitement at the sight of the spring.

The water was crystal clear, and I could see the smooth stones lining the bottom. A wall of tall, thick ferns and boulders partially concealed the spring, almost as if the primordial forest sought to protect the hidden sanctuary.

I rushed toward the water and dipped my fingers in.

It was cold but not biting.

"Cadence, be careful near the edge," Malesh warned.

Lost in the spring's beauty, I'd forgotten about the men trailing me. I turned to appraise him, and a wicked grin spread across my face. Malesh groaned as if he already knew what was coming next.

"Eyes downcast."

His panicked tone made me chuckle, but their obvious discomfort did not dissuade me. The spring was so inviting that it felt wrong not to bask in nature's beauty.

I wasted no time as I kicked off my boots and slid my dress from my shoulders until it pooled in a soft heap on the ground. When I reached for my undergarments, I hesitated, debating whether or not to remove them, knowing Ryker would lose his mind if he learned I was naked in front of his men.

Then I reminded myself that Ryker was a bastard, and I didn't care what he thought about my choices. He could do with some discomfort in his life. The gods knew he had more than earned it.

I slipped out of my panties and stepped toward the spring. The smooth stones were cold against my feet as I slowly waded into the water. A shiver raced through me as it reached my knees, then my thighs.

I took a deep breath before diving forward until I was fully submerged beneath the cool liquid. When I broke the surface, my wet strands clung to my skin as droplets streamed down my cheeks.

I tipped my head toward the heavens as I let the sun warm my face. Swimming to the center of the pool, I rolled onto my back and allowed the gentle current to move me as I floated on the surface. The weightlessness of my body was freeing. For a moment, I could forget everything and allow my mind to escape.

I laughed softly to myself, and the sound echoed in the stillness.

I didn't know how long I lay there, letting the water lap at my bare skin as it loosened my tight, achy muscles.

The feeling of unseen eyes raked over me, and I dipped beneath the water. Not that it would do much to conceal my nakedness, given its pristine state.

I glanced toward the shore, and my eyes clashed with murderous, grey ones.

Ryker stood before his men, his corded arms crossed over his broad chest as he clenched his jaw tight. I fought the urge to slink away from the fuming prince. He had no right to be upset. I would make the most of my gilded prison, irrespective of his fragile feelings.

"Come here, Cadence. Now."

His voice rumbled over my flesh with a ferocity that was more tantalizing than it was intimidating, and gods damn it, my nipples pebbled.

I waded toward the shore and raised my chin before striding out of the water, making no effort to conceal my nakedness.

Ryker's gaze darkened as he took me in, and then, remembering we had an audience, he growled, "If you value breathing, you will keep your eyes off my mate."

The violence that dripped from his tone should have terrified me, but it didn't.

Instead, my core throbbed, and liquid fire pooled at the apex of my thighs.

Ryker stormed toward me, and I heard him mutter, "I cannot kill my men. I cannot kill my men. I cannot kill my men."

His large hands reached for me, and he pulled my damp body against his chest. Ryker's warm breath fanned across the shell of my ear, and he whispered, "Oh, sweet Cadence. You are in so much trouble."

Before I could respond, dark shadows formed around us, and then everything disappeared.

Chapter Sixteen

CADENCE

My feet hit solid ground, and I fell forward as I struggled to right myself.

Traversing Ryker's shadows had been a disconcerting experience, and I felt the need to hold myself together as though I had somehow broken apart and then reformed on the other side.

Of course, Ryker had no such qualms. He moved with a predator's grace, not the least bit ruffled by our journey.

I glanced around, realizing that I now stood in the middle of Ryker's bedchamber.

Naked.

A shudder ran through me as I tried to cover myself, and when I met Ryker's steel-grey eyes, a malicious glint stared back at me.

Ryker reached for his belt. With steady fingers, he undid the clasp and pulled the leather free from his waist.

What the hell did he intend to do with that?

"On your knees, Cadence."

There were moments in life when you had to make choices that could alter the very fabric of your being.

This was one of those moments.

I knew I should fight Ryker, defy his command to obey, and reassert my authority over my being. If I gave in to him, he would only be emboldened. He would take it as an act of submission. That I accepted the bond he insisted we shared.

That couldn't be further from the truth.

Still, there was a part of me, and not a small part, that desperately wanted to know what Ryker intended to do to me.

Despite my better judgment, I lowered myself to my knees before him, not once breaking eye contact.

Ryker smirked down at me, and he cupped my cheek with his calloused palm.

"So, you can be trained," he purred as he cocked his head to the side to study me.

I wanted to return a scathing retort, but I was so transfixed by the intensity glinting in Ryker's grey eyes to risk him stopping whatever this was. Instead, I bit my tongue and glared back at him.

“There she is,” Ryker cooed as he stroked my cheek. “My Temptress. My mate.”

He ran his eyes over my naked form, and he hummed in appreciation.

“You don’t seem to understand your place, sweet Cadence. But don’t worry, I intend to show you.”

Ryker seemed to vibrate with anticipation, and I knew I should be concerned, but I wasn’t.

“You are my mate. Mine. Only I get to gaze upon your perfect skin. To see the way your breasts rise and fall in time with each accelerated heartbeat.”

Ryker took a step back and reached behind him as he tugged off his tunic before discarding it on the floor.

My throat bobbed as I swallowed.

“I won’t fucking share you,” he snarled.

Ryker prowled toward me, his leather belt pulled taut between his fists. He leaned down and wrapped it around my neck before securing it in place with the buckle.

He pulled on the end still clasped in his hand, and I gasped.

My body caught ablaze, and I had to bite the inside of my cheek to keep from moaning out loud.

Gods, what the hell was wrong with me?

Why did I like this?

A knowing smirk pulled up the side of Ryker’s mouth. The hand not holding his belt reached down and loosened the ties of his trousers. Then it dipped inside his pants and freed his cock.

Fuck.

I'd forgotten how huge he was.

I pushed my nerves away, too curious, and if I was being honest with myself, too turned on to back down now.

Ryker tugged on the belt, pulling me forward so his cock pressed against my mouth.

"Open."

The authority in his voice went straight to my core, and I parted my lips.

Ryker dipped the engorged head inside my mouth, letting me taste him before he slammed all the way to the back of my throat.

I gagged around his length, and tears sprang to my eyes.

Ryker grinned, but he pulled back until only the tip remained pressed between my lips.

"Suck," he commanded.

I took more of him into my mouth and used my tongue to massage the underside of his cock. Ryker groaned, and I intensified my efforts, bobbing up and down as I tasted him.

"This is what happens when you disobey me, Cadence. You get punished."

Ryker thrust his hips in time with each bob of my head. I hollowed my cheeks, sucking him into my mouth with vigor. He tapped my cheek, and I looked up at him as he waggled his finger at me like I was a misbehaving child.

"This won't be over quickly, Cadence."

Ryker tugged on the belt once more, and then he wrapped it around his knuckles. I straightened, extending my body to avoid being choked by the leather.

He chuckled above me, and I knew he was enjoying the way I was forced to bend to his will just as much as he enjoyed having my mouth wrapped around his cock.

Despite knowing this, tingles danced through my core, and I had to rub my thighs together to alleviate the tension building there.

But it wasn't enough.

My hand moved toward the juncture between my thighs, and I pressed a finger against my entrance.

Ryker ripped my hand away and snarled. "This is a punishment, Cadence. You don't get to come unless I allow it."

Ryker's movements sped up, and I gagged as I tried to suck in air. Drool spilled from my mouth, and the tears that had been pooling in my eyes streaked down my cheeks as I struggled to breathe.

"Cry for me, Temptress. Your tears will only make me come that much harder."

I couldn't help myself. I moaned around his length, and Ryker shuddered.

There was something about the way he used me, treated me as an object for his pleasure, that turned my core molten.

Ryker slammed his cock into my mouth, and with a deep, masculine groan, he came down my throat.

His salty taste exploded on my tongue, and I was surprised to realize I didn't hate it. I swallowed him down, and Ryker preened above me.

He stepped back, his cock jutting out in front of me as his come dribbled from the tip.

"Clean it up," he demanded. "Every drop."

And gods help me, I did. I swirled my tongue around his cock as I licked up every drop of his come until there was none left.

"Good girl," Ryker growled, and my nipples tightened under his praise.

"Get on all fours, Cadence," he commanded as he circled me, the belt still clutched firmly in his grasp.

I lowered my arms to the ground, and I choked as the leather pulled taut against my throat.

Ryker didn't release his grip on the belt. Instead, he watched me flail, my face turning crimson as I struggled to breathe. I tried to straighten, but Ryker placed a hand between my shoulders, keeping me in place.

"You need to understand that I own you, Cadence," he whispered as he crouched behind me. "I set the rules, and you obey. The very first rule is that you never, *never* show anyone else what belongs to me."

Panic gripped me, even though I knew Ryker wouldn't kill me. He'd made it clear that he wanted me.

No.

Needed me.

"The sooner you accept that, the better your life will become. In return, I promise to give you everything you need, to protect you and keep you safe. We can have a good life together, Cadence. All you have to do is embrace it."

The hold Ryker had on the belt slackened, and I sagged forward as I greedily sucked air into my starving lungs.

I drew my knee up before sending my foot backward, straight into Ryker's chest.

"You're a fucking bastard," I wheezed. "Has anyone ever told you that?"

Ryker groaned and then barked out a laugh.

Rising to my elbows, I went to stand just as Ryker gripped the belt and tugged me back down on all fours.

"Let me show you what it means to be mine," he said huskily.

Before I could even consider his words, Ryker's tongue dipped inside me, and a low, wanton moan burst free. I arched my back, and his teeth grazed my clit. I knew it wouldn't take long before I was coming.

The belt tightened around my throat, cutting off my oxygen once more, just as Ryker pushed a finger inside me.

He wasn't gentle about it, either.

He thrust his finger forward with brutal force, and my hips moved of their own volition as they rocked against his hand.

"That's it, Temptress," he panted. "Now, make yourself come."

His words were muted as I lost myself in the sensations he created inside of me. Ryker thrust another finger into my core as he lapped at my entrance, licking the entire length of me.

Just as I thought I might pass out from a lack of air, he released his hold on the belt, and I came so hard my vision darkened.

My orgasm tore through me with the force of a raging storm, and I screamed, unable to contain the sounds I was making.

I collapsed on the floor, my arms giving way as aftershocks continued to wrack my body.

Ryker unclasped the belt and then scooped me into his arms. He strode toward the bed and gently set me down beneath the covers. His large, muscular frame wrapped around me, and he stroked my hair away from my face.

A soft kiss landed on the corner of my mouth, and I couldn't even convey my confusion as my body gave in to the need for rest.

"Sleep, Cadence. I've got you."

My eyelids shuttered closed, and I surrendered myself to the darkness.

Chapter Seventeen

RYKER

I woke to the feel of Cadence's supple flesh beneath my palm. I ran my hand over the smooth, silky skin of her hip, and it was so soft I found myself unable to stop touching her. The bond surged inside me, and I felt an inexplicable urge to claim her, mark her, make her mine. The thought had my cock thickening against her ass.

Yesterday, I had finally broken her.

My Temptress had gotten to her knees for me and had given me her submission. And then I'd fucked her so hard, she'd passed out. A satisfied growl rumbled in my chest as I recalled how beautifully she had shattered for me.

Cadence murmured in her sleep and pressed herself against me. My cock throbbed in response. I was ready to repeat every sordid thing we'd done the day before, but just as I shifted to pull her closer, the growl that had vibrated up my throat tore its way free, and Cadence stiffened.

"Don't be coy now, Temptress. I've already tasted your submission."

Cadence rolled onto her back and glared at me. She studied me for the longest time, and then her features softened.

I moved to position myself on top of her, but Cadence placed her small palm against my sternum. My eyes narrowed, and she smiled up at me, the picture of innocence.

"I want to try something," she whispered. A thrill shot through me with her words. Her fingers danced down my chest as she shifted before she rolled me onto my back, straddling my waist.

Her eyes glinted with mischief as she glanced around the room. She furrowed her brows as she gazed at something I could not see.

"I'll be right back."

Her broad grin was so captivating that I felt my own lips tug upward in response.

My gaze tracked her every movement as she rushed to the other side of my chambers. The way her naked ass bounced, and her hips swayed had my cock begging for attention. A moment later, she returned to the bed, a triumphant smile on her face. She held my leather belt in one hand and a scarf in the other.

I raised a curious brow as I smirked at her, and Cadence bit her lower lip, looking nervous. She didn't let it deter her, though. She climbed back onto the bed, straddling me once again. Her fingers worked quickly as she secured my wrists to the headboard, first with the belt and then the scarf.

I tugged against the restraints. They were tight, but not painful. Still, an excited thrill ran through me at the way she took control. I was eager to explore whatever fantasies she could conjure.

Cadence beamed down at me before her gaze darkened with desire. She lowered herself to my chest as she kissed a path from my throat to my navel. The feel of her breasts pressed against my bare skin almost drove me insane with need. I resisted the urge to fight my bindings and grab her. Something about the way she moved, commanding the moment, made me want to let her enjoy herself.

Cadence glanced up at me from under her lashes, her smile sexy yet taunting. She placed her lips around the crown of my hard cock and sucked lightly. I groaned, nearly coming as though I were a boy experiencing his first woman.

Instead of taking my cock into her throat like I expected her to, Cadence kissed the tip before she pulled away and jumped off the bed with a wicked grin.

"What are you doing?" I demanded, as she searched the room again before ducking out of sight.

"Aha!" she exclaimed as she stood.

Her eyes were alight with victory, and she held a pair of tight leather trousers in her hands that I certainly did not have commissioned for her. A moment later, she retrieved an emerald green tunic and a brown corset.

She dressed quickly before pulling on her boots.

"Cadence," I growled, the warning clear in my tone.

I didn't know what game she was playing, but I wasn't about to let her get away with it.

She grinned, completely unfazed, as she placed her hands on her hips.

Even though she was clearly scheming, I couldn't help but admire how fucking sexy she looked in her fighting leathers.

"You've got a little something..."

Cadence trailed off as she flicked her thumb against the corner of her mouth.

Was she suggesting I was drooling?

I nearly choked on a laugh.

Wait, was I?

"Whatever you think you're doing, I promise it won't work," I warned, "and it'll just earn you another punishment."

Cadence's eyes sparkled with defiance, but I noticed the subtle way she pressed her thighs together, and I smirked.

"You know what, Ryker," she hissed, her voice trembling with fury. "You abduct me, hold me captive, control my every move, and you still think you have the right to punish me."

Cadence stalked toward me, and she leaned down until she was mere inches from my face.

"Fuck. You."

I could feel the heat radiating from her body, and I inched closer, eager to have her sear my flesh.

"Let this be *your* first lesson. I do not belong to you. My body is my own. My mind is my own. My magic is my own. I will *never* bond with you. I will *never* fuel your power. You're not a good man, Ryker. You are the villain in our story."

"Ah, but you accept it is *our* story."

Cadence's eyes widened in disbelief before she threw her arms up in the air with a frustrated cry.

She stomped toward the door, but before she opened it, she glanced over her shoulder, her lips curving into a sly smirk.

"Be a good boy and use this time to reflect on how you might improve your unpleasant demeanor."

With a final haughty glance, she slipped through the doorway and shut it behind her.

I threw my head back and laughed. My little mate surprised me, but I'd be lying if I said I didn't enjoy it. Her defiance was fucking intoxicating.

I let my power flood my veins, and my shadows spilled from me. In an instant, the belt and scarf fell away as my restraints loosened. I dropped my arms, a dark thrill coursing through me at what lay ahead.

Cadence wanted to fight, and that knowledge did not disappoint me. I inhaled deeply, savoring the ecstasy of her impending submission.

The thought of breaking her entirely was fucking thrilling.

Chapter Eighteen

RYKER

I'd barely stepped foot outside my chambers when Riordan approached me.

"Father is expecting you in his study."

"For what reason?" I snapped.

"Your guess is as good as mine," he said with a shrug.

Remembering that Riordan was only the messenger, I inhaled a deep breath to soothe my agitation.

"Has he learned of Cadence's presence here?"

My father would most certainly try to use her to control me.

"I doubt it, but like you, I avoid his company, so I can't be sure."

I grunted in answer.

For the first time in years, my heart ached for the loss of my mother. My father had been a different man while she was still alive.

He'd been kind once. Loving. Doting even.

Now, he was harsh and paranoid, seeing an enemy in every face that surrounded him, including his sons.

That was what happened to someone who lost their fated mate. Not only did your power weaken, but your mind also followed. The decline was slow, like an insidious disease. It was the cruelest of fates, and he had been suffering from it for decades.

In the beginning, I'd felt only compassion for his plight. Then, all traces of my father slowly faded, leaving a tyrant in his place.

"Ryker," Riordan called, and I got the impression it was not the first time he had tried to gain my attention. "I asked what you intend to do if he has learned of her."

"Like we discussed, I will pretend she is your... courtesan."

The word tasted sour on my tongue.

"You might want to work on your expression if you have any hope of selling it," Riordan chuckled.

I grunted again.

It seemed that was my preferred method of communication today.

We walked in companionable silence as we headed toward our father's study. When we arrived, I didn't bother to wait for the guards to open the doors as I pushed past them.

The air in the dimly lit room was thick with tension, and the flickering candlelight illuminated the stern features of my father's face.

He was sitting in one of the armchairs on either side of the fireplace, and opposite him was Lord Barrington.

Hatred burned through my veins, and Riordan placed a hand on my forearm.

"Easy," he warned.

It was then that I realized I had curled my hands into fists at my sides as I ground my teeth together.

Few people had earned my disdain more than Lord Barrington.

He was a snake. Always slithering around, waiting for an opportunity to strike. He was the type of man to rejoice in the suffering of others, and unfortunately, he was my father's closest ally.

He was also the mastermind behind my father's recent notions regarding how I would best fulfill my duties to the crown.

Of course, Lord Barrington benefited greatly from his stroke of genius.

"Ah, my sons have arrived."

My father's voice was icy as he studied me.

I noted the absence of any seating for Riordan and me, which was likely the point. He wanted us to be uncomfortable for this discussion.

"Lord Barrington and I have been discussing our strengthening allegiance," my father drawled.

"Have you now?" I retorted.

My father narrowed his eyes at me, his irritation at my interruption written all over his face.

"You have a duty to the Unseelie, Ryker. To this family, and to the crown."

Lord Barrington smirked at me, and I stared back at him until he shifted uncomfortably before glancing away.

A sick satisfaction rushed through me at his obvious fear.

"Is it duty that motivates you, Father?"

My gaze flicked back to Lord Barrington before I added, "Or is it just another move in your endless game of power?"

My father's gaze sharpened, and he straightened in his seat. "You will watch your tone when you speak to me, Son. I may be your father, but I am also your King, and I won't tolerate disrespect from any of my subjects."

I resisted the urge to roll my eyes. My father was well aware that my strength was greater than his, and if I wanted to, I could dethrone him with little effort.

But I had no desire to sit on his throne and spend my days indulging the council's every whim.

This performance was solely for Lord Barrington, who would be wise to remember the danger he was courting.

"Lord Barrington has been aiding the kingdom with our efforts to dispel the rebels."

"The Crimson Enclave? You can say their name, Father," I taunted.

He tsked, still unwilling to concede the reemergence of the Wraith Borne. Despite the passage of time, their attack on the palace had unsettled him in ways I couldn't fully understand.

"Lord Barrington would like to see a return on his investment," my father said pointedly. "In two weeks, we will host a ball to celebrate our alliance."

My gaze flicked to Lord Barrington, and the smugness I saw in his features made me want to strangle him. My shadows pulsed inside my veins as though they agreed.

I didn't bother to object. Instead, I kept my expression clear of the simmering rage that threatened to burn me.

I hadn't much cared when their intentions were first revealed to me, save for the fact that I loathed anything that might benefit Lord Barrington. However, with Cadence now in play, I was no longer content to remain... disinterested.

I contemplated murdering both men and ridding myself of the burden they had become, but I quickly dismissed the thought. I had neither the time nor patience for a civil war.

"Is that all?"

My father's disapproval was evident in the way his nostrils flared and how he pressed his lips into a thin line.

For a moment, the silence was suffocating.

"For now."

My father's voice was low and quiet, but I didn't miss the threat that rang out loud and clear.

I didn't wait to be dismissed before turning on my heels and striding toward the door. As my palm rested on the doorknob, my father called out behind me.

"And Ryker."

Warning bells sounded inside my head as my father's bitter voice settled over me.

"Don't think I'm unaware of the secrets you keep, Son."

An icy chill ran down my spine, but I ignored it as I pushed the doors wide and strode from my father's study.

Riordan had to jog to catch up with my long strides. "I hate to tell you I told you so, Brother, but I did, in fact, tell you so."

"Not now, Riordan," I snarled.

"All I'm saying is —"

Riordan slammed his mouth shut as I rounded on him, and he raised his hands in surrender.

I didn't know what I looked like, but judging by Riordan's reaction, I was sure that my expression reflected my deadly mood.

"I'll. Take. Care. Of. It."

"All right, Ryker," Riordan placated. "I only mentioned it because I want to help you. I'm not trying to be a dick."

My brow rose in challenge.

"Fine. I was being a bit of a dick, but can you blame me? Riling you up has always been one of my favorite pastimes."

Despite myself, I laughed.

"I love you too, Little Brother."

Riordan screwed up his face.

"What?"

"Whenever you express emotion, your face does this thing, which kind of makes you look like you're struggling to make a bowel movement," he said with complete seriousness.

"Fuck off," I chuckled as I shoved him.

Riordan's own laughter followed me down the hall.

"Oh, look," he called and pointed to the courtyard.

My gaze followed the direction of his outstretched arm.

In the middle of the square, Malesh had a practice sword raised, his footsteps confident and seamless, as another soldier prepared to defend against the strike.

Only it wasn't a soldier.

Cadence stood with her back to me. She wore her long brown hair in a braid that I desperately wanted to wrap around my fist as I did wicked things to her body.

She thrust her practice blade high, deflecting Malesh's strike before dancing out of range.

Riordan let out a low whistle from beside me. "Looks like you've got more to worry about than you thought," he mused. "She already nearly stabbed you with your *own* dagger. What will she be capable of once Malesh has finished with her?"

"I should have left him to die," I grumbled.

Riordan chuckled as he slapped a hand on my shoulder. "Good luck," he said in a saccharine tone.

As I continued to watch Cadence trade blows with Malesh, I realized that I just might need it.

Chapter Nineteen

CADENCE

"That's it for today," Malesh said as he stowed his practice sword away.

Drenched in sweat and panting hard, I was grateful for the reprieve.

"Thank you, Malesh."

The stoic Fae male inclined his head, acknowledging my thanks.

I returned my weapon to the rack and forced my uncooperative limbs toward the walkway that led to the interior of the palace.

It felt like my whole body was rebelling against the torturous training I had subjected it to. I ached in places I didn't even know could ache. But if it meant that I had a fighting chance at escaping this place one day, I'd endure it.

Ryker's chambers lay at the far end of the eastern wing, yet they could have been a world away as I forced my feet forward.

Just another grievance to add to my ever-growing list against Ryker.

The air vibrated with distant music, and ordinarily, I'd be curious as to its source. Tonight, however, all I wanted to do was slip into the quiet safety of Ryker's chambers before collapsing onto the bed and never moving from it again.

When I finally reached his chambers, I traced the intricate carvings that adorned the wood paneling of the door. A relieved sigh left me as I pushed the door open, and I slipped inside, eager for rest.

As I crossed the threshold, I immediately sensed that something wasn't right.

I swept my gaze over my surroundings, and a tingle of awareness shot up my spine. My heart hammered against my ribs, and sweat that had nothing to do with my earlier exertion beaded on my brow.

The setting sun cast long shadows through the lone window, that stretched across the room. There was nothing out of order, yet I could sense an unseen presence lingering just beyond my sight.

I took another step inside the space, and then a familiar scent hit my nostrils.

The sharp, metallic aroma was unmistakable.

Blood.

My breath caught in my throat as I peered at Ryker's desk.

A single piece of parchment sat atop it, and even though it was folded in half, I knew it was the source of the smell.

My chest tightened as I approached. I reached out to take the paper, but hesitated.

Did I even want to know what it said?

I pushed my unease aside and gripped it between my fingers. Taking a deep breath, I opened it.

The letters were written in thick, jagged strokes, and the sight had bile creeping up my throat.

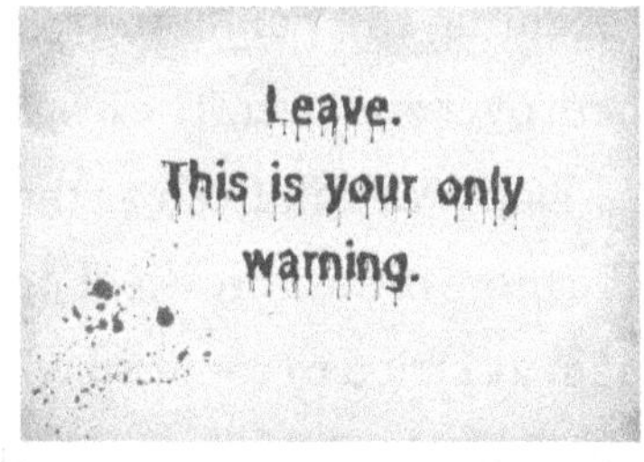

The message had been written in blood, and the coppery scent turned my stomach.

My mind raced as I tried to make sense of the threat.

Was it intended for me?

I doubted anyone would be foolish enough to forewarn Ryker if they were planning an attack.

The note had to be intended for me, but I had no clue who had sent it.

"I would leave in a heartbeat if I could."

If the situation weren't so serious, I might have laughed at its absurdity.

Unsure of what to do next, I stood there, frozen, as I stared at the bloodied note in my hand. The silence that permeated the room felt suffocating, and I gave the collar at my throat an involuntary tug.

My instincts screamed at me to run, to flee this kingdom and escape.

But Ryker would never allow me to get far. He'd hunt me down and drag me right back here, and I'd be in the same position I now found myself.

I continued to examine the parchment, letting the words soak in as I read them over and over. The bright crimson letters indicated that the blood was still fresh as they had yet to pale and shift toward the more muted brown of decay.

I wracked my brain as I tried to come up with a list of potential suspects for the author of the note. I quickly realized it was futile. Few knew of my presence, and I had done nothing to earn their ire.

I abandoned that line of thought as I wondered whether I should alert Ryker to what I had found waiting for me inside his chambers.

What if someone knows your secret?

The insidious notion struck me without warning, and I staggered back a step.

My vision swam in front of me, and my body trembled as I willed myself not to vomit. My pulse spiked, sending adrenaline coursing through my veins, and I leaned over my knees as I gulped a lungful of air.

"Get it together, Cadence."

No matter how much I chastised myself, however, I couldn't rein in my terror.

The low groan of a floorboard snapped me out of my spiraling thoughts, and I straightened as I surveyed the room.

I pulled my magic around me and turned in a slow circle. My eyes flicked to the corner, where shadows deepened with the setting sun.

Even with my heightened Fae vision, I couldn't detect anything hiding within the darkness.

"Is there someone there?"

Only silence answered me.

I crossed the floor to the large arched window, my gaze settling on the last few stragglers in the courtyard as they wrapped up their business and wandered home for the night.

As I leaned forward, I rested my head on the cool glass and allowed my breathing to even out.

"You're jumping at shadows now, Cadence. If you ever hope to leave this place, you'll need to strengthen that backbone," I chided.

I straightened and studied my reflection in the window.

Then I let out a blood-curdling scream.

A figure stood behind me, their face hidden beneath the cowl of their hood, and their black clothing blended seamlessly into the night.

I spun around, my magic thrumming wildly inside me as I prepared to defend myself.

But when I turned, the person was gone, leaving nothing but empty space and the crippling weight of unseen eyes.

My breath came fast and shallow as my heart hammered in my chest.

Had I imagined it?

I glanced down and realized I was still clutching the note in my palm.

That, at least, had been real.

Leave. This is your only warning.

The unspoken threat was apparent.

There was little I could do to heed the warning, however, when Ryker held me prisoner inside the palace.

I would leave if I could. I *wanted* to do just that.

Resolve settled in the pit of my stomach, and I set my jaw. I couldn't escape this place, but I sure as hell wouldn't sit around waiting to be ambushed if the note's author returned.

Next time, I would be ready for them.

Chapter Twenty

CADENCE

The door to the outer chamber creaked open, and I stiffened. I'd been on edge ever since I found the note.

The sound of heavy footfalls followed, but I was now so familiar with Ryker's gait that I instantly relaxed.

Then I remembered it was his fault that I was in this situation, and anger flooded my system like a wild maelstrom.

A moment later, the door swung wide, and Ryker stepped inside.

I bristled at the sight of him.

He had pulled the strands of his light-colored hair into a messy knot atop his head. No care or attention had gone into the updo, and yet, it made him look even *more* attractive.

Fucking asshole.

His tight leather trousers did nothing to lessen that impression. His thick, muscular thighs and toned ass hinted at the hours he spent training, honing, and enhancing his skills. With his white tunic loose, he flaunted his muscular chest, and I fought the urge to lick my lips.

No. Absolutely not. I was not going there.

This man was my enemy, and my body needed to get on board with that notion and stop betraying me.

I snapped the book I had been reading shut and tossed it onto the bed.

"Well, if it isn't the King of Assholes himself," I taunted.

"I'm in no mood for your antics tonight, Cadence," he growled, marching toward the washroom.

"Good. Then you can let me go, and I'll be out of your hair," I said, crossing my arms over my chest.

Ryker disappeared behind the door that led to the bathing chamber, and I heard the sound of water splashing.

I flicked the covers back and got out of bed as I waited for him to reemerge. I hated it when he ignored me like I was nothing more than a mere nuisance. As if he hadn't upended my whole life only to discard me in the next moment.

Ryker returned from the washroom, his tunic nowhere in sight as he leaned against the door frame. His gaze raked over my body, and a hungry glint entered his eyes, which had me pressing my thighs together.

"I love how my gifts look on you, Temptress," he said with a low rumble I felt in my core.

I glanced down at the lace nightgown I wore. It revealed more skin than the occasion called for, but the silky fabric was impossible to resist. It was like I had pulled on a slice of heaven when I slipped it down my body.

Suddenly uncomfortable, I glowered at Ryker, channeling my disquiet into the familiar rage I felt whenever I was in his presence.

"Don't change the fucking subject, Ryker!"

He pushed off the wall and strode towards me. "I see you haven't learned your lesson from the last time you mouthed off at me."

My flesh heated at the memory.

When Ryker reached me, he circled me like a predator sizing up its prey. The warmth of his body caressed my bare skin, and I shivered.

"Or is it that you want a repeat?" he whispered against the shell of my ear.

"Fuck you!" I spat.

Before I could turn to face him, Ryker gripped my hip with one hand and cradled the back of my head with the other, then pinned me against the wall.

I gasped in surprise, and he seized the advantage, locking both my hands in one of his much larger ones at the base of my spine. He tapped my ankles apart, spreading my legs wider as he stepped closer to me. His hard chest pressed against my back, and I could feel his cock thickening against my ass.

"Are you sure this is the game you want to play, my vicious Temptress?" he growled.

"I'm not your anything, Ryker."

A deep chuckle vibrated down my spine and settled between my thighs with a pulsing intensity that had me rubbing my legs together to ease the tension.

"I guess it is."

His weight lifted off me, no longer pressing me into the wall as he released my hands. I tried to get away, but Ryker's palms came down on either side of my head, caging me in.

"Did I fucking say you could move, Cadence?" he snarled.

My heart raced. Not from fear, but from anticipation.

"Answer me!"

"No," I bit out.

Ryker moved his hand to my shoulder, gathering my hair and pushing it aside. His fingers grazed the collar at my throat before he placed a soft kiss on my neck.

"I do like the visual reminder of my ownership," he purred.

The memory of what he'd done had me seeing red. "You can't own me, Ryker! I'm a fucking person!"

"On the contrary, Cadence. I do own you. I own every fucking inch of this sweet flesh," he said as he slid the band of my nightgown down my arm, exposing my breast. He repeated the action with the other strap until the garment pooled at my waist.

"You're so fucking beautiful," he murmured.

His hands gripped the fabric bunching at my hips before he pushed it down my body until it reached the floor. Ryker took a step back, his gaze burning a path down my flesh as he assessed me. I didn't turn around. I stayed perfectly still, waiting to see what he would do next.

"Good girl," he praised when he realized I would not resist him.

Ryker unbuckled his belt, and I stiffened.

"What are you doing?"

I had intended to sound demanding, but it came out breathy, wanton.

Ryker chuckled darkly. "There are consequences for your actions, Cadence, or did you already forget about your little stunt from this morning? You continue to defy me, and so I am forced to remind you of your place."

Goosebumps erupted all over my body. His last *lesson* had been more enjoyable than I would ever admit, especially to him.

A whipping sound cut through the air and a moment later, pain flared on my ass cheek. I jolted forward, my breasts grazing against the roughened wall, bringing my nipples to a peak.

Fuck! Did he just spank me with his belt? More importantly, did I like it?

Before I could dwell on it, another slap hit my ass, and my body shot forward again. The contact sent waves of exquisite agony through me, and I had to bite my lip to prevent a moan from escaping.

I did like it. I liked it a lot.

Six more strikes followed in quick succession, and I was a panting mess by the time Ryker's belt hit the floor. My ass felt as though it was on fire, but I couldn't deny the slickness between my thighs.

Ryker's warmth surrounded me as he pressed against my back once more. He must have removed his pants at some point, because I could feel the swell of his cock as it jutted against my ass.

I hissed as fiery pain exploded across both cheeks. Ryker's breath came heavy, though I couldn't tell if it was from exertion or excitement.

Probably both.

"I'm proud of you, Cadence," he murmured. "You took your punishment so well."

I scoffed as I rested my head against the wall.

"Are you ready to learn what else you can take?"

"I'm ready for you to go to hell, Ryker."

He tsked. "And here I thought we were making progress."

His teeth sank into my earlobe as he whispered, "Tell me, is my pussy soaking wet right now?"

"No," I snapped and rubbed my thighs together as if doing so would erase the evidence of my arousal.

Ryker chuckled. "Let's find out, shall we?"

A calloused finger danced across my folds before dipping inside me.

"You're dripping, little liar," he growled.

I bit my bottom lip hard enough to draw blood, but when Ryker pushed another finger inside me, I couldn't stop the moan that left my lips.

"Mmm," he hummed. "You like that, don't you? You like it when my fingers fuck you so hard that you're moaning like a common whore."

I couldn't deny it. I did like it. I liked it very much.

Ryker pumped his fingers in and out of me roughly, and my walls tightened around him, trying to hold the digits in place. He withdrew his fingers abruptly, leaving me feeling empty and unfulfilled.

"W-what?" I muttered, not sure what I was asking.

A moment later, the head of his engorged cock nudged my entrance, and I inhaled a sharp breath as I lost myself to the delirium of the lust coursing through my veins.

Ryker's hips thrust forward as he sheathed himself to the hilt. Pain flared in my core with the sudden intrusion as my body struggled to accommodate his size. Ryker groaned as he laid his forehead between my shoulders.

"Fuck Cadence," he gritted out. "Your pussy was fucking made for me."

I said nothing.

I couldn't.

The sense of him filling me so completely, stretching me wide, it was all-consuming, overwhelming, to the point that I forgot how to breathe.

"Can you feel how your body tightens around me, strangling my cock as she welcomes me home?"

And then he started moving.

Ryker rocked his hips, impaling himself inside me over and over until he had me seeing stars.

I sucked in a ragged breath.

"That's it, Cadence. Let me in. Let me claim what belongs to me."

A large palm landed on my hip, gripping tightly, while the other trailed up my side before cupping my throat. The cool metal of the collar dug into my flesh as Ryker anchored himself so he could pound into me.

"You're taking me so well, Cadence. Every fucking inch. I am going to coat your womb with my come. I'm going to bury myself so deep inside you that you'll never be able to get rid of me."

My orgasm began to build, and I moaned.

"Fuck, Cadence. Yes! Squeeze my fucking cock. Come all over my dick like the whore I know you can be."

I cried out as my release tore through me with a ferocity that left me trembling.

"Good. Fucking. Girl." Ryker bellowed as he thrust inside me. "Take every fucking drop I have to give you."

Ryker came with a roar. His body tensed around me, and then he stilled.

We were both breathing heavily as I remained caged against the wall under the weight of Ryker's enormous frame.

When I had recovered enough to speak, I whispered, "Are you ever going to free me?"

"No," Ryker answered without hesitation.

"I hate you!"

"Hate me all you like, Cadence, so long as you're by my side."

Ryker pushed off the wall and disappeared from behind me. I didn't move. My emotions were waging war inside me, and I couldn't tell if my anger or my despair would win out on this occasion.

A warm cloth was pressed between my thighs, startling me. Peering over my shoulder, my eyes locked with Ryker's as he cleaned up the mess he'd made.

Without a word, he tossed the cloth on the floor and lowered onto his haunches as he pulled my nightgown back up my body. When he was done, he took my hand and tugged me towards the bed.

He settled me beneath the covers and wrapped an arm around my middle, pulling me flush against his chest.

I listened to Ryker's quiet breathing as I attempted to settle my wildly beating heart. When his breaths evened out, I gave in to the need to follow him into sleep, feeling dejected for being unable to reconcile my raging emotions.

Chapter Twenty-One

RYKER

My brother stood before me, his blade drawn and his stance poised. He shifted his weight from foot to foot, his dark eyes glinting with steady determination.

"Are you planning to fight me this century, or do you intend to stand there admiring my pretty face?"

I grinned at Riordan as I tossed my sword from hand to hand. My blade was slender but lethal, and it glistened in the bright sunlight as I angled it toward my younger brother.

Riordan tightened his hold on the pommel of his sword. His grip was firm, but not tense. Relaxed, but ready. He wore a loose, sleeveless tunic, which allowed him the freedom to move quickly and without restriction. I preferred to train shirtless, a decision I regretted as the women who lined the training ground whooped and hollered.

Riordan flashed a roguish grin, his white-blond hair falling into his eyes as he returned their eager gazes.

With a burst of speed, I lunged at him, cutting my blade through the air toward his shoulder. Riordan deflected the blow, but only barely. He sidestepped my advance, but stumbled as he fought to regain his footing.

I tsked. "What's the first rule of fighting, Riordan?"

"Never allow yourself to get distracted."

His sullen tone yanked me back to our boyhood when I began teaching him to wield a blade. Those days felt distant now, mere echoes of a time when we were free and unburdened.

I raised my sword again and swung my blade in a wide arc. Riordan deflected, twisting his body to flank my exposed side, but before he could strike, I stepped out of range and then pressed forward as I closed the distance with a grin.

"You're much faster than I recall, Little Brother," I said as our blades clashed.

"He has to be," Eamon called out from the sidelines, his deep voice rumbling with laughter. "Your ruthlessness knows no bounds, and you're just as likely to skewer him to teach him a lesson," the hulking man said with a grin.

"True," Malesh added.

I shook my head, but I couldn't stop the grin that spread across my face.

"You see, that right there," Riordan said as he gestured toward me with his sword. "That's why Cadence is my new favorite."

I struck Riordan's blade hard, harder than I should have for a practice session, and the sound of steel grating against steel rang out around us.

Riordan parried before he stepped past me to reset his stance.

"Something on your mind, Brother?" Riordan cooed as he arched a brow.

I heard Eamon and Malesh trying to muffle their laughter from where they stood behind me.

"Should there be?" I grunted as I thrust forward.

Riordan exhaled an exasperated sigh. "You're an emotional void, you know that, Ryker?"

"Not true. I like you," I countered, a smirk tugging at my lips.

"Barely," he muttered. "And I'm almost certain it's out of familial obligation."

I barked out a laugh. He wasn't wrong.

"All right then," I said as I pointed my sword in Malesh and Eamon's direction. "I like them, too."

"That's because you know we have to follow every rule you set," Eamon hollered back. "You're controlling ass wouldn't have a clue how to make friends with anyone you couldn't coerce."

"I can remove you from that list, Eamon," I warned.

The brute tossed his head back and howled with laughter. When he regained his composure, he wheezed, "My point exactly."

"How is it going with Cadence?" Riordan asked.

His tone was deceptively light, and my eyes narrowed in suspicion. He lowered his sword, resting his forearm on the pommel.

Apparently, our training session was over.

A chorus of disgruntled groans came from the women watching before they resumed their day.

Sweat coated every inch of me, and Malesh handed me a waterskin. Eamon moved to my other side as all three men watched me expectantly.

"Fine," I grumbled.

Knowing smirks spread across their faces, and I snarled before I lifted the waterskin to my lips and drank greedily.

These fuckers were far too pleased with my current predicament.

"Is the bond developing?" Malesh pressed, his tone turning serious.

The bond was growing despite Cadence's reluctance to embrace it. Even now, I could feel it flourishing inside me as it beckoned me to her.

The bond's pull could drive a man insane.

"It is."

"But?" Eamon pushed.

"But... I'm no closer to convincing Cadence to accept it."

For a moment, everyone was silent. Then deafening laughter erupted all around me.

"You thought she'd just fall into line after you forced her to stay," Eamon teased.

When I said nothing, Eamon balked. "Gods, you did, didn't you?"

I shrugged as I met Riordan's concerned gaze.

"Ryker, you need to make this work," he almost pleaded. "Not only for the power it gives you — though that's reason enough — but because she's a weakness."

The thought of anyone harming Cadence to get to me, pulled a growl from my throat before I could stop it.

"You can't protect her, and therefore yourself, if she is always trying to escape," Riordan finished, ignoring my interruption.

"He has a point," Malesh added.

"Let me ask you this," Riordan said, as he gripped his chin between his thumb and forefinger. "Do you love her?"

Love?

My feelings for Cadence were violent and unrelenting, searing my flesh and destroying everything in their wake. She was the only constant in my mind, immovable and uncompromising.

But love?

That word felt too pure, too sweet, too... mundane.

What I felt for Cadence... it was an unyielding obsession.

"How do you know if you're in love?" I asked instead of answering.

A collective groan sounded at my question.

"Is she always on your mind?" Malesh asked.

I thought about the way her lips wrapped around my cock and how her tight little body fit against mine.

"Yes."

"Do you ache at the prospect of being separated from her?" Eamon added.

The thought of her slipping through my carefully woven web or some other bastard taking my Temptress away from me made my blood boil with fury, almost to the point of pain.

"Yes."

"Do you find yourself needing to touch her, to be close to her, anytime she's near?" Malesh asked as though he was recalling a fond memory.

Fuck yes, I did.

My cock agreed as it strained against my trousers. "Absolutely."

"Then you love her," Eamon declared.

Riordan snorted. "Or his dick does."

The three men began bickering, but their voices faded as my mind drifted to my Temptress.

She had crawled under my skin, into my blood, into my very soul.

With a growl, I set my waterskin down. Now that Cadence had invaded my thoughts, there was only one thing I wanted to do.

Claim my mate.

Chapter Twenty-Two

CADENCE

Something had shifted between me and Ryker, and I couldn't quite put my finger on it. Somewhere along the way, we'd fallen into a semblance of cooperation. It wasn't a truce exactly, more like a cease-fire.

Which was why I found it odd that Riordan, not Ryker, would be my escort for the ball that night.

To be honest, my invitation caught me by surprise.

Ryker hadn't taken me to any formal events since I had arrived in the Unseelie Kingdom almost a month ago. In fact, he seemed determined to downplay my presence here at every opportunity.

Then, unexpectedly, I received an invitation to a prestigious ball celebrating an alliance between the crown and a prominent family on the governing council.

I wasn't sure what to expect, but the gown Ryker had gifted me suggested the event was for the kingdom's elite.

I studied my reflection in the mirror. My long brown hair cascaded in gentle waves over my shoulders, and I could make out the rich chestnut hues that captured the light from the candelabra.

The deep navy-blue dress that I wore shimmered with each subtle movement, and it flowed around my feet like liquid midnight. The fitted bodice hugged my form, pushing up my breasts until I thought I might very well topple out of it, before flaring elegantly at my waist and flowing to the floor.

Trust Ryker to choose something that was borderline scandalous.

Intricate silver patterns adorned the top of the gown, and they sparkled in the light like a constellation of stars against a cloudless night. Delicate gossamer sleeves billowed from my upper arms, drawing attention to the graceful curve of my collarbone.

My gaze snagged on the rose gold collar around my throat, and my mood soured.

Despite the relative peace Ryker and I had found as we coexisted side by side, he still didn't trust me enough to remove the damn thing.

His instincts were correct. The moment he took it off, I'd try to escape.

A small pang erupted behind my ribcage when I thought about fleeing Ryker. The intrusive feeling left me gasping, and I clutched the table for support.

What the hell was wrong with me?

I decided I didn't want to ruminate on it and, instead, returned my attention to my reflection in the mirror. Scarlette had visited earlier to do my makeup, and I had to admit, she had done a masterful job.

The light dusting of blush accentuated my high cheekbones, and the kohl that lined my eyes gave them a seductive allure I was rather fond of. The bright red lipstick that had been painted on my lips only worked to enhance the appeal.

I looked beautiful, and the thought made me miss home.

My mother would have been beside herself to see me dressed so elegantly. She'd often encouraged me to embrace the beauty I was half convinced only she saw, but now I could finally understand what she'd been saying all along.

A loud knock at the door startled me and drew me out of my reverie.

Riordan didn't wait for me to answer before he strode into the room. He stopped halfway toward me, his mouth gaping open before he scrubbed a hand down his face.

"Gods, Cadence," he groaned. "Keeping unwanted attention off you tonight is going to be an impossible task."

I shifted nervously on my feet, unsure what to make of his reaction.

"Fuck! Keeping my hands to myself, and thereby my head attached to my shoulders, will be a godsdamned miracle," he muttered.

"So do I look all right?"

"Do I look all right, she asks."

Riordan blew out a breath before meeting my eyes.

"Cadence, sweetheart, you're the most beautiful woman I've ever seen. You are a goddess made real. Every man in that hall would trip over himself for a sliver of your attention, and if one succeeds, Ryker will surely skin me alive."

"So, that's a yes, then?"

"That's a fucking hell yes!"

My shoulders relaxed, and I chuckled at Riordan's response.

"Good, because I'm awful at these types of events. Honestly, I've never been to anything this fancy. The closest I have come is the Beltane festival back home."

I was rambling. My nerves were getting the best of me.

Riordan crossed the room and clasped my hands.

"Stay at my side, and you will have nothing to worry about," he grinned. "And I'll be the most envied fucker there," he added with a wink.

I laughed despite myself.

"Shall we?" he asked, as he waggled his eyebrows.

"We shall," I confirmed, feeling more confident.

As we made our way toward the ballroom, we drew more than our fair share of stares from other partygoers.

"Why are they staring?" I mumbled to Riordan.

"I told you, you're gorgeous."

A blond woman with a pixie cut stopped in front of us, and she reached out to place her hand on Riordan's forearm.

"Will I be seeing you after the festivities, Your Highness?" she purred.

"What do you think, Cadence? You up for it?"

Before I could answer, he winked at the woman and breezed past her. I could feel her piercing glare at my back as we walked into the hall.

I almost gasped when I took in the lavish space before me.

The ballroom was a dazzling display of grandeur and opulence. Tall, arched windows lined the walls, and they were draped in heavy velvet curtains that were the color of midnight. Crystal chandeliers hung from the lofty, vaulted ceiling, casting a luminescent glow over the space as they caught and reflected the candlelight.

At the far end of the room, a raised dais held a grand throne made of the richest mahogany, inlaid with mother-of-pearl and adorned with plush, golden cushions. Around the throne, fresh bouquets of the most beautiful flowers I had ever seen stood in tall gold vases, and their enticing fragrance permeated the space.

Waiters drifted in and out, offering glasses of Fae wine and platters of exotic fruits, delicate pastries, and skewered meats that made my mouth water.

Before I could make my way toward the nearest waiter, a gong sounded, and the ballroom fell quiet.

"What's going on?" I whispered to Riordan.

"The King has arrived."

The guests parted, creating a path down the center of the enormous chamber, which led to the dais. A moment later, a man with dark, cropped hair wearing a silver crown atop his head strode down the aisle. He didn't stop and acknowledge his son as he passed us.

"I'm guessing you and Ryker take after your mother," I whispered.

"Something like that," Riordan smirked.

The King ascended the platform and settled onto the throne. Once he had arranged his cloak around himself, he gave a curt nod of his head. "You may begin."

Chapter Twenty-Three

CADENCE

The herald's voice rang out loudly in the silence of the room.

"His Royal Highness, Ryker Ashborne, The Crown Prince of the Unseelie."

Heads turned toward the entrance as Ryker strode inside. His face was handsome, but expressionless as he stared straight ahead at the dais. Tall and composed, he looked every inch the king in waiting, but I didn't miss the slight tension around his jaw.

"Why is he just standing there?"

Before Riordan could answer my question, the herald continued.

"And introducing His Royal Highness's betrothed, Lady Celeste of House Barrington."

Applause broke out across the ballroom, and the rowdier attendees cheered and hollered for their future king and queen.

But I heard none of it as my vision swam in front of me.

My heart pounded against my ribcage as though it were trying to tear its way out of my chest. I inhaled a sharp breath, and I willed my feet to move, to flee this kingdom of lies, but my body remained rooted in place.

"Cadence," Riordan murmured, concern lacing the single word. "Are you all right?"

"I... I..." My words died on my tongue.

"Fuck," he groaned. "Please tell me that my brother did not let you loose among the wolves tonight, with no hint of what was coming."

The woman in question, Lady Celeste, saved me from answering as she stepped forward and placed her hand on Ryker's outstretched palm.

She wore a dazzling silk gown of soft violet that complemented her regal beauty. Her curly blond hair was styled in an elegant updo, and she wore a gold circlet across her forehead.

She looked every inch the queen she would someday become.

Celeste beamed at Ryker as she dipped into a practiced curtsy I could never perfect, and the pair started toward the dais hand in hand.

Ryker's gaze roamed over the crowd as though he were searching for someone. When his steel-grey eyes landed on me, a shiver raced down my spine. His stare narrowed as if warning me not to make a scene.

I straightened my shoulders and raised my chin as I glared right back at him.

"That's the little fighter I've heard so much about," Riordan chuckled from beside me.

Despite my composed exterior, the room spun, and I felt as if a hand was wrapped around my throat, cutting off my oxygen.

I desperately needed the reprieve that only the cool night air could offer me.

I remained in place until Ryker and Celeste took their seats alongside the King on the dais, and with the formalities over, the party resumed.

"Join me outside?" Riordan asked as he jutted his chin in the balcony's direction.

I didn't trust myself to speak, so I gave him a curt nod, and he gripped my hand in his as he pulled me through the crowd. On my way out, I glanced toward Ryker and saw that he had once again donned the mask of indifference he so often wore.

A rush of anger pulsed through me, sharp and cutting.

What game did Ryker think he was playing? Keeping me at his mercy, *fucking me*, and all the while he had a godsdamned fiancée waiting in the shadows?

Riordan placed his palm on the small of my back and guided me through the doors to the balcony. The cool night air washed over me like a tidal wave, leaving me gasping and shaking all over.

"It's all right," he soothed as he rubbed his hand up and down my spine. "You're all right, Cadence."

When I regained control of my breathing, I flashed Riordan an embarrassed smile.

"I don't know why I'm so shaken. You might not know this, but I can't stand your brother."

Riordan chuckled, but there was a knowing look that twinkled in his eyes as he gazed at me.

"Just taken by surprise, I guess," I muttered.

Riordan made a sound of affirmation, and I pulled my gaze from his as I peered down at the courtyard below. We stood in companionable silence as Riordan allowed me the space to gather myself.

"Do you want to get back at him?"

When I glanced in Riordan's direction, mischief gleamed from his smoke-grey eyes, and his lips were pulled up in a wicked grin.

"What did you have in mind?"

Pushing off the banister, Riordan raised his hand and extended his palm to me. I studied it for a moment, and Riordan's grin only widened.

"Come on," he cajoled. "You know you want to."

Dimples appeared in his cheeks, and I knew I was done for.

With a resigned sigh, I placed my hand in his and let him lead me back inside. My gaze drifted toward the dais, and when my eyes locked with Ryker's angry ones, I internally chastised myself for caring.

"See, it's already working," Riordan whispered conspiratorially.

I laughed, feeling much lighter.

The music softened, and couples flocked to the dance floor as they prepared to join in the waltz.

"I'm not the best dancer," I confessed.

"Lucky for you, I am. Just follow my lead."

Riordan's hand rested firmly on my hip as he guided me about with quiet confidence, his eyes never leaving mine.

Soon, I found myself relinquishing my burdens, and I relaxed into his embrace.

"There you go," he said with approval.

I smiled up at him. "You're a reasonable teacher."

"Only Reasonable?"

I shrugged and then grinned as his brows furrowed.

"Oh, I see how it is, sweetheart," Riordan teased.

I didn't answer him, simply raising a brow in challenge.

"You're taking advantage of me," he said with complete seriousness.

Laughter burst from my lips, and a moment later, Riordan's deep chuckle followed. He spun me around the room, his fingers interlaced with mine as his thumb gently brushed my skin.

With each step and graceful spin, I realized I was enjoying myself despite everything. The music built to a crescendo, and Riordan lowered me toward the ground, my back arching beneath his strong fingertips. He didn't release me immediately when he brought me back up. Instead, he pulled me flush against his powerful frame as he pressed his lips to my ear.

"Are you ready for the grand finale, sweetheart?" he murmured, and an involuntary shiver wracked my body.

I had no idea what he was talking about, but when he slanted his mouth over mine, I found myself suddenly breathless.

Before Riordan's lips could meet mine, a large shadow loomed over us. We both glanced toward it, only to be greeted by Ryker's simmering rage.

"May I cut in, Brother?"

"I don't know," Riordan taunted him. "I was just about to get to know Cadence on a more *personal* level."

He turned to me and winked.

Ryker pulled his brother away from me before his large palm landed on my waist, and he gripped my hand in his.

"Have fun," Riordan called as Ryker spun us into the middle of the dance floor.

"You're playing with fire, Temptress," he growled.

I glared back at him.

The gall of this man.

"Don't you dare speak to me about playing games when you have a fucking fiancée, Ryker!"

"Is that jealousy I detect, Cadence?" he purred.

I opened my mouth to argue, but changed my mind.

"Fuck. You. Ryker."

Before he could respond, I turned away from him and strode from the dance floor, leaving him behind.

Chapter Twenty-Four

CADENCE

I fled toward the balcony, desperate to put as much distance between us as possible. He had the uncanny ability to set my world on fire before casually waltzing out, stomping on the ashes he left behind.

I forced myself to take a deep breath, needing to regain control of my emotions. It wasn't as though I cared for Ryker. He'd kidnapped me from my home and refused to let me go, despite how much I begged and pleaded.

The man had *collared* me like some fucking pet for the gods' sake.

I didn't care about Ryker; I hated him.

Then why did my heart splinter at the reminder of his fiancée?

Could it be the bond pulling me to him?

I chastised myself for even entertaining the thought. There was no bond. Ryker was not my mate. He was an entitled asshole who took what he wanted whenever he pleased. I couldn't lose sight of what was at stake. The man would kill me if he knew the real me.

The door creaked open behind me, and I stiffened, not yet ready for the confrontation I was certain Ryker was preparing to unleash.

I'd hoped for a moment of peace, a brief escape from the suffocating reality that had become my life.

I exhaled a resigned sigh and turned toward my nemesis. Only it wasn't Ryker's gorgeous face that awaited me.

Eight Fae males stepped onto the balcony, each moving with a calculated ease as they formed a loose circle around me. They were an imposing wall of amused grins and curious gazes.

A gentle breeze lifted the hem of my gown, the soft fabric flowing around my ankles, as if in reassurance. But it did nothing to alleviate the sweat beading on the back of my neck.

Dressed in their finery, the men exuded confidence and grace. But there was a heavy feeling in the pit of my stomach that warned me whatever their intentions were, I'd only find trouble.

One man stepped forward. He was tall, with dark hair and a mischievous glint in his eye that lacked the warmth Riordan so often emitted. The man leaned against the railing, never taking his gaze off me as he assessed me with a lazy charm. When his eyes returned to mine, a wolfish grin spread over his face.

"A woman as beautiful as you and I don't even know your name."

The man was arrogant enough to expect an answer.

Another man stepped forward. He was shorter than the first, and his smile was playful, almost flirtatious. But he stared at me with an intensity that made me uncomfortable.

"You didn't think your absence would go unnoticed, did you?"

The two men exchanged a predatory grin, and their companions chuckled behind them.

A third man watched me from a distance as he crossed his arms over his broad chest. He stayed silent, his lips curved in a smirk as if daring me to play a game where only he knew the rules.

"What's a lovely woman like you doing out here all alone?" another man asked, drawing my attention.

I stepped back, and the cool metal of the banister pressed into the base of my spine.

The first man leered at me, his pleasure in my discomfort gleaming in the dark depths of his eyes.

A fourth man, perhaps the least threatening one of the group, stuffed his hands into his pockets as he turned his head slightly to observe me.

Cursing my cowardice, I straightened and adopted a relaxed aura as I allowed a small smile to play on my lips. Underneath the surface of my calm veneer, a raging inferno was burning as I calculated the best way to extricate myself from the situation.

"I'm still waiting."

"How presumptuous of you."

Laughter burst from the group, and the first man's face flushed crimson.

Despite my discomfort, a small thrill coursed through me as I matched their audacity with my poise.

"She's too smart to be overcome by your charms, Lucas," a fifth man chuckled as he slapped his friend on the shoulder.

"And what are you gallant men hoping to achieve by following me out here?"

Surprised laughter broke out at my forwardness, but I didn't miss the hint of aggression present in the sound.

The first man leaned into my space, and I pulled my magic to me, ready to defend myself should the need arise. His hand darted forward as he wrapped a lock of my hair around his finger.

"We are only here to ensure that you enjoy your night, My Lady," he murmured.

Then his lips were on me, and he was pushing his tongue into my mouth. I struggled against him, but he wasn't having it. He thrust his tongue deeper as he cupped the back of my head, holding me in place.

I sank my teeth into his bottom lip, hard enough to draw blood, and he released me. The metallic taste coated my taste buds, and I recoiled as I spat the vile substance on the ground.

"Fucking bitch!" he gasped as he raised his hand and slapped me across the face.

As if his strike somehow gave the rest of them permission, the men descended on me in unison.

Hands reached for me, groping me above my dress. Whenever I pushed one away, more appeared to take its place.

"No need for that," one man cooed as I slapped his arm. "We only want to show you a good time."

"Let me go!"

"Your struggle is only making my dick harder," another man preened. "I bet your cunt tastes all the sweeter because of it."

A hand slipped underneath the neckline of my dress, and a rough palm squeezed my breast.

Closing my eyes, I sent a silent apology to my mother for what I was about to do next.

Before I could unleash my magic, a low growl rumbled behind the group, and tension drained from my body before I could think better of it.

The night deepened into an unnatural black, and the stars vanished from the sky.

Cool air kissed my exposed flesh as I felt the weight of the man in front of me being violently torn away.

A snarl shattered the stillness, followed by a bloodcurdling scream.

Panicked cries erupted all around me, but no matter how hard I tried, I couldn't see through the mass of darkness engulfing me.

A tearing sound assaulted my ears, only to be replaced by a wet gurgling noise.

Terrified screams and groans of pain filled the night, and it sounded like the men were being ripped apart by a feral beast driven by animalistic bloodlust.

A small whimper sliced through the haunting sounds before everything fell silent once more.

The darkness ebbed, and light flooded my senses. The scene that greeted me had me turning toward the railing and expelling the contents of my stomach.

Butchered and mutilated bodies littered the marble floor of the balcony, and rivers of blood flowed over the edge.

All eight men lay before me, dead.

Not just dead.

Torn apart.

Obliterated.

Hardly recognizable as human.

A high-pitched scream erupted from inside the ballroom, but I scarcely heard it.

My gaze swept over the massacre before my eyes settled on Ryker.

He stood among the carnage, covered from head to toe in blood. Shadows snaked around his hands, awaiting their next command, and enormous, black wings extended from his back.

When I locked my gaze with his, a gasp slipped between my lips. Ryker's eyes were obsidian, no trace of his steel-grey irises peeked through.

That wasn't what drew the gasp from my throat, however.

Elongated fangs protruded from his gums, sharp and glistening with blood. Suddenly, the feral, animalistic sounds I had heard earlier made perfect sense.

"What are you?" I breathed, unable to tear my gaze away.

Ryker strode toward me, not caring about the pulverized remains he was treading through. When I was within reaching distance, his hand darted out, and he collared my throat with his large palm.

"Mine," he growled.

Then his lips slammed against my own, and darkness swallowed me whole.

Chapter Twenty-Five

CADENCE

When the darkness dissipated, we were standing in Ryker's chambers. The familiar environment immediately calmed my racing heart.

That was until I turned around and caught sight of Ryker.

Blood coated every inch of him, but his eyes had returned to the steel-grey color I was used to. His fangs had receded, and there was no sign of the shadowy wings that had cradled me protectively.

I could feel Ryker's anger radiating from him, and that may have been a cause for concern if my own rage wasn't morphing into a maelstrom of wrath.

Raising my hand, I sent my palm sailing toward him until it connected with his cheek. A sharp stinging sensation erupted on my flesh, but I ignored it as I slapped him again and again.

Unsatisfied with the damage I was inflicting, I refocused my efforts on pummeling my fists against his hard chest. I was almost certain that the blows hurt me more than they hurt him, but I refused to give up the only outlet I had for my anger.

Ryker's hands moved between us, and he wrapped his fingers around my wrists in a punishing hold.

"That's enough," he growled.

My head reared back before I drove it into his face. Blood erupted from his nose, yet the sight was less satisfying than I'd hoped, tainted by the blood of his victims.

Ryker released me and staggered back. He pinched the bridge of his nose as he stemmed the flow of blood. I watched in silence. My chest heaved as I glared at him.

After a few tense moments, he removed his coat and tossed it to the ground. Next, he reached his hand behind his head and pulled his tunic over his bulky frame. He used the garment to mop up the blood on his face and hands before discarding it to the floor alongside his coat.

"You want it rough, Cadence?" he snarled. "Fine by me."

Ryker prowled toward me, and I stepped out of reach.

"Don't think for one second you're putting your fucking hands on me, Ryker," I spat.

"Oh, I'm thinking about it, Cadence. It's all I ever think about. Every second of every godsdamned day."

I darted behind his desk, trying to create distance between us.

"That's what you have a fiancée for."

Ryker let out a low, menacing growl, the sound vibrating with a warning before he swept his arm across the surface of his desk. Parchment fluttered, and the inkpot toppled, spilling its contents all over the ground.

"If I want to take a wife, Cadence, I'll take a fucking wife. And you know what? You'll still be here, waiting obediently in my chambers, because no version of our story ends with me giving you up."

"You don't get to marry her *and* keep me as your unwilling mistress, Ryker," I shrieked.

The word tasted foul in my mouth, and I wanted to retch all over again. "I'm not that type of woman."

"What you are, Cadence, is MY fucking woman," Ryker growled as he slammed a palm against his bare chest.

"That's where you're wrong, Ryker," I said in a sultry tone. "I belong to no man, and when I escape this place, you'll see that for the truth it is."

Ryker lunged for me, his hand wrapping around my throat as he dragged me to him. My legs landed on either side of his thick thighs and my ass rested on the edge of the desk.

I gasped, unable to conceal the excited sound.

"You say that I don't own you, Temptress," Ryker sneered as he gathered my skirt in his grasp and pulled it up to my waist.

His fingers dipped inside my panties, and he groaned against my throat as he found me dripping wet for him.

"But your cunt tells a different story."

I raised my knee and slammed it awkwardly into his side. Ryker jolted, and it was enough to break his hold. I raced across the room and jumped onto the bed in a desperate attempt to escape him. Futile, as it was.

"I don't care how much my body betrays me. My mind will never stop fighting you."

Ryker straightened, pain pinching the corner of his eyes as he rubbed his side.

"You'll pay for that, Cadence."

"I'll kill you, Ryker. If you lay your hands on me, I'll fucking kill you!"

"All this because of an insignificant fiancée?" he scoffed as he threw his arms wide. "She's a figurehead, Cadence. Nothing more."

It was my turn to scoff.

"You're marrying her, Ryker. That will undoubtedly come with some responsibilities, no. Unless I'm mistaken, you'll need to fuck an heir into her to ensure the line of succession. I suspect the kingdom won't look favorably on you if you outsource that task."

Ryker stared at me before breaking out into a wicked grin.

"My, my, my, Cadence. You can deny it all you want, but your jealousy is showing."

I ground my teeth together because fuck him, he was right.

I was jealous. And that made me the stupidest woman in the realm.

"Besides, with everyone's attention on her, they won't be looking at you. My marriage to Celeste protects you, Cadence."

"Oh, my apologies," I said in a saccharine tone. "I guess I should thank you then."

With a sudden burst of speed, Ryker was across the room and standing right in front of me. An undignified squeal escaped me, and I grabbed the closest thing I could find and hurled it at him.

He ducked his head and avoided being struck by the book I'd been reading the night prior. He didn't hesitate as he reached out and gripped my ankle before tugging me toward him.

I tumbled to the mattress, my fall cushioned by the soft pillows and comforter. A tearing sound filled the room, and I peered down, surprised to see the front of my bodice torn in two.

"Oh no, you don't," I hissed as I scrambled away from him.

I was no match for his strength, however, and he proved it a moment later when he flipped me onto my stomach and pinned my hands at the base of my spine.

"Stop. Fucking. Fighting. Me."

His words only egged me on. I bucked and kicked and even scratched whatever part of him I could reach from my restrained position.

"Fuck!" he snapped. "Those claws of yours are sharp, Temptress."

"Good," I said with a ragged breath. "I hope you bleed to death."

Ryker chuckled above me, right before he tore the rest of my dress away from my body.

The cool night air nipped at my bare skin, and I shuddered. From the cold or anticipation, I couldn't tell.

Ryker's palm landed with a bruising force on my ass cheek and my whole body jerked up the mattress. Three more slaps quickly followed, and my core had turned molten by the time he'd finished.

"Tell me, Temptress, is my pussy ready for me?" Ryker taunted.

She was, the traitorous bitch. But I'd sooner die than admit it.

The rustling of clothing sounded behind me, and then Ryker's free hand was in my hair, pulling my back flush against his chest. His hot breath caressed the shell of my ear before he bit down, making me cry out.

"I'm going to fuck this disobedience out of you, Temptress. And if you're a good girl, I might even let you come."

Ryker shoved me down roughly, and then he entered me from behind. He slammed inside me, all the way to the hilt, and my pussy burned as I stretched to accommodate him.

He didn't give me any time to adjust to the intrusion. He pounded into me with a ferocity that both thrilled and terrified me.

The sound of skin slapping against skin filled my ears, and my breaths became shallow pants as I climbed toward my climax.

"Don't you dare fucking come, Cadence," he bit out.

I didn't answer him, couldn't answer him, as a moan slipped between my lips.

"Cadence," he growled in warning, but I was too far gone.

I crested the peak, my orgasm tearing through me as I clung on, simply trying to survive the waves of euphoria crashing down on me.

"Oh, gods," I moaned as I drowned in a sea of pleasure.

Ryker covered my body with his as he leaned down and growled in my ear. "The gods don't own your pleasure, Cadence, I do."

He picked up his pace, abandoning his hold on my wrists and hair as he gripped my hips. Ryker slammed into me, going faster and deeper than ever before. I could feel the stirrings of another orgasm as he impaled me on his cock.

"Mine," he snarled. "My fucking pussy."

He snapped his hips forward, driving into me.

"You hear me, Cadence? Your pussy belongs to me. Your body belongs to me. There is no part of you I don't own."

His grip on my waist tightened, and I could tell he was getting close.

"You'll never own my heart, Ryker," I panted. "No matter how long you keep me trapped here, I'll never stop trying to escape you. I'll fight you every step of the way. Do you hear me?"

Ryker let out a sound somewhere between a groan and a snarl as he emptied himself inside me.

A sharp sensation pierced the delicate curve of my neck, slicing through the tender flesh with searing precision, and I cried out as another orgasm was violently wrenched from me. This one was unlike anything I had ever experienced in my life. Stars exploded behind my eyes, and my whole body trembled as indescribable pleasure coursed through my veins.

I didn't need to turn around to know that Ryker had sunk his fangs into my neck. The deeper they pierced my flesh, the more my body writhed against him.

My orgasm went on and on until I was sobbing and begging him to stop. When he withdrew his fangs, he flipped me over, and he pulled me against his broad chest. Sobs continued to wrack my frame as I came down from my high.

"You did so well, Cadence," Ryker soothed as he ran his fingers over my hair. "My perfect fucking goddess."

His warm mouth covered the wound on my shoulder, and his tongue darted out to lap up the blood. When my sobs receded, Ryker laid us down on the bed, his arm curled over me protectively.

As I surrendered to the darkness, I thought I heard him whisper, "I can never let you go, Cadence. My world would be empty without you in it."

Chapter Twenty-Six

RYKER

The tension inside the throne room was stifling. The fact that we were having this conversation in the throne room instead of my father's private study was telling in itself.

My footsteps echoed in the vast chamber as I made my way toward the dais. Every eye was trained on me, but I ignored them, keeping my attention fixed on the man ahead.

My father's narrowed gaze tracked my movements as I approached him. Lord Barrington stood at his side, his features twisted into a sneer. The man was dancing dangerously close to death, but he was too foolish to recognize it.

I donned my usual mask and kept my face void of all expression as I stood before my father. With my chin raised, I stared him down, daring him to do his worst.

My father's summons had been curt and public, leaving no doubt about the reason behind it. If that hadn't been evidence enough, the soft whimpers coming from the families of the men I had killed would have washed away any lingering suspicions.

If he thought hauling me before the court to answer for my actions would rattle me, he was sorely mistaken. This little charade was for the people, not me.

My father and I both knew who held the real power between us, and he'd do well to remember it.

"Prince Ryker," my father's voice boomed in the silence of the room.

His words were bitter and cutting.

"Step forward."

Obeying his command, I moved closer, but I refused to take a knee before him. I felt my father's anger rolling off him in waves, even from a distance.

"Son, you disappoint me," my father said.

His eyes were dark, and his mouth was set in a thin line.

Likewise, I thought bitterly.

"You understand why I have summoned you here?"

I gave a curt nod of my head in confirmation.

"Then tell me, what justification could there be for the brutal murder of your subjects?"

It amused me that my father was even asking this question as if he hadn't ordered me to take the same action in the past.

"The men you killed were all from noble families. Respectable citizens of the Unseelie Kingdom, and the future representatives of the council."

I could feel the eager eyes of the courtiers on me as they waited with bated breath for my next words. They weren't foolish enough to demand I answer, but I felt the weight of their judgment all the same.

"It's quite simple," I said with a shrug. "They attacked a woman under my protection, and I responded in kind."

My father's eyes narrowed as he looked down his nose at me.

"You call tearing eight men to ribbons with nothing more than your bare hands, responding in kind?" my father scoffed.

I'd also used my fangs, but... semantics.

A soft cry pierced the air from somewhere to the left of me, but I kept my gaze locked on my father.

"They're lucky that's all I did to them," I said, my voice low but deadly.

My father's eyes widened in surprise, but he said nothing.

"They were trying to force themselves on an unwilling female, and they may well have succeeded had I not intervened."

"Lies!" a woman screamed, and I turned to face her.

A man, most likely her husband, tried to quiet her, but she refused to heed his warnings.

"My Lucas would never do such a thing!"

In a blur of movement, I was standing in front of her before she could blink. I allowed my shadows to encase my eyes and tilted my head to the side as I studied her.

The woman paled, realizing the mistake she'd made.

"Please," she whimpered.

"Your Lucas," I snarled, remembering the dark-haired man who struck my mate, "was the ringleader of the group." I leaned closer, invading her space. "If I had my time again, I would have ensured his death lasted days for touching what belonged to me. He would have suffered until he begged for me to end him, only to discover I'm not that merciful."

The woman fainted, collapsing into her husband's waiting arms, who bowed his head before he carried her away.

I fixed my gaze on the rest of the families standing between the stone pillars. "Does anyone else have something to say?"

They remained silent, their heads lowered as they studied the floor.

"Leave us," my father commanded.

Feet shuffled around me as courtiers rushed for the door, desperate to escape the tension permeating the room.

"Ryker," my father rumbled.

I turned to face him and noted that Lord Barrington still stood at his side. I closed the distance between us, baring my teeth.

"You are a prince, Ryker. Heir to this throne. You need to prove yourself worthy to the people you just threatened. One day, you will come to rely on their influence. Everything you do must serve to better the kingdom."

"Is that what you do, Father?" I scoffed. "Work for the betterment of the kingdom?"

"Who is this woman?" he asked, ignoring my question.

"She is not your concern," I growled.

"I knew you were keeping a whore of sorts," he said dismissively. "But this is an overreaction, even for you."

I was moving before I was aware of it. My fingers tightened around my father's throat as I glared at him.

"Call her that again, Father, and it will be the last word to ever pass between your lips."

My father's eyes widened in fear, and Lord Barrington recoiled.

"I am your King," my father spat.

"Be grateful that you are. If you were anyone else, your head would already be on the floor."

Releasing my father, I stepped back and descended the dais.

"She is your mate, isn't she?"

His words stopped me in my tracks. When I turned, triumph was written all over his face.

The fear that I had glimpsed only moments before was long forgotten as he eyed me.

"What about my daughter?" Lord Barrington demanded.

My father relaxed against the backrest of the throne, his posture confident.

"Ryker will marry Celeste, won't you, Son?"

I curled my palms into fists as I inwardly cursed my stupidity for playing right into his game.

"Careful, Father," I warned. "Lest you forget what you stand to lose."

Namely, your head.

"Oh, I know exactly what's at stake here, Ryker," he smirked. "And so do you."

"I hope you're not threatening me, Father. That would be extremely unwise."

My father chuckled without mirth. "There's no need for threats, my son."

He leaned forward and steepled his fingers under his chin.

"As long as you obey my commands, you don't have to worry. No harm will come to your pretty little mate."

A low growl erupted from my throat, and I stalked toward him.

"What makes you think I won't end your reign here and now for even entertaining the idea?"

My father smirked up at me.

"This kingdom has your loyalty, Ryker, though they don't know it. But I do."

My father gripped the armrests of his throne, and his voice became hard and cold.

"I know the lengths you've gone to in protecting the Unseelie. Killing me now would only plunge the kingdom into civil war. I'm betting on the fact that you don't want that."

I wanted to throw my head back and laugh at his foolishness. He had no idea what motivated me. I had gone to extreme lengths to defend the kingdom, but not for the Unseelie Fae, as he so arrogantly assumed.

"I wouldn't be so sure, Father. It might just be worth it."

He lifted his shoulder in a half-shrug, calling my bluff.

Silence stretched between us, and the longer I didn't tear him limb from limb, the more confident my father became.

"I don't care if that woman is your mate. You *will* marry Celeste, and soon."

"You will live to regret this day, Father," I sneered.

"Perhaps," he mused. "But today is not that day."

I studied the man before me, searching for the father he had once been.

But that man was no longer living.

He had died right alongside my mother.

I turned on my heel and marched out of the throne room. I'd painted a target on Cadence's back, and I would need to do everything in my power to keep her safe.

Chapter Twenty-Seven

RYKER

I paced the dimly lit library. Shadows flickered along the wall, and the light cast by the sconces made them appear monstrous, malevolent.

The familiar smell of leather-bound books and parchment did little to soothe my raging emotions. I'd been a fool today and had shown my hand to the one man who would stop at nothing to use it against me.

I ran my fingers through my hair in agitation, gripping the strands and pulling tight. My anger was a living, breathing entity inside me, and all I wanted to do was scream my wrath to the heavens above.

"You'll wear a hole in the carpet if you keep that up."

I turned to face the newcomer who'd intruded on my tumultuous self-reflection.

"I'm in no mood, Riordan," I warned.

My brother pushed off the door frame he'd been leaning against and headed toward the cabinet, where we kept an assortment of liquor.

"I can see that," he remarked as he grabbed two tumblers, filling them with whiskey.

Riordan offered me a glass, and I took it, emptying the contents in one swallow. The liquor burned my throat, and I relished the sting. The pain grounded me, strengthening my resolve.

My brother studied me from where he stood, his muscular arms folded against his chest, and his gaze sharp and thoughtful.

"Tell me what happened."

"Father figured out that Cadence is my mate."

The words tasted bitter on my tongue, and I marched toward the cabinet to refill my tumbler.

"Not to add insult to injury, Brother, but you made that obvious when you slaughtered eight men for her."

I glared at my younger brother. He was right, but that didn't ease my irritation. Ignoring his observation, I lifted the whiskey to my lips and drank greedily.

"That won't help anything, Ryker," he chastised.

Silence stretched between us as we both considered this new turn of events.

"Did he threaten her?" Riordan asked.

"He commanded me to follow through with my marriage to Celeste or risk Cadence."

Riordan groaned. "This is exactly what I was trying to forewarn you about."

"Do not test me, Little Brother," I warned. "You and I both know why I'm in this predicament."

A muscle feathered in Riordan's jaw, but he didn't push the matter further.

"What do you intend to do, Ryker?" he asked instead. "You took her from her home. You exposed her to this. Now you need to protect her."

"Don't you think I know that?" I snapped. "She's my mate, Riordan. Mine. And I *always* protect what's mine."

I gave my brother a pointed look, and this time, he dipped his chin in acknowledgment.

I exhaled a defeated sigh as I ran a hand down my face.

"If I keep her locked in my chambers, she's no better than a prisoner."

Riordan snorted. "Of course, your mind goes straight to restraining her."

I smirked, but didn't defend myself. "While I'm not against that idea, the prospect will undoubtedly displease Cadence. Doing it would only push her further away, and I am trying to make the stubborn woman submit to me and accept the bond."

"You don't have to make her a prisoner, Ryker. You only need to guard her. Your men are loyal to you. Use them. They'll ensure her safety when you cannot."

A growl rumbled up my throat, and I glared at my brother.

"Are you suggesting I cannot protect my mate, Riordan?"

My brother rolled his eyes.

"No, you primitive barbarian, but you won't always be around to keep her safe."

I considered Riordan's words. I trusted Malesh and Eamon with my life, and I knew that if I asked it of them, they would protect Cadence above their duty to the crown. But I wasn't so confident my remaining men would feel the same.

The weight of my brother's gaze bore into me as I resumed my pacing. My shadows burst free, and they swirled around me, twisting and writhing as though they sought to soothe my agitation.

"Assigning guards to her is only going to bring more unwanted attention her way."

My voice sounded rough, laced with the frustration burning through me like acid.

"The entire court was present when Father summoned you to answer for the massacre, were they not? The news that Cadence is your mate will spread."

An involuntary smile pulled up the corner of my mouth. My brother spoke of my murderous deeds with such casual indifference.

"No," I answered. "Father dismissed the courtiers after I'd described the way I would have slowly tortured Lucas to death for daring to touch Cadence had I more time, which made his mother faint."

"You did not," Riordan chuckled.

"I did, and I don't regret it. Not even a little. She was spewing nonsense about how her precious Lucas would never harm a woman, and she needed to be set straight," I grunted.

"And I'm sure it pained you greatly to be the one to undertake such a delicate task," he drawled.

"You know me, Brother, I am a prince devoted to his people. I live to serve my subjects," I said as I spread my arms wide and dipped into a bow.

Riordan, who had just taken a swallow of his whiskey, choked on the amber liquid, and I stepped back to avoid being in the firing line.

"For fuck's sake," I muttered. "You really ought to work on that, Little Brother. Your penchant for choking is not only annoying, but it also leaves you vulnerable."

"Hilarious Ryker," he scowled.

"Who's joking?" I said as I crossed my arms over my chest.

"Let's get back on topic," Riordan grumbled. "I hate to break it to you, Brother, but if you will not install guards, then you'll need allies in the council."

"The council is full of vipers who wouldn't hesitate to offer up Cadence if it meant putting a leash on me and my powers," I growled.

"Precisely."

I narrowed my eyes at my brother. "Explain yourself," I demanded.

"Who better to expose the council's schemes than one of their own? Just offer them something they crave more than your obedience."

I absentmindedly scratched at the stubble along my jaw. "I assume you have someone in mind."

Riordan's grin was downright devilish. "Lord Hanzel has a son he is trying to move up in the military ranks. The problem is, the man is useless."

"And?" I pressed.

"And," Riordan said, rolling his eyes. "Give him a contingent to oversee."

"If the man is incompetent, he'll only endanger my other soldiers."

"Not if you pair him with someone more experienced," Riordan countered, the mirth twinkling in his eyes.

"Are you suggesting I play Lord Hanzel, Little Brother?" I asked, my amusement infecting my tone.

"Me?" Riordan said, aghast, as he placed a hand over his heart. "I would never."

I snorted and shook my head, already feeling much better about the situation.

"All I'm saying is that you could treat the appointment as a traineeship of sorts. Pair the son with someone high-ranking and give him shared responsibility for the contingent. Make it clear he is to defer to his senior commander until he's ready to take over. If that day never comes, well..." Riordan trailed off.

"I like the way you think, Little Brother."

"Why thank you," he beamed. "In the meantime, use your advantage wisely. Come up with a plan to keep Cadence safe."

I nodded in agreement, my mind already working through the possibilities.

"Make it happen," I ordered.

"You know, the point was for *you* to make allies, Ryker. That's not something you can delegate."

I gave my brother a pointed look, and he sighed.

"Fine, I'll do it."

He cast a glance in my direction, taking me in from head to toe.

"You'd probably fuck it up anyway with all that overt approachability you're exuding."

I barked out a laugh, unbothered by the insult. He wasn't wrong.

My mind turned to the other task I still had to complete.

Riordan narrowed his gaze as he studied me.

"An all too pleased glint just entered your eyes. What's that about?" he said, suspicion clear in his tone.

I walked over to him and clapped a hand on his shoulder.

"I have a mate to tame," I said, not even attempting to hide my excitement.

Riordan's groan followed me as I strolled out of the library, ready to execute the next step in my plan.

Chapter Twenty-Eight

CADENCE

As the sun set over the palace courtyard, a warm orange hue draped the trimmed hedges that lined the stone wall. The fading light made the bushes appear as though they were on fire — flames flickering across the greenery as the inferno slowly devoured them.

The open space was peaceful, the air fresh and invigorating, as a gentle breeze caressed my cheek.

Until it wasn't.

"Well, well, what have we here?"

My shoulders tensed, and I turned in my seat, angling my body toward the newcomers.

Standing in front of me, her hair pulled into an elegant twist and her gown trailing behind her in a shimmer of pale blue, was Celeste. Two women stood at her back, their shared look of disdain letting me know we wouldn't be sharing court gossip over tea anytime soon.

A knot tightened in my chest as I watched them. I wanted no part in the impending territorial display.

"Lady Barrington," I said politely. "What can I do for you?"

"You can stay the hell away from my fiancée for a start."

I sighed, hating that I was right.

"You'll need to discuss that with the prince."

Fucking Ryker.

I doubted it would matter if I told them I was here against my will, and that I'd gladly leave if the prince would kindly remove the contraption from my throat.

"You don't even have the decency to be ashamed of yourself," Celeste scoffed.

I felt my temper flare at her words, but I forced myself to remain calm. Getting into a shouting match with Lady Barrington would do me no favors.

Her eyes narrowed at my lack of response, and she took a step closer, her manicured hands clenching into fists at her sides.

"You think you're so special, don't you? That you can waltz in here and steal what's mine?"

"What I think," I drawled, "is that this conversation is pointless. I am a guest of the Crown Prince. Any objections you may have should be raised with him directly."

Guest was a stretch, but the venomous viper before me didn't need to know the details of my captivity.

Celeste's eyes dropped to the collar that adorned my throat, and a cruel smile twisted her lips.

My stomach sank with dread as I braced for her next words.

"A guest? Is that what they're calling royal pets these days?"

Her companions tittered behind her, and I felt heat rush to my cheeks. I longed to slap the smug look off her face, but I knew better than to raise my hand to her. Her betrothal to the Crown Prince made it clear she held a position of influence within the Unseelie Court.

Instead, I stood, smoothing my skirts as I faced her.

One of Celeste's companions, a redhead with features pinched in perpetual disapproval, piped up. "I heard she's not even Unseelie. How the prince could lower himself to indulge in Seelie scum is beyond me."

My spine stiffened with her words. I didn't know how she knew about my heritage, but that knowledge put me in imminent danger.

The animosity between the Seelie and Unseelie kingdoms was legendary, and it wasn't unusual for innocent bystanders to be caught up in the crosshairs of that enmity.

"That got your attention, didn't it?" Celeste sneered.

Her lips curled into a predatory smile as her eyes glinted with excitement. I felt my power swirl to life inside me. The familiar hum comforted me as it pleaded with me to let it loose. To let it show these vain bitches who they were messing with.

But I needed a viable escape plan before unleashing my magic, and right now, I had none.

"Here's how this is going to go," Celeste purred. "You'll make the prince lose interest in you. Run away, disappear, or fall into another man's bed, I don't care. But you will clear my path to the throne, or I'll expose your little secret to the Unseelie Court and let them tear you to shreds."

I fought the urge to roll my eyes. If I could get the prince to lose interest in me, I'd have done it already. The man was controlling and possessive. I doubted there was anything I could do to make him leave me alone. He had already ensured I couldn't run, and if I fell into another man's arms, he'd sooner kill them and fuck me on their corpse just to remind me who I belonged to.

The man was unhinged like that.

Despite the impossibility of the task Celeste was asking of me, I was unable to deny the very serious nature of her threat against me.

But I also couldn't cower before this woman. Those who thrived on intimidation and control never relented unless someone forced them. Even if, by some miracle, I convinced Ryker to let me go, she wouldn't be satisfied until I was crushed beneath her boots, with no chance of ever rising to threaten her ambition.

Decision made, I squared my shoulders and lifted my chin.

"Lady Barrington," I began cordially. "It speaks volumes about your own insecurities if you feel the need to resort to threats just to hold the attention of a man."

Celeste gasped and took a step back as though I had slapped her.

Pressing my advantage, I reclaimed the space between us before continuing. "Have you ever considered that perhaps the prince's desire to be rid of you has nothing to do with me, and everything to do with the vile person you've proven yourself to be?"

Celeste's face flushed with anger, and her eyes narrowed to slits.

"How dare you speak to me that way! You're just a common whore, unworthy to even breathe the same air as nobility."

Her voice quivered with rage, and I quirked a brow in amusement.

"And yet, here I am, breathing just fine."

Celeste raised her palm as if to strike me, and my magic pulsed in my veins. Before she could land her blow, however, a large masculine hand caught her wrist in mid-air.

Celeste turned, her face paling when she realized who had seized her arm.

"Careful, My Lady," Riordan purred. "Trust me when I tell you that my brother does not take kindly to anyone mistreating his things."

Riordan glanced my way and sent a cheeky wink in my direction. This time, I didn't stop the eye roll from escaping.

"Your Highness, you misunderstand the situation. This insolent little witch," she snarled as she pointed at me.

"On the contrary, Lady Barrington," Riordan said, cutting her off. "I understand it perfectly. I see you for the desperate woman you are. One trying to cling to power that should never be yours."

Celeste wrenched her arm from Riordan's grasp, her chest heaving with outrage.

For a moment, she looked ready to lunge at the prince. Consequences be damned. But then her attention returned to me, and a cold smile spread across her lips.

"Enjoy your position while you can. I don't make idle threats. Soon enough, everyone in this court will know the worthless blood that runs through your veins."

An icy shiver raced down my spine, but I refused to let it show. I pushed aside my fear and tilted my head to the side as I smiled maniacally at Celeste.

"I welcome it, Lady Barrington." I leaned in closer as I whispered against her ear, "You see, that's not the only secret I've been hiding."

When I pulled back, I saw the terror flashing across her eyes. For the first time since she accosted me, uncertainty tightened her features.

I lunged forward, gnashing my teeth together mere inches from her face.

Celeste squealed as she retreated, her companions turning as pale as she had before they scurried off, muttering among themselves.

A dark chuckle drew my attention, and I whirled on Riordan.

"I had everything under control! You didn't need to come in and play the hero."

"I see that," he grinned. "What did you say to unsettle her so much?"

"None of your business." I crossed my arms over my chest for emphasis.

"Fair, fair," Riordan chuckled as he extended an elbow to me. "Shall we?"

I huffed, but accepted his proffered arm as I let him lead me away from the courtyard.

Chapter Twenty-Nine

RYKER

The long, winding corridors were quiet as I made my way toward the healer's quarters. Secluded from the main dining hall and the bustling guest chambers, the healer's wing lay at the farthest end of the palace.

It was well past midnight, and the only discernible sound in the darkness was the echo of distant footfalls from the patrolling guards.

Tonight, the isolation suited my needs.

I couldn't risk curious ears overhearing what they should not, or questioning glances perceiving more than they should.

As the door to the healer's quarters came into view, I pulled the hood of my cloak back, allowing the faint shimmer of moonlight to illuminate my features.

My father's ambitions and Cadence's disobedience fueled the storm lurking inside me. I could feel the tension pulling tight across my shoulders as I rapped my knuckles against the heavy oak door.

Whoever stood on the other side would know exactly which version of their prince they faced tonight.

When the door creaked open, it revealed a young woman, bleary-eyed and disheveled, as she blinked up at me. Her eyes widened with recognition, and she bowed hastily, her soft golden curls bouncing as they fell over her shoulder.

"Your Highness," she stammered as she dipped even lower into her bow. "How may I be of service to you?"

Without waiting for the woman to straighten, I marched into the antechamber behind her and crossed my arms over my chest.

"I need to speak with your matron," I demanded.

"Of course, Your Highness," the woman said, as she twisted her fingers in front of her.

I arched an impatient brow, and she flinched before spinning around and darting from the room.

I perused the medicinal herbs that hung along the walls to cure as I waited. The scent of turmeric, sage, and mint filled the air. To most, the aromas would be calming. Tonight, they were cloying and oppressive, as if they sat in judgment of my intentions.

Something sharp tugged at the center of my chest, and I reached up to rub at the spot.

Was that... guilt?

I shook my head as if that would ease the sensation. Before I could sink further into the strange feeling, the young woman returned with another Fae in tow. Her hair was as white as snow, and her eyes were as sharp as any bird of prey. She looked up at me with a mix of surprise and curiosity, but more importantly... suspicion.

A smile curved the corner of my mouth despite myself. She was correct in questioning my intentions.

"This is Mistress Odette," the younger woman said.

"Thank you, Gemma," Odette murmured. "You may return to your quarters."

Gemma gave me a final cursory glance before she bowed and left the room.

Odette continued to assess me as the silence stretched between us. I had to admit, I admired her obstinance.

"Your Highness," she said, breaking the tension. "This is unexpected. What brings you to me at this hour?"

I stepped forward, invading her space as I towered over her. Odette stared up at me, her neck craning as she kept her gaze focused on me.

She knew a predator when she saw one.

My admiration for her soared. Battle-hardened warriors were less daring.

"What I need from you requires a certain level of discretion," I murmured.

She raised her brows, her interest piqued, as she folded her hands before her.

"Discretion is but one of our many talents here in the healer's wing, Your Highness." Her tone was low but measured.

"A woman is staying in my quarters." I paused and waited for her to confirm she knew of whom I spoke.

When she dipped her head in acknowledgment, I continued. "She receives the daily fertility tonic as part of her morning regime."

My gaze hardened on Odette, and she shifted her weight from foot to foot.

"I am told that you prepare them."

Odette nodded, understanding beginning to dawn in her eyes.

"Yes, that is correct," she intoned. "It is standard for the courtesans of high-ranking members of the Unseelie Court to wish to avoid pregnancy during their time with their benefactors."

A low growl rumbled from my chest, and Odette retreated a step before she could stop herself.

"Cadence is not a courtesan," I snarled. "Refer to her like that again, and you will find yourself seeking employment elsewhere. Do I make myself clear?"

"Yes, Your Highness."

I reached a hand over my head and pulled my neck in the opposite direction. A sharp *crack* shattered the tense silence, and I mirrored the motion on the other side. The action went some way to alleviate my anger. I forced myself to remember that I needed this woman alive to carry out my plan.

When I returned my gaze to Odette, she was waiting patiently for me to continue. All traces of her earlier fear had vanished.

"I need you to prepare her tonic, as usual. However, I want you to alter it. Replace the ingredients with something harmless that mimics the taste, color, and texture exactly, but will not prevent pregnancy."

Odette stared at me for the longest moment. My request caught her off guard, leaving her speechless.

Just as I thought she wouldn't answer, she drew a breath and said, "Your Highness, forgive me, but shouldn't we discuss this with your lady first?"

My palms clenched into fists, and I allowed my shadows to coat my eyes with obsidian. Odette swallowed, and her posture stiffened, but she did not back away from me.

Once more, I was forced to appreciate her resolve. Odette was fierce, and a woman like that made a better ally than an enemy.

Softening my tone, I tried again. "The situation is... complicated. If it helps ease your conscience, this is what's best for her."

Her gaze held mine, and I could see the conflict warring in her eyes. "Your Highness, I am a healer. What you are asking me to do goes against the oath I swore to protect those in my care."

"And what of your oath to serve the Royal Family?"

I could always make Odette do as I commanded, but I knew her discretion would be more potent if she felt she played a willing role in my deception.

"I am loyal to the Monarchs, Your Highness," she said, her voice softer now. "If this is your command, I shall do as you ask."

I fought to contain the smile that threatened to spread across my face at my victory.

"Thank you, Odette. I will not forget your loyalty."

I dipped my head in a slight bow and headed towards the door. When I reached for the handle, I paused and glanced back over my shoulder.

"I trust you know what happens if you breathe a word of this."

Odette's lips thinned, and she grimaced. "I do."

"Excellent."

I crossed the threshold of the healer's wing and set off toward my chambers without another word. She may not like my methods, but once Cadence was carrying my heir, the future King of the Unseelie Fae, I'd be one step closer to ensuring she was untouchable.

As I slipped into the shadows of my quarters and saw Cadence curled up on my bed, sleeping peacefully, that same sharp tugging erupted from my chest.

It wasn't guilt.

I was doing what needed to be done. Cadence thought she could escape me, but I would ensure she was bound to me so tightly she could never break free.

I would see this through, no matter the cost — even if that cost was my peace.

Chapter Thirty

CADENCE

Warm rays of sunshine peeked around the edges of the thick black curtains, shielding me from the outside world that was slowly coming to life.

My altercation with Celeste had left my muscles coiled tight, and my body ached all over.

I was ready to call it a day before it had even begun.

With a groan, I rolled onto my back and flung my arm wide... where it collided with a hard, muscular chest.

"Oof."

It appeared Ryker had returned to his chambers after all.

"Was that necessary, Cadence?" he rumbled, his voice still thick with sleep.

"That depends. Have you done anything to warrant my ire this early in the day?"

Ryker chuckled. "Who am I kidding? Of course you have."

Then I recalled I already had reason enough to be irate where he was concerned.

"I had a pleasant chat with Lady Barrington yesterday. Care to guess the topic of our conversation?"

"The impressive length of my cock," Ryker murmured as he buried his face in his pillow.

My anger simmered beneath a thin veneer of calm, and I sat up before reaching over and ripping the pillow away from him.

"This is serious," I yelled as I slammed it into his head again and again.

"Cadence, fuck!" Ryker growled. "Give me the damn pillow."

He gripped the silken edge of the cover and tore it out of my grasp. Ryker ran a palm through his messy hair, and for the briefest moment, I forgot why I was so angry with him.

But Ryker being Ryker reminded me of exactly why I detested the man.

"Well, don't keep me in suspense. What were you and my fiancée chatting about?"

The faint smirk he wore, and the amused glint in his eyes, made me damn near homicidal.

"This isn't a game, Ryker! The woman knows I am Seelie, and she threatened to divulge that tidbit to the whole godsdamn Unseelie Court!"

Ryker's smirk faltered, and a shadow crossed his handsome features. But he remained composed, not allowing any further sign of his displeasure to slip past his calm mask of indifference.

"Celeste knows better than to cross me, Cadence," Ryker said.

He sat up and made himself comfortable against the headboard, one arm slung behind his head, the picture of relaxed ease.

My hands curled into fists at my side, and I leaned in, invading Ryker's space.

That was a mistake.

His intoxicating scent hit me with full force. The heady blend of wild earth and something… darker overwhelmed me, and I had to shake myself out of my reverie.

"Celeste warned that if I didn't leave, she would expose me to the entire court and let them tear me to shreds. Does that sound like a woman who's afraid to defy you?"

I glared at Ryker, allowing him to feel the full weight of my fury. "And you and I both know that her words are no idle threat. The hatred between the two kingdoms is renowned."

Before I even registered what he was doing, Ryker gripped my waist in his large, calloused hand and pulled me beneath him. His face was close to my own, and his expression was so dark, I couldn't tell if he intended to kiss me or devour me whole.

"There is no escaping me, Cadence," he said in a low, dangerous tone.

My body stiffened before I pushed against his chest.

"Of course that's all you heard?"

"You keep entertaining the idea that you can escape me, so I will continue to remind you of your place."

Furious tears burned behind my eyes, but I refused to let them fall.

"How could I ever forget? You collared me like a fucking animal."

I wrapped my fingers around the cool metal that adorned my throat. "Whenever I see this, I am reminded of how little you think of me."

My breath was coming in short, sharp gasps, and I was losing the battle to keep my tears at bay.

"She called me your pet, Ryker."

I'd meant to fire the words at him so he would feel them like a physical blow, but my emotions had taken over, and they escaped me on a broken sob.

Ryker's eyes hardened, and he stared down at me as though I were a puzzle he needed to solve. But a flicker of some emotion, something dark, crossed his features, and then he lifted his thumb to catch the tears sliding down my cheek. Unable to bear the weight of his penetrating gaze any longer, I turned away from him, burying my face in the pillows.

"Celeste overstepped, Cadence, and I will ensure she knows just how badly she fucked up," he murmured.

He didn't get it. How could he? He'd never experienced the loss of anything as precious as his autonomy.

I wasn't crying because Celeste had threatened my life. My tears flowed because he had finally broken me, and the man was too arrogant to understand the difference.

"What am I to you, Ryker?" I murmured, cutting through the tense silence.

"What do you mean?"

"I mean, you are betrothed to Celeste, and you intend to marry her, no? She will be your queen, she will bear your heirs, and she will stand at your side when it is time for you to sit on the throne. Where will that leave me? Your dirty little secret? Your mistress, concubine, what? Do you have so little regard for me you would rob me of my future for your own selfish desires?"

When he didn't answer, I turned to look at him.

Ryker studied me for the longest moment before he released a resigned sigh.

"It's not that simple, Cadence."

"Of course it is," I scoffed.

Ryker's eyes narrowed, and a muscle in his jaw twitched. He pushed off me and resumed his place against the headboard.

"There are things at play that you aren't aware of, Cadence. Celeste's family maintains a position of power in the Unseelie Court, and they contribute many resources to the kingdom's coffers. Disavowing her right now would be extremely unwise."

I barked out a laugh. The sound was harsh as it reverberated throughout the room.

"So, you keep her close while I'm to suffer the consequences?" I lifted my chin, my voice hard as I stared him down.

"How very noble of you, Ryker. You get the benefits of power, the stability of her family's resources, and me."

"Mind your tone, Cadence," Ryker warned, his voice dangerously low, but I refused to concede.

"What will you do?" I challenged. "Kill me? If I am to suffer the life you so graciously offer me, I think I would prefer the freedom of death than remaining in your vile company for a second longer."

Ryker jumped from the bed, his shoulders heaving as he ground his teeth together. Then he closed his eyes and inhaled a deep breath. When he opened them again, pain, or remorse perhaps, stared back at me. For a moment, he looked almost vulnerable, as if my words had cut straight to his core.

Then his usual mask of coldness fell into place, and he retreated behind the walls he wore like armor.

"This is about survival, Cadence. I will not jeopardize that for your petty jealousies."

"Jealousy," I breathed. "You think this is about jealousy?"

My voice rose as indignant fury washed through me once more.

"This is about my life, Ryker. You've stolen my future from me! And you don't even have the decency to treat me with respect. You collared me, so I can't leave, yet you parade another woman around in front of the masses. You have made sure I am dependent on you for everything, keeping me at your mercy while you entertain yourself with your cruel games."

My chin quivered, and I cursed myself for showing any weakness. I didn't know how to make him understand. Ryker had never been denied anything in his life, including me.

"You claim I am your mate, yet you treat me as though I am your whore. You say I am to endure your oppression because it means I am safe, yet you allow threats against me to go unpunished."

I stood from the bed and began pacing, unable to stay still any longer.

"You're a coward, Ryker! The terrifying Night Cursed Prince is a coward. Where is the man whose name alone makes people tremble? Because I don't see him."

Ryker rounded the bed and gripped my chin between his thumb and forefinger.

"No one will touch you, Cadence," he rumbled. "I protect what's mine."

"Have you ever considered that you're the one I need protection from?"

Ryker's heated gaze bore into me, and I felt as though my whole body might catch ablaze under his scrutiny.

"I said I'd take care of it, Cadence."

Ryker leaned in to kiss me, but I turned away. His lips grazed my cheek, and a small blossom of warmth spread across my chest.

I was a godsdamned fool, and if I didn't harden myself against the effect he had on me, it would cost me my life.

"Wait here for me, Temptress."

With that, he disappeared, leaving me alone in his cold, empty chambers.

Chapter Thirty-One

RYKER

Fury roiled inside of me as my feet pounded against the marble floors of the palace. Servants and guards alike stepped out of my way, giving me a wide berth when they saw me coming.

I hadn't even attempted to conceal the wrath that radiated from me.

As I rounded the corner of the hallway that led to Celeste's wing, I heard high-pitched laughter emanating from behind closed doors.

The telltale sign that Lady Barrington was serving tea.

I hadn't bothered to announce myself as I pushed the ornate doors wide and stepped into an antechamber filled with the overpowering scent of perfume.

Celeste sat at a small breakfast table, her gown a rich crimson, almost the shade of spilled wine. Her hair was perfectly groomed, with not a stray strand in sight, and her pouty lips were coated in thick paint, the same color as her dress.

She arched a single brow in surprise before placing her teacup on the saucer in front of her.

"Ryker," she purred. "What an unexpected delight."

She beamed up at me, her smile as fake as her wide-eyed innocence.

"Leave us," I barked, not bothering to look at the women surrounding Celeste.

They shuffled nervously in their seats, their eyes darting between me and Celeste, unsure of what to do.

"Do not make me repeat myself."

Celeste nodded sharply, and they leaped from their chairs, almost sprinting for the door.

I kept my gaze trained on Celeste. The memory of Cadence sobbing as she recalled what Celeste had said to her fueled my rage.

Celeste folded her hands in her lap and waited for me to speak. She was the picture of poise and elegance, but I knew the cruelty that lay beneath the surface.

She was a Barrington, after all.

"You know why I am here," I stated, each word as cold as steel.

"I am certain I do not."

I lunged forward, gripping the armrests on her chair and forcing her into the backrest.

"Do not play games with me, Celeste. You threatened Cadence's life."

Celeste let her mask fall away, the feigned innocence disappearing from her eyes, only to be replaced by a glint of cold fury.

"Cadence? Is that the name of the pet you've been entertaining yourself with?" she scoffed.

A low growl forced its way up my throat, the sound dangerous and threatening. She swallowed thickly, but lifted her chin and pointed her nose in the air as though she smelled something that displeased her.

"I warned her, yes. I informed her of what would happen should she endeavor to take what is rightfully mine."

"Are you in the mood to meet the gods?" I asked with a calmness that belied the lethal anger I was feeling.

Celeste laughed, a mocking, hollow sound that filled the room. When I remained silent, her eyes rounded in fear, and she sucked in a sharp breath.

"You can't be serious, Ryker."

"Try me."

"My father will not stand for this," she warned. "Our betrothal is a condition of his continued support for the King."

"Cadence has nothing to do with that."

"I am to be your wife and the future Queen of the Unseelie. I refuse to be made a fool of by your dalliances."

Shadows coated my vision, and I felt the sharp prick of pain as my fangs descended.

With one look, Celeste crumbled.

"Ryker, p-please," she stammered. "This has all been a huge misunderstanding."

She reached for me but thought better of it, letting her hand fall to her lap.

"Then let me clear it up for you, Celeste."

A sinister smile spread across my face, and a small whimper escaped her.

"This is your only warning. If you make any attempt to harm Cadence or incite any violence toward her, you will suffer a fate worse than death."

I leaned in closer, my lips brushing against the shell of her ear.

"There is a reason that men like your father seek to leash me, Celeste. I promise you, you do not want to discover what that reason is."

I pushed off the chair and met her terrified gaze.

"Have I made myself clear?"

"Yes," she whispered as she nodded her head.

"Excellent," I purred, but the word was laced with venom.

Without a second glance, I strode from the room, leaving Celeste behind to contemplate my warning.

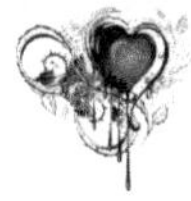

My thoughts raced as I made my way back to my chambers. I wanted to reassure Cadence that I had eliminated the threat against her. My earlier rage still simmered beneath the surface, but it had abated enough that I could shift my focus to the next pressing matter.

As I turned toward my wing, however, a figure stepped out of the shadows and into my path.

"Impressive performance you put on back there," Riordan said.

He leaned against a column, his arms crossed over his chest and an amused smile on his face.

"Eavesdropping again, Brother?" I glared at him, but there was no real heat behind it.

Riordan shrugged. "Someone has to keep an eye on you. The gods know you are unpredictable when you're in a mood."

"Fuck off!"

I pushed my brother out of my way and continued on my path. His cackling laughter followed in my wake.

"She's different, you know," Riordan said as he stepped into place beside me.

I cast a sideways glance at him, and he rolled his eyes.

"You can stop imagining my bloody demise, Brother. All I meant was that she's genuine. She's the kind of person who would stand at your side not because of your title and what she can gain from it, but because she thinks you're worthy."

Riordan nodded, as a thoughtful expression crossed his face. "That's rare in our world," he mused.

"Sounds like you've been spending too much time with *my* mate," I grumbled.

"Ha! If you recall, Brother, that was by your command."

And damn it all to hell, he was right.

A knowing smirk lifted the corner of Riordan's lips, but he didn't rub salt on the wound, which was remarkably restrained for him.

We continued in silence for a while, both lost in our musings.

"You can't push her too far, Ryker. Once she tips over that edge, I don't know if you'll ever be able to pull her back."

I bristled, but Riordan held up a hand to stop me.

"I'm not criticizing you, Ryker. Though your methods leave a lot to be desired," he murmured.

"Get to the point, Riordan," I demanded as I pinched the bridge of my nose.

"I can see Cadence means something to you. Whether it's pure desire, the needs of the bond driving you, or, dare I say it, love," he grinned wickedly, and I narrowed my eyes at him. "It's clear that you want to keep her beside you."

"That's a lot of words to say absolutely nothing," I grumbled.

"If you want her to stay... willingly."

My brother gave me a disapproving look, which I ignored.

"If you want her to accept the bond, you need to meet her halfway. Stop treating her like she's your property and start treating her like she's your mate."

Cadence *was* my property.

Mine.

I didn't voice that aloud, however, as it seemed like it might be counter-intuitive to Riordan's point.

"And how do I do that?" I asked instead.

"May the gods have mercy," Riordan muttered under his breath. "You must court the woman, Ryker. Let her get to know you. Show her there is more to you than the disagreeable asshole you've presented her with so far... despite how tiny that fraction of your personality may be."

"Even when you mutter, Riordan, I can still hear you."

"Lords and ladies, behold! The man *can* listen."

"You're lucky you are my brother, or else I would have killed you eons ago."

"A thank you would suffice."

"Thank you," I deadpanned.

"You're welcome," my brother beamed. "Just don't fuck it up!"

Riordan clapped me on the shoulder, then turned and strode down the hall, disappearing into the shadows from which he'd emerged.

I took a deep breath and steeled myself for the task ahead.

I could do this.

I could court my mate.

Chapter Thirty-Two

CADENCE

A knock at the door pulled me from my misery. I'd burrowed beneath the covers of Ryker's impossibly comfortable bed, and I was content to stay there.

A second knock sounded, and I released a resigned sigh. The sooner I handled whoever was at the door, the sooner I could return to my pity party.

"Come in."

I didn't bother getting out of bed. If their visit was so urgent, they could deal with my current bedraggled state.

The door creaked open, revealing a woman I'd never seen before. She was tall and slender, with pale skin and even paler hair, which she had pulled back into a tight braid. Her clothing was simple, her dress a muted shade of green. It was the kind of practical attire that marked her as a servant of the palace.

She moved further into the room with soft steps and practiced grace. In her hands, she carried a small silver tray with a glass vial resting in the center.

"Good morning, My Lady," she greeted. "My name is Odette, and I have come to deliver your daily fertility tonic."

Her sweet, reassuring tone contrasted sharply with her alert gaze, making me uneasy. I kept my eyes fixed on her as she lowered the tray to the nightstand.

"Scarlette is usually the one who brings me my treatment."

Odette straightened and gave me an encouraging smile. "I am the Matron of the healers who work within the palace. Normally, I'd have another healer or maid bring your tonic, but I like to check in on my patients myself now and then."

She picked up the glass vial and offered it to me. Her eyes flicked over me with a hint of something I couldn't quite place.

I shifted my position on the bed so that I was upright and leaning against the headboard.

"Thank you," I said as I took the small bottle.

I studied the amber liquid inside it before removing the stopper. A familiar herbal scent wafted from it, but it did little to appease my suspicions.

I wouldn't put it past Celeste to try to poison me at the first opportunity. But Odette didn't know I was a healer, capable of identifying countless toxins even in my sleep.

Deciding this was the perfect time to see if Celeste was so bold, I feigned ignorance and played along.

"Should I look for anything specific?"

"Hmm?"

"You said you checked in to monitor the treatment's progress. Should I watch for any particular symptoms?"

"Oh no, nothing like that," Odette said, quick to reassure me. "Occasionally, some women experience unpleasant side effects such as headaches or stomach troubles, that type of thing. Fertility treatments also require great attention to detail to ensure the best outcome, so I prefer to monitor the dosage. That way, if any adjustments are required, I can action them to avoid unintended consequences."

All true.

That didn't mean this dose wasn't laced with something sinister, however.

I lifted the vial to my nose and inhaled deeply. There was nothing unusual about the various aromas, so I took a tentative sip. The bitter, earthy taste slid over my tongue, and I tried in vain not to grimace. While the tonic tasted the same, it was more potent than usual.

I drew upon my magic and sent it delving into every corner of my body. When I detected nothing amiss, I released a relieved breath.

My gaze lingered on Odette, and I studied her as I spoke.

"It's stronger than my normal dose."

Odette's expression remained neutral, but her eyes held an intensity that left me feeling exposed.

"Bodies are ever-changing, and they often build up a tolerance for any medicines we rely on regularly," she supplied. "It is necessary to increase the dosage from time to time to maintain effectiveness."

Another truth.

The bitterness settled unpleasantly in my stomach, and I downed the rest of the tonic before I could talk myself out of taking it. I set the vial down on the silver tray and returned my attention to Odette.

"How was that?" she asked.

"Fine, I suppose."

"No complaints then," she said with a slight grin.

"I'm not sure I would go that far," I mumbled, the bitter taste still coating my tongue.

She barked out a laugh but quickly sobered. "It's important, especially for someone in your position, that everything remains... balanced."

She flashed me an apologetic smile, and I wondered just what she thought I was doing in Ryker's chambers.

Did she think I was his courtesan?

I nodded, not wanting to voice my question aloud. It wasn't her fault that Ryker had kept my presence here a mystery, and I didn't want to appear rude or ungrateful. Instead, I waded into safer waters.

"Is it a common practice then?"

Odette knitted her brows.

"Adjusting the ingredients, I mean."

The healer seemed relieved when I clarified my line of questioning, and, for some unknown reason, that observation had dread swirling to life within me.

"Oh, yes," she beamed. "Every woman's constitution is different, so the blend must be tailored accordingly."

Once again, her words rang true.

Odette leaned forward and placed her hand on my knee in a comforting gesture.

"My Lady, your wellbeing is paramount. I assure you, I craft each dose with care, but if there's anything I should know..." she trailed off, unsure what else to say.

Something in her tone made my insides plummet, but I forced a polite smile. "I'm fine, truly. My stomach is just a little unsettled from the higher dosage. I'm sure I'll get used to it."

Odette's gaze lingered on me for a moment longer than necessary before she straightened and nodded.

"Of course, My Lady."

She moved to collect the silver tray and empty vial, her fingers brushing the glass with something akin to reverence.

"I'll leave you to get on with your day."

I watched as Odette turned, her movements almost eerie in their rigidity, a complete contrast to the poise she had displayed upon entering. She strode for the door, but as she reached for the handle, she paused and cast a glance back in my direction.

"If you feel anything... unusual... do not hesitate to summon me. I will always make myself available for your needs."

An involuntary shiver raced down my spine, but I forced myself to ignore it.

"Thank you. I'll keep that in mind."

With a final dip of her chin, Odette slipped out of Ryker's chambers, the door closing softly behind her.

I exhaled slowly, surprised that I felt even tenser than before. Odette's parting words echoed inside my head, and there was an undercurrent that lingered, a warning perhaps, that I couldn't put my finger on. Her appearance, so close after my confrontation with Celeste, seemed orchestrated. Her demeanor had been polite, but tense.

Yet, everything she said was true.

Had my distrust grown so strong that I now saw enemies where none existed?

I shivered as I dismissed the notion. I glanced back toward the door, half expecting Odette to reappear. She had seemed so invested, so watchful, as she attended to me.

I shook my head to dispel my lingering doubts. The woman was only trying to help.

Even as the thought formed, I couldn't shake the feeling that I was missing something crucial.

Chapter Thirty-Three

CADENCE

When the door burst open soon after Odette left, I expected to see the strange woman lingering in the doorway.

Instead, I found a hulking Fae male with a brooding aura looking unsure as he surveyed me with apparent nervousness.

"Go away, Ryker," I muttered. "I'm in no mood for company, least of all yours."

"Cadence," he rumbled in that tone that had my nipples puckering.

Not today, hormones.

"Are you deaf as well as an asshole?"

A dark chuckle was my only answer, and the sound filled the room with a tantalizing mixture of danger and allure, daring me to come closer despite my every instinct screaming at me to stay away.

I could hear the rustle of clothing as Ryker moved nearer, but I was determined to ignore him.

That was, until he ripped the covers from me, exposing my skin to the cool morning air.

"What the hell, Ryker!"

"You will not spend the day sulking in bed, Cadence. Get up. Now."

He waved his hand in the air as if he expected me to jump at his command. Hell, he most likely did.

"I said no, Ryker. I realize it's not a word you are familiar with, but it means fuck off."

Ryker sighed.

The man fucking sighed.

It was almost as if it was *his* life that had been uprooted.

"Cadence," he said, the single word a plea. "Can we agree to put our differences aside for one day and just enjoy ourselves?"

Enjoy ourselves? The man was delusional!

"Please," he added when I didn't respond.

I eyed him, and a hopeful grin pulled up his lips.

"I promise I have no untoward intentions, Cadence. I only want to show you something I think you will appreciate."

"What kind of something?"

Ryker extended his hand to me, and his grin turned predatory. "You'll have to come with me to find out."

I debated with myself for a moment, but my curiosity won out.

"Fine."

I dressed quickly, not bothering to brush my hair. Instead, I ran my fingers through the mane of knots and hoped for the best.

"Ready?" Ryker asked as he extended his palm once more.

"Is there a reason I am required to touch you?"

"Yes," he chuckled as he took my hand in his and pulled me to him. "Even if that weren't the case, I'd still want to touch you, Cadence. I always want to touch you."

I couldn't even be mad that my body was betraying me. My mind was also on board for whatever dark and delicious thoughts were occupying Ryker's head.

How could I hate the man and crave him at the same time?

Too caught up in my musings, I didn't notice when the room darkened.

"Oh no," I began, but it was too late.

Shadows as black as night surrounded me, suffocating any hint of light as Ryker moved us through the darkness.

Mercifully, it was over as quickly as it started.

"Not my favorite pastime," I grumbled, and Ryker laughed.

The sound was so genuine, with no trace of his usual cynicism or cruelty, that I was momentarily stunned.

"Come on," he called as he gripped my hand and tugged me along behind him.

I scanned my surroundings and gasped when I realized we stood atop a mountain range.

"Stunning, isn't it?" Ryker murmured.

"It is."

The valley below was breathtaking. The rolling hills cradled the valley's basin while the shimmering threads of the river wound their way across the terrain, catching and reflecting the sunlight as it traversed the landscape.

Villages and farms dotted the horizon, their red roofs blending seamlessly with the vibrant greens of the forest lining the valley. I peered up at the sky, an infinite canvas of shifting white clouds that only served to highlight the beauty of everything below.

Ryker tugged on my hand, and I realized I had stopped walking to take in the view. He led me down a well-worn path, and the trees grew denser as we walked. Branches arched overhead, and the small slivers of sunlight that peeked through the canopy gave the forest an ethereal appearance.

I cast a glance toward Ryker out of the corner of my eye. His usual hard demeanor had disappeared, and his features softened as he navigated the familiar path.

"Do you come here a lot?"

Ryker smiled. And not just any smile. This one was a panty-melting, I'll-charm-you-out-of-your-first-born type of smile.

"This place," he murmured, nostalgia lacing his voice, "is where Riordan and I escaped to as children."

He paused and glanced over his shoulder at me. "It was our secret," he finished with a crooked grin.

I raised an eyebrow, unable to contain my next question.

"And you're sharing it with me?"

Ryker stopped walking and turned to face me. His hand, which had felt warm wrapped around my own, now felt searing as heat banked between us.

"I am."

I swallowed around the lump forming in my throat.

Mercifully, Ryker spared me from having to respond as he pushed aside an overhanging branch to reveal the mouth of a cave nestled against the rocky hillside. A trail of moss wound its way over the rugged stone, and I sucked in a deep breath, relishing the scent of damp earth and fresh rain.

Ryker stepped forward, but I hesitated.

"Is it safe?" I jutted my chin toward the entrance. "Inside, I mean."

"Perfectly," he grinned.

His eyes sparkled with mischief, and he tugged me closer. "Trust me."

I gave him a look that portrayed exactly how little I trusted him, and he laughed, not perturbed in the least.

"Fair," he conceded. "But you can trust me in this."

Excitement and apprehension warred within me, but once again, my curiosity won out, and I followed him inside.

The further we ventured, the more difficult it became to see. I found myself trusting Ryker to lead me through unscathed, and for the first time since meeting him, the thought of putting my faith in him didn't terrify me.

We rounded a corner, and the path opened into a wide cavern. There was a narrow opening above us, and the sunlight filtered down, highlighting the space and giving it an otherworldly glow.

A small pool of water sat at the center of the cave. Gentle ripples danced across the surface and reflected off the stone walls.

"It's beautiful," I whispered, afraid that if I spoke too loudly, I'd break the spell.

"The most beautiful thing I've ever seen," Ryker murmured.

But when I turned to him, Ryker's gaze wasn't on the cave or the inviting pool.

He was staring at me.

Chapter Thirty-Four

CADENCE

I cleared my throat for no other reason than to escape the intensity of Ryker's gaze.

"You said you came here to get away." I turned in his direction and glanced up at him from under my lashes. "From what?"

Ryker sighed. He had been doing that a lot today.

"Expectations. The sense that nothing I did would ever be enough. My father. Take your pick."

He gripped the back of his neck before burying his hand into his hair and tugging the tie free. His snow-colored tresses flowed over his shoulders, and he shook his head to clear the errant strands that had fallen into his eyes.

"I tried to shield Riordan from the worst of it." His entire body sagged as if he felt the weight of the realm bearing down on him. "I wasn't always successful."

He murmured the last part as if he were speaking to himself, and I wondered if he meant to say it out loud.

"At least here I knew he was safe."

Ryker shrugged, brushing off the confession. Though I could still see the vulnerability that clung to him. I wanted to probe further, but it was clear he was done talking.

He gripped the back of his tunic and tore it from his body before discarding it on the damp cave floor. His hands dropped to his belt as he unfastened it with slow, deliberate movements. He slipped the leather free, and I swallowed roughly.

"What are you doing?" I asked, when I couldn't take the tension any longer.

Ryker lifted his eyes, and I didn't miss the spark of amusement that shone back at me.

The man was well aware of the effect he had on me.

A playful grin spread across his lips as he said, "Going for a swim." He toed off his boots as he added, "Care to join me?"

I glanced at the pool. Its allure was stronger than ever. But the thought of stepping into its depths with him so close, looking like a god... had me fighting the urge to press my thighs together.

I couldn't trust myself around him.

The air between us was heavy, as if we stood on the edge of something inevitable, and I wasn't sure I was ready to cross that line.

"You promised me one day, Cadence."

Ryker's smooth voice caressed my exposed flesh like an old lover.

"I promised you nothing," I retorted, distracting myself from my body's reaction to him.

"Come on," he urged, his tone low and tantalizing. "Give in to me, just this once."

Ryker didn't wait for my response. Instead, he pulled his trousers down his muscled thighs and stepped out of them before striding into the clear water. When the water reached his waist, he dipped his head under the surface, only to reemerge a moment later.

Water droplets ran down his chiseled torso, and he pushed his hands through his hair as he brushed the wet strands out of his face.

I never imagined I could envy a mere water droplet. And yet, I desperately wanted to take its place, preferably with my tongue.

Ryker quirked a brow at my obvious ogling. "Well?" he challenged.

With a deep breath, I kicked off my boots and slipped out of my dress. My hands moved to cover my breasts as the cool air of the cave left me shivering. I could feel the blazing heat of Ryker's gaze on me, but I didn't dare meet his eyes.

Ryker had seen me naked more than once already, and I'd stripped down to my skin before his men when I'd found the spring, but this felt different.

This time, I was choosing to bare myself to him.

Pushing aside my reservations, I discarded my panties and moved toward the water. Ryker's heated gaze tracked me, his eyes never leaving me as I approached. When I reached the edge of the pool, I dipped a toe in to test the temperature, and to my surprise, it was warm. I lowered myself onto the edge and slid my feet in until the water kissed my knees.

Ryker waded toward me, and I could see his erect cock through the pristine water. He leaned into me and placed his forearms on either side of my thighs.

"You're so fucking beautiful, Cadence," he whispered reverently. "When I look at you, I have to remind myself to breathe because your very presence steals the air from my lungs."

Something tugged at my chest, but the sensation quickly faded.

"Ryker," I murmured, at a loss for words.

Ryker gripped my hips and pulled me into the pool with him. The water was smooth as silk as it embraced me, and a slight gasp slipped between my lips as I felt the tip of Ryker's length brush against my entrance.

Ryker swallowed the sound as he sealed his lips over mine, and I wrapped my arms around him.

The kiss wasn't gentle, but it lacked his usual dominance. Instead, it was probing, as if he wanted to taste every inch of my mouth.

When we broke apart, he pressed his forehead against mine as he sucked in ragged breaths.

"I want to do better, Cadence."

His words were so quiet, it was as though he was afraid to speak them aloud. Ryker pulled back and met my gaze. The intensity in his eyes caused my heart to skip a beat.

"I know I've made things difficult for you, and I'm not the easiest person to be around, but I never meant to hurt you."

It wasn't an apology, nor was it a promise to free me.

But he was trying.

"We could be good together, Cadence. I could give you the world if you'd let me."

The question was, did I want that? I had many reasons to despise Ryker, yet something kept tugging me back to him. Unable to come up with an answer, I redirected the conversation.

"How Ryker? How can you say that when you're marrying someone else?"

Not to mention he'd kill me without hesitation if he knew the truth, but I kept that thought to myself.

"I won't be marrying Celeste, Cadence."

"That's not what you said this morning," I countered.

"I have a plan. I've set things in motion to secure our future. I can't tell you everything yet, but trust me when I say I'll take care of you, and I'll keep you safe."

"How can you ask me to trust you after all you have done?"

Ryker's gaze held mine, imploring and earnest. There was a rawness there, too. Something unguarded that had me *wanting* to trust him, to give in to him.

"You're right," he said, breaking the silence. "Let me prove it to you instead."

His words settled over me, and I felt the weight of his sincerity.

But I would never trust Ryker. How could I after everything he'd put me through? Yet, for the very first time, I wished I could.

And that thought terrified me.

I was losing myself to him, and it enraged me that my hatred was not enough to overpower his intoxicating presence.

"All right," I murmured.

The words escaped before I could stop them, and there was no taking them back.

Ryker squeezed my side, and the water rippled around us. He trailed his fingers over my waist, tracing a slow path to my back.

As he caressed my spine, he tucked my head beneath his chin. The action both comforted and confused me, but I felt myself sinking further into his embrace.

"I promise you, Cadence," he whispered, "everything will be as the fates intended it."

Chapter Thirty-Five

CADENCE

The only sound discernible inside the cave was the slow trickle of water as it dripped from the ceiling.

That, and the rasp of my ragged breathing.

We stood chest-deep in the still water, and anticipation flooded my veins as Ryker watched me. He raised his fingers and traced a path down my neck to my collarbone. His touch lingered when he reached the pulse point at the base of my throat, and his gaze darkened when he felt the rapid beat that had settled there.

My breathing hitched, and my lips parted as he lifted his eyes to meet mine. Primal need burned in his gaze, and I was certain he saw the same in me.

"How I feel about you, Cadence, is unlike anything I've ever felt before," he murmured.

He pressed his mouth to my throat as he left a trail of wet kisses all the way to the shell of my ear.

"You've buried yourself beneath my skin. Your presence has invaded my thoughts to the point of insanity. Not even my dreams are safe from your presence, and it feels as though you are haunting me," he breathed. "Are you Cadence? Are you haunting me?"

Before I could say anything, he sucked my earlobe into his hot mouth and bit down. A shudder ran through my body and Ryker pressed closer, the head of his cock nudging at my entrance.

"You've become my addiction, my obsession, and I fear there are no lengths I wouldn't go to, no boundaries I wouldn't cross to keep you at my side."

He'd proven that time and time again, and I hated it.

But at that moment, with him, I felt anything but hatred. It wasn't disgust that had me pulling him closer, needing to eliminate any space between us.

Without warning, Ryker lifted me from the water and placed me on the ledge. He stepped between my thighs and stared down at me, open and bare before him.

"And none of this is a choice," he murmured so quietly I almost didn't hear him. "It's a descent into madness. A pull I'm unable to resist, even as it threatens to bring me to the edge of myself."

Ryker lifted his gaze, and his eyes locked with mine. Obsidian had consumed the whites of his eyes, and I inhaled sharply.

Not from fear, though.

From anticipation.

"I know it will tear me apart, and yet, I would never escape it because, in that darkness, you are mine, and mine alone."

Then his mouth was on me.

He placed a hand on my lower abdomen and gently pushed me until my back hit the cold, wet earth as his tongue swirled inside my opening. Ryker licked the length of my slit before he sucked my clit into his mouth.

A needy sound that I hardly recognized as my own escaped me, and I almost exploded then and there.

"You make the most delicious sounds, Temptress," he purred, and as his warm breath hit my center, I whimpered.

"You'll be a good girl for me, won't you, Temptress?" he drawled, emphasizing each word. "When I give an order, you will obey. Isn't that right?"

"Yes," I breathed, desperate to feel his hands on me again.

Ryker chuckled darkly, pleased with my obedience.

"Now play with your nipples while I devour your needy cunt."

I slid my fingers up my body and pinched one puckered nipple and then the other. When Ryker dipped his tongue back inside me, I cried out at the intense pleasure the competing sensations created.

Then he went to war on my pussy and everything else faded away.

I cupped my breasts, feeling the full weight of them as I continued to circle my nipples, pinching and squeezing as he'd instructed me.

The world could have crumbled around us, and I wouldn't have noticed... or cared.

All I could focus on was the way he made me feel.

The stirrings of an orgasm began to build, and I reached down to run my fingers through Ryker's hair, partly needing to touch him and partly to make sure he didn't stop his ministrations.

I was close.

So, so, close.

And unabashedly desperate.

"That's it, Temptress," he growled against my pussy.

The vibration sent shock waves pulsing through my core.

"Shatter for me."

My inner muscles clenched, creating a tingling sensation before waves of pleasure crashed into me. Violent tremors wracked my body, and a wanton moan, long and guttural, passed between my lips as a sense of euphoria washed over me.

I was panting hard, trying to catch my breath as I came down from my high, and I didn't even realize Ryker had pulled me into the water until the cool liquid assaulted my sensitive nipples.

Ryker spun me in his arms so that my back was to his chest, and he placed my hands on the edge of the pool to steady me.

"My turn," he snarled against my ear, and that was the only warning I got before he thrust into me, long and hard.

I screamed Ryker's name, but that only encouraged him to go faster, deeper. With one hand on my hip, he wound my hair around his fist, anchoring me to him as he pounded into me without restraint.

"You take me so well, Cadence," he praised. "So. Fucking. Well."

Each word was punctuated with a thrust so harsh I could feel it in my womb.

The sound of flesh meeting flesh bounced off the walls of the cave and echoed around the chamber as Ryker ruthlessly fucked me.

The pull on my hair disappeared, and a moment later, Ryker's fingertips danced across my collarbone before his large hand gripped my throat.

"This fucking pussy is mine," he rumbled.

The hand on my waist crept higher, stroking my side until his palm kneaded my breast with no hint of tenderness or gentility.

I doubted Ryker even knew how to be gentle.

And I wasn't sure that I cared.

His grip was rough and punishing as he squeezed my tender flesh, tugging and twisting my sensitive nipple.

"Oh, gods, Ryker, please," I gasped, unsure of what I was even asking for.

"I told you I'd have you begging, Cadence," he taunted. "What is it you need, hmm? Do you want me to fuck you so hard that you won't be able to sit down for the next week without remembering where I've been?"

His hips slammed forward, and the force of it made my whole body jolt toward the edge of the pool.

"Yes," I whimpered.

"You want me to fill up this needy cunt with my come until you're drowning in it?"

His movements slowed, and I was on the verge of sobbing and promising him anything he wanted if he'd just keep moving inside me.

"Ryker."

His name fell from lips as the plea it was.

"You want me to own you, don't you, Cadence?"

His thrust was long but languid, not enough to bring me to the edge of oblivion.

"You want me to own this pussy so completely that no other cock will ever satisfy you?"

"Yes, Ryker. Yes, to all of it."

I might have been embarrassed by the desperation in my voice if not for my all-consuming need for him.

"Beg me to make you come, Cadence."

"Please, Ryker," I begged. "Please make me come."

Ryker snarled behind me, the sound animalistic and savage, leaving no doubt about its meaning.

It was a sound of claiming.

The predator preparing to conquer its prey.

The hand on my breast moved to the side of my neck, and with both palms wrapped around my throat, Ryker unleashed on me.

He slammed into me with a ferocity that left my body shaking and my lungs struggling to suck in my next breath.

There was nothing between us except the raw, electric tension that heightened my senses and made me feel as though I had never truly lived until that moment.

"You'll give me one more, Temptress," Ryker demanded right before his fangs sank into the juncture between my neck and shoulder.

I screamed in ecstasy as bursts of light flashed behind my eyes, and my body gave out, crashing against the rocky ledge of the pool.

"Good fucking girl," Ryker shouted as he spilled himself inside me.

My breathing was choppy, and I felt as though I might pass out from the sheer bliss raging through me.

A slight buzzing noise sounded in my ears, and I barely heard Ryker when he asked if I was all right.

Beneath the noise and stimulation, something else stirred.

It started as a gentle tug in my chest before growing frantic, insistent.

Oh gods, it couldn't be true.

Not him.

Not now.

But no matter how I longed for ignorance, I was unable to deny the pull or what it meant.

Ryker was my fated mate, and whether or not I liked it, the bond had just taken root inside me.

Chapter Thirty-Six

CADENCE

A fragile sense of peace had settled between me and Ryker since our trip to the cave. Despite my calm exterior, however, there was a war raging inside me. And it was one that I was losing.

The more I tried to hold on to my anger for Ryker, the more I felt it slipping away.

I hadn't informed him I'd sensed the first stirrings of the bond, but I couldn't shake the feeling that he already knew. I was unable to ask him about it, though. Doing so would make it too real, undeniable.

Now, as I peered down at the courtyard, I wondered if that peace was about to shatter.

"You're being unreasonable, Ryker," I huffed.

"The Wild Hunt is no place for you, Cadence."

"And why is that?"

"There are men there, and... it just isn't."

He grabbed the nape of his neck as if the action would soothe his irritation. He wasn't easily riled, and my curiosity only grew.

"What is it you don't want me to witness?"

"More like what I won't stand for anyone else to see," he muttered.

"What was that?"

Ryker blew out a long breath. "As the Crown Prince, it is my duty to lead the Wild Hunt. I'll be unable to focus knowing you're out there... and that others will be participating."

I didn't know what he meant, but I wasn't above begging.

"Please, Ryker. You said you wanted to prove to me that I could trust you. Locking me away again doesn't achieve that."

That was clearly the wrong thing to say.

Ryker's expression hardened, and he crossed his arms over his chest. His presence filled the room in a way it hadn't before. He appeared larger now, more imposing.

He strode across his chambers, his dark gaze fixed upon me, and I couldn't help but retreat a few steps.

That didn't deter Ryker, though. He kept on coming until he had me pinned against the wall, his towering frame caging me in as his hand reached up to caress my cheek.

The gesture could be mistaken as gentle, loving, even.

But I recognized it for what it was.

The calm before the storm.

Ryker's thumb and forefinger tightened around my chin, and he angled my face until his steel-grey eyes locked with mine.

"Do not try to play me, Cadence," he warned. "You won't win."

"Ryker," I protested, but he cut me off.

"Perhaps you've misunderstood me."

I glared at him, letting him see my displeasure for himself.

As angry as I may have been, however, that didn't stop the gentle throbbing that had started up in my core at his domineering tone.

He exuded power, and gods help me, that was the sexiest thing I'd ever seen on a man.

My lust was going to get me killed. I had grown too complacent, and I needed to remember what was at stake here.

"So let me be abundantly clear," he purred. "Everything I shared with you inside that cave was true, but I am still the one in control. I order, and you obey."

A shiver raced down my spine, and I tried my best to suppress it. The knowing smirk that curved Ryker's lips told me I'd done a poor job.

Frustration and desire swirled within me. My secrets weren't safe around this man. Hell, I wasn't safe around this man.

"I said that I would prove you could trust me to take care of you, that I would keep you safe. This is me keeping that promise."

He leaned in and brushed his lips against mine. When his tongue darted out and swiped at my bottom lip, demanding entrance, I opened for him. Ryker kissed me with a punishing force, as though his tongue alone could make me submit to him.

Before he could pull away from me, I bit down on his lower lip hard enough to draw blood. The metallic taste exploded across my tongue, and I let my satisfied smirk lift the corner of my mouth.

Ryker lifted a finger to his brutalized lip and brushed the crimson substance aside with his thumb. His eyes darkened, but not from rage.

A low, raspy chuckle escaped him, and I felt it all the way to my toes.

"Behave yourself, Cadence," he warned before he placed a chaste kiss on my forehead.

He pushed off the wall and stepped back. "I'll return in a few hours."

Without another word, he left the room.

I moved to face the window as I watched the preparations continue to unfold in the courtyard beneath me. Men were saddling horses, loading them with various weapons and furs, while the women inspected their footwear and stashed small drinking skins about their person.

Not for the first time, I wondered what the Wild Hunt entailed.

A familiar mane of white-blond hair came into view as Ryker stepped into the courtyard. Malesh moved toward him as he led a large obsidian warhorse by the reins. Ryker took the proffered reins from Malesh's outstretched hand and swung into the saddle.

As if sensing my eyes on him, Ryker twisted in his seat and glanced up at me. Mirth sparkled in his gaze, and he winked at me.

I rolled my eyes in response, but I was secretly pleased I still held his attention.

My gaze darted to another familiar head of hair, and I scowled as my eyes locked with Celeste's. She gave me a victorious grin and a condescending wave as she headed toward Ryker. When she reached him, she placed her small palm on his forearm. I didn't get the chance to see Ryker's response as a deep masculine voice sounded from behind me.

"That's a very short leash you allow him to keep you on, sweetheart."

I spun around, my fingers flying to the base of my throat as I screamed. Riordan shushed me as he waved his hands in my direction.

"You don't want him storming back in here, do you? It would ruin all the fun I have planned for us."

"Riordan, what the hell are you doing lurking in Ryker's chambers?" I panted when I finally regained the capacity to speak.

"From what I saw earlier, they're as much your chambers now as they are his."

He made a sickening kissing sound, and I cringed.

“Stalking is unbecoming, Riordan.”

He snorted. “Have you mentioned that to Ryker? Because in case you forgot, he’s the one with the problem.”

I couldn’t argue with that.

“Tell me what you’re doing here,” I demanded. “And next time, announce yourself like a normal person. Better still, use the cursed door.”

Riordan shook his head and chuckled as if I were being ridiculous. A broad grin spread across his face, and he threw his arms wide.

“I have come to rescue you from your tower, dear Maiden,” he said with an exaggerated bow.

He lifted his gaze to mine, and the teasing glint I saw in his eyes told me that whatever his plans were, they would most certainly lead to trouble.

“The Wild Hunt awaits, My Lady.”

Oh, Ryker would not be pleased.

And that thought only heightened my anticipation.

Chapter Thirty-Seven

CADENCE

Riordan led me down a labyrinth of stone passageways I had no hope of navigating on my own.

"You'll be there to guide me back through this when we return, right?" I asked, giving voice to my concern.

"Cadence, sweetheart, do I look like the type of man who would lead you into danger if I didn't have a backup plan?"

"Yes."

"Ungrateful fiend," he muttered before releasing a dramatic sigh.

Despite my legitimate concerns, I laughed at Riordan's antics. He was quickly becoming my favorite person in the Unseelie Kingdom. A small flicker of guilt assaulted me when I thought about all the time Malesh had devoted to helping me train, but I pushed it aside. It wasn't him sneaking me out of my gilded prison.

"If you need a way back in, I'll wait by the eastern gate," Riordan said.

"What does that mean? What other alternative is there?"

"You won't require my help if Ryker finds you first."

The salacious grin he sent me had me questioning my sanity for even agreeing to this.

"What will he do if he catches me?" I asked, unable to hide the unease in my voice.

Riordan stopped walking and turned to glance at me.

"I know I tease my brother mercilessly, Cadence, but I promise he is a good man."

When I cast him a skeptical look, he added, "Good... ish?"

"Why did that sound like a question?"

Riordan chuckled.

"All right, all right. He may not be a good man, but for those he cares about, he would level any kingdom, destroy any monster, slay any villain to keep them safe."

Sadness flickered in Riordan's gaze, and I sensed he was referring to the same thing Ryker had hinted at in the cave.

"Will you tell me?" I asked, not wanting to be insensitive, but also finding myself desperate to understand who Ryker really was.

Riordan hesitated for a moment before he spoke. "My mother is dead. Did you know that?"

I shook my head.

"She died when Ryker and I were children. She was my father's fated mate, so when she passed, he became..." Riordan pursed his lips as if he was trying to find the right word. "Different."

"Different how?"

"When a person loses their fated mate, their mind soon follows."

I knew losing a mate had dire consequences, but I had never witnessed it firsthand.

"He changed from a loving father, a kind man, and a just ruler to someone cruel, distant, and ruthless."

"I'm sorry, Riordan. I didn't know."

He shrugged, but I could tell it was painful for him to speak about.

"Anyway, whenever he had an... episode, he often became violent. One day, Ryker walked in on him beating me half to death."

I gasped, and my fingers flew to my mouth. Overwhelming sorrow filled me at the thought of something so horrible happening to Riordan. His carefree, charismatic nature masked a dark past, and I'd been none the wiser.

"I was nine, Ryker was thirteen, and he didn't hesitate to jump between us. He shielded my body with his and took whatever blows my father dished out. He didn't so much as move to protect himself. All he cared about was protecting me."

An icy gust of wind blasted us, and an eerie howl tore through the corridor with Riordan's words, as though the stone walls were crying out in protest.

"When Ryker turned fifteen, he truly came into his power. He could have leveled the kingdom, bathed the land in blood, and taken the throne from my father that day." Riordan sucked in a sharp breath. "And every day since."

He murmured the last part so softly I couldn't tell if he meant for me to hear it.

Having seen Ryker's strength, I shuddered at the thought of what he may be capable of when pushed too far.

"Why didn't he?" The words slipped free before I could stop them.

Riordan raised his head to look at me. Sadness lingered in his eyes, shadowed by something else... regret, perhaps.

"I was at my mother's side when she took her final breath. She gripped my tiny hand in hers and made me promise that I would take care of the kingdom and our people. My mother was a good queen, someone who loved passionately and cared deeply. She also knew her sons. Ryker had little interest in becoming king, but she knew he would become what the Unseelie Fae needed. My mother asked me to guide Ryker, to stand by him and help him, even when his pride kept him from asking."

Riordan's grin was infectious, and a slow smile spread across my own lips despite myself.

"So," he continued, "I made Ryker promise me he would never do anything to compromise the kingdom. That he wouldn't let his impulses destroy the very thing our mother fought so hard to protect."

Riordan sighed and ran his hand through his hair.

"I know Ryker is a dick and a pain to be around, but not everything he does comes from selfishness."

"Only most things," I teased, and Riordan rolled his eyes with dramatic effect, making me chuckle.

"A part of him still clings to the oath he swore to his baby brother," he said sheepishly. "If you give him the chance to show you the side of him that I see, you won't regret it."

"Those descriptions are far too mild for Ryker," I mused. "How about evil incarnate? Or a demon made flesh?"

Riordan barked out a laugh, then said, "You're right, but you know what I mean."

I smiled back at him, glad to see the earlier shadow of sadness had disappeared from his features.

"Now, are we joining the Wild Hunt or not?"

I met his eager grin with one of my own.

"Lead on."

I swept my hand out in front of me, and Riordan stepped past me as he continued down the corridor. We walked for another ten minutes or so, taking four more turns before we reached... a wall.

I studied the tapestry that adorned the stone. A headless man stood tall, sword raised, as battle raged around him.

"Interesting choice," I muttered.

Riordan chuckled under his breath before pushing the woven cloth aside to reveal a passageway.

"Come on."

We stepped into a dark tunnel, and a flame appeared in Riordan's palm.

"Fire Fae," he grinned.

"Impressive," I said, inclining my head. "What is this place?"

As I scanned my surroundings, I found no windows or exits. Only unending darkness.

"This tunnel runs underneath the castle. It's the quickest way to reach the outer walls."

I remained quiet as I followed him. My mind was busy processing and storing the information I had gathered for later. When I stumbled in the dark, Riordan's hand flung out to catch me.

"Stay close. We're almost there."

We made the rest of the journey in companionable silence, and my heartbeat picked up speed the closer we came to the end. Ryker hadn't wanted me to witness the Wild Hunt, which only strengthened my resolve to see it through.

The tunnel ended abruptly up ahead, and before I could question Riordan, he said, "This is it."

He reached for a heavy steel lock and slid it out of the way. As he pushed the door open, moonlight flooded the narrow tunnel, and I was surprised at how late it had gotten.

The frigid night air kissed my exposed flesh, and I shivered. Riordan shrugged off his cloak and wrapped it around me.

"Won't you get cold without your cloak?" I asked, even as I snuggled deeper into its warmth.

"Fire Fae, remember. I can always warm up."

"Hmm, that's handy."

Riordan winked at me before he reached out and took my hand in his.

"Where is everyone?" I asked as I searched the surrounding forest.

"There is a clearing up ahead. If we hurry, we'll make it in time for The Howl."

"The Howl?"

"You'll see," Riordan smirked.

We moved through the forest, careful to avoid making any noise. The task proved harder than first anticipated, as every hidden branch in the darkness threatened to betray us.

"See there?" Riordan asked, and I followed his outstretched hand to where he pointed.

Through the trees, a large bonfire roared toward the heavens as men and women danced, laughed, and teased one another.

Then I did a double take.

Some women were completely naked. Not a stitch to be seen anywhere on their person.

"What kind of hunt is this?"

"It's a fertility ritual. The women call upon the gods to bless their wombs, and then they run off into the forest. After a short head start, the men quickly follow, and whoever they catch, they—"

"I get it," I said, interrupting him.

Riordan flashed me a mischievous grin, and right when I thought he was going to finish his sentence regardless, a commanding voice from within the clearing called the gathering to order.

Ryker.

"Ladies and lords, if I could have your attention," he called.

The crowd grew quiet as the anticipation grew. People buzzed with excitement, shifting restlessly as they awaited the commencement of the hunt.

"Tonight, we stand on the threshold of two worlds: the civilized and the untamed."

I could hear the smirk in Ryker's voice, and the participants whooped and cheered for their prince.

"Tonight," he continued. "We shed the societal expectations of our stations and become creatures of the darkness."

More cheering erupted, and excited chatter broke out.

"Let us run until we feel nothing but the thunderous beat of our hearts. Let us chase until no thoughts remain, only instinct."

Ryker paused for dramatic effect, then added, "Tonight, we belong to the hunt."

No wonder Ryker didn't want me to come.

He said he was leading the Wild Hunt, which meant he was planning on catching a woman and rutting with her in the forest like godsdamned animals.

Well, if he thought he could have his fun and still expect me to be waiting for him, ready and willing to serve him when he returned, he had another thing coming.

"What's that look for?" Riordan asked, a hint of panic in his voice.

He glanced toward Ryker and then back at me.

"Oh no, it's not what you're —"

His words were drowned out when Ryker bellowed, "Let the Wild Hunt begin!"

A series of howls rent the air as the women darted into the forest. I jumped to my feet and quickly followed them.

"Cadence," Riordan hissed behind me. "You can't go out there alone."

But I didn't stop.

I ran and let the Wild Hunt claim me.

Chapter Thirty-Eight

RYKER

The sharp night air bit through the fire's lingering warmth at my back. Clouds had swallowed the moon, casting the forest into an abyss of shadows.

My lips tugged up into a smirk. The darkness was my playground.

The low murmurs of the men behind me grated on my nerves as their anticipation reached a fever pitch. They droned on, their voices becoming a cacophony of laughter and obnoxious noises that made it difficult to think.

I drifted from the group, imagining the thrill of tearing through the woods, navigating each twist and turn in pursuit of

Cadence. When I found her, I'd reclaim her on the forest floor, showing her again and again what it meant to be *mine*.

My blood ran hot with need, and every instinct in my body called for me to abandon my post and go to Cadence. The laces of my trousers tightened uncomfortably, and I shifted my position, attempting to adjust myself discreetly. Once I was confident that I had tamed my raging erection, I turned my attention to the lords waiting for my command.

"Hunters!" I shouted, and the men's excitement grew palpable. "Time to chase your prey!"

They launched themselves onto their horses before diving into the forest, their figures quickly disappearing from view.

Now that the men were free to hunt their willing prey, all I wanted was to return to my mate and fuck her senseless. Standing in the cold while the Unseelie elite screwed each other was not my idea of a night well spent.

Cadence would likely be furious with me when I returned to my chambers, but I would let no one who wasn't me hunt her.

Not that a single soul would dare touch her after what happened at the ball.

Still, I didn't want them so much as glancing at her, let alone imagining her naked.

The gods knew I'd killed for less.

My younger brother pulled me from my ruminations when he stepped out of the tree line, a guilty expression on his face.

"Riordan, so kind of you to join us," I drawled.

"Sorry," he mumbled as he gripped the back of his neck.

"What kept you?"

"Ahh," Riordan said before he trailed off.

He glanced to the side before his gaze returned to me. I didn't miss the way he looked right above my head, not making eye contact. Malesh and Eamon, having sensed trouble brewing, moved to stand beside me.

"What's wrong, Riordan?" Malesh asked.

"Why do you look like you're about to be sick?" Eamon added.

"Well, I may have done something, and before you jump down my throat, Ryker, I did not encourage her to do anything."

My eyes drifted closed for the briefest moment, and I ground my teeth together to stop myself from murdering my brother. I knew without a doubt that whatever Riordan was about to say, I would not like it.

"What did you help her do?" I gritted out.

Riordan shuffled in place as he directed his gaze toward the ground.

"I wouldn't say I —"

"Riordan," I snapped, interrupting him. "Tell me what Cadence has done."

Riordan cleared his throat. "She may have, ah... joined the Wild Hunt."

My brother stepped back, and it was then that I realized I had advanced on him. I dug my heels into the damp forest floor and forced myself to take a deep, calming breath.

"I'm sorry, Little Brother, but I need you to repeat yourself. I could have sworn that you said, Cadence, my Seelie mate, who I know for a fact is being guarded inside my chambers, had joined the Wild Hunt."

Riordan made a pained noise in the back of his throat before he said, "I, ah, may have snuck her out of the castle."

He winced as the last word left his mouth, and I realized no amount of deep breathing was going to keep me calm.

"And what the fuck led you to believe that was a good idea?" I hissed, barely managing to contain my rage.

My hands flexed at my sides, each muscle coiled like a spring ready to snap.

Malesh's gaze bore into the side of my brother's head as if he were begging him not to answer, but knowing Riordan as I did, I knew he wouldn't be able to help himself.

"Because you keep her couped up inside your tower, refusing to let her experience any of the good things our kingdom has to offer."

He puffed out his chest and if I hadn't been so pissed off at him, I might have appreciated the fact that he was trying to make my mate feel welcome in our home.

"Did you ever consider what would happen to her if our people discovered who she is to me, or worse, that she's Seelie?" I said through gritted teeth.

Riordan opened his mouth as though he was going to protest, but then understanding dawned on him, and he closed it again.

"Being my mate makes her a target, but being Seelie makes her a traitor to the kingdom. You and I both know that those who wish to harm me would readily use her against me."

"Ryker, I —"

"Didn't think! Yes, Riordan, I established that for myself."

I regretted the words immediately.

Riordan swallowed hard and dropped his gaze to the forest floor. "I didn't mean for it to go this far, Ryker. She only wanted a chance to explore our world. To better understand it — to understand you."

A bitter laugh slipped from my lips. "And what do you think she'll understand if some bastard from court stumbles across her before I do and considers her fair game?"

Riordan flinched, and I fought to control my anger. However foolish, Riordan's intention stemmed from a desire to help Cadence feel more at home in our dark world, and I couldn't fault him for that.

Sighing, I said, "There is a reason I keep her on such a tight leash, Riordan. I can grant her some freedom, but only when my men or I are there to protect her. Out here," — I waved my hand toward the trees — "anything goes."

The forest grew eerily quiet, and the sound of distant hooves faded as the hunters moved further away. But the silence only amplified the feeling that something sinister waited inside the woods. Every rustling leaf was a warning. Every whisper of the wind carried an echo of the hunt. I had to reach her before the night stole her from me.

"I'm going after her," I declared, leaving no room for argument. "Nobody touches her, understood? If you catch even the slightest hint that a hunter is closing in on her, stop them by any means necessary."

Malesh gave a single nod, his eyes steady and dark. "Understood."

"What do you need me to do?" Riordan asked as he lifted his chin and straightened his shoulders.

"I need you to stay here with Malesh and Eamon. Take over my post as Warden of the Hunt. Can you do that for me?"

Riordan nodded his head in agreement. "What are you going to do?"

My body thrummed with a wicked sort of excitement as the thrill of the chase coursed through my veins. My senses became sharper, more primal, and I listened to the sounds of the forest as I tried to discern which way she may have gone. The sounds of pleasure met my ears as the revelers immersed themselves in the hunt, allowing all their dark and depraved desires to flow freely.

Cadence was out there somewhere, hidden and waiting. Anticipation coiled tight in my gut, and I swung my leg over my mount. I wouldn't stop until she was back in my grasp.

The knowledge that she had defied my every order, every warning, just so she could throw herself among the chaos, made a shiver of desire race down my spine. Her defiance was both infuriating and arousing.

I would find her. And when I did, I would ensure that she understood the consequences of defying me.

"I'm going to hunt down my mate."

Chapter Thirty-Nine

CADENCE

"You just had to run headfirst into the forest, completely unprepared and ill-equipped, didn't you, Cadence?" I berated myself as my dress snagged on another outstretched branch that almost had me kissing the dirt beneath my boots.

"I'm sure Ryker will learn his lesson when you fall and break your neck, all because you couldn't see a godsdamned thing in this cursed forest and tripped over your own feet! Too bad you won't be around to enjoy it."

As if to demonstrate my point, my boot got caught in a gnarled root, and I went careening to the ground. The impact knocked the air from my lungs, and I gasped as I tried to suck in oxygen so frigid it burned.

I screamed to the heavens, cursing the gods for my current predicament, even though I knew this one was entirely my fault. Nearby, a shrill squeal sounded, followed by masculine laughter that seemed to reverberate off every tree trunk as they drew closer.

"Perfect! Just announce to everyone where you are. Well done, Cadence."

I pushed myself up from the ground, but the foliage beneath my boots was slick, and I stumbled, catching myself on a low-hanging branch.

A hiss of pain escaped me as the limb scraped against my hand. Even in the dim lighting, I could make out the blood gathering in my palm.

Focusing my attention on the sounds of the forest, I listened intently as I tried to determine if anyone was close. The couple I'd heard a moment ago had changed course, moving in the opposite direction. When no other noises met my ears, I spared some time to heal my hand.

My magic rumbled to life beneath my skin, and I sighed with relief. I wasn't used to going so long without summoning it, and the rush of euphoria I felt was like wildfire racing through my veins, igniting every nerve until I hummed with raw, unbridled energy.

My injured palm pulsed as the torn edges of my flesh knitted themselves back together. Slowly, the blood stopped pooling as the unseen threads of my power drew it back into my body. The skin on my hand reformed as my magic set about mending the assaulted tissue until my flesh was unblemished once more.

My legs, trembling with exhaustion moments ago, now felt strong and revitalized. Even my breath flowed easier. I retracted my earlier curses and thanked the gods for gifting me with the ability to keep myself whole and set off again with renewed vigor.

I'd only been running for a few minutes when I spotted the outline of a large fallen tree. When I reached it, I slipped beneath it as I pressed myself into the narrow crevice where the roots met the ground.

It wasn't much, but it was enough to shield me from prying eyes while I took stock of my surroundings and planned my escape route. I was bowing out of the Wild Hunt at the earliest opportunity. I craved a warm mug of tea and the comfort of Ryker's bed more than I needed to assert myself, at least for now.

The snap of a branch nearby had me sucking in a ragged breath. The crunch of dead leaves quickly followed, and I made out the low murmur of voices. Closing my eyes, I willed myself to disappear into the shadows.

Then, a new sound shattered the silence. It was a woman's voice, distant but unmistakable.

"Ryker," Celeste sang.

Her voice sounded almost deafening to my ears.

"I know you're out there."

I could hear the note of longing in her tone and something dark twisted inside my chest.

He wouldn't. Not after everything he promised.

But he kept you out of the hunt for a reason, my inner voice taunted.

My heart clenched, and I was caught between the urge to flee and morbid curiosity. I shifted in place, craning my neck as I peered out through a gap in the roots. I could see Celeste moving through the trees, but Ryker was nowhere in sight.

The sound of hooves hitting the hard earth startled me, and I watched as Celeste froze where she stood.

From deep within the forest, an enormous black war horse strode past the tree line. Its movements were graceful, and its powerful muscles rippled beneath its shimmering coat. Steam curled from its nostrils with each breath as it scanned the shadows, searching for unseen eyes.

It was the most beautiful creature I had ever seen.

And atop the magnificent beast sat Ryker.

Celeste straightened and marched toward him. He slid from the horse, his movements practiced and fluid, showcasing his years of training.

Ryker stepped away from his mount, crossed his corded forearms over his broad chest, and waited for Celeste to come to him.

"I've been looking for you," she purred as she reached him.

Celeste placed her hand on his arm, and a seductive smirk flitted across her lips. Ryker didn't respond to her touch, but he didn't move to shake her off, either.

Emboldened, Celeste reached out to trace the edge of Ryker's jaw. Her fingers lingered there, almost possessively, before she trailed them down his throat.

"What do you want, Celeste?" Ryker asked, sounding bored.

"I thought we could have a little fun," she said suggestively.

"You're well aware of the rules prohibiting members of the royal family from participating in the hunt."

Ryker couldn't join the hunt?

Celeste's high-pitched laughter interrupted my wayward thoughts.

"You needn't worry about conceiving a bastard when we're to be married, Ryker. Any child I bear you will be heir to the throne following our union."

Celeste's fingers danced down Ryker's arm, but this time, he gripped her wrist as his eyes narrowed on her with disdain.

"Do. Not. Touch. Me."

His voice was low and calm, but the threat underlying his words couldn't have been louder.

"Ryker," Celeste whined. "You aren't still mad at me about your little pet, are you?"

Ryker's hand darted forward and grabbed Celeste by the throat. "If you know what's good for you, Celeste, you'll turn around now and get back behind the palace walls."

The sinister undertone to Ryker's voice raised the small hairs on my nape as he said, "Before I change my mind about letting you leave here alive."

When Ryker let her go, Celeste coughed and spluttered as she sucked in one lungful of air after another. Without sparing him a second glance, she raced into the forest as quickly as she could.

A cruel smile played on Ryker's lips, and I had to question my sanity when I discovered I rather liked this unhinged side of him.

"You can come out now, Cadence." Ryker's deep voice rumbled over my flesh, and I froze, not daring to breathe in case he was bluffing.

"Or you could continue hiding behind that tree trunk, making it even easier to catch you."

Not bluffing, then.

I stood from my hiding place and dusted off the debris that had clung to my cloak. When I raised my head and met Ryker's gaze, I could see the burning fury blazing there.

"What are you wearing?" he growled.

I peered down at the cloak Riordan had given me, but I couldn't find anything amiss with it.

"Riordan's cloak," I shrugged.

"Take it off."

"No. It's cold."

"Take. It. Off."

The command in Ryker's voice was difficult to resist, but I did.

"I said no," I retorted as I straightened my spine.

A low, throaty chuckle erupted from Ryker, and for the briefest moment, I wondered if I'd made a grave mistake.

"Run, Temptress."

"I'm sorry?" I asked, confused.

"Not yet, you're not. But you will be."

Ryker's words settled over me, and warmth flooded my core.

What had he done to me? Was I now the type of person who got aroused by being threatened?

"Don't let me catch you, Temptress," Ryker said as he pulled his tunic over his head.

"What happens if you do?"

My mouth was dry, and a faint heat flushed my skin.

"Oh, I think you know," he crooned, as he slapped the hindquarters of his massive war horse, sending it racing back toward the palace.

Ryker stretched the muscles in his arms, and I watched, transfixed, as they bulged under the strain.

"Three."

Panic gripped my chest, but I pushed it aside to survey my surroundings.

"Two."

I wasted no time as I rushed into the forest, heedless of the noise or the obvious trail I left in my wake.

I needed to put as much distance between me and Ryker as I could manage.

"One."

The true hunt had begun.

Chapter Forty

CADENCE

The forest was conspiring against me.

Twisted branches reached out to me like claws trying to hinder my escape, and the damp ground made each step unsteady. But I didn't stop running. I pumped my arms as hard as I could, ignoring the way my breathing grew ragged with each passing second.

I could hear Ryker closing the distance between us. His footfalls were deliberate and unhurried, a predator savoring the chase.

My heart hammered away inside my chest, the wild beat of terror mixing with something much more dangerous.

Exhilaration.

The thrill of the hunt made me feel more alive than I'd ever felt before, and even though my mind screamed at me to flee, my body was telling a very different story.

A twig snapped somewhere nearby, and I quickened my pace as I wove between the trees. My hand brushed against the rough bark, and I almost stumbled as a root ensnared my foot for the second time that night.

"The faster you run, the more I crave catching you, Cadence," Ryker called, his voice thick with unmistakable hunger.

A tremor raced down my spine, and I didn't know if I was more afraid that he would catch me... or that he wouldn't.

"And when I do, I am going to punish you for your disobedience."

Thorns snagged at my dress, but I tore myself free, not willing to let him claim victory so easily. Shadows stalked my every move, drawing nearer and snaking around me as they gently caressed my skin.

I felt him before I saw him. My skin prickled, and my blood heated, sensing his gaze in the darkness.

A large hand encircled my waist while the other pressed against my mouth. I tried to scream, to fight him off, but Ryker was as immovable as stone.

His warm breath fanned against my neck as he pulled me against his taut chest.

"Caught you."

Ryker's words were little more than a whisper, but they were edged with menace.

My pulse raced, and I trembled in his arms. The dark forest seemed to close in around us, and I felt trapped, unable to break his hold on me.

I felt like prey.

Without warning, Ryker threw me to the ground, and I barely had time to brace my fall. Before I could regain my footing, the weight of his body pressed into mine, his larger frame caging me in as he rubbed his hard length against my ass.

"Do you feel that, Cadence?" he asked, his voice hoarse. "That's what hunting you down like a fucking animal does to me."

My breathing hitched, and to my horror, I realized I was pushing against him, meeting him thrust for thrust.

Ryker chuckled darkly.

"I knew there was a wanton whore beneath your self-righteous indignation," he mocked.

"Are you going to talk all night, or are you going to fuck me, Ryker?"

"You'd like that, wouldn't you? You want to feel my cock tearing into your cunt and forcing you to come because you're unable to deny the pleasure I rip from you."

I swallowed roughly. I did want that, but I'd take my last breath before I ever gave him the satisfaction of hearing me say the words.

"Answer me, Cadence!"

When I remained silent, he pushed his fingers into my hair and yanked me to my feet. I bit my lip to stifle the scream that built at the back of my throat with the sudden burst of pain.

Ryker shoved me into the trunk of a tree, the bark biting into my flesh despite the layers that protected me. When my gaze clashed with his, obsidian eyes glared at me.

"Take off your clothes," he demanded.

"No!" I said, and jutted my chin out in defiance.

"You either remove them yourself, Cadence, or I tear them from your body and force you to walk back to the palace in your skin."

I gulped, knowing that Ryker meant every word, but needing to push him anyway.

"People will see me. I thought only you got to gaze upon my perfect skin," I taunted, throwing his own words back at him.

I arched an eyebrow to emphasize the challenge I was laying at his feet. A cruel grin twisted his mouth, and I knew I had made a fatal over calculation.

"They would," he purred. "And as a result, I'd be forced to rip their eyes from their sockets."

He raised a brow just as I had, mocking me.

I didn't question whether he was serious. It was written all over his face.

With trembling hands, I unfastened the hook of my cloak, allowing it to pool at my feet. Next, I reached around and untied the ribbon of my dress before pulling it down my arms.

The biting cold wind kissed my nipples, and I shivered.

"All the way down," Ryker commanded, and I narrowed my eyes at him.

I slid the fabric over my hips and let it fall to the forest floor. Stepping out of it, I kicked off my boots and nudged them to the side. Ryker gave me a pointed look, and I huffed before discarding my panties.

Naked, I stood before him, vulnerable and exposed.

He curled a finger at me, signaling for me to move closer. As I did, I couldn't deny the bolt of anticipation that coursed through me and settled between my thighs.

Ryker studied me for a long moment before he prowled around me in a wide circle, assessing me as though I were a piece of prized livestock. Once he was done, he planted his feet right in front of me and crossed his arms over his bare chest.

He didn't speak as he placed a firm hand on top of my head and forced me to kneel. He peered down at me reverently, stroking my cheek with his thumb.

"You look so pretty on your knees for me, Cadence."

It was a strange contrast, having this vicious-looking man with his eyes as black as night touch me so tenderly. Yet, the dangerous glint in his gaze had me swallowing hard.

Ryker unbuckled his belt, slipping the leather free, as he crouched down in front of me. I thought he was going to fasten it around my throat as he had done before, but he leaned behind me and secured my hands in a tight knot at the base of my spine. I resisted the urge to test my restraints, not wanting to give him any hint of my discomfort.

Ryker stood as he slipped his hand beneath his trousers and released his massive cock. I stared at it eagerly, licking my lips before I could stop myself. Ryker didn't have to command me to open for him. I did it willingly. The underside of his cock slid against my tongue, and he groaned.

"Your mouth feels so good, Cadence," he rasped above me.

Encouraged by his reaction, I closed my mouth around his length and sucked in earnest. My head bobbed up and down as I tasted every inch of him. Pressure built between my thighs, and I rubbed them together to ease the tension.

Then Ryker ripped himself away from me before he leaned down and wrenched my legs apart. I whimpered at the loss of friction, and he smiled.

"This isn't for your pleasure, Cadence. It's a punishment. You won't come until I say you can."

Before I could respond, Ryker shoved his cock between my lips and gripped either side of my head as he fucked my mouth without mercy.

"You think you can disobey me without consequence? You think you can put yourself in danger whenever the desire takes you."

He thrust deep into my mouth until the tip of his cock hit the back of my throat. I choked around him, but Ryker didn't ease up.

"I put these rules in place to protect you, Cadence, and what do you do? You throw it back in my face and force me to abandon my post to come and find you."

Drool spilled down my chin, and I could feel my cheeks growing hot as my lungs screamed out for air. I tried to pull away from him, but Ryker only tightened his grip.

"You breathe when I say you can breathe," he spat as he slammed his hips forward once more.

When Ryker pulled out, I greedily sucked air into my starving lungs. Once my breathing had evened out, I glared up at him.

"Oh, you think *you're* angry," he growled, the sound deep and terrifying.

Ryker gripped the base of his cock and stroked his length up and down with rough, furious movements.

"What do you suppose would have happened to you if one of the other men from court had found you, hmm?"

I knew exactly what was going to happen. In fact, I'd been counting on it. I had planned to show Ryker that I wouldn't simply warm his bed while he sought gratification elsewhere. Now, though, as I stared into his murderous gaze, I had to admit it had been reckless, if not dangerous.

"Or what if Celeste had revealed that you are Seelie to any of the men taking part tonight?"

Ryker's movements became jerky, and I was distracted by the way the vein on the underside of his cock throbbed, that it took a second for his words to sink in.

My head snapped up, and I locked my gaze with Ryker's. His upper lip was curled, and he was pumping his shaft with a brutality that almost had me wincing.

I let his earlier remark wash over me. If Celeste had told anyone about me, then coming out here alone and unprotected had been more than foolish.

It was suicidal.

Suddenly, I understood Ryker's rage, and it must have shown on my face.

"Now you understand, Temptress," he said roughly. "No one, not even the gods, gets to take you away from me."

Ryker's gaze never left mine as hot ropes of his come hit my chest and face. He continued to pump his cock furiously, draining every last drop of his orgasm.

Breathing heavily, Ryker leaned down and smeared his come all over me. The intensity with which he worked made it appear as though he was an artist and I was his masterpiece.

Satisfied, his eyes returned to mine.

"Tell me, Temptress. How wet are you for me right now?"

Without waiting for a response, Ryker slipped his hand between my thighs and gathered the evidence of my arousal. He raised his glistening fingers to his lips and sucked them clean.

Then he invaded my space, his mouth brushing against my ear as he whispered, "Now the real fun can begin."

Chapter Forty-One

RYKER

I had promised Cadence I would take care of her, so forcing her to choke on my cock in a moment of fury probably wasn't the best idea in the circumstances.

Then again, seeing how much she enjoyed it made me think she wouldn't hold it against me. My mate wanted to submit to me; her mind just couldn't rationalize her body's desires.

According to Malesh, she was a well-respected healer in her village, and many people relied on her for help. Perhaps the thought of giving up all of that responsibility and letting someone else take control for her, *of her*, was an attractive one.

And I had many plans for how that could play out.

I rose to my feet, drawing a startled gasp from Cadence at the abrupt motion. Kicking my boots free, I ripped my trousers down my legs and wrapped my fingers around the base of my cock as I stroked leisurely. Already eager for another round, it stood to attention, a drop of pre-come glistening from the tip.

Cadence watched my every move as though I were a viper ready to strike. A sinful smirk curled my lip at the thought. My Temptress sensed the predator lurking just beneath my skin, and she was right to be wary.

I fisted her hair in my hand and dragged her to her feet. She grunted at my rough handling, but she didn't cry out or ask me to release her.

She was so fucking perfect.

With my back pressed against the trunk of a wide tree, I lowered Cadence to my lap. Her hands were still bound, and she struggled to balance her weight, so I gripped her hips to steady her.

"Climb on."

I stared pointedly at my cock and Cadence glared at me before she slid down my length, burying me in her tight heat. A low groan rumbled up my chest, and Cadence threw her head back as her lips parted with a gasp.

Fucking perfect.

I pressed my mouth to the column of her throat, kissing and nipping at her flesh as I made my way to her ear.

"How much do you need to come right now, Cadence?"

A whimper escaped her before she clamped her mouth shut, denying me the sound of her moans and small cries of pleasure.

"Is that how you want to play this game?"

I thrust my hips upward, driving my cock further into her eager cunt. Cadence bit her lip, but I didn't miss the way her body trembled in my hold.

A dark chuckle escaped me, and I couldn't deny the excitement that rushed through me at the idea of wrenching every delectable sound from her. I gripped her hips hard enough to bruise as I lifted her in my lap, only to slam her back down, impaling her on my cock.

As I leaned forward, I sucked a pointed nipple into my mouth, lavishing it with my tongue before sinking my teeth in.

This time, Cadence cried out, unable to deny me.

"I'm only getting started, Temptress," I purred.

The sound of rustling leaves caught my attention, and I let my wings free, encasing Cadence in darkness and shielding her from unworthy eyes.

I hadn't been lying when I said I'd tear the eyes out of anyone who dared to look upon her naked form.

A moment later, a man stepped forward from the brush, and he froze the second our gazes locked.

"If you'd like your heart to remain inside your chest, you'll turn around and leave right now," I growled, my voice low and menacing.

The man didn't hesitate as he darted away from us, his gaze downcast as he ran in the opposite direction.

When I unfurled my wings, Cadence was staring at me with a cocked brow and a smug look on her face.

"Keep going," I warned, "because I intend to fuck the brat out of you."

To emphasize my point, I slapped her ass cheek as I drove back into her, forcing her to give me a long, sultry moan.

"That's it, Temptress. I want to hear you sing for me."

"Stop talking, Ryker," she panted. "You're ruining the moment."

Before she could protest, I let my fangs elongate and sank them deep into the juncture between her neck and shoulder.

Cadence's resistance evaporated, her body softening in my hold as she gave in to the pleasure my bite had forced on her.

Moan after moan spilled from her lips as she rocked against me with abandon. I didn't relent, instead driving my fangs in deeper and forcing another orgasm to drown her.

Her words became incoherent, her forehead beaded with sweat as she came undone, her pussy strangling my cock with every tremor.

"P-please," she breathed. "I can't take it anymore."

I withdrew my fangs, and Cadence collapsed against my chest. If she thought that was the end, she was sorely mistaken. Shadows emerged from my fingertips, and I let my magic caress her flesh as it slowly made its way down her body. Cadence shivered, and I grinned.

This was far from over.

My shadows danced across her flushed skin, teasing and stroking her as they moved lower. Her breath hitched when they reached her inner thighs, so close to where she was still joined with me. I guided the shadowy tendrils between her sensitive folds and let them swirl around the base of my cock.

Cadence jerked in my arms, her eyes wide with a mix of fear and arousal.

"Ryker," she whimpered, her voice trembling.

I nuzzled her neck, inhaling her intoxicating scent. "Yes, Temptress?"

Cadence squirmed in my lap, taking me deeper. We both groaned at the sensation, and I tightened my hold on her hips.

"I... I can't."

"You can," I purred, nipping at her earlobe. "And you will."

My shadows coiled and pulsed, stroking her clit and teasing her entrance. I could feel her inner walls squeezing me, her body betraying her desire even as she tried to protest.

I directed my shadows to wrap around her thighs, spreading them wider and giving me more room to angle my cock deeper. Cadence groaned, and the sound was exhilarating. As I sent my shadows to tease her back hole, she stiffened, her eyes swinging back to mine as she glared at me.

Little did she realize that her defiance only made me want to take her that much harder. I cocked a brow, pushing my magic further inside her, challenging her to deny me.

"Ryker," she growled. "Don't."

I leaned in, licking between her breasts before making my way to the pulse point at the base of her throat.

"Stop fighting it, Temptress," I murmured against her skin. "Stop fighting me."

I pushed more of my magic into her ass and Cadence cried out, her face contorted in a mix of pain and pleasure.

"It's," she hissed before her words trailed off into incoherent mumbling.

"It's what, Temptress? Tell me exactly how I make you feel."

"I feel," she panted, "unbearably full."

I sent both my shadows and my cock driving into her, forcing her to feel my overwhelming presence as I owned her body. When Cadence pushed back against my magic, I knew I needed to feel her tight ass choking my cock.

I let my shadows fall away, and I gripped Cadence's hips as I turned her and pressed her back against my chest. Then I drove my length inside her puckered hole.

Cadence screamed, and I sank my fangs into the side of her throat, letting her pain transform into pleasure. My shadows pressed against her clit and a moment later, she was coming undone...*for me.*

That was all the invitation I needed to unleash on her. I pounded into Cadence's ass with an animalistic fury that I knew would have pained her if not for the euphoria of my bite. My balls tightened, and I retracted my fangs as I spilled myself inside her.

Cadence fell forward, her body sagging against the ground as she fought to control the trembling that wracked her frame.

"You're... an... asshole," she panted. "That hurt."

I chuckled, not apologetic in the least. "What's a punishment without a little pain?"

"Fucking asshole," she muttered, and I swatted her bare ass cheek.

The sight of my come dripping down her thighs was enough to make me hard again. I watched, transfixed, as it slowly trickled down her smooth skin.

Deep inside me, something primordial stirred.

"Mine!" it snarled.

If looks could kill, Cadence would have me withering on the ground as my flesh rotted from my bones. It was cute that she thought her murderous stare would have any impact on me.

"Come, Temptress," I said as I removed the belt that had bound her hands.

My fingertips softly caressed the sensitive flesh of her wrists until a pink flush warmed her skin.

I stood from my crouched position and extended my hand to Cadence. To my surprise, she took it and allowed me to help her stand.

My Temptress was already surrendering herself to me, and she didn't even realize it.

Chapter Forty-Two

CADENCE

Ryker was a godsdamned animal.

A dangerous beast who couldn't be tamed. He showed no regard for my discomfort. In fact, if the knowing smirk he wore was anything to go by, he reveled in it.

I yanked the laces of my boots tight, nearly snapping them, before straightening and snatching up Riordan's cloak.

"What do you think you're doing?" Ryker growled.

I stared at him in confusion, unsure of what had offended the unhinged asshole now. Ryker scowled, then marched over to me and ripped the cloak from my hand.

"You're not wearing that."

My mouth dropped open, but no words came out as I gawked at him.

"You can't be serious," I protested. "He's your brother."

Ryker stalked closer, eliminating the little space left between us. "Oh, I am. And if you want to see just how serious I am, continue to press me, Cadence. You are *my* mate, and I won't see you draped in the clothing of another man. Brother or not."

"Ryker, there is something seriously —"

My words were cut off as Ryker's calloused palm covered my mouth. I struggled against his hold but stilled when he whispered in my ear.

"We're not alone in these woods."

My eyes widened as I glanced around, trying to locate any movement in the shadows, but the forest was silent.

"Wraith Borne," Ryker hissed.

The venom that dripped from Ryker's tongue had my spine straightening and my magic stirring to life beneath my skin.

"Don't make a sound," he murmured as he let his hand fall away.

He reached down, his fingers disappearing inside his boot, and reemerging a moment later with a small, pointed dagger.

"Take it," he said as he pressed the cool steel into my palm. "And Cadence."

I raised my eyes to meet his grey ones, and the concern I saw reflected there made my brows furrow.

"If anyone comes near you, you end their lives, no hesitation. Understood?"

When I remained silent, he added, "Tell me you understand."

I swallowed the lump forming in my throat and nodded. "I understand."

Ryker's mouth crashed against mine, and his tongue pushed at the seam of my lips until they parted for him. He kissed me like he was going to war, and I was the enemy. Ryker conquered me with his tongue, destroying me until I yielded to him.

All too soon, he pulled away, leaving me breathless and wanting.

Ryker pressed his forehead to mine, his hand moving through my hair until he found the nape of my neck.

"No one takes you from me, Temptress. Not even the gods. Remember that."

I watched in awe and slight trepidation as Ryker's emotions drained from his face, only to be replaced by deadly determination. His shadows bled into the whites of his eyes until only obsidian remained. The black wings that had embraced me earlier sprang free, but there was a distinct lethality to them now. The tips were pointed and sharp, and as he unfurled them to their full span, the surrounding space seemed to darken. It was as though every beam of moonlight had been consumed by his presence.

I took in the sight before me. Ryker was terrifying, yet beautiful.

Instinctively, I stepped back, my heart racing. Ryker tilted his head as he considered me before his gaze fixed on something in the distance.

His lips curled into a snarl, revealing the tips of his elongated fangs. When he spoke, his deep voice vibrated with power.

"Stay behind me," he commanded. "They're coming."

As if on cue, a shrill shriek broke through the silence of the night. An icy wind raced through the branches surrounding me, carrying the faint scent of decay.

Those who could mend bodies or preserve life could always detect the acrid smell of death. After all, we worked hard to deny the God of Death his rightful bounty.

I gripped the hilt of my dagger, its silver blade catching the moonlight that dared to pierce the darkness of the night. The crunch of leaves and the rustle of footsteps surrounded us — a haunting chorus that drifted through the trees, growing louder with every step the enemy took in our direction. I fixed my eyes on the tree line ahead, but I still couldn't make out anyone approaching.

The clash of steel meeting steel rang out, and I gripped my dagger so tight that my knuckles turned white, almost translucent.

"I won't let any harm come to you, Cadence," Ryker murmured, misunderstanding my anticipation for fear.

This moment had been a long time coming.

Ryker stepped forward, his power rippling through the forest as his shadows coiled around him. The tendrils writhed and pulsed, eagerly awaiting his command. He raised his hand, and his shadows surged from his palm. They glided through the night effortlessly, twisting and dancing as they became one with the darkness.

A low hiss sliced through the air, followed by an ear-splitting scream.

I swung my head back in Ryker's direction, and the cruel smile making its way across his lips left me shivering.

I didn't get the chance to question what he had done as a dozen of the Wraith Borne charged through the underbrush. One figure lunged for me, his hand swiping at my chest, his blade missing me by mere inches as he tried to end my life.

I twisted out of reach, stumbling over my boots in my haste, but I righted myself before I crashed to the ground. Flicking my wrist as Malesh had taught me, I slashed my dagger at my attacker, grazing his cheek before he jumped back.

I didn't hesitate as I darted forward and sliced my blade through the air once more. The man blinked in surprise, and I mimicked the action, unsure I could trust what I was seeing. Crimson droplets beaded across the man's throat like rubies as they danced along his skin. The red substance gleamed under the dim light, and the macabre display was both dazzling and disturbing.

I couldn't tear my eyes away as I watched the color leach from his face. His ragged breathing was the only sound I could hear as he struggled to fight against the inevitable. My hand moved without my permission, and my fingers slid against the wetness coating his skin. His blood was hot and sticky, and

I could smell the metallic tang in the air, intermingled with sweat and fear.

Horrified, I jumped back and hastily wiped my hands against my dress, desperate to rid myself of the slick substance. The man fell to his knees, gravity pulling him to the ground, where he collapsed, unmoving.

As if I had been holding my breath, oxygen filled my lungs so rapidly that it felt as though they might burst. Grunts of pain and cries of terror reached my ears, but they were muted by the buzzing that had started up inside my head.

Shit, was I going to faint?

Tingles broke out all over my body, and a cold sweat quickly followed.

I was definitely going to faint.

I didn't have time to panic, though, because someone yanked on my hair so hard that black dots marred my vision.

"What do we have here?"

A man leered down at me, and I shook off any lingering dizziness as revulsion took over. Before I could make a move against him, however, I caught sight of Ryker, covered head to foot in blood, as he stared me down.

He was the embodiment of deadly wrath.

His whole body vibrated before dissolving into a swirl of darkness. A moment later, he reformed behind the man in front of me.

As if he could sense the danger closing in on him, the man turned to face Ryker.

His hand fell away from my hair, and he stumbled as he tried to put distance between himself and the furious Fae male.

“Stay back,” he said as he waved his hands in the air.

The threat was obvious.

Should Ryker advance, he would release his magic.

Ryker smirked at the man, and his arms trembled as his resolve wavered. With a flick of his wrist, a shard made of shadow flew from Ryker’s hand before it pierced the man’s rib cage.

He was dead before he even hit the ground.

Then Ryker turned his deadly wrath on me.

“What did I tell you, Cadence?” he demanded.

I raised my chin and folded my arms over my chest in defiance.

“I killed one,” I defended.

Ryker barked out a harsh laugh. He closed the distance between us as he wrapped his hand around my throat, forcing me backward until my body collided with a tree.

“You killed a man, and then you allowed your shock to hold you captive.”

The accusatory tone of his voice had me bristling.

“Well, forgive me for not being a trained assassin!”

Ryker lowered his head, his lips a hair’s breadth from meeting mine.

“You’re forgiven,” he whispered. “Just don’t let it happen again.”

He brushed his mouth against mine in a soft kiss, and I could feel the smug smile tugging up his lips. Then he pulled away from me, turning on his heels and disappearing into the darkened forest.

"Hurry up," he called over his shoulder, not bothering to wait for me.

"Ryker," I hissed, but the man had been consumed by the darkness.

"Fuck!"

I let out a frustrated breath before following him.

Chapter Forty-Three

CADENCE

The sound of fighting intensified, and I could hear the faint echo of weapons colliding, sharp cries of pain, and the guttural roars of warriors locked in a violent struggle.

I stepped into the small clearing where the Wild Hunt began and sucked in a ragged breath at the sight before me.

Desiccated bodies littered the ground, their shriveled and withered remains beyond recognition. There wasn't time to dwell on the senseless loss of life, however, as the battle raged around me. There would be a chance to mourn later.

First, I had to survive the night.

"Behind you," someone who I hoped was Riordan called out.

I spun, ducking just in time to avoid the strike meant for my head. I didn't hesitate as I drove my dagger upward, plunging it into my would-be killer's chest. The Fae woman fell backward as she screamed.

I reached down and plucked my blade from her body before I turned to face the clearing. More of the Wraith Borne broke through the tree line, and Ryker sent out a wave of shadows. I watched, unable to pull my gaze away, as the darkness consumed everything in its path.

Even as Ryker extinguished one life after another, more Wraith Borne charged forward.

"There are too many of them!" Malesh yelled. His voice was barely audible over the cacophony of battle.

I moved with a speed I didn't know I possessed as I threw myself into the fray. My dagger flashed in front of me as I cut down the enemy one by one. My movements were more confident than they had been when the Wraith Borne first appeared, but each strike brought me closer to the edge of exhaustion. I hadn't been training long enough to build up my stamina.

When I made my way to Malesh, his face paled as he took me in.

"Cadence, what are you still doing here?"

"I can help!"

He opened his mouth to speak, but his words were cut off as another Wraith Borne ran towards him.

Without thinking, I sent my dagger sailing through the air, and it landed with a sickening thud at the base of the man's throat. Fountains of crimson spurted from the wound, and the man clutched it, trying to stem the flow. He leaned forward, swaying on his feet before he careened towards the ground. The bloodied tip of my blade was pushed through the back of his neck as his body met the earth.

"Shit, that was my only weapon," I hissed.

Steel glinted in my periphery, and I turned to face Malesh. His hand was outstretched, offering me another dagger. This one was longer than my last, and when I picked it up, it felt heavier in my palm.

I grinned, and Malesh shook his head.

"Anytime you want to end this, Ryker," Riordan called, driving his sword into the gut of the warrior who had tried to sneak up on him. "Would be fine by me."

Ryker sank his teeth into one combatant as he decapitated another. When he stepped back, an enormous chunk of flesh dangled from his mouth before he spat it on the ground. I pressed a hand to my stomach in a futile attempt to settle the nausea churning inside me.

"When I'm having so much fun?" he replied, the blood painting his face, making his wicked grin seem even more sinister.

As I tried to dispel the image, an eerie sensation crept up my spine, and my hands moved instinctively as I rubbed the nape of my neck. It felt as though unseen eyes were boring into me, watching and assessing my every move.

I was drawn out of my reverie when a woman stepped forward, the sharp edge of her blade swinging in a wide arc before she brought it down toward me. I raised my dagger to meet the biting steel of her sword, and my arm shook from the force of it. But I refused to give up, if only to prove to myself that I could survive and that Ryker was a fool to underestimate me. I lifted my knee and drove it into her lower abdomen. She stumbled back, clutching her stomach tight.

The woman was formidable. I knew I'd have to act quickly if I had any hope of overpowering her. With a battle cry, I charged forward and jumped on her back. I wrapped my legs around her waist and plunged my dagger into her carotid artery. When warm liquid gushed from the wound, drenching my hand, I knew my strike had found its mark. I tore my dagger free as I awkwardly slid down the woman's body and surveyed the damage.

I never imagined that the knowledge I'd gained as a healer would serve me on the battlefield.

The same sensation from earlier returned tenfold, and the hairs on the back of my neck stood up as I scanned the area, searching for the source of my unease.

My gaze locked on a cloaked figure standing at the edge of the tree line. It was a man, judging by his height. There was something about the way he carried himself that felt oddly familiar. The man raised his hand, and I braced for an attack, but when nothing happened, I took a tentative step forward.

"Cadence!" Ryker hollered, and I turned to see him stalking towards me.

Three of the Wraith Borne used Ryker's distraction to their advantage. Two circled him from the sides as another stepped into his path, their arms outstretched as they reached for him.

But they had forgotten who they were facing.

They had forgotten that Ryker was the Night Cursed Prince.

And it was a lesson they would pay for with blood.

Ryker crouched low as the first warrior descended on him. Shadows snaked from his palms before they crawled their way up the warrior's body, binding his hands in place.

As Ryker rose from the ground, he pulled his wings tight against his sides before snapping them out again, impaling the other two assailants on the sharpened points. Their screams rang out all around me, suffocating me as their agony pierced the night air.

I stumbled forward, my palms pressed to my ears as I tried to block out the noise, but it did nothing to mute the sounds of their anguish. A moment later, Ryker stood to his full height, and a tearing sound filled the clearing. I watched in horror as the pointed tips of Ryker's wings ripped the warriors in half. Their mangled bodies fell to the ground, yet Ryker hardly noticed as he snarled at the one still fighting the hold of his shadows.

The man opened his mouth to scream, but Ryker was faster. He darted forward, his fangs sinking into the side of the Wraith Borne's neck as he tore out his jugular. A torrent of blood spilled down the man's tunic, and I could no longer deny the needs of my body. I hunched over my knees just in time to empty the contents of my stomach onto the ground.

More terrified screams broke out, and I didn't have to guess the cause. Dark shadows swirled across the ground, twisting and thrashing as they grew. Darkness engulfed the clearing, and the sounds of the Wraith Borne dying ebbed and flowed until only silence remained.

Ryker's shadows receded, and when I raised my head, steel-grey eyes peered down at me.

"Are you all right?" he asked as he lifted me into his arms.

"I'm fine," I protested, my cheeks heating at the way Ryker cradled me against his chest. "Can you *please* put me down?"

Ryker grinned, and it would have been charming if not for the copious amounts of blood staining his hair and painting his handsome face.

"Worried what would happen if I got my hands on you again?"

"No," I lied.

"About time," Riordan grumbled as he sauntered up to us.

Mercifully, Ryker lowered me to the ground, but he didn't let me get far as he pulled me into his side, his palm firmly planted on my hip.

"I thought you could use the exercise, Little Brother," Ryker teased.

Riordan mumbled a curse under his breath, but I tuned them out as the prickling sensation of unseen eyes assaulted me once more.

I turned to the spot where I had seen the cloaked figure, but he was gone. Still, the feeling didn't abate. It only grew stronger.

Unease crept over me, and something told me that whoever he was, he wasn't finished with me yet.

Chapter Forty-Four

CADENCE

By the time we reached Ryker's chambers, I was exhausted. My whole body ached, and muscles that I didn't even know existed protested in pain.

Still, I was alive, so that was something.

The room was quiet compared to the soft noises of the forest and the violent sounds of battle. Everything had been amplified out in the woods. The sound of my blood pounding in my ears had been a constant companion as I lurched from one moment to the next.

Now, the silence was deafening. Eerily so.

As I peered around, taking in the velvet drapes and ornate furnishings, it seemed like they had lost their opulence. As if the night's events had dimmed them somehow.

Ryker set me on the edge of his chaise before disappearing into the bathing chamber. My clothing was ruined, and I was smeared with blood and grime from the battle. I'd stain the soft fabric of the lounge in my current state, but I couldn't bring myself to care.

A moment later, Ryker returned with a washcloth in hand. He lowered himself to his knees before me, then pressed it to my temple. I hissed as pain radiated from the site, and when he pulled the cloth away, I was surprised to see it was bloody.

I hadn't even realized I'd been injured.

"You held your ground out there," Ryker murmured as he continued cleaning the dirt from my face.

I blinked, unsure how to take the praise.

"Did I?"

Ryker nodded, his eyes never leaving mine as he worked.

"I've seen more seasoned warriors falter when confronted with such odds."

A humorless laugh escaped my lips.

"It was terrifying, and I'm not entirely sure how I made it out alive," I admitted.

"I knew you would."

"How?"

I quirked a brow, ready to hear him repeat his earlier declaration that not even the gods could take me from him.

"Because you're strong, Cadence," he said, dropping the washcloth to the ground.

"You are stronger than you give yourself credit for. You were forced to make a choice tonight, and you chose to survive."

I opened my mouth to respond but closed it again when words escaped me.

"And you're stubborn," he continued with a mischievous grin. "Far too stubborn to die, that's for sure."

A laugh bubbled up my throat, and before I could stop myself, it burst free. Ryker's grin widened, and he cupped my cheeks in his palms.

"You are my mate, Cadence," he whispered almost reverently. "You were created to stand at my side, and the gods would never have sent someone weak to tame the Night Cursed Prince."

"Have I?" I purred, surprising myself.

I cleared my throat and tried again. "Tamed the Night Cursed Prince, I mean?"

I studied Ryker's face, but his expression gave nothing away. His gaze dropped to my lips, and my tongue darted out to wet them.

Ryker leaned in close, his warm breath fanning across my cheek, and I inhaled sharply. His mouth moved to the shell of my ear, and he murmured, "Not even a little."

It took a moment for my mind to clear from the lust-induced fog and to register his words. When I finally processed what he said, I shoved him in irritation. He fell to the ground, his back colliding with the hard stone floor as he laughed raucously.

I was defenseless against his boyish charm. He so rarely showed that part of himself that I longed for it every moment in between.

I grinned down at him, my annoyance fading away as I watched him struggle to rein in his laughter.

“You should have seen your face, Cadence.”

“You’re an idiot, Ryker,” I snapped, but there was no bite to it.

“No one has ever dared to call me an idiot before,” Ryker mused. “Well, except Riordan.”

“Yes, well, Riordan is an excellent judge of character.”

“Does your opinion of his judgment extend to all the good things he has been saying about me?”

“How do you know about that?” I demanded, crossing my arms over my chest.

Ryker lifted a hand, letting shadows pool in his palm. The reminder of what those dark tendrils could do sent a shiver of excitement racing down my spine.

“My shadows hear everything,” Ryker said absently as he played with the black mass.

Wisps of darkness danced between his fingers and wrapped around his forearm as if embracing him.

“And they trade in secrets.”

“Well, that’s hardly fair.”

“You didn’t answer my question, Cadence,” Ryker rumbled as he sat up, bracing his arms on either side of my thighs.

“I don’t know,” I admitted. “I’m still trying to figure that out.”

Ryker hummed, and liquid heat coiled between my legs.

The man had trained me to respond to his commanding tone. Even now, after everything I had endured tonight and how exhausted I felt, my body burned for him.

The intensity churning in Ryker's gaze had me glancing sideways to escape the overwhelming heat that seemed to pin me in place.

My eyes locked on a crimson stain that had soaked through his tunic.

"You're hurt," I said, and I could hear the disbelief in my tone.

"It's a scratch."

I clawed at the garment as I pulled Ryker's shirt over his head. An angry red gash marred his side, the steady flow of blood letting me know just how deep it was.

"If you wanted to get me naked, Cadence, all you had to do was ask," Ryker teased.

I gave him a look that warned I wasn't playing around before I returned my gaze to his injury. He sucked in a breath as I prodded the wound gently and more blood welled at the site.

"You should have said something," I grumbled as I laid my palm over the gash.

The rush of power had me sighing in contentment, and I leaned into the feeling as I pushed more of my magic into Ryker. The swelling around the injury lessened, and the constant trickle of blood dried up.

Ryker's eyebrows bunched as he watched me work, my magic weaving his broken flesh back together. As the final pulse left my palm, the thrumming in my veins slowly faded, and I looked up to see Ryker staring down at me.

"You're incredible," he said hoarsely.

"You've seen me work before, Ryker."

"It's different when you can feel it, too."

Ryker plucked the washcloth off the ground and resumed his ministration on the cut at my temple.

"I can heal that myself, you know," I teased.

"I'm aware, but I want to do it."

The bond flared inside my chest, and I gasped.

"Did I hurt you?" he asked, concern lacing his tone.

"No, I... it's fine," I muttered, as I forced myself to keep my hands at my sides instead of rubbing at the spot like I wanted.

Ryker gave me an indiscernible look but said nothing.

Once he was satisfied that he'd cleaned out the cut, Ryker stood and offered me his hand.

"Where are you taking me?" I asked as I placed my palm in his much larger one.

"For a bath. You're a mess."

"As if you can talk," I scoffed, and I pointed to the blood still covering his body and matting his hair.

Ryker simply shrugged and tugged me along after him.

Warmth spread throughout my chest, and I had to wonder if I was finally softening toward my mate.

Chapter Forty-Five

CADENCE

In the weeks following the attack, the Unseelie Court was in turmoil. The Crimson Enclave had been a distant threat to the ruling class, if not pure fiction. Now, they had come dangerously close to the palace, shattering any illusions of safety.

Ryker had been tasked with discovering how they made it so close without detection, and with him preoccupied, my days had been spent alongside Riordan or Malesh. While I enjoyed their company, the time away from Ryker also created an ache in my chest I couldn't quite alleviate.

The days dragged on, yet every night he would return to his chambers and fuck me with a savagery that I was beginning to crave. My body was deliciously sore, but I was starting to think his rough treatment was more than I could bear. My breasts were tender from his vicious ministrations, and the man kept me awake until the small hours so that I could hardly function the next morning.

He was insatiable, and I was ready to concede defeat.

A prickling sensation burned behind my eyes, and to my shock, I realized I was crying. Fat tears rolled down my face, and my body trembled as sobs built inside my chest. No matter how many deep breaths I inhaled, I couldn't stop the flow as they traced their way down my cheeks.

A low creak caught my attention, and I turned to the door as Riordan entered.

"Good morning, Sunshine," he beamed, but his expression fell when he saw me burying my face in my palms.

His footfalls were barely audible over the sound of my heaving sobs, but his gentle fingers gripped my wrists as he lowered my hands. He took one look at me and pressed me against the hard planes of his chest.

"Shh, Cadence. It's alright. Whatever Ryker did, I'll make sure he pays."

A strangled laugh escaped me, but the sound only made me cry harder. Riordan rubbed his palm up and down my back in a soothing gesture as he tried in vain to calm me.

"Can you tell me what's wrong?" he murmured.

"I don't know," I wailed.

Riordan's movements paused as he struggled to comprehend my words.

"Did you say you don't know?"

I nodded against his chest, and I was horrified to see how my tears had stained his tunic.

"Then why are you crying?"

I pulled out of his grasp and quickly dabbed my eyes.

"I have no idea," I admitted, and I tried to laugh it off, but the sound was forced.

Riordan furrowed his brows in confusion, but he merely shrugged and opened his arms wide for me to hug him once more. I didn't hesitate as I dove into his embrace. More tears welled, and this time, I let them fall. The rhythmic beating of his heart was a welcome distraction, and I found his woodsy scent oddly calming.

"You smell good," I murmured against his chest.

"Don't let Ryker hear you saying that," he chuckled.

I inhaled deeply, letting Riordan's scent fill my lungs, and a contented sigh escaped between my lips.

"Seriously, you smell amazing."

"Thank you... I guess," Riordan said, confusion lacing his tone.

I settled into Riordan's embrace and allowed his soothing touch to help me overcome whatever mental breakdown I was experiencing. His friendship was a comfort in this land of schemes and enemies.

When the door creaked for a second time, we both froze before turning to face the irate Fae prince standing in the doorway.

"It's not what you —" Riordan began, but Ryker moved before he could finish his sentence.

In a mass of shadows and fury, Ryker crossed the floor in seconds and pulled me from Riordan's arms. When my mind caught up with what I was seeing, Ryker had his brother slammed against the stone wall, his forearm pressed against the base of Riordan's throat.

"Ryker, let him go."

Ryker turned his murderous gaze on me, his obsidian eyes twin pools of wrath.

"I'll deal with you in a moment," he gritted out.

Turning back to Riordan, he snarled, "You know better than to touch what belongs to me, Little Brother."

Riordan scoffed, and Ryker pressed harder against his throat.

"Sure do, you psychopathic tyrant," he said in a strangled tone.

"Then tell me why I walked into *my* chambers to find *my* brother holding *my* mate."

"Because," he wheezed, "you're an asshole, and you did something to upset her, so being the good brother that I am, I tried to comfort her."

Riordan pushed against Ryker and he released his hold, as his younger brother sucked in large gulps of air.

Ryker crossed his arms over his chest and angled his body so that he had both of us within view.

"Cadence," he rumbled. "Speak."

I straightened my shoulders and mimicked his pose. "Why should I? You come in here acting like a godsdamned animal and think you can command me at your will."

A low chuckle sounded beside Ryker, and he turned his gaze back to Riordan.

"Get out," he barked as he jutted his chin toward the door.

Riordan glanced in my direction as though he were waiting for my approval. Ryker growled at his brother, but I ignored him and nodded at Riordan.

"All right, I'll leave you two lovebirds to sort through your issues," he said. "Of which there are many," he added under his breath.

"Meet me at the training grounds," Ryker called after him.

"Of course, My Lord. Anything you command, My Lord," Riordan replied without looking back in our direction.

When the snick of the lock sounded, Ryker stormed toward me. "Why were you upset?" he demanded.

I raised my chin and met his steely gaze with a glare of my own.

"I owe you no explanation," I said, unwilling to confess to this maniac that I did not know why I had been crying.

"Cadence," he growled as he pinched the bridge of his nose. "You will tell me why I almost murdered my brother."

"All right. It's because you have a toxic sense of entitlement, and you have deluded yourself into believing that you own me."

"There is no delusion involved. I do own you," Ryker deadpanned.

Warmth spread across my cheeks, and I flung my arms out wide.

"You can't own a person, Ryker!" I snapped.

Ryker smirked, and my vision turned red.

"Gods! I hate you," I screamed. "Everything about you is obnoxious and irritating," I ranted.

He cocked an amused brow that sent my blood boiling inside my veins.

"You know what's wrong with you," I said as I poked a finger into his firm chest.

The digit flared in pain, meanwhile, it appeared as though Ryker hadn't even felt it.

"You've had everything handed to you on a silver platter your entire life, and now you think you're entitled to whatever you want."

Ryker scoffed and uncrossed his arms. "Hardly, Cadence. There are things I have endured which would make your blood run cold."

One moment, I was fired up, righteous anger engulfing me. In the next, a torrent of fresh tears streamed down my face at the thought of Ryker in pain.

Gods, what was wrong with me?

"Cadence, I'm... not sure what to do here," he admitted.

He moved closer to me, but I held up my palm to stop him.

"I don't know why I'm crying, Ryker, but right now, your presence aggravates me, and I need you to leave."

"All right," he drawled. "I'll give you some space."

He glanced towards the door, and I sensed that he couldn't escape the room fast enough.

I didn't acknowledge him as I threw myself on the bed and screamed into the pillows.

The sound of the door shutting behind him was a welcome reprieve, and I let all of my pent-up emotions flow free.

All I needed was a good cry, and I'd feel better.

Well, that, and a long nap.

Chapter Forty-Six

RYKER

I stormed toward the practice grounds, sword in hand, ready to release my frustration. Arguably, my brother was not to blame for my darkening mood, but I wouldn't pass up the chance to put him in his place.

I didn't bother with the usual pre-training exercises, instead opting to dive straight in. Riordan raised his sword to meet mine, and the clang of steel rang out around us, sharp and rhythmic, like the heartbeat of battle.

Dust stirred beneath our feet, our relentless attacks not giving the well-worn ground a moment to settle.

"Correct me if I'm mistaken, Brother, but it seems you are aiming for blood on this fine day," Riordan grunted. "My blood, to be precise."

I didn't answer him as I adjusted my grip on my sword, the leather-bound hilt slick with sweat. My strikes came fast and furious, the weight of my anger carrying every blow.

"Of course not, Riordan," my brother said in a mocking tone as he danced out of reach with infuriating ease. "I'd never do anything to harm you under the guise of misplaced rage."

His grin was as wide as a crescent moon, and I ground my teeth together to stop myself from taking his head off.

"Come on, Ryker. Not even the hint of a smile."

A growl worked its way up my throat, and my jaw tightened as I redoubled my efforts. The sun was high in the sky as it bore down on us, and the relentless heat had my tunic soaked in minutes.

But I hardly noticed as I focused all my attention on my little brother.

"Stop grinning like an idiot, Riordan. You crossed a line, and you know it."

I feigned left but brought my blade down on Riordan's right. He stumbled back but caught himself in time to parry my strike, and the clash of our swords reverberated through the training yard.

"Ryker," Eamon called, the concern evident in his tone.

I hadn't even noticed his presence when I'd marched into the square. My mind had been consumed by the thought of Cadence in Riordan's arms.

"Stay out of this, Eamon," I warned. "This is between me and my brother."

I lunged forward, aiming my sword at Riordan's midsection. My simmering rage had boiled over, making my movements reckless.

Riordan barely deflected the strike before he spun out of reach. His eyes darted down to his stomach, and pain pinched his features as he stared at the red substance seeping through his tunic.

Riordan's gaze snapped to mine, and he scowled. He launched himself at me, attacking with renewed ferocity as our swords met in a flurry of sparks and grating steel.

"You're mad, Ryker, and I get it."

I parried, returning the intensity of Riordan's strikes.

"Do you, Little Brother? Because if you were anyone else, you would be dead with your entrails spread across my chamber floor."

Riordan swung his sword in a wide arc before bringing it down on my blade in a vicious assault. I pushed back, our faces meeting in the middle of our swords before I shoved him away, only to advance on him again.

"This is only practice," Eamon yelled, but we both ignored him.

"You upset her, and I stumbled upon the mess you'd created. Would you have preferred I left her to her misery?"

Anger surged through me like wildfire, consuming everything in its path.

"I did nothing to upset her! She told me she had no idea why she was even crying."

Riordan reared back before slamming his head into mine. Blood burst from my nose, dripping down my chin and onto my tunic.

"Riordan," Malesh called, sounding almost panicked.

I didn't know when he had sauntered into the training grounds, nor did I care. My little brother had drawn blood, and I was about to show him why that was a very bad idea.

The look on my face must have betrayed my intentions, because Riordan's scowl deepened as he tightened his hold on his blade.

"You deserved that," he shouted. "Blood for blood, Brother."

With a flourish, I prowled toward Riordan, and he settled into his stance, ready to meet my attack head-on.

"Oh, no you don't! No creepy shadow eyes. You face me like a man."

My control was slipping.

Cadence may very well be the death of me.

Recalling my shadows, I raised my blade and swung hard. Riordan deflected as he spun. He came at me from my other side, and I stepped out of range before advancing on him. Once again, steel grated against steel. Our movements became a blur as we traded blows, neither one of us willing to concede defeat.

We were both panting heavily as we circled each other.

"What did you expect would happen, Brother?" Riordan demanded. "That Cadence would simply fall into life here at the Unseelie Palace and forget that she had ever had a home before you?"

Yes.

Now that he said it out loud, it did seem a little unrealistic.

"You may have done nothing in particular to upset her on this occasion, but she's hurting all the same."

I wanted to argue, to deny his accusations, but how could I?

Everything he said was true.

Before I could respond, a wave of dizziness washed over me. My head felt light, and as I glanced around, my world tilted.

"Are you all right?" Riordan called.

I couldn't answer him. Nausea twisted inside me, sharp and relentless, unfurling from my gut like a serpent coiling tighter with every breath. I stumbled, and I lowered my sword before my knees buckled.

Had I been poisoned? Was this the way I would leave this plane?

I staggered toward the edge of the training grounds as I clutched my stomach. I only just made it to the shade of the nearby trees before I doubled over, retching violently.

Riordan followed behind, and his concern quickly turned to laughter.

"Please tell me Cadence finally poisoned you," he teased.

I glared up at him through watery eyes as I wiped my mouth with the back of my hand.

"Fuck off, Riordan."

This only made him laugh harder.

"Seriously though, what's wrong? Did you eat something questionable at breakfast?"

The thought of food made me groan as nausea churned my gut. I sank to the ground and closed my eyes as I rested against the tree. Sweat coated my brow, and I had to focus on my breathing to dispel the bile threatening to come up.

"Do you want me to fetch a healer?"

"I'm fine," I muttered, not at all sure that I was.

"You don't look fine," said Eamon, joining the conversation.

"Should I get Cadence?" Malesh asked.

Cadence.

An odd sensation flared inside me at the mention of my mate, and the nausea began to fade. It wasn't gone completely, but it was as if I was experiencing it second-hand.

I cracked open one eye and then the other.

The bond surged again, and I realized with a start that the nauseous feeling was not coming from me.

I could feel Cadence through the bond.

"It's not me," I murmured.

"What?" Riordan asked.

"It's not me," I repeated. "It's Cadence. She's sick, and I can feel it through the bond."

"She didn't seem sick this morning," Riordan mused.

"Fae rarely get sick," Eamon added.

"Not unless she's pregnant," Malesh muttered to himself.

The word jolted through me, setting me ablaze from the inside.

Could she be?

I couldn't stop the slow grin spreading across my face.

"Ryker," Riordan growled. "What the fuck did you do?"

Chapter Forty-Seven

CADENCE

Once I'd finished dispelling my breakfast, I dragged myself back to bed. I performed a cursory evaluation of my body and was relieved when I detected no poison in my system. I still didn't understand why I was feeling so unwell, but I figured I could make a proper assessment after my nap.

I was so damned tired.

My plans were rudely interrupted when the door to Ryker's chambers burst open. It hit the stone wall and rattled on its hinges from the force of the collision.

I sat bolt upright, calling my magic to my fingertips as I prepared to defend myself.

"Cadence," Ryker growled, and I let my hands fall to the bed.

"Gods, Ryker, you scared me half to death."

I fell back on the mattress, throwing an arm over my eyes as I blocked out the oppressive daylight. My stomach had settled somewhat, but there was an underlying queasiness that I was eager to sleep off.

Apparently, Ryker wasn't content to leave me be.

His rough fingers tightened around my wrist as he pulled my arm away from my face. The weight of his presence filled the room as he gazed down at me, and his steel-grey eyes were swimming with some emotion I couldn't identify.

"How are you feeling, Cadence?" he rumbled.

His question caught me off guard, and my eyes narrowed as I studied him.

"I'm a little under the weather, actually. How did you know I wasn't well?"

"The bond," he said with a shrug.

I blinked at him, not understanding what he meant. Then realization slammed into me, and I gasped.

"You felt me through the bond?"

Ryker nodded but didn't elaborate.

"Gods, there is no going back now, is there?"

Ryker curled his upper lip, and I realized I had spoken the last part out loud.

"There was never any going back, Cadence," he snarled. "Especially when you are carrying my heir."

My breath caught in my throat, and I felt my whole body tense as my heart slammed against my ribcage.

"What did you say?"

"You're pregnant, Cadence."

My mouth opened and closed as I tried to form words, but nothing came out. Ryker leaned over me, his hands wrapping around my shoulders as he pulled me to my feet.

"Do not deny it," he warned.

I was spared from responding when the door was thrown open once more, and Riordan stormed inside.

"Tell me what you did!" he demanded, and it took me a moment to realize he was talking to Ryker.

I stumbled back as my legs trembled, threatening to send me careening to the floor. The brothers continued to bicker, but I heard none of it. Pulling on my magic, I delved into every corner of my body as I searched for any sign that something was amiss.

Nausea still swirled in my stomach, but the feeling was less intense than it had been earlier. My breasts were tender, and a little swollen, and I had a higher temperature than normal. Not enough to be considered a fever, but enough to notice. Then, there was my heightened sense of smell. The way Riordan's woodsy scent had been all-consuming, despite never really noticing it before.

I closed my eyes and let out a shaky breath. Focusing on my abdomen, I sent out small tendrils of power, searching for any sign that Ryker might be right.

Then I felt it.

The slight flutter of something pressing against my magic. It raced up the thread of my power as if reaching for me. My eyes flew open, and the room spun around me.

"Oh gods," I breathed, reaching out for the bed frame to steady myself. "This isn't possible."

"Cadence?" Ryker asked, his brows furrowing. "What's wrong?"

"It's true."

How had I missed the signs? I was a godsdamned healer, and I failed to heed every single message my body had sent me.

"Sweetheart," Riordan said gently.

Ryker snarled at his brother and pushed him away.

"Fuck off, Ryker, this isn't about you," Riordan snapped.

Ryker ignored his younger brother and extended his hand to me. When I recoiled, his jaw tightened, but he let his hand drop.

"Get dressed, Cadence," he barked.

"W-what?"

"I said get dressed. You have five minutes before I drag you out of here in what you're wearing, vomit and all."

I glanced down at my dress, only now noticing the damp patch I'd rather not name.

"Ryker!" Riordan protested, but his brother simply dragged him out of the room after him.

I changed quickly as I tried not to let panic overwhelm me. As much as Ryker and I had settled into a peaceful coexistence, I had never given up on my plans to break free from him. I wanted my old life back. I longed to go home and see my family, to resume my work at the apothecary.

With the bond strengthening and now this... I felt desperation clawing at my throat.

How would I ever escape him now?

I didn't have time to fall apart, though. Ryker, true to his word, barged into his chambers exactly five minutes later. He'd changed his clothes, swapping out his training garb for one of his more formal tunics and trousers.

Unease crept over me. Where was he taking me?

His gaze raked over my body, assessing me from head to toe. He nodded, seemingly pleased with what he saw.

Ryker marched toward me, threading his fingers through mine.

"Where are we going?" I demanded, but the stubborn man remained silent.

As we crossed the threshold of his chambers, I was met with a wall of muscle. Riordan, Malesh, and Eamon stood guard just outside the door, and serious expressions adorned each of their faces.

The hairs on the back of my neck rose, and my senses were immediately alert.

"What's going on?" I asked, unable to hide the tremor in my voice.

"Come, Cadence," Ryker said as he tugged me along behind him.

"Ryker, wait," Riordan called after us, but Ryker didn't slow his strides.

We moved through the palace in silence as I continued to steal glances at Ryker from under my lashes. His footsteps were unhurried, and his expression betrayed no hint of what he was feeling.

When we stopped outside a set of unfamiliar doors, I peered up at Ryker in confusion. He pushed the heavy wooden panes aside and pulled me inside. The air was thick with incense, and the marble floors glowed faintly, illuminated by the sconces lining the walls. I could make out runes carved deep into the stone, the Fae symbols for eternity and prosperity, catching my attention.

The sound of a throat clearing startled me, and I looked up to see a man who I assumed was one of the High Priests, standing before an altar.

"Prince Ryker," he said, sounding unsure. "I wasn't expecting you."

I peered over my shoulder at the others who had followed us inside, but none of them would meet my eye.

"Tell me what is going on, Ryker, or so help me —"

My words died on my tongue as Ryker announced, "You will marry us."

His tone brooked no argument, and the Priest swallowed hard.

"Your Highness," he began, but Ryker held up a hand to silence him.

"Right now."

My shock gave way to anger, and I wrenched myself free of Ryker's grasp.

"Are you insane?" I hissed. "I'm not marrying you."

Ryker spun toward me. His movements were so fast that I almost missed them. His hand darted forward, wrapping around my throat as he pulled me to him.

"This is not up for discussion, Cadence," he snarled. "You will take my name, my protection, and my power. You *will* become my wife, and once it is done, there is not a single person inside this kingdom who would dare harm you," — his gaze flicked to my flat stomach and then back to me — "or our child."

"I won't do it," I said, my resolve strengthening. "And you can't force me to do this. Fae law is absolute. The binding won't be true if I do not consent."

Ryker smirked and stepped closer, invading my space.

"Ryker," Riordan warned, but the man before me gave no indication that he had even heard his brother.

Ryker's warm breath tickled the side of my neck as he leaned in close to my ear.

"Fight me on this, and I will return to the Seelie Kingdom. While I'm there, I will make sure that I call on your parents in their brownstone house that's nestled only two streets back from your apothecary."

I inhaled sharply, but Ryker wasn't done.

"Then I'll be sure to visit your brother, Callum, right?"

My palms landed on Ryker's chest, and I shoved him, but he didn't budge. His calloused hands wrapped around my wrists as a wicked grin spread across his face.

Dread settled in my stomach. "How?" I whispered.

"You don't live this long in my world without always staying one step ahead of your opponent at all times."

Tears filled my eyes, but I refused to let them fall.

"You truly are a monster," I choked out.

"*Your* monster. And I won't risk your life, or the life of our child, for your pride, Temptress."

Turning to the Priest, he nodded his head. "You may begin."

Chapter Forty-Eight

CADENCE

"Prince Ryker," the Priest intoned, his voice echoing throughout the chamber. "You stand before the gods, ready to tether your fate to the woman before you?"

Sweat beaded on my upper lip, and I felt as though I was drowning.

"Ryker, please," I begged. "You can't do this."

"I can, and I will," he said before returning his gaze to the Priest and giving him a single nod.

"Very well. Declare your vows at the table of the gods."

Ryker's steel-grey eyes locked on me.

"I, Ryker Ashborne, Crown Prince of the Unseelie Fae, bind myself to you, Cadence Tiernan."

His voice was steady as his words rang out around us.

"Before the gods and those who bear witness here today, I vow to protect you, to honor you, and to keep you at my side until my dying breath."

The Priest turned to me, his gaze expectant. When I said nothing, Ryker squeezed my hand. Whether in warning or reassurance, I didn't know.

"My Lady," the Priest murmured. "It is your turn to say your vows."

"Cadence," Ryker growled, and I lifted my chin in defiance.

Before he could threaten me further, Riordan stepped forward, his head bowed.

"Cadence," he said gently. "Can I have a word?"

Ryker ran a hand through his hair, his agitation plain to see.

"You should talk some sense into her, Brother, before I resort to more unpleasant means."

The warning was not lost on me, but I couldn't bring myself to concede to him.

Riordan gripped my elbow and steered me to the corner of the chamber.

"You better not even think of defending his actions to me, Riordan," I snapped.

He raised his hands in surrender, and some of the tension left my shoulders.

"The way my brother went about this is inexcusable," he admitted. "But he isn't wrong."

A growl tore free from my throat, and Riordan rushed to continue.

"News of your pregnancy will put a target on your back."

"I already have a target on my back because of your brother."

"True, but if the Unseelie Council learns that you carry his heir, that danger will only grow. They'll stop at nothing to protect the advantages they believe his betrothal to Lady Barrington brings to the kingdom."

As much as I hated Ryker, I couldn't deny the irrational flicker of jealousy that coursed through me with Riordan's words. Riordan gave me a meaningful look, and I didn't miss the message he conveyed.

I threatened their engagement, and a child only strengthened that threat.

"They'll still feel the same way, even if I marry him."

Riordan shook his head. "They might risk Ryker's wrath for a mistress, but never a wife."

When I raised an irritated brow at him, Riordan only shrugged.

"Ryker hasn't announced you as his mate, therefore, most people believe you are his courtesan."

I released a frustrated sigh as my fate closed in around me, strangling me into submission.

"Let him protect you, Cadence. He owes you that much."

"If I marry him, I'll never be free from him, Riordan," I said, my voice sounding small, even to me.

Riordan gave me a pained smile as he cupped my cheek in his palm.

"There was never any escaping him, sweetheart," he murmured. "You and I both know that once Ryker got his hands on you, he'd never let you go. I promise you I am going to do whatever I can to help you regain yourself along the way, but for now, we need to focus on keeping you safe."

Concern tightened Riordan's features, and a small piece of my armor fell away.

While he might be right, I still wasn't ready to lose myself to Ryker's will.

Though it didn't seem like I had much of a choice.

Riordan wrapped my hand in his as he led me back to Ryker, who was pacing in front of the altar. He gave me one last nod before he stepped aside, rejoining Malesh and Eamon.

"Are you ready, dear?" the Priest asked.

I dipped my chin, and Ryker reclaimed my hands as he stared down at me.

Letting out a controlled breath, I said, "I, Cadence Tiernan, bind myself to you, Ryker Ashborne."

I didn't bother with his title because the gods knew he deserved nothing further from me.

"With the gods as my witness, I vow to be your ruination and make you regret ever treating me less than I deserve."

A groan sounded behind me, but I didn't pull my gaze away from the Fae prince standing before me. The ghost of a smile flickered across Ryker's face, and he nodded for the Priest to continue.

The man raised his arms and chanted in the old Fae tongue. When he was done, a golden light shone from his palms, and he placed his hands over our joined ones.

"The gods accept your vows and bind you as Husband and Wife, in this life and the next."

A jolt of pain ran through me with his declaration before it slowly receded. Ryker pulled me close and pressed his forehead to mine.

"You're mine, Cadence."

Both triumph and relief colored his tone.

"Forever," he murmured.

I closed my eyes, and a small tear streaked down my cheek at the finality of his words.

Ryker gripped my chin with his thumb and forefinger, forcing me to look at him. His penetrating gaze searched my face before he crashed his lips against mine.

I didn't fight him, instead letting him devour me as I lost myself in the distraction his kiss provided.

When he pulled away, I rested my cheek against his muscular chest.

"I will never forgive you for this, Ryker," I whispered, and I felt his body stiffen at my words.

"I don't seek your forgiveness, Cadence, only your safety."

He thought he was protecting me, but he was the biggest threat of all.

Ryker stepped back, his large hand once again engulfing mine.

"Come, wife. You need to rest."

As Ryker led me out of the chamber, I replayed the events that had brought me to this moment. My mind was a riot of emotions, each fighting for dominance as I tried to quiet the noise inside my head. Ryker's actions ignited a furious blaze within me, leaving me reeling from the chaos he created.

Above all that, however, was a tiny sliver of emotion I hadn't dared to name until now.

I was going to have a child, Ryker's child, and that knowledge filled me with… hope.

Hope that I would not suffer a life in Ryker's shadow, miserable and alone.

My fingers brushed against my stomach as the reality settled deep into my soul. A life now grew inside me, and that both frightened me and gave me strength.

I hadn't asked for any of this, but I already felt a fierce sense of protectiveness toward my child budding within me.

Ryker glanced at me from the corner of his eye, his fingers tightening around mine. It wasn't painful, but possessive, as if he feared I'd vanish the moment he let me go.

"You're quiet," he said, his voice soft but cautious.

I snatched my hand from his grip and wrapped my arms around myself in a tight embrace. Glancing over my shoulder, I found the hallway empty behind us. The others had slipped away, and I hadn't even noticed, too consumed by my churning thoughts.

"What would you like me to say, Ryker?" I spat. "That I'm happy? Grateful? I'm not."

Ryker's jaw tightened, and I could feel his anger radiating from him as he struggled to maintain his mask of indifference.

"I did what I had to, Cadence, and I won't apologize for it."

We walked in silence as we made our way back to his chamber, the tension between us thick and unrelenting.

But beneath my fury, a quiet, insidious thought lingered.

The game had only just begun.

Chapter Forty-Nine

RYKER

The door clicked shut behind me, and I rested my back against the smooth wood as I crossed my arms. Cadence disappeared into the bathing chamber, and I waited for her to finally let go, to release some of her simmering rage.

Once she had gotten it out of her system, we could both move forward with our lives.

Not a minute later, Cadence returned, her hands balled into fists at her side.

"Why Ryker?"

"You know why," I said as I studied her.

My gaze landed on her belly and the vision of her swollen with my child had my cock stiffening. I'd never thought about having children before, never particularly cared for them.

But I was now.

And only because it was her.

"Are you trying to tell me that the Night Cursed Prince, the most feared Fae in all the kingdoms, can't protect his mate?"

She cocked her hip to the side and folded her arms over her chest. At least she had given up the pretense that I wasn't her mate.

"Well," she demanded.

"I told you I had a plan, Cadence."

"And what plan would —" her words fell away, and she swayed on her feet.

I pushed off the door as I crossed the room to help her.

"Cadence, are you all right?"

"Don't come any closer," she snarled.

Her wild eyes locked on me as her face drained of color.

"You knew," she whispered.

"Knew what?"

"When you came in here earlier, you knew why I was sick. You knew I was pregnant."

Fuck.

I hadn't planned on revealing the circumstances behind her current state. When I didn't respond, she closed the distance between us, her chest heaving as she brandished her hand in the air like it was a weapon.

"What did you do, Ryker?" she demanded.

I scrubbed a hand over my face, knowing this conversation was about to turn ugly.

"I swapped out your fertility tonic," I admitted.

Cadence reeled back as if I had slapped her. Her mouth hung open as she gasped in shock.

"I told you I had a plan to secure our future. I promised you I would look after you. This is me keeping that promise, Cadence."

"You... you think that justifies any of this?" she asked incredulously.

Cadence threw her arms out wide as she gaped at me. "You had no right to take away my choice, Ryker!"

"I did it for us. For our child," I said through gritted teeth.

A bitter laugh erupted from Cadence, and tears streaked down her face.

"You only learned I was carrying your child mere hours ago. A child *you* forced me to conceive without my knowledge or consent."

Her eyes narrowed on me, pinning me in place.

"So, don't you dare say you did this for *me*," she said, her voice cracking. "You did this *to me* because it benefited *you*!"

My patience was wearing thin. I prowled toward her, forcing her to retreat until her back hit the wall. Leaning into her space, I placed my forearms on either side of her head, caging her in.

A dark, mirthless chuckle rumbled up my chest. "I did this because you refused to accept our bond. You refused to stop fighting the inevitable and surrender to your fate. At every opportunity, you reminded me you were going to leave me. That one way or another, you would escape me."

My fingers traced the intricate links of her collar, and she shivered beneath my touch.

"So yes, I stacked the deck in my favor because I couldn't stand the thought of losing you so soon after finding you."

The confession slipped free without my permission, and Cadence inhaled a sharp breath. Her chocolate-brown eyes searched mine, but whatever she was looking for, she didn't find it. Her shoulders slumped as more tears slipped down her cheeks.

"Your words are meaningless, Ryker. Everything that flows from your mouth is nothing but a sweet lie."

My hand reached toward her face, the pad of my thumb brushing the soft flesh beneath her eye. Her tears soaked my finger, and I lifted it to my lips, tasting her pain.

"Was any of it real?"

"Was any of what real?"

Her tongue darted out, and she wet her bottom lip. "At the cave, when we visited the pool, were any of the things you told me... real?"

"Every. Fucking. Word."

Cadence closed her eyes and rested her head against the wall. More tears slid down her face, and I leaned in, running my tongue up her cheek as I caught them.

My lips hovered over hers as I whispered, "I told you that you could trust me to protect you. That I would take care of you. But I warned you I would do things my way. I never lied to you, Temptress."

"A lie by omission is still a lie."

I wanted her to scream and lash out at me until all her anger dissipated. Then I'd pick up all her shattered pieces and put her back together again.

We'd move past this, and we'd be stronger for it.

But Cadence did none of that. I had destroyed the strong, confident woman who was my mate, and I had no idea how to fix what I'd broken.

"Temptress," I started, but she cut me off.

"Leave, Ryker."

It wasn't ideal, but if she needed space, I'd give her space.

I pressed my lips to her forehead, soaking in her warmth as I squeezed her hip.

"All right, Cadence, I can give you space."

She didn't meet my eyes as I stepped away, giving her the room she needed to move.

"I have some things to tend to. I'll be back soon. If you need anything, call for Scarlette."

Cadence nodded, but still didn't look in my direction. With a heavy sigh, I headed for the door.

When the lock clicked shut behind me, I rested my forehead on the wood as I took a deep breath.

A broken sob met my ears, and then Cadence started screaming. The sound was filled with so much pain, so much agony, it hurt my fucking soul.

Unable to bear it any longer, I turned away from my chambers and marched toward my father's study.

I was angry, and I needed an outlet for the raging emotions I was harboring.

If nothing else, this conversation was long overdue.

Chapter Fifty

RYKER

The hallways of the palace were silent as I walked through the towering columns, my footsteps echoing off the marble floors as I went. It was as if the entire palace could feel the energy radiating from me in waves and steered clear of my destructive wrath.

That wouldn't spare my father, though.

I pushed through the heavy wooden doors that led to his private study and took in the scene before me. My father sat perched in his armchair by the fireplace, and occupying the seat next to him was Lord Barrington.

Two for one, perfect.

I headed over to the wine cabinet and retrieved my father's favorite vintage before pouring myself a generous serving.

"By all means, Ryker, help yourself," my father drawled.

Ignoring him, I raised the goblet to my lips and drank greedily. The earthy taste slid over my tongue, and I savored the mix of flavors as I organized my thoughts.

After I had drained the contents, I lowered my cup and met my father's icy stare. His demeanor was cold, as though he could freeze the very air around him. He leaned forward in his chair, his piercing gaze fixed on me.

"Well, boy, don't keep us in suspense," my father taunted, and Lord Barrington snickered.

A malicious smile lifted my lips, and Lord Barrington cleared his throat. I ignored him, instead meeting my father's gaze.

The tension grew taut between us. One wrong move, and it would snap.

"Say whatever it is you have come to say, Ryker," my father demanded, his voice deep and authoritative.

I rolled my empty goblet lazily in my palm as I continued to stare at him.

"I have come to inform you that I have chosen to end my engagement to Lady Barrington."

My tone was even, giving away no hint of my turbulent emotions as my shadows simmered beneath the surface of my skin.

"I will not marry Celeste."

The silence that followed my declaration was deafening.

My father's expression didn't change, but Lord Barrington's face grew crimson with rage.

"Care to repeat yourself, Son?"

I shrugged, unbothered. "You heard me well enough the first time."

A vein at my father's temple began to hammer wildly as he clenched his jaw. I could feel the weight of his ire like a physical presence, but he no longer held the upper hand. While I may not be salivating at the thought of provoking civil unrest, with Cadence and my child in the mix, I would face it head-on.

"I have taken another wife, and she carries the heir to the Unseelie throne. The bond has been sealed, and it cannot be undone."

"You did what?" my father said, his voice low and brimming with venom.

I straightened to my full height and let my shadows darken my eyes as I reminded my father exactly who he was dealing with.

My father stood, too enraged to heed the warning.

"YOU DARE DEFY ME!" he roared. "I am your King. Do you have any idea what you have done?"

"I understand perfectly," I said, letting him hear the amusement in my tone. "I have undermined your efforts to leash me, and while I can appreciate that may upset you, I would caution you against doing *anything* you'd regret."

My voice was sharp and dangerous, denoting the threat that my words promised.

“Strengthening our alliance with the Barringtons was crucial for safeguarding your path to the throne, boy. Yet you cast it aside as if it were meaningless.”

I tossed my head back and laughed without restraint. I wondered if my father even heard himself.

As I reined in my laughter, I stared him down, letting him see the truth of my words.

“There is no threat to my ascension, Father. Even if there was, there is no Fae within this kingdom who could challenge me and win. My betrothal has always been about what benefited you. I only indulged your whims because I saw no reason to refuse them. Now that has changed.”

“Foolish boy,” my father scoffed. “You risk a civil war for some whore.”

I grinned at him, but it was far from friendly.

“Careful, Father,” I warned. “You’re dancing awfully close to death.”

Lord Barrington jumped from his seat, indignant rage mottling his features, and seemingly unaware of the tension that had built to a breaking point.

“You humiliate my daughter by ending your betrothal, and I won’t allow such an offense to go unanswered.”

He breathed in heaving pants, and sweat covered his face.

“Have the problem taken care of, and then do your duty to the Unseelie Fae and prove you’re fit to rule them,” he demanded.

I turned toward him, my shadows seeping from me as they spread throughout the room. My fangs descended, and the sharp prick of pain was a welcome distraction from the fury that was tearing through my body. I lifted my shoulders, and my wings burst free, causing the man in front of me to stumble back as he called on the gods to protect him.

I tsked as I prowled toward the sniveling man, and his face contorted with terror. The smell of piss filled my nostrils, and I peered down at the man's trousers, which were steadily growing damper.

My lip curled in disgust. I'd pity the man if I were capable of such an emotion.

"You forget yourself, Lord Barrington," I taunted, as I moved closer. "For far too long, you have bathed in the false radiance of the crown, believing yourself untouchable."

"P-please," Lord Barrington stammered.

"But you forget the true power of the Unseelie Kingdom hides in the shadows. And try as you might, there is no keeping the shadows at bay."

With a flick of my wrist, I sent my shadows surging forward. They extinguished the light in the room as they wrapped around Lord Barrington with terrifying speed, holding him in place.

The man struggled against his bindings, and his fear fueled my power.

"Not so demanding now, are you, Lord Barrington?"

His struggles became frantic as I plunged the chamber into darkness, my shadows spreading to each corner, swallowing every remnant of light.

"You thought you'd leashed the Night Cursed Prince," I said as I barked out a laugh.

The sound was unhinged, deranged, tortured even. I should have been concerned that I was enjoying myself so much.

But I wasn't.

Instead, I let the madness in and embraced it like an old friend.

"You thought you could intimidate me. You thought you could pull on my leash, and I would bow my head in submission," I mocked.

My shadows pulsed as they snaked around the man's throat, and a strangled sound passed between his lips.

I cocked my head to the side as I listened to Lord Barrington beseeching the gods to save him.

"Lord Barrington," I teased. "I never knew you took your faith so seriously."

I could hear my father calling out to me, begging for me to put an end to things as he struggled to see past my shadows.

Moving around the trembling Lord, I positioned myself at his back and brought my lips to the shell of his ear.

"I'll let you in on a little secret," I whispered, as desperate sobs wracked the man's body. "The gods aren't listening."

I threw my head back and slammed my fangs into the side of his neck, piercing his jugular. Blood gushed from the wound, drenching his tunic, and I felt his pulse slow as his life left him.

When his heart ceased beating, I retracted my fangs and let his body fall unceremoniously to the floor.

I didn't bother to clean the blood smearing my face as I recalled my shadows, letting the light flood the room once more.

My father's gaze landed on the crumpled body of Lord Barrington, and he sucked in a ragged breath. He lifted his head to look at me, and his eyes were wild with fear.

"What have you done?"

I stalked toward him, planting myself right in front of him as I stared him down. My father shrank away from me, and the action gave me a sick sense of satisfaction.

"The same thing I will do to anyone who threatens my wife or child," I growled.

I waved my hand in Lord Barrington's direction, and my father's eyes followed before he could stop himself.

"Let this serve as a warning," I said, never taking my eyes off him. "Father or not, if you come after Cadence, I will end you."

With the threat of my words hanging between us, I stalked from my father's study, eager to return to my wife.

Chapter Fifty-One

RYKER

It had been six days, fourteen hours, and thirty-three minutes since Cadence had uttered a single word to me.

After I had dealt with my father, I'd returned to my chambers to find her staring out the window. When I spoke, she didn't even look at me. It had been that way ever since.

But she didn't maintain her silence entirely.

She gladly entertained Riordan or Malesh whenever they checked on her. She spent her days laughing and chatting with my brother and best friend as though she'd known them all of her life and their company was all she needed to be happy in this world.

Had I thought about murdering both of them and laying their heads at her feet as some kind of ceremonial offering?

Absolutely.

More than once.

But I also knew that this was my fault. I just didn't know how to fix it.

Cadence's silence was slowly killing me. Every second I went without her sweet voice filling my ears was like having a dull blade slice into my chest. My blackened heart, which I'd long since believed incapable of beating, now thundered madly as though it were trying to tear its way free in a vain attempt to get to her.

And it was fucking agony.

I peered at myself in the mirror over the wash basin. Dark circles colored the skin beneath my eyes, and my hair was begging for a comb. My tunic was rumpled, and I couldn't remember changing it from the previous day.

I looked like shit.

My thoughts were too consumed with the woman who loathed my presence.

I dipped my hands into the basin and cupped some water. The cool liquid felt refreshing as I splashed it across my face, clearing my mind and sharpening my focus.

This couldn't go on. I needed to end this impasse. Right fucking now.

I strode from the bathing chamber and found Cadence in the same spot I'd left her — staring out the window.

"Cadence," I said, my tone measured.

When she didn't respond or even glance my way, I released a controlled breath as I ran my hand through my hair. My gaze traced the curve of her face and the set of her jaw. She was stubborn and unyielding, my mate.

I moved across the room and retrieved a tumbler from the cabinet. I poured myself two fingers of whisky and raised the glass to my lips. The burn of the alcohol went some way to temper my mounting frustration.

"Cadence," I tried again, softer this time. "Talk to me. Yell and scream if you want to. Call me a bastard and curse me in this life and the next. Hit me, punch me, cut me. I don't care. Just... say *something*. Anything."

My voice dropped to a whisper as I pleaded with her. "Please, Temptress."

Still, she said nothing.

Cadence continued to stare out the window as though I didn't exist.

My hands curled into fists, and shadows flowed from me without permission. My magic was restless, mirroring my inner turmoil.

I was losing my fucking mind.

I marched toward her, stopping a few feet away, and waited for her to acknowledge me as I looked down at her small frame.

She didn't look up.

"Cadence," I growled, my frustration getting the best of me. "I can't..."

My words died on my tongue, not wanting her to hear the desperation in my tone.

But then my resolve snapped.

Fuck it. I was desperate.

"Cadence, I can't withstand this anymore. Your silence is worse than any torture I've ever endured."

Her jaw tightened, but she did not speak.

I dropped to my knees in front of her, casting aside my pride as desperation clawed at me, tearing me apart from the inside. My hands gripped the arms of her chair, and I turned it toward me.

I leaned in, my face mere inches from hers.

"Fuck, Cadence, I need you," I whispered. "I need to hear your voice. Hurt me if it'll bring you some godsdamn peace, but don't sit there and pretend I don't exist."

Cadence's eyes flicked to mine, and the brief acknowledgment made my heart stutter. But her gaze was cold and unreadable. It pierced deeper than any blade ever could.

For a moment, I thought I saw a shimmer of emotion in her chocolate depths, but it vanished as quickly as it had appeared. Her lips parted, and I inhaled sharply, praying to the gods for the first time in my life that she was about to end my misery and speak to me.

Instead, she exhaled a soft breath and turned away from me, staring back out the window into nothingness.

"What would you have me do, Cadence?" I begged. "Do you want me to carve my heart from my chest and place it in your hands? I'll do it. Just say the words."

Cadence rolled her eyes as if I wasn't ready to do just that.

"Tell me how to fix this."

But Cadence only pressed her lips together in a tight line, denying me any hope of my salvation.

A low growl rumbled in my chest as frustration and despair warred within me. I sat back on my heels before pushing myself to my feet and pacing the room as if I were a caged animal. My magic thrummed beneath my skin like a furious tempest, and I resisted the urge to pull Cadence across my knee and spank the defiance out of her.

As much as my cock stirred at the thought, something told me she wouldn't be agreeable to that idea.

I raked my fingers through my hair, gripping the strands as I tugged.

I welcomed the pain.

Any distraction from the thick, oppressive silence that stretched between us was a welcome one. My control was slipping under the weight of her indifference, and I knew that if I didn't rein myself in, I'd only push her further away.

I stalked toward her again, my footsteps light but deliberate. Cadence tensed, and her body went rigid. But she still wouldn't look at me.

Once more, I lowered myself to my knees. I took her hands in mine, and when she didn't pull away, I thanked the gods for that small mercy.

"If you don't want to speak to me, that's fine."

It wasn't.

I figured I had one day left in me at best before I lost it and did something foolish.

"I'll talk, and you can listen."

Cadence shifted in her seat, and that was all the encouragement I needed to continue.

"I know I fucked up. I understand my actions have hurt you, and while you may not believe me, my main priority has always been your safety."

Cadence snorted, and I couldn't help the smirk that lifted my lips.

"Fine, I was also driven by an insatiable need to keep you at my side. To mark you in a way that everyone would know exactly who you belonged to."

That got a reaction out of her.

Cadence turned to face me. Her eyes narrowed in disapproval, and her lips pulled up in a sneer.

Fuck!

She was most beautiful when she looked ready to end my life with her bare hands.

"I might be a monster, Cadence, but I'm a monster who'd do anything to keep you safe. No matter how reprehensible. Even if it means you hate me for it."

I paused, searching her eyes for any sign that my words were getting through.

"I won't lie to you and tell you that I regret stealing you away or deceiving you into carrying my child or making you my wife."

Cadence stiffened, but I pressed on.

"But I do regret that my actions hurt you."

I waved my hand between us as I said, "This is all new to me, Temptress. Despite how it looks, I am trying to be the man you need. It won't happen overnight, and I'll probably fuck up more than I succeed, but I'm committed to doing better by you. I want to be the mate you deserve."

Cadence met my determined gaze, and this time, she saw me, really saw me. She scanned my face, studying every detail as if seeing me for the first time.

My heart hammered inside my chest, and I bit my tongue to stop myself from filling the silence, giving her the space to come to me of her own volition.

Any hope of reaching Cadence vanished as she turned away.

Just like every time before.

With a resigned sigh, I stood and headed toward the door.

It was time for a different approach.

Chapter Fifty-Two

CADENCE

Ryker had left me alone for the rest of the day, only returning late in the afternoon to inform me that the King had requested our attendance at dinner.

As he led me into the dining hall, the grandeur of the space was impossible to ignore.

The high vaulted ceilings drew my gaze upward, and I studied the intricate patterns carved into the beams overhead. I couldn't make out the finer details of the design from where I stood, and yet, it captivated me, reeling me in and making it difficult to look away.

In the center of the hall, a grand table stretched the length of the room, set with glittering crystal goblets and the finest porcelain I had ever seen. An array of mouthwatering dishes lined the tabletop, and I had to wonder if we were expecting company, given the amount of food that had been prepared.

The entire dining hall was designed with comfort in mind, and yet, no room had ever felt more oppressive.

Tension rippled beneath Ryker's composed exterior as he pulled my chair out for me. All the while, his father, the King of the Unseelie, glared at him from his seat at the table.

"Your Majesty," I said as I bowed my head in acknowledgment of his station.

He grunted in answer, but his eyes never strayed from his son.

As we sat in awkward silence, the only saving grace I could find was that Riordan had also been summoned to join us. I shifted uncomfortably in my seat, and the King's piercing gaze turned to me. He had stormy grey eyes, the same shade as Ryker's, and they seemed to bore into me as if he were searching for all my secrets.

"Cadence," Ryker rumbled next to me, but I studiously ignored him, instead focusing my attention on his brother.

"I didn't see you today, Riordan. What mischief did you get up to in my absence?"

Ryker's expression was unreadable as he piled my plate with every sort of vegetable and meat imaginable, but the faint tick of his jaw betrayed his displeasure. I speared a baked potato and popped it into my mouth as I waited for him to answer. Riordan chuckled and shook his head, but he was enjoying himself more than he'd admit.

"I missed you too, sweetheart," he winked. "Alas, your tiresome husband had me tending to some matters on his behalf."

He tipped his goblet in Ryker's direction before taking a sip.

"You know how wonderful his people skills are."

"What business?" the King called, reclaiming our attention.

"It's a personal matter," Ryker snapped.

The King raised an eyebrow, but he didn't challenge his eldest son. The air between them was charged, crackling like a storm on the brink of unleashing.

"So," the King began as he heaped food onto his plate. "This is the woman you have chosen for your wife, Ryker."

It wasn't a question but a statement, and it was dripping with disapproval.

"Careful, Father," Ryker warned, but the man appeared unfazed.

"Tell me, Cadence, what qualifies you to be the future Queen of the Unseelie?"

"The fact that she is my wife," Ryker barked before I could answer.

For a moment, his shadows broke through his hold, curling around the base of his chair before he forced them to retreat.

Riordan gave me a conspiratorial grin as he said, "Aren't you glad that you accepted Father's invitation to dinner?"

As much as I tried, I couldn't help the small smile that pulled up my lips.

"Riordan," his father snarled, but whatever he was about to say was interrupted when the heavy doors at the far end of the hall creaked open.

Everyone turned to see the newcomer, and dread filled the pit of my stomach when Celeste strolled into the room.

"My apologies, My King," she said demurely. "I was delayed as the healers stopped by my chambers to discuss funeral arrangements."

Her gaze flicked to Ryker, but she didn't look upon him with the hatred I had expected.

That, she saved for me.

Her upper lip curled in disdain as she approached the table, her narrowed eyes never leaving mine.

Gods, you would think that *I* was the one who had murdered her father in cold blood.

"No apology necessary, Celeste," the King said. "Come. Join us."

Celeste's white gown trailed behind her, and her alabaster skin glowed beneath the light as she took her seat.

It wasn't lost on me that she looked like a bride joining her wedding feast.

Ryker's expression darkened, and his fingers twitched as he reached for his goblet.

"How are you finding my seat, Cadence?" Celeste asked with feigned innocence.

"It's rather fitting. Thank you for asking."

Across from me, Riordan spluttered into his goblet, and I could feel the heat of Ryker's gaze on the side of my face.

"That's news to me," he whispered against my ear so that only I could hear.

Ignoring him, I kept my focus fixed on Celeste. A scowl twisted her delicate features, and she looked as though she was a moment away from jumping across the table to strangle me.

Then she turned her attention to the King, her expression softening. "You must understand my frustration, Your Majesty. My family has given so much to this court, only to be discarded with no explanation."

Ryker's large palm ran down my thigh before he gripped the fabric of my skirt in his fist and tugged it up my leg.

"What the hell are you doing?" I hissed as I adjusted myself to face him.

Ryker smirked back at me, one eyebrow lifted in amusement. "She speaks," he gasped, as he raised the material higher.

"Yes, my son's actions have been most disappointing," the King replied as Ryker slipped his hand beneath my skirt, his fingers brushing the edge of my panties.

My throat tightened, and I reached for my goblet. The cool liquid did little to ease the heat now rushing to my face. Ryker's fingertips dipped below my waistband, and I tried to clench my thighs together to prevent him from going any further.

"The Barringtons have been loyal subjects of the crown, and I am aghast that things between our families have ended this way," the King continued.

Celeste nodded in agreement, and the hungry shimmer in her eyes betrayed her intentions.

Ryker's calloused finger traced the length of my entrance, and my cheeks flamed, knowing he would find me wet and ready for him.

"You're soaked, Temptress," he rumbled before he pushed a finger inside me.

I gripped the edge of the table to steady myself as I inhaled a shaky breath.

"There must be something that can be done," Celeste pleaded, and the King glanced in our direction.

I kept my eyes trained on my plate, and Ryker chuckled beside me.

"Don't beg, Celeste. It makes you look pathetic," he snickered as he pushed another finger inside me.

"Stop. Now."

I hardly got the words out as I ground my teeth together. Ryker ignored me as he rubbed circles around my clit, and I had to bite the inside of my cheek to keep from moaning out loud.

"Cadence?" Riordan asked. "Are you all right?"

My hand shook as I gripped my goblet, and the moment the cool crystal met my lips, I drank greedily.

"Mm-hmm," I hummed, unable to form words.

I could hear how wet I was as Ryker pumped his fingers in and out of me, and I was certain everyone else could hear it, too.

"How much do you need to come right now, Temptress?" Ryker murmured as he increased his pace.

My hand moved of its own volition as I gripped Ryker's forearm. I didn't know if I was trying to push him away or hold him in place. My mind needed him to stop, but my body screamed that I might die if he did.

Ryker had played me so effortlessly, winding me up until I was vibrating with the need for release. And judging by the predatory grin that spread across his face, the sick bastard knew it too.

"I can keep going all night, Temptress. If this is the only way I can get you to speak to me, then I'm happy to oblige."

Ryker swirled the pad of his thumb around my sensitive nub, and I damn near saw stars.

"Ryker."

I'd meant for the single word to be a warning, but I panted his name like I was begging for more.

"What do you need, Temptress? Do you even know?"

"No," I admitted before I could stop myself.

Ryker's grin widened in triumph as he pushed his fingers inside me with vigor. This time, I did moan, but I covered the sound with a cough. I had no idea if I was fooling anyone, but at that moment, I didn't care. It had been almost a week since I'd let Ryker touch me, and my body was starved for him.

The sounds of murmured chatter surrounded me, but it was indistinguishable as the blood pounding in my ears drowned out everything else.

I was close.

Ryker pinched my clit, and I turned toward him, burying my face in his tunic as I came undone. His fingers continued to move inside me as waves of pleasure wracked my body. As the tremors slowly waned, my breathing evened out, and I was thrust back to reality.

Now that it was over, my cheeks burned with embarrassment, and I refused to lift my head from Ryker's chest. Understanding my distress, Ryker lifted me into his arms and cradled me against him.

"Cadence isn't feeling well," he announced before pressing his mouth to my forehead.

"Do you need me to do anything?" Riordan asked, and I could feel the twitch of Ryker's lips against my skin. "I have it in hand, Brother."

Without another word, Ryker strode from the dining hall, taking me and my mortification with him.

Chapter Fifty-Three

CADENCE

As soon as Ryker crossed the threshold of his chambers, I sprang from his arms, my body trembling with rage and the need to destroy him.

"What the hell was that?"

Ryker stalked toward me, and I backed away, all too familiar with the game he was playing.

"That, sweet Cadence," he purred as he moved closer, "was me putting an end to this godsforsaken impasse we have been dancing around for days."

"And you think simply declaring it will make me obey," I scoffed.

Without warning, Ryker lunged for me, his muscular arms wrapped around my body as he tossed me over his shoulder and strode toward the bed.

"Put me down!"

Ryker's hand came down on my ass with a punishing force and I jolted forward.

"What... what the hell was that for?"

"This has gone on for too long, Cadence, and we're going to thrash this out right now."

Ryker dropped me onto the mattress before he climbed on top of me, straddling my waist. He gathered my hands in his larger ones and pinned them above my head. I struggled against his grip, but quickly realized I wasn't going anywhere.

Huffing out a breath, I returned my gaze to his. Steel-grey eyes stared down at me, and a smirk twisted his lips.

"Are you ready to behave?" he rumbled, the sound vibrating up his chest and settling in my core.

"Say whatever it is you have to say, Ryker."

I pressed my thighs together to alleviate the mounting tension, and Ryker's nostrils flared.

"Is there something you need, Cadence?"

"For you to get off me," I snapped.

Ryker chuckled, letting me know that my attempt to distract him had failed miserably.

"How about this?" he mused.

He leaned in close as he pressed his lips to the pulse point at the base of my throat. His tongue darted out, and he made his way to the shell of my ear before biting down.

"For every answer you give me, I'll reward you."

"What kind of reward?" I blurted, before I could think better of it.

I stifled the groan that fought to break free in admonishment of my stupidity.

"The kind that will have you screaming my name."

My breath hitched as his words sent a shiver racing down my spine. I tried to maintain my composure, but my body betrayed me, arching into his and begging him for more.

"And if I refuse to answer?" I challenged, my voice just above a whisper.

Ryker's eyes darkened, and a predatory gleam flickered in their stormy depths.

"Then, Temptress, I'll be forced to punish you."

"That's not the deterrent you think it is."

Ryker threw his head back and laughed raucously. It was then that I realized I'd voiced that thought aloud. My cheeks heated, and I looked away.

Rough fingers pinched my chin as Ryker angled my face toward him.

"Do not hide from me, Temptress," he murmured, his free hand trailing down my side.

His fingertips ghosted over my ribcage, igniting a trail of fire in their wake. I swallowed hard as my mind raced. Part of me wanted to give in, to surrender to the desire that had been building between us.

It was torture, denying yourself the one thing you craved.

But another part of me, the part that was stubborn and defiant, refused to yield so easily. Ryker had violated me in ways he could never understand, and I wasn't sure I could ever forgive him for that.

"Your first question," Ryker whispered. "Why are you so determined to deny fate?"

"Because you're an insufferable fool who takes what he wants despite the cost to anyone else," I deadpanned.

Ryker shifted above me, and his hard length pressed against my center. He rolled his hips, and I bit my lip to stifle a moan.

"See? That wasn't so difficult now, was it, Cadence?"

I watched, transfixed, as he slid further down my body and bunched my skirt around my hips. His fingers gripped the waistband of my panties, and he slowly drew them down my legs. His touch ignited a fire in my core, and I was ablaze with need.

"Are you afraid of me, Cadence?"

"Afraid of you?" I scoffed.

"I see how you struggle. The way you're constantly fighting this pull between us. Even after everything I have done to you, you're terrified that I could be exactly what you need."

I opened my mouth to retort, but quickly shut it.

I wanted to deny it, to deny him. But there was a part of me, buried deep inside, that knew he was right.

I was afraid.

I was afraid that all the pain and suffering I had clung to over the years wasn't enough to overcome the visceral need I felt toward Ryker. Every part of him called to me, and the longer I stayed with him, the closer I came to giving in.

After all this time, what did that mean for me? That I could fall so easily into the arms of my enemy.

Ryker pressed his tongue flat against my entrance, and my hips bucked, begging for more.

"You may not always agree with my methods, Cadence. So fight me, scream at me, hate me if you must. But I won't let you push me away again. Not now, not ever. Do you understand?"

The conviction in his voice terrified me as much as it excited me.

"You drive me mad, woman," he snarled before he thrust his tongue inside me, setting an unrelenting rhythm.

"Gods, Ryker," I cried as he brought me to oblivion.

My thighs trembled under the intensity of my orgasm, and I didn't have time to catch my breath before Ryker crashed his lips against mine, forcing me to taste myself.

When he broke the kiss, he was panting heavily, his chest heaving with emotion as he stared down at me.

"I can't live without your fire, your defiance, your voice," he murmured. "I can't live without you."

His words struck me like a boulder to the chest, and I felt my armor crack under the weight of his declaration.

"If I have to drag you to the edge of reason to get you to speak to me, then so be it."

"You're infuriating," I whispered, my voice trembling.

"And you're intoxicating."

"I still can't forgive you, Ryker."

"I can wait."

The outline of Ryker's erect cock pressed against my entrance, and I rubbed myself against him, inviting him closer.

"Cadence," he groaned. "Stop trying to distract me."

"Is it working?"

"You know it is."

The air grew heavy around us, and I didn't dare breathe in case it shattered the fragile peace we'd achieved as we teetered on the edge of something I couldn't quite name.

Ryker pulled back, his eyes searching mine.

"I am going to fix what I broke between us, Cadence," he promised.

"How can you fix it when I don't trust you, Ryker?"

"Do you trust me enough to let me try?"

I hesitated, feeling the weight of my answer bearing down on me.

"Maybe," I whispered, unsure if that was the truth.

A wide grin split Ryker's handsome face as he said, "That's good enough for now."

Reaching into his trousers, Ryker freed his thick cock as he groaned, "I need to be inside you."

I spread my legs wider and purred, "Then what are you waiting for?"

"There will be no more secrets, Cadence," he rumbled as he lined himself up with my center. "From here on out, I'll tell you everything."

Ryker thrust his hips forward, and the sensation of him filling me felt like coming home.

As much as I wished it were different, Ryker's vow changed nothing. Because his vow was built upon deception. There were things he didn't know about me, and I had no intention of changing that.

Chapter Fifty-Four

CADENCE

Something was wrong.

I could feel a shift in the air that told me danger lurked nearby, but I couldn't detect the source of my unease. Apprehension wrapped around me, choking me until I felt like I was unable to breathe.

Not even the palace escaped the eerie sense of foreboding.

Instead of the usual opulence, a light fog obscured the daylight, muting everything. The crystal chandeliers hung overhead, but their soft glow did little to illuminate the space. The polished marble floors echoed louder than they should, making it seem like faint whispers were brushing against my flesh.

My skin prickled, and the hairs on the back of my neck stood on end. As I peered around me, I noticed the corridor was completely desolate. I couldn't recall when I last encountered a servant or a guard.

I picked up my pace and headed toward the chambers I shared with Ryker. The silence was suffocating. With each step, the feeling of unseen eyes grew more oppressive. As I rounded the corner, I couldn't contain my sigh of relief.

The comfort was short-lived, however, as the surrounding air turned frigid. It was as though my body was trying to warn me, but no matter how hard I tried, I couldn't understand the sense of dread that was pulling me under.

My eyes darted around, and my pulse quickened as I searched for something, anything, that would explain my mounting panic.

"Pull yourself together, Cadence," I snapped, but the words sounded hollow, as if my mind remembered the last time I dismissed my instincts.

All those months ago, when I had ventured home from the marketplace, I knew that danger had followed me to my apothecary. I had played it off as a trick of my imagination, and the next thing I knew, I woke to find myself trapped in the Unseelie Kingdom.

I wouldn't be so foolish a second time.

I drew my magic around me as I reached for the door handle, but something made me hesitate. My fingers trembled as they brushed against the cool metal, and then I noticed a faint odor in the air. I couldn't discern what it was exactly, but the smell churned my stomach.

I braced myself, pushed the door open, and stepped inside.

Unnatural darkness bathed the room, but through the bond, I sensed it wasn't Ryker's doing.

My attention snapped to the billowing curtains. The window I had closed this morning was now wide open.

Cautiously, I inched toward the window. I peered down at the courtyard, which was devoid of its usual hustle and bustle, and repressed the shiver that threatened to break free. I slammed the pane shut, hoping it would block out the unsettling feelings slowly drowning me.

But I was wrong.

Very wrong.

I felt their presence before I saw them, lurking in the shadows, waiting to strike.

As though they sensed my revelation, a low hiss broke the silence, and I spun around as a figure lunged from the darkness.

Dressed in black with their face concealed underneath the hood of their cloak, the figure aimed a strike at my throat. I thanked the gods for Malesh's dedication to my training as my reflexes kicked in, and I deflected the blow with my forearm before darting to the side.

I scanned the room for a weapon but found none.

A faint throb began in my arm, and I glanced down to see that I hadn't escaped the assault unscathed. Crimson stained my tunic, and I sent my magic racing to the site to stem the flow.

As I faced my assailant again, an unexpected kick to my ribcage flung me across the room, slamming me into the edge of the bedpost. I groaned in pain as breathing became difficult.

That fucking hurt.

I diverted my power to the fresh injury, and, as expected, I found three broken ribs. The figure prowled toward me, their movements fluid and graceful, as a feral grin stretched across their face.

"You were told to leave," a low, masculine voice taunted me.

I stood on shaky feet, keeping the man's attention trained on me as I worked my magic.

"Yeah, well, I've been told I'm stubborn like that."

"Foolish," the man hissed.

His tone was chilling, and goosebumps rose on my skin.

"Did you think being bonded to the prince meant you were safe here?"

I didn't get the chance to respond as he lunged again, slashing his blade at me. I ducked in time to avoid the brunt of his strike, but I still wasn't fast enough to escape without injury. Red hot pain seared my shoulder, and I could feel the warmth of my blood as it trickled down my arm.

The man laughed maniacally, and the sound grated against my ears like broken glass.

"Who sent you?" I demanded, trying to inject as much authority as I could manage into my tone.

"You should worry more about what I intend to do to you."

I rolled my eyes despite the fear that gnawed at me. "It's pretty obvious, don't you think?"

The man sneered, his upper lip curling as he glared at me from beneath his hood. Without warning, he lunged at me again. I raised my arm in a feeble attempt to block the strike, and this time, he didn't simply graze me with his blade. He drove it into my forearm with such force that the tip pierced the other side.

Pain surged through me, and I fought the overwhelming urge to vomit. I could hear the man moving around me, but the sound was muffled. A buzzing sound erupted in my ears, and my vision blurred as I stumbled away from my attacker.

He gripped the hilt of the dagger before he ripped it from my arm. Agony shot through my entire body, and I cried out, unable to contain the sound of my pain. Cruel laughter surrounded me as I fought to remain conscious. I needed a reprieve, a moment where I could focus on healing my injuries without the threat of my death looming over me.

Today was not my day, however.

The man charged straight for me, gripping my hips as he lifted me before driving me into the ground. One swift movement knocked the breath out of me, and it took a while for my mind to catch up. Then my lungs inflated, and it was as if I was inhaling fire, the burning pain almost unbearable.

But I refused to lie down and die that easily.

My heart pounded against my ribs as I scrambled to my feet and prepared to break the oath I'd made to my mother. I called on my dormant magic, and my veins flooded with power. I could feel my body repairing itself as I faced off against the man sent to end my life.

"You look far too confident for someone about to die," he mocked.

I grinned, letting the menace show in my expression. "I could say the same about you."

He barked out a laugh before he surged toward me.

My hand clasped his wrists, and a shockwave of energy burst free on contact. My magic seeped into him before he had the chance to utter a single word. His jaw dropped, and his skin tightened as I drained the life from his body. His fingers curled into skeletal claws as they pressed against the gaunt, shriveled skin. His flesh withered, and his eyes rolled back, leaving only the black abyss of his sockets.

When it was done, all that remained was an empty, fragile husk that was beyond recognition.

I was panting heavily when I released my hold on my attacker, and his remains fell to the cold, hard floor.

"Cadence," a familiar voice whispered from the doorway.

I spun around to see Ryker staring at the man lying at my feet. His mouth opened and closed as he took in the scene before his steel-grey eyes settled on me.

His gaze narrowed, and his lips pressed into a thin line.

Then he rumbled the two words I'd been hiding from my entire life.

"Wraith Borne."

Chapter Fifty-Five

CADENCE

Ryker slammed the door with such force that the walls vibrated, and I flinched, unable to hide my terror.

I took in his rigid stance. His broad shoulders were tense, and his hands were clenched into fists at his sides. His storm-grey eyes surveyed me, wild and furious.

I stepped back as my heart hammered inside my chest. The heat of his anger was palpable, radiating in waves that made the walls press in around me.

Shadows swirled at Ryker's feet, thick and menacing, as they slowly climbed up his body. He didn't seem to realize that his hold on his power was slipping.

His entire focus was locked on me.

"You lied to me," he growled.

His voice was low, and it was edged with some emotion I couldn't discern.

"Last night, you sat here and agreed we'd keep no more secrets from each other."

I swallowed hard, forcing myself to meet his gaze.

"I agreed to nothing, Ryker, and I didn't lie."

The words sounded weak, even to my ears.

Ryker chuckled, but there was no humor in it. His expression darkened, and he curled his lip in a sneer.

"What was it you said to me, Cadence?" he mused. "A lie by omission is still a lie."

The venom in his tone made my chest tighten.

"Yet, you wove the greatest deception of all."

He glanced at the dead man, then at me, his gaze heavy with condemnation.

My spine stiffened as outrage and defiance rose within me. I kept my secret because I knew if it got out, I would be killed without question. Our situation was not the same.

"I owe you nothing, Ryker," I snarled.

My blood pounded in my veins as my anger anchored me.

"Try again, Cadence."

"You think just because you made promises to me after you did something unforgivable that I'm supposed to give in and share every secret of my own?"

"Yes!"

"Then you're delusional." My chest heaved as I glared at him, and he glared right back.

"You are responsible for the near eradication of the Wraith Borne," I spat. "You're the last person I would ever confide in."

For the briefest moment, hurt flickered across Ryker's face, but he quickly schooled his features.

"And I'd do it again."

His words were sharper than any blade, and I flinched despite myself.

"So, you admit to massacring my family," I said, as I built a wall around my heart.

"What are you talking about, Cadence? Your family is very much alive last I checked."

"I'm talking about my parents."

"Again, they're safe and well in the Seelie Kingdom."

"They're not my parents," I murmured.

"Cut the bullshit, Cadence, and tell me what the fuck you're talking about."

"They're not my parents," I repeated. "They're my aunt and uncle."

For a moment, Ryker's anger faltered, and something softer shone in his eyes.

"Are you Unseelie?"

"Half," I admitted. "My father was Unseelie and one of the Wraith Borne."

"But I've seen you heal others. Fuck, you've healed me. How can that be if you're Wraith Borne?"

"I'm not *only* Wraith Borne. My mother was Seelie. I inherited my healing abilities from her."

"You received both strains of magic?" Ryker asked, and I could hear the wonder in his tone.

A child usually inherited their magical abilities from one of their parents, but rarely both. Of course, the fact that most Fae married within their kingdom meant it wasn't unusual for their parents to share similar magic.

To suggest a Seelie Fae wed an Unseelie Fae was almost tantamount to treason. But my parents had been mates, and for that, they persevered.

I nodded in answer to Ryker's question as he continued to stare at me.

"Tell me what happened to them."

I sucked in a ragged breath. Decades had passed since I'd lost my parents, but time did little to lessen the pain.

"They were killed in the uprising of the Wraith Borne. I was only five when it happened, and I'd been left with my aunt and uncle when they joined the rebellion. Their leader had convinced my father to fight, and where my father went, my mother followed."

Tears pricked the back of my eyes, but I bit my tongue, refusing to let them fall.

"They died in the attack on the palace?" Ryker asked, the pain in his voice pulling my gaze to his.

"Yes," I whispered. "It's why I can't embrace the bond we share. Because you led the assault that resulted in their deaths."

"They attacked us, Cadence," he growled as he raked a hand through his hair.

"I know," I murmured. "And I hate the Wraith Borne just as much as you do. If not for the uprising, my parents might still be alive."

Ryker's shoulders slumped as though my words brought him some relief.

"Even so, I can't forgive the role you played in their demise. Besides, it wasn't as if the rebellion was without cause."

Ryker's gaze snapped back to mine as he stalked toward me.

"What are you trying to say, Cadence?"

He was within reach now, but I kept my arms locked at my sides.

"You know as well as I do that your father had been turning the Unseelie against the Wraith Borne long before the rebellion. He feared their power, and so he wove a narrative that suited his end goal, which was the cleansing of my kind. I may despise the Wraith Borne, but can you honestly say that your family's hands are any less bloodied?"

Ryker's eyes narrowed dangerously, and the tension coiled tight between us.

"Don't pretend you know my story, Cadence."

"Oh, because you're such an open book," I scoffed.

I crossed my arms over my chest and glared at him as my anger intensified, matching his.

"I never wanted this, Ryker. I didn't ask for this magic, this bond, this fucking life. But I'm here, trying to survive it the only way I know how."

Ryker eliminated the space between us, his hot breath fanning across my lips as he exhaled.

"Survive?" he repeated, his voice deadly calm. "You think keeping secrets like this from me is how you survive? Do you know what would have happened to you if anyone had found out about this before I did?"

"Do you think me a fool?" I snapped. "This has been my entire life, Ryker, hence the secret. I promised my aunt that I would never reveal my magic to anyone, and I've kept that promise. Until now."

Ryker's hand shot out, and he gripped my chin as he forced me to look at him. I raised my hands in defense, the threat lingering between us. If Ryker intended to end me, I wouldn't go down without a fight.

"You think you could kill me, Temptress?" he asked with a dark edge underlying his tone.

"Yes," I lied.

"Then do it," he gritted out. "Free me from this godsforsaken bond and spare me the agony of craving your touch, every minute of every day, but knowing I'll never truly have you, because your hatred is stronger than your affection. Do. It. Cadence."

We stared at each other, our ragged breaths the only sound that cut through the suffocating silence.

"Fuck," Ryker growled, and then he slammed his lips against mine.

He laced one hand through my hair, and he squeezed the nape of my neck to the point of pain. His other hand gripped my hip, pulling me flush against his muscular frame.

Despite my better judgment, I melted into his touch. My arms wrapped around his neck, and he groaned as I deepened the kiss. His tongue warred with mine, and his teeth sank into my lip hard enough to draw blood.

Ryker stepped back, breaking our connection and leaving me panting. He ran a hand through his hair, and for a long moment, he was silent, his gaze distant as he processed my confession.

When he finally spoke, his tone was rough but confident.

"You need to stay here, Cadence," he said, his voice dripping with authority. "I mean it. Do not leave this room."

"What are you going to do?" I asked, the suspicion in my tone making him bristle.

"I'm going to ensure your safety," he rumbled as he strode toward the door.

His hand reached out and gripped the doorknob. His shoulders rose and fell with a deep breath, and he cast one last glance in my direction before he left the room.

I released a shaky breath and placed a hand on my stomach to settle the unease whirling inside me.

It was going to be all right. Ryker would protect me, just as he had promised.

But the illusion dissolved when I heard a noise that condemned Ryker forever.

The sound of the lock sliding into place.

Chapter Fifty-Six

RYKER

Wraith Borne.

Cadence was one of the Wraith Borne.

No matter how many times I repeated the words, I struggled to accept that my mate belonged to the Fae who had tried to take everything from me.

She'd killed a man with her bare hands. His body had been an empty shell by the time she finished. I wouldn't deny that such power in a mate was extremely alluring. However, I couldn't overlook the risk it posed to her safety.

As I rounded the corner of the hallway, Riordan's chambers came into view. I didn't bother knocking as I pushed his doors open and strode inside.

My first mistake.

Loud moans greeted me, and I came face to face with my little brother's naked ass. He was taking a redheaded woman from behind, and the sound of skin slapping against skin had me wanting to rip my ears off. Despite my horror, I found myself unable to look away as I tried to discern where all the limbs were coming from.

My second mistake.

"Switch," Riordan panted, and another man appeared from underneath the redhead as my brother moved in to take his place.

As the trio shuffled on the four-poster bed, a third man emerged, and I blinked to make sure I wasn't seeing things.

"What the fuck, Riordan!" I shouted, and they all froze.

My brother turned to face me, his usual carefree air clinging to him as he raised a brow in my direction.

"I would invite you to join us, Brother, but I'm fairly certain Cadence is not the type to share."

"Get out," I barked at the onlookers, and they groaned in unison as they scurried around in search of their clothes.

"I was promised an earth-shattering orgasm," the redhead complained as she slid her dress over her head.

I glanced toward my brother, and the little demon winked.

"Next time, Scarlette," Riordan cooed, and I had to do a double take.

"Is that Cadence's maid?"

"Ah, perhaps," he answered as he gripped the back of his neck.

"Get dressed," I chuckled as I grabbed his tunic from the floor and tossed it at him.

"So, to what do I owe this poorly timed visit, Ryker?" he asked as he pushed his legs through his trousers.

"I need your help."

"Oh?"

"Don't sound so cocky," I grumbled.

"It's not every day you recognize my superior intellect," he teased.

I glanced around to make sure Riordan's guests were not still lingering within earshot.

"Cadence is one of the Wraith Borne."

His smile fell, and he moved toward his armchair before dropping into it unceremoniously. He ran his hand through his already tousled hair as he fought to stifle his unease.

The look on his face made my gut clench. I was reminded of the young boy I'd protected from our father's violent fits of rage.

To say Riordan's history with the Wraith Borne was complicated would be an understatement.

I crossed the room and took the chair opposite him. Steepling my fingers, I focused on my brother as I prepared to relay everything I knew.

"Someone sent an assassin to kill her, but she took him out before he got the chance. His body is lying on my chamber floor, withered beyond recognition."

A shudder ran through Riordan, but he met my gaze.

"Is there any other explanation for how she could have killed him? A dark manifestation of her healing abilities, perhaps?"

"She's one of the Wraith Borne, Riordan. She confirmed it herself."

"Fuck."

He blew out a breath as he rubbed a hand over his jaw. I felt much the same as I sank further into the armchair.

"That's... complicated."

"Complicated doesn't begin to cover it," I scoffed.

Leaning forward in his chair, Riordan rested his elbows on his thighs.

"What do you need me to do, Ryker?" he asked, and the sincerity in his tone made my chest tighten.

"The fact that she's Wraith Borne doesn't give you pause?"

"Of course not!" he scowled as he eyed me.

I had hoped my brother wouldn't hesitate to help Cadence, but I still wanted him to know he had a choice. I would not force him to confront the ghosts of his past.

"I need access to your network. I need to find out who sent that assassin after her and if it's connected to her magic."

Riordan nodded in agreement. "If anyone else is aware of her power..."

"I know," I growled. "She'll be hunted by the Court, our father, and everyone in between."

Riordan offered me a pained smile. "If there's even a whisper out there, I promise you, Ryker, I'll find it."

"Thank you, Riordan."

My brother angled his head as he appraised me. "Where is Cadence now?"

When I failed to respond, Riordan groaned as he ran a hand down his face.

"You locked her in your chambers again, didn't you?"

"For her safety," I said through gritted teeth. "I needed her to stay put until I figured out what to do. My chambers are the safest place for her right now."

"The same place an assassin entered undetected and almost killed her?" he challenged.

I opened my mouth to argue, but fuck him, he was right.

"Besides, that's not safety, Ryker. That's imprisonment."

I stiffened, my whole body bristling at his challenge.

Riordan waved a dismissive hand between us. "Let's set aside your draconian methods for now and focus on the real problem. Do you have any idea who could have sent an assassin after her?"

"My immediate thought was Celeste, but it's not her style."

Riordan grunted in agreement, and I scratched at the stubble lining my chin.

"Whoever it was, they knew enough to get close," I mused. "It wasn't random. They understood when to attack and where."

"Do you think they know about her magic?" he pressed.

"I didn't even know about her magic," I muttered, "but I guess it's a possibility."

Riordan's eyes darkened, and I saw the wheels turning in his mind. "I'll start digging."

Unable to take being idle for a moment longer, I stood and began pacing.

"You'll need her cooperation if you're going to get to the bottom of this," Riordan said, breaking the tense silence. "Locking her up won't help you achieve that."

"I fucking know that, Riordan. You think I enjoy locking her away?"

Riordan gave me a pointed look.

I exhaled, but it came out sounding more like a growl.

"The point is, the palace isn't safe right now. I don't trust anyone."

"You can always leave her with me. I'm pretty sure she prefers my company anyway, and we'd have fun together. We could braid each other's hair, share your darkest secrets, and practice cursing you," he offered with a smile.

I stopped my pacing and turned toward my brother.

"Not a time for jokes. Noted," he muttered under his breath.

When he returned his gaze to mine, he studied me for the longest time. "Gods, you're scared, aren't you?"

It wasn't really a question, but a statement.

"I can't recall a single occasion when you were ever afraid... until now."

I shook my head and resumed my pacing, not wanting him to see the truth of his words.

"We'll protect her, Ryker, but not by smothering her. You'll need to trust her enough to let her be a part of this. She's not some fragile damsel, and you know it."

"She's resilient," I agreed. "But she is reckless. Not telling me about her magic wasn't a smart choice."

Riordan rose from his armchair and came to stand in front of me. "Try to see it from her perspective," he said, clapping his hand on my shoulder. "Our kingdom has hunted the Wraith Borne for decades, and you've led that charge."

I glared at my brother, but he merely shrugged.

"When did you become so fucking reasonable?" I sighed.

"I've always been the reasonable one. Your thick head just never appreciated it."

A laugh broke free of my chest, and I felt lighter, like some of the weight had been lifted from my shoulders.

"I'm going to get started," Riordan announced as he moved toward his desk. "I'll spread some misinformation about unrest in the outer regions, too. That way, if anyone's sniffing around, they'll have something else to chase."

"Thank you, Riordan."

As I headed for the door, Riordan called after me, stopping me in my tracks.

"Let Cadence out of your chambers, Ryker. Tell her what's going on and invite her input. If you treat her like a child or as if she's a problem you need to solve, you're going to lose her. And a woman like Cadence, well, you'd be foolish to let her slip between your fingers."

Without another word, I opened the door and stepped into the hallway.

I hated that he was right.

What I hated even more was the insidious voice in my head telling me it was already too late.

Chapter Fifty-Seven

CADENCE

Ryker had confined me to his chambers, disappearing without any hint of where he was going, and left me to stew in my roiling emotions.

Again.

He'd cut me off from the outside world with no means of escape, holding me prisoner until he decided my fate.

That thought churned in my mind as I paced before the locked door.

My body was rigid with tension, and the collar that adorned my throat felt tighter and tighter as the minutes ticked by. I pressed my fingers to the cool metal, and a shudder raced down my spine. The delicate twists and knots were a cruel reminder of the power Ryker held over me.

Shuffling behind the door halted my pacing mid-stride.

Had he returned?

Was he alone, or was I about to face my execution?

My ears strained as I pulled my magic around me, ready to defend myself no matter what odds I faced.

Fear gnawed at my gut, and my heart pounded in my chest as I waited for the telltale *snick* of the lock. When it finally came, I sucked in a sharp breath and stepped back.

The door swung wide, but instead of an army ready to seize me, a tall woman with raven-colored hair and crimson eyes greeted me. Her pale skin shone under the light pouring into the room, and her smile sent a ripple of unease through my body.

Every instinct told me to run, but before I could, the woman spoke.

"Cadence, I presume?" she asked as she stepped inside, closing the door behind her.

Her voice was smooth and unhurried, and her posture radiated quiet confidence.

"Who are you?" I demanded as I created distance between us.

"I'm here to get you out."

Her words were as unexpected as they were alarming. I narrowed my eyes at the woman as I gripped the edge of Ryker's desk.

"Who are you?" I repeated. "And how do you know my name?"

Her lips curled into a wicked smile as she sized me up.

"I am Eleanor, and I'm one of the last Blood Fae to serve the palace. I have learned many things about you, Cadence, since creating that shackle for the prince."

Eleanor pointed to the collar around my throat, and I bristled.

"You made this?" I snarled, as my fingers gripped the metal.

Eleanor nodded, not at all alarmed by my hostility.

"When the prince demanded I make that collar, I took it upon myself to learn everything I could about the woman he held captive."

She stepped toward me, and I mimicked the movement as I backed away.

"You had to be important for His Highness to invest so much energy to keep you contained," she mused.

My breath hitched, and my pulse quickened. There was something not quite right about the woman before me. I sensed her magic in the room, dark and wicked.

"You should go," I said, sounding more authoritative than I felt.

Eleanor took a step closer. "If I leave, who will spare you from the executioner's block?"

I reeled back as though I'd been struck, and I could feel the blood draining from my face.

"Don't look so alarmed, Cadence," she chuckled. "I am not here to harm you, and I have no intention of revealing your secret. As I said, I'm here to help you."

"Why?"

I cursed myself for the tremor that accompanied my words. Something warned me that showing weakness to this woman would be a fatal mistake.

"Does it matter?" she asked as she raised a brow. "If I can free you from this place, *from him*, are you in any position to refuse me?"

She was right, and I hated it.

"It matters," I snapped. "Especially if your intentions are more nefarious than those of the prince."

Eleanor cackled and the sound made me recoil. "More nefarious than the prince? I'm not sure if you are aware, child, but for the past eight decades, His Highness has had sole responsibility for hunting down and slaughtering your kind."

Her words made me flinch, but I couldn't argue with the truth of them.

"Why?" I asked again. "Why would you help me? What do you have to gain?"

Eleanor's crimson eyes settled on me, and something akin to rage flashed across her features.

"Because," she spat, "this kingdom has systematically annihilated any type of Fae that possesses more power than the King. First, they came for the Wraith Borne, isolating them from the rest of the Unseelie until the perfect storm of fear, hatred, and uncertainty allowed them to make their move."

Eleanor's gaze was distant, as if she was reliving a moment long since passed. Then her eyes refocused on me as she continued.

"The Blood Fae learned from the suffering of the Wraith Borne, and they gradually left the confines of the palace and surrounding villages, moving far from their reach. The writing was on the wall. Once they'd eliminated the Wraith Borne, the Blood Fae would be next."

My mind raced as I processed Eleanor's words.

"So, you could say I'm helping you out of a sense of duty. I did nothing back then, but maybe the gods put you in my path as an opportunity for redemption."

Despite the sincerity in her tone, I couldn't help but wonder if this was all an elaborate ploy to lead me into another cage.

"How did you know I was Wraith Borne?" I asked, buying myself time.

"Your collar," she said simply.

My fingers drifted back to the cool metal. "What do you mean?"

Eleanor rolled her eyes as if my lack of understanding offended her.

"When I was performing the enchantment, I may have taken a few liberties," she said with a conspiratorial smile. "I not only tethered the collar to the prince, but also to myself. When you drew on your power earlier, I recognized it."

Eleanor's gaze drifted to the dead man still lying motionless on the floor. I crossed my arms over my chest and narrowed my eyes as I scrutinized the woman for any signs of deceit.

"Ryker told me only he could release it."

"True," Eleanor said with a shrug.

"Then how do you propose to free me?"

Eleanor's hand disappeared beneath her skirts, and a moment later, she lifted a vial in the air with a triumphant smirk.

"What is that supposed to be?"

"This vial contains the prince's blood," she beamed. "I needed his blood to perform the binding, and I saved the remnants left behind in case they one day proved useful."

The offer lingered between us, tempting but terrifying. My mind turned to Ryker, his heated gaze and possessive touch. He had promised he would protect me, but more often than not, it was him who had exposed me to danger. He took with little regard for the consequences, and he had betrayed my trust more than once.

Yet, my heart cried out at the thought of leaving him. How could I loathe someone while also needing them the way I needed my next breath?

"Tick Tock, Cadence."

The energy radiating from her was dark, and it thrummed with a power that felt... wrong. Trusting her felt like stepping into a pit of vipers.

Eleanor smiled viciously, as though she could hear my thoughts. "What's it going to be?"

"And if I say no?"

"You'll remain here, shackled and suffocated, until the prince decides your fate. But I suspect you already know what your future looks like in that scenario."

My mouth felt dry, and sweat beaded on the back of my neck. She was right. I knew exactly what my future held if I stayed behind. Ryker had shown me as much when he told me I could trust him in one breath and then locked me up like a prisoner with the next.

Decision made, I straightened my shoulders. "I'll come with you, but if this is some kind of trap, I won't hesitate to end you."

Eleanor smiled as if my murderous intentions pleased her. "I'd expect nothing less."

She moved to the desk, rummaged through its contents, and found a small bowl. With one swipe of her hand, she sent all sorts of instruments, parchment, and ink sailing to the floor. Eleanor emptied the vial of Ryker's blood into the bowl and looked up at me expectantly.

"Come," she said as she clasped my hands in hers. "It's time."

My heart pounded as Eleanor chanted, her voice low and melodic, as her words wrapped around me like an embrace. I glanced at the bowl and swallowed the bile creeping up my throat as I saw the blood boiling.

Eleanor's chanting grew louder, and her brows furrowed in concentration. Then, without warning, a searing pain burned my neck as the metal of the collar heated. My hands moved instinctively as I clawed at it, trying desperately to free myself from its fiery grip.

"Hold still," Eleanor chastised, but I was beyond hearing her.

I could smell the acrid scent of my flesh burning as Eleanor's magic surged, igniting the collar anew. The metal burned hotter, and I sank my teeth into my bottom lip to keep from succumbing to the pain. I couldn't afford to lose consciousness or be otherwise distracted when I still wasn't sure if I could trust her.

A deafening snap filled the room, and the collar broke apart before falling to the floor.

I was panting heavily, the pain slowly receding, and when I glanced in Eleanor's direction, she appeared to be faring no better.

"We have to go," she said between ragged breaths.

"Where are we going?"

"Somewhere he'll never find you."

Chapter Fifty-Eight

RYKER

My mind raced as I marched through the palace back to Cadence. A weight had been lifted from me, knowing that Riordan had made his connections available for my purposes. Yet, so much still needed to be done before I would be satisfied that she was safe.

My footsteps faltered for the briefest moment as a strange sensation washed over me. It wasn't painful, but I'd experienced nothing like it before in my life.

A feeling in my gut told me it had to do with Cadence, and I wasted no time as I stepped inside my shadows, reappearing outside my chambers.

I swung the door wide open, and I had to clutch the door frame for support when I was confronted by the sight before me.

Lying in a small pile on the floor, mottled and charred, was the collar I had placed around Cadence's delicate throat to prevent her from ever leaving me.

My mind struggled to make sense of it all, but a single thought drowned out the rest.

Cadence had finally broken free from me.

Only one person besides Riordan knew about the collar and its purpose. No doubt, Eleanor's chambers were as empty as my own now were.

My heart thundered against my chest, and my vision blurred as rage consumed me. I could smell the magic that still lingered in the air, and it set every nerve ending ablaze. Eleanor had dared to enter my private rooms and take what belonged to me.

With a guttural roar, I swept my arm over my desk, upending the last remnants that remained. The action didn't dissipate my mounting rage, so I picked up the table and threw it across the room. It crashed against the wall, splintering on impact and sending small particles of wood sailing in every direction. Shadows sprang free from my palms, and I slammed my fists into the cold stone walls.

But it wasn't enough.

My shadows slithered around my bed frame, and I tugged, tearing through the carved posts like a blade through flesh.

"Fuck!" I bellowed.

But no matter how much I raged and tore the place apart, the wrath I felt at Cadence's betrayal remained.

I took a deep, calming breath, and I tried to get a hold of my anger. As I surveyed the damage I'd caused, my eyes fell on the collar. I stalked toward it before crouching to pick up the remnants of the broken metal.

My fingers traced the intricate links as if I could somehow feel her there if I pressed hard enough. When that didn't work, I curled my hand around the jagged pieces, the sharp edges cutting my palm.

But I felt no pain.

With every drop of my blood that splattered onto the tiled floor, my resolve strengthened. My shadows writhed around me as if the dark tendrils were feeding my growing ire.

Cadence had been here. She'd been mine. And now she was gone.

The door slammed against the wall, jolting me from my thoughts. I looked up and found Riordan standing in the doorway.

His gaze swept over the destruction, and he raised an amused brow.

"Redecorating?"

A low growl traveled up my throat, and I pushed myself to my feet.

"Cadence is gone."

All amusement drained from Riordan's face, and I opened my bloodied palm to reveal the shattered pieces of the collar.

"Well, that explains why the entire staff was fleeing for their lives," he muttered.

"What the fuck are you talking about?"

"You didn't think I just stumbled by your chambers so soon after you left mine, did you?"

A menacing snarl lifted my upper lip, and Riordan rushed to continue.

"I was told that you were unleashing all kinds of hell and tearing the palace apart. No one wanted to ask what had upset you, so they sent me," he finished with a sheepish grin, though it lacked its usual calming effect.

"We will figure this out, Ryker," he said in a soothing tone. "Now tell me, was she taken, or did she escape?"

"Escape," I admitted begrudgingly.

"How can you be so sure?"

"She hated the collar. Hated me for putting it on her. But she doesn't understand the danger she has put herself in by running."

"You locked her in a gilded cage, Ryker," Riordan sighed as he rubbed a hand over his face. "Did you expect her to love you for it?"

"SHE IS MY MATE!" I roared, my hands clenching into fists at my sides. "She belongs to me. And now she's out there, unprotected, conspiring with the fucking Blood Fae."

Riordan stared at me intently, his eyes narrowed as he appraised me. It was as if he could see the desperation lurking beneath the mask of my anger.

"Why haven't you used the bond to find her?" he asked quietly.

I glanced away, unable to answer.

"You're afraid, but what is it that truly frightens you?" he muttered, as if he hadn't meant to ask the question aloud.

I stiffened, and my whole body prickled at the accusation. "I'm fucking furious is what I am."

"No, you're scared that she ran because she hates you. That she'll never forgive you for the things you've done."

The silence that stretched between us was telling.

"And you're terrified that if you use the bond to find her and drag her back here, she will never be yours."

I turned away from my brother, my hands trembling as I gripped the armchair.

"There is no reality in this life or the next where Cadence isn't mine. I don't care if she hates me," I said, my voice straining. "All that matters is that she's alive. So long as she is safe, she can hate me to her heart's content."

When Riordan remained silent, I turned to face him. His gaze was trained on me, and his eyes were full of pity.

I didn't want his fucking pity. I wanted my mate.

"Then we need to move," he said, sensing my thoughts.

Riordan stalked toward the door, but paused. "What will you do when we bring her back?"

I clenched my jaw at his unspoken accusation. "She is safest with me, Riordan."

"She's safest when she trusts you, and right now, you're giving her every reason to keep running."

He didn't spare me a second glance as he strode from the room.

My shadows writhed, feeding off my agitation. Riordan was right, but that knowledge did nothing to quell the incessant urge I felt to bind Cadence to me in any way I could. A primal drive pushed me to possess her, control her, and keep her by my side forever.

I suddenly understood what it might feel like to lose your mate. How your mind would descend into madness until only a rotten soul remained.

I gained a newfound understanding of what my father endured, though I could never forgive him for what he'd done.

As I strode from my chambers with renewed purpose, I was once again consumed by a single focus.

Find Cadence and return her to where she belongs.

Chapter Fifty-Nine

CADENCE

My breathing was ragged as I ran through the forest, reminding me once more that my stamina needed improvement. Regret clenched my chest at the thought of never training with Malesh again. The stoic warrior had grown on me despite his disinterest in the spoken word.

A twig snapped in the distance, and the sound of heavy boots trampling through the undergrowth reached me. Blood pounded in my ears, and my heart slammed against my ribcage frantically.

I knew exactly who was pursuing me. I could feel Ryker closing in around me through the bond.

“We have to move faster,” Eleanor hissed as she dragged me through the trees. “They are gaining on us.”

My lungs burned with every inhale, and my legs trembled under the unrelenting pace. We weren’t going to outrun Ryker. It was only a matter of time before he caught us.

“You go. I’ll create a diversion so you can escape,” I said.

“After all the effort I exerted to free you, not a chance.”

The tip of my boot got hooked on an exposed root, and I stumbled. I would have fallen if not for Eleanor’s quick reflexes. She gripped my upper arm and yanked me upright with surprising strength.

“I don’t understand how he’s still tracking us. The binding of the collar was broken.”

“It’s the bond,” I heaved out between ragged breaths.

Eleanor stopped abruptly, and I slammed into her.

“What did you just say?”

She flattened her lips into a grimace, and her tone sent a wave of unease crashing into me.

“He is my mate,” I whispered, and I realized it was the first time I had acknowledged it out loud.

Eleanor studied me intently, and an unsettling glint entered her eyes. It disappeared as quickly as it had formed before she barked out a harsh laugh.

“Then this is a futile endeavor. If he’s using the bond to track you, then he’ll be able to find you no matter where you go.”

My stomach sank with her declaration, but there was also another part of me that rejoiced. I chose to ignore that part and focus on the immediate problem.

"Isn't there anything you can do?"

Eleanor eyed me before she blew out a breath.

"I could try to mask the bond, but that kind of magic, one that interferes with fate's design, is not without risk."

Her eyes dipped to my lower abdomen, and my hand moved to the spot without my permission.

"You know?" I gasped.

"As I said, when I forged the collar, I tethered myself to you just as I had done for the prince."

A surge of frustration overwhelmed me, and it took me a moment to realize it was coming from the bond. I could feel Ryker's anger, his desperation, and it terrified me.

"Do it."

Eleanor scanned the forest, her eyes sharp and discerning, before she tugged my hand and pulled me toward a small clearing.

"We have to be quick," she urged, as she settled on the ground.

I dropped to my knees in front of her, and the damp earth soaked through my dress. An icy shiver tore through me, and I pulled my cloak tighter around me to ward off the chill. Eleanor withdrew a dagger from her belt, and the blade gleamed dangerously under the moonlight. Dark runes etched its edges, and I swallowed, unable to conceal my apprehension.

“Give me your hand,” she demanded, and I turned my palm heavenward before extending it to her.

Without any preamble, Eleanor sliced the blade across my flesh, and crimson beads pooled in my open palm. The coppery scent of my blood filled the air, and a sharp stinging sensation erupted at the site. I tried to ignore it by focusing on Eleanor’s murmuring as she flicked the red droplets from the knife in a rhythmic pattern, but the sound was guttural, making my skin crawl.

Eleanor then pressed the blade to her hand, cutting deep. She rose from her position on the ground, her blood dripping onto the forest floor as she circled me. The runes on the dagger glowed faintly in the dark, and a slight tingle broke out over my body.

The bond screamed in protest, and a searing pain tore through my chest. I gasped, unable to breathe through the agony as I clutched my heart. Tears streamed down my face, and I cried out as choked pleas fell from my lips.

“Stop, please,” I begged. “The pain, it’s unbearable.”

“That means it’s working,” Eleanor reassured me, but her words fell flat as my body warred with my mind, both begging for relief.

Then, mercifully, the pain ebbed before fading away. My breathing was labored, and sweat coated my forehead, but I forced myself to stand on unsteady feet.

In the distance, a visceral roar of anguish echoed through the forest, and the creatures of the night fled in panic. My vision blurred, and I swiped away the tears that betrayed me. For the first time since meeting Ryker, I felt... alone.

"We have to keep going," Eleanor said as she wiped the blade clean and tucked it back into the sheath at her hip.

"How long will it last?" I asked as I forced my legs to follow her.

"Long enough," she said. "Now move. We're not safe yet."

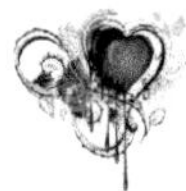

We'd been traipsing through the forest for hours, and the further we delved, the more oppressive it grew. My limbs ached, and my dress was torn and bloodied from our desperate escape. I'd gathered countless abrasions along the way and would have given anything for a moment's rest to mend my wounds.

"We're almost there," Eleanor said, her voice soft but urgent.

"Almost where?" I asked, as a feeling of foreboding settled over me.

"To safety."

I'd put my faith in Eleanor because I'd had no other option. But now, with the bond concealed and Ryker unable to track me, doubt began to creep in.

"Where are you taking me?"

She huffed like I was a misbehaving child, and she waved a dismissive hand in the air.

"I told you already, somewhere safe."

There was something in her tone that made my stomach twist, and my footsteps slowed in response. But before I could turn and flee, shadows emerged from the forest surrounding us.

"You led me into a trap," I hissed, and Eleanor glanced over her shoulder at me.

A broad smile split her face, but it was far from reassuring. Several figures stepped forward, their faces obscured under their cloaks and their weapons reflecting the moonlight.

My magic stirred beneath my skin, and my pulse quickened.

This was no sanctuary.

"You lied to me," I spat in Eleanor's direction as I took a step back.

More figures emerged from the shrubbery, crowding me from behind and cutting off my retreat. Eleanor turned to face me, and she planted her hands on her hips.

"It was foolish of you to reveal such a deadly secret. But it's far too late to run now."

My hands clenched into fists, and my magic thrummed wildly as it danced across my fingertips, ready to do my bidding.

"What do you want from me?"

"For you to die," she said sweetly. "We've been searching for a way to weaken the prince, and then you fell into my lap, as if the gods themselves willed our victory."

"What are you talking about?" I demanded through gritted teeth.

"The death of his mate will be the prince's undoing."

Murmured conversations broke out all around me, but I blocked them out as I focused on the woman before me.

"This has been your plan all along."

"Not quite. I truly freed you to spare you from the cruel fate of your people, but then you made the fatal miscalculation of revealing you were the prince's mate. I wasn't about to let such a prize slip through my fingers." Her grin was downright disturbing as she stared at me, practically vibrating with excitement.

Realization struck me, and I suddenly understood who these people were.

I was standing amid the Crimson Enclave.

Bile rose up my throat, and I wanted to lunge across the space separating us and force my magic into her body until she withered and died.

Before I could act on my wayward thoughts, the crowd parted, revealing a tall man draped in a dark cloak. He had broad shoulders, and he angled his head as he looked me over.

There was something oddly familiar about the gesture, but I couldn't place it. As he lifted his hand to lower the hood of his cloak, I noticed his skin was littered with fading scars, and for reasons I couldn't understand, that made my chest tighten.

When he let his hood fall away, my eyes clashed with chocolate-brown ones that were full of compassion and regret.

"No," I whispered, as I stumbled back.

I shook my head, trying to dispel the image in front of me, but it remained stubbornly unchanged.

"This isn't real," I whimpered as tears pricked my eyes.

The man's features softened as he stepped closer.

"Cadence," he said, his voice a low rumble that caressed me like a tight hug.

I closed my eyes, letting the tears stream down my cheeks as I sank into the sound. When I opened my eyes again, the man watched me with concern, his brows furrowed, unsure what to do.

I launched myself at him, my arms wrapping around his neck as I buried my face against his chest.

"Papa!"

His arms encircled me, and he hugged me just as tightly, gently stroking my hair.

"I'm here, Cadence. Everything is going to be all right."

Chapter Sixty

RYKER

Our footsteps were silent as we moved through the dense forest, the moss-covered ground concealing the sounds of our approach. The tall trees that loomed above us blocked out the inky night sky, plunging the woods into darkness.

Instead of being a hindrance, I thrived among the shadows. The blackness called to my soul, welcoming me home.

I didn't have to worry about losing my way. The bond beckoned me to Cadence as a moth to a flame, guiding me through the wilderness with ease.

It was also a constant reminder that she'd left me, spurring my anger as I hunted her down like prey. My mind kept returning to the various ways I would punish her for disobeying me. All of them involved her being naked and on her knees.

A twig snapped behind me, and I spun on my heels to scowl at my younger brother.

"You need to get out of the palace more often, Little Brother. You're losing your edge."

Riordan scowled back at me, but he didn't deny it.

The bond blazed inside my chest, reclaiming my attention, and I could tell she was close. My muscles ached from being coiled tight as I hunted my mate, but it was comforting to know the end was near.

She wouldn't be able to evade me for much longer. I'd have Cadence back at my side where she belonged.

As soon as the thought formed, the air shifted. The forest grew unnaturally quiet, and the night became thick and oppressive. My shadows danced and writhed around me, hovering at the edge of my vision, waiting for the command to strike.

"Something's wrong," Malesh whispered, and I gave him a curt nod in agreement.

"It could be a trap," Eamon added.

But he knew me well enough to know that wouldn't stop me.

"Keep your eyes peeled and your weapons at the ready. No harm comes to Cadence. If you get the chance, take her and flee."

"And what about you?" Riordan asked.

"I'll dispose of the Blood Fae."

"On your own?"

I gave my brother an amused smirk, telling him exactly what I thought of his concern.

"I'm surprised you can stand upright with the inflated ego you're carrying around," he muttered under his breath.

A laugh threatened to explode from my chest, but I suppressed it, not wanting to draw attention to our presence.

"Come on. It's time to retrieve my woman."

I took a single step forward, and then my entire world shifted on its axis.

One moment, my connection with Cadence flared, tethering my life to hers and leading me toward her.

And the next, it was gone.

A violent tearing sensation erupted behind my ribcage, and the force was so potent that it brought me to my knees. My hands clawed at my chest as a raw, animalistic howl tore from my throat. My vision blurred, and my mind reeled as an unbearable emptiness spread throughout my body.

Riordan dropped to the ground beside me, his face pale as he tried to capture my attention.

"Ryker, what's happening? Did something happen to Cadence?"

I could hear the panic in his tone, and as I glanced around me, I saw twin expressions of concern contorting Malesh and Eamon's features.

My hands curled into fists, and my nails dug into my palms until blood trickled between my fingers.

"No," I snarled as the surrounding space darkened, my shadows twisting in response to my anguish.

"No, what?" Riordan pressed. "Tell me what's going on."

But I couldn't bring myself to say the words. I refused to accept that Cadence was gone or the knowledge that I'd failed her.

"FUCK!" I roared, and the forest recoiled as the pulse of my anger washed over it.

The surrounding trees wavered, their limbs shaking as they resisted the pull of my power. But not even the primordial strength of nature was enough to resist my agony as my shadows forced the forest to its knees, flattening the trees around us.

I no longer cared if we were discovered.

Let them come. I would show them what a fucking monumental mistake they had made by taking what belonged to me.

The thought didn't bring me as much comfort as I'd hoped it would, as the truth continued to claw at me, undeniable and cruel. The bond had been a constant reminder that no matter how fiercely Cadence fought me, she was still mine.

But now... now it was gone.

"Ryker, tell me what's going on," Riordan pleaded.

"She's gone," I whispered, unable to hide the tremor in my voice. "Cadence is gone."

"What do you mean, she's gone?" Malesh pressed.

"She's fucking gone! The bond is broken. I can't feel her anymore."

My voice hitched on the last word, and Riordan's eyes misted over.

"A bond can only be broken if—"

A menacing growl worked its way up my throat, cutting him off. I staggered to my feet, my breathing shallow and uneven as I steadied myself.

I had taken my time with Cadence for granted, too comfortable in the notion that she was mine and would remain by my side until our dying days. I'd envisioned our entire future. One where she ruled alongside me as we watched our children flourish and grow.

Now that future had been stolen from us, and every step felt as though I was trudging through quicksand. My body was weighed down by my unbearable grief, and I had no idea how I would survive this.

Memories of Cadence swam in my mind like a tormented dream — one you longed to escape, but knew you'd have to endure before the reprieve of consciousness found you. My vision wavered as rage and sorrow battled for dominance.

I threaded my fingers through my hair, tugging on the strands with such fury that I was surprised they hadn't been pulled free.

Not even the pain could ground me. I was adrift, with no land in sight, hoping the waves would drown me.

"What do we do now?" Riordan asked, barely above a whisper.

My gaze landed on him, and I took in his pained expression and wet cheeks. The image made my heart clench, but I didn't have any space left to absorb Riordan's suffering.

Not this time.

Then my eyes darted to Malesh. He was muttering curses under his breath as he paced back and forth, wearing a hole in the hard ground.

Eamon sat beside him, his head in his hands as though he couldn't comprehend what was happening.

In such a short time, Cadence had become an irreplaceable feature in all our lives, and her loss was excruciating.

The ache in my chest twisted into something sharper, something more volatile. My grief gave way to rage, burning brightly until it became an unrelenting tempest that consumed me whole.

If the fates deemed it acceptable to allow Cadence to be taken from me, then they could watch as the world burned in her absence.

"I'm going to kill them all. Every. Fucking. One. Of. Them."

Chapter Sixty-One

CADENCE

I followed my father's footsteps as we broke through the tree line of the dark forest. A large clearing lay ahead, where a makeshift camp had been set up. People milled about preparing bedding and tending to chores, while others sat in small groups, enjoying the warmth of the fire.

The camp appeared calm, even relaxed, but subtle hints suggested they were ready to flee at any moment. Packs were carefully arranged next to bedrolls, horses were tethered but saddled, and their weapons were all within arm's reach, their sharp edges gleaming in the firelight.

My father led me to a nearby log, his massive frame taking up most of the space. Every set of eyes in the camp followed my movements, as if waiting for me to attack. Their distrust and resentment bore into me, making my skin prickle under the intensity of their glares.

I focused my attention on the man I had long believed dead as I tried to block out the feeling of the narrowed gazes still lingering on me. My father appeared older, a rare feat for a Fae, hinting at a life that was far from easy. His once golden skin looked weathered and was littered with scars. His piercing brown eyes, so similar to my own, stared back at me, but they lacked the warmth I'd clung to as a child.

The man before me was not the father I remembered, but a stranger forged by hardship and vengeance.

"Tell me how you're not dead," I demanded, not bothering to soften the blow.

He winced, but he didn't shy away from my question.

"I was badly injured during the assault on the Unseelie Palace, and I would have died, if not for the Wraith Borne who risked their lives to bring me to safety."

"And my mother?" I asked, unable to hide the vulnerability in my voice.

My father shook his head and averted his gaze. I watched as he stared into the fire, tracking the tiny embers as they danced along the wind. When his gaze returned to mine, all softness had disappeared, and in its place was unyielding fury.

"Dead," he said without emotion.

I swallowed hard. This had been my reality for years, but hearing it confirmed after a glimmer of hope had taken hold was just as crippling as the first time those words reached my ears.

"So, you survived the Cleansing, hid in the shadows, and let me believe you were dead," I accused.

Those gathered around the fire were doing all they could to pretend they weren't eavesdropping, but the way their bodies leaned toward us gave away their intentions.

My father placed his elbows on his knees as he clasped his hands together. The firelight danced across his hollow cheekbones, and he studied me for a long moment before speaking.

"I did what I had to, Cadence," he said, his voice calm but devoid of remorse. "Surviving wasn't a choice, but a necessity."

My hands curled into fists as years of grief and anger flared within me.

"And what, your only child, who had just lost everything she loved, whose world had been turned upside down, would have derailed your chances?"

"Yes," he said, and I couldn't mask the hurt that stabbed through my chest.

My father exhaled as he scratched at the light stubble adorning his cheeks.

"I didn't want to leave you, Cadence, but it wasn't safe for you to join me. This life," he said, waving a hand around the camp, "is no way to raise a wee one. You were better off where you were."

"It's been eight decades! I haven't been a child for a long time."

Tears pricked my eyes as a flurry of emotions crashed into me. Anger, resentment, sadness, and hope all warred within me, fighting for their right to be set free.

Then my thoughts turned to my aunt and uncle waiting for me in the Seelie Kingdom. They'd been forced to leave their home and their families and settle in another village to give me a chance at a better life. Somewhere, no one would think to question my different features, allowing me to become their daughter in every way that matters. They had given me a home, a family, and an infuriating brother whom I adored more than anything, and at that moment I realized my father was right.

My anger seeped from me, and I suddenly felt exhausted from the upheaval of the day. My limbs were heavy with fatigue and my eyes burned as they begged for sleep.

"Why didn't you ever send word that you were alive?" I asked in a small voice.

My father's expression softened, as if he'd sensed the change in my emotions.

"Because I knew the path I was taking wasn't one I could share with you, at least not then. I needed to stay hidden, to gather what remained of our people, and to plan. The Cleansing destroyed our world, our way of life, Cadence. The Unseelie King and those who followed him, took everything from us. But now... now it's time to take it back."

Murmurs of agreement broke out around me, and my gaze flicked to the Fae meandering about the camp. They were no longer pretending not to listen, but were actively following along, nodding their heads at my father's sentiment. They looked at my father with a kind of reverence that made my stomach knot as realization washed over me.

"You're the leader of the Crimson Enclave, aren't you?"

My father narrowed his gaze as he studied me. His thoughts swirled behind his eyes, and it appeared as though he was assessing me, evaluating my worth, as he tried to determine if I could be trusted.

He didn't look at me like a daughter.

"I am," he said, and my mind whirled.

I'd heard of the atrocities the Crimson Enclave had committed, all in the name of retribution. While I understood their anger, they'd inflicted the same suffering they had experienced during the Cleansing on their fellow fae. The people they killed and the lives they ruined were as innocent as they had been.

Unease gripped my chest, but I tempered my features, not letting it show on my face.

"What do you mean, take it back?"

My father's eyes flared with interest, and the faintest hint of a smile tugged at his lips.

"We've waited long enough."

Cheers of agreement broke out around the group, but I kept my gaze locked on my father.

"We have allies now, strength we didn't have before. But before we strike, we need an advantage."

The way my father looked at me, as if I were no longer a person but a weapon, raised the hairs on the back of my neck. Whatever he was about to say, I was certain I wouldn't like it.

"And you, my daughter, are that advantage."

My blood ran cold.

I hated that I was right.

"What are you talking about?"

"The prince is your mate."

My gaze darted to Eleanor, and the smug smirk that painted her lips had my eyes narrowing with resentment.

"You intend to kill me?" I asked in disbelief.

My father stared at me as if he was considering his options. I pulled my magic around me, ready to defend myself despite the overwhelming odds.

It had been eight decades since my father had lost his mate. There was no telling how far the sickness of his mind had progressed. I could no longer depend on him to protect me as I once had.

"While that's one way to bring about the prince's demise, there's another option. One that might prove significantly more beneficial."

His shrewd gaze assessed me, and a shiver of revulsion coursed through my body. The camp followers protested angrily, but my father's eyes remained locked on me.

"You can get close to him. You've earned his trust, and infiltrated his world whether or not you intended to."

An undignified snort escaped me at his declaration, and his brows furrowed in confusion.

"The prince does not trust me," I clarified. "He keeps me close because he has to."

My father considered my words, his fingers tracing his jawline as he mulled everything over.

"Then you must earn his confidence and get him to open up to you," he insisted.

"For what purpose?"

"We require information, Cadence. We need to undermine the royal family from within as we prepare to make our final stand."

My stomach churned, and bile rose in my throat. My father wanted me to help him stage a coup. As I glanced around the camp, I could see that their earlier anger had transformed, and a hungry glint now stared back at me.

This moment had been years in the making. The Wraith Borne had been biding their time until the perfect opportunity presented itself for them to seize control and exact their retribution.

And I had foolishly wandered right into their midst, giving them everything they had been waiting for.

Chapter Sixty-Two

CADENCE

"You want me to betray him?" I whispered, aware that everyone around us was hanging on to our every word.

"I need you to do what is necessary," my father corrected. "He is not your ally, Cadence. Nor is he your protector, your lover, or your friend. He's the enemy."

"He is my mate, and if you kill him, you will be condemning me to a fate worse than death."

My father was already living the fate I described, and yet, he'd condemn me to suffer the same agony.

Anger flared in my father's brown eyes, and I fought the urge to flee. There was something dangerous lurking behind his calm demeanor and I was in no hurry to discover what it was.

"He is the reason my mate, your mother, is dead."

I reeled back from the impact of his words. My father's shoulders trembled violently. It was taking considerable effort for him to contain his raging emotions, and the entire camp seemed to notice. Silence enveloped the clearing as though everyone was too afraid to even breathe.

"What are you saying?" I asked, fearing I already knew the answer.

"The prince didn't just lead the charge against us when we attacked the palace."

I inhaled sharply, preparing myself for the devastating blow he was about to deliver.

"He killed your mother with his own hands."

My breath caught in my throat, and my world darkened. The sounds of the camp became muted, giving way to my thundering heart. I had always blamed Ryker for my parents' deaths, hated him for it even. I knew he led the charge against the Wraith Borne. But knowing he took the life of the one who loved me most was a torment all its own.

Disbelief turned to rage in the blink of an eye, and I watched as an eerie grin spread across my father's face.

"Now you understand, Daughter."

My father rose to his feet, towering above me, but I couldn't meet his gaze. The weight of Ryker's betrayal was slowly suffocating me, and I didn't know if I wanted to survive it.

"What is it you expect me to do? I am only one person."

"You're not just one person, you are my daughter. And you're powerful. More so than you realize. You are Wraith Borne, Cadence. You're a weapon he can't control, and he likely fears you more than he lets on. Use that against him."

I didn't feel powerful.

I felt trapped.

There were very few things that frightened Ryker, and I doubted I was one of them. I couldn't voice those concerns, however. The wild look in my father's eyes told me I had to tread carefully or risk his ire.

"It's not that simple," I murmured as I gnawed on my bottom lip.

My father crouched before me, his hand reaching out as he tugged my lip from between my teeth.

"Revolutions never are," he whispered, reminding me of the man who once read me bedtime stories.

The shift in his demeanor was startling, standing in sharp contrast to the man he'd been moments ago.

"She's carrying his heir," Eleanor interjected as she watched us from across the fire.

The camp fell silent, then erupted in a flurry of voices.

"If that's true, then she can't be trusted," one man called. "I say we kill her now and take our chances against the prince."

"She's already chosen a side," another man added.

"If we kill his mate and his heir, we will either cripple him or give him the strength he needs to end us once and for all," an older woman reasoned.

"Enough!" my father bellowed, and all conversation fell away.

His eyes darkened with anger, and I could see his thoughts churning as he tried to decide how best to use this new information. Then he returned his gaze to mine, and something akin to insatiable greed stared back at me.

"Is that true?" he asked, his voice a low rumble.

I nodded, unable to form words past the dread clogging my throat.

A slow grin spread across my father's face, and the sight had every instinct inside me screaming at me to run.

"Then the timing is perfect."

My nose crinkled with confusion, not understanding where his thoughts had traveled.

"Why?" I asked, suspicion lacing my tone.

"Once we remove the royal family, you will have a claim to the Unseelie throne."

His eyes lowered to my flat stomach, and unfettered ambition simmered in his chocolate depths as he stared at me. My hand darted forward protectively as if it could shield my unborn child from his hungry gaze.

"You will rule as Regent until your child comes of age."

My father stood, extending his hand to me. "And I will stand at your side," he said as he pulled me to my feet.

"Return to the Prince," my father ordered, his voice hard and unwavering. "Earn his trust, dig deeper into his world, and when the time is right, you will launch our strike from the inside."

The way he commanded me, as though I were merely a puppet, left me seething. Despite my better judgment, I straightened my spine as I glared at him in defiance.

"And if I refuse?" I whispered so that no one else could hear.

My father stiffened, a dangerous edge creeping into his expression.

"Then I'll be forced to consider you a liability," he whispered back, glancing around the camp pointedly.

That look told me everything I needed to know. I was balancing on a tightrope, and one wrong move would seal my fate.

My father leaned in closer, "And Cadence, liabilities do not survive long in my world."

A whole body shiver tore through me as the threat hung heavy in the air between us.

Sorrow washed over me anew as I realized my father really was dead. The man before me was a stranger, a mere shadow of the one I had lost.

I gave a curt nod, and my father's grin returned.

"Excellent," he said as he rubbed his hands together. "Now sleep, Daughter. You will need it for what comes tomorrow."

I lifted my chin and followed after him. Whatever came next, the only person I could rely on was myself.

Ryker wanted to own me, and my father intended to use me.

I would do as my father asked. I'd find out Ryker's secrets, but I wouldn't hand them over to him blindly.

I'd do whatever needed to be done to protect myself and the life of my child.

Chapter Sixty-Three

CADENCE

The weight of inevitability pressed down on me, and I struggled to stay upright. I wasn't sure how Ryker would react when he found me, but I knew our reunion would be emotionally charged.

Whether that emotion was anger or relief, I couldn't predict.

I took a steadying breath and let the sounds of nature soothe me. The crunch of dead leaves beneath my boots mixed with the shuffling and scraping of the creatures that called the forest home.

The wind twisted through the trees, making the woods seem as though they were alive — as if the whispers of all those who had traveled the same path now sang out to me.

Crisp, clean air filled my lungs, going some way to ease my mind, which raced with a thousand fractured thoughts. But it did little to uncoil the tight knot of tension that wrapped around my throat, suffocating me.

I could feel the concealment spell fade as the bond surged to life inside me.

And if I had felt it, so had Ryker.

He was close, and it wouldn't take him long to find me.

A shudder wracked my frame, and I knew my time was up.

His presence cut through the air like lightning, sharp and impossible to ignore, electrifying my body in his wake.

My magic rose to the surface, dangerous and alert.

"Cadence."

His voice was a low growl that sent an icy shiver racing down my spine.

The single word was a warning.

I froze, every muscle locking into place, before I willed myself to calm down and turned to face him. He narrowed his steel-grey eyes, and his nostrils flared wide. The corner of his mouth was lifted as though he were forcing himself to contain a snarl. His jaw was clenched, and I could hear his teeth grinding together.

His face was a mask of barely concealed fury.

"You've been busy, wife."

Ryker's tone was deceptively calm, and I tensed as he stepped toward me. My heart thudded in my chest, but I forced myself to straighten my spine.

I would not cower before him.

Ryker stopped a few paces in front of me, his towering frame looming over me, forcing me to crane my neck to look up at him.

"You left," he hissed. "You ran, Cadence. After all we've been through, you ran."

Defiance stirred in my gut, and I scowled at him.

"After everything you've done to me, you mean. Did you expect me to stay put like a good little pet?" I taunted.

"Yes," he snapped, his voice rising. "That's exactly what I expected you to do. You're my mate. *My wife*. You don't get to just walk away."

"You left me with no choice," I shouted back, shoving him.

Ryker gripped my wrists in a tight hold as he pulled me flush against his body.

"No choice? You had a choice, Cadence, and you chose to betray me."

"Do you hear yourself, Ryker? You discovered my truth, and then you locked me in your chambers. You told me I could trust you, and then the minute you had a chance to prove yourself, you showed me with your actions that I couldn't."

My chest was heaving as the sense of betrayal washed over me anew. There had been a fleeting moment where I'd chosen to put my faith in Ryker. I trusted him, despite everything he'd done, and I thought for the first time since we'd met, we were finally moving in the same direction.

But he shattered that illusion the instant he slid the metal lock into place, trapping me as his prisoner.

We both glared at each other, the silence stretching between us as the air grew thick with the weight of old wounds and unspoken words.

Ryker was the one to break the silence.

"Fuck Cadence," he whispered, and then his lips were crashing against mine.

Ryker kissed me like a man possessed. One hand slid down my arm, his rough touch leaving a burning flame of desire in its wake as he settled his palm on my hip. His other hand snaked into my hair, pulling me close as he devoured me.

Mind, body, and soul.

When our need for oxygen overwhelmed us, Ryker broke the kiss, his forehead pressing against mine as we caught our breath.

"I thought I'd lost you, Cadence. I thought you were dead."

His voice cracked on the last word, and a small part of me felt guilty for what I had done. Then my father's words rose in my mind, unbidden.

He killed your mother with his own hands.

My guilt morphed into something else entirely.

I pushed against Ryker with all my strength, and he stumbled back, not expecting it. My gaze shifted to the three men I'd overlooked standing behind him, and I gasped.

Riordan, Malesh, and Eamon stood watching our interaction, their faces a mix of relief, amusement, and concern.

"Hi there, sweetheart," Riordan said as he rubbed the nape of his neck. "You gave us quite the fright."

A fresh wave of guilt assaulted me, but this time, I knew I deserved it.

"I'm sorry."

Something cold brushed against my wrists, and I glanced down to see Ryker securing twin bracelets in place. Lifting my hands in the air, I studied the silver bands as they shimmered in the moonlight. A strange sensation coursed through me, and trepidation gripped me tight.

"What is this?" I demanded, shaking my hands in front of Ryker's face.

"They are magic nullifying cuffs."

"Ryker," Riordan hissed, but I ignored him.

My blood pounded in my ears, and I desperately tried to call upon my power, to no avail. Fear clogged my throat, and I fought the sting of tears that threatened to break free.

"So, you intend to bring me to trial," I said, ashamed of the way my bottom lip trembled.

Ryker chuckled without mirth. The sound made me recoil, and I felt an overwhelming urge to flee, to hide where he could never find me.

"Oh, sweet Cadence," he murmured, his voice a dark caress. "I couldn't care less if you slaughtered every fucking being in the Unseelie Palace and then bathed in their blood."

The coldness of his stare sent my heart racing, and I retreated a step before I could stop myself.

"I'm not angry that you're one of the Wraith Borne, Cadence. I am fucking enraged that you thought you could leave me."

His calm demeanor was even more terrifying than any act of violence I'd ever witnessed.

"Not only that, but you conspired to have me believe you were dead."

Ryker reclaimed the step between us as he leaned into my space. His lips brushed against the shell of my ear, and his warm breath tickled my neck.

"How. Fucking. Dare. You."

Ryker pushed his hand into my hair and gripped my nape with a bruising force.

"You are never going to be free of me, Cadence, and your new accessories will ensure you can't use your magic to escape me," he said as his free hand slid over the cuffs. "You *will* sit beside me when I take the throne, or so help me, Cadence, I'll hunt down every single person you love and remove them from this world."

"Brother," Riordan murmured, the shock audible in his tone.

"Stay the fuck out of this, Riordan," Ryker snarled, never taking his eyes off me.

Inhaling deeply, I allowed all the pain and sorrow I had experienced in my life to flow through me. I drowned in it. Rejoiced in the suffering because once it had subsided, I would be reborn.

Then I exhaled a measured breath and narrowed my gaze at Ryker.

"With the gods as my witness, Ryker, you will rue the day you walked into my life. I am going to destroy you. I will take back everything you've stolen from me, and then I'm going to burn your world down around you."

A ghost of a smirk curved Ryker's mouth as he extinguished the remaining space between us.

"Anything for you, Temptress. If you want to burn my world down, I'll hand you the fucking match."

Ryker pressed his lips against mine, sealing his vow with a kiss. His tongue invaded my mouth, and I bit down, tasting blood. That didn't stop him, though. He kissed me as if I was the very air he needed to breathe.

His hands gripped my waist with a possessiveness that was both infuriating and intoxicating. I wanted to pull away, to resist, but once again, my body betrayed me.

His kiss softened, his aggression giving way to something deeper, something that felt like desperation.

When he broke the kiss, he reached between us and clasped my hand in his. His free hand drifted up to swipe at the blood staining his lips, and when he peered down at the crimson substance smeared across his thumb, he rumbled in approval.

Without another word, he turned in the direction of the Unseelie Kingdom.

"Come, Cadence, we're going home."

His kingdom would never be my home, and he'd realize that soon enough.

Chapter Sixty-Four

CALLUM

Months prior...

There had been no sign of Cadence in weeks, and despite my best efforts, my search had been futile. I couldn't find her, and I was running out of places to look.

Her apartment above the apothecary remained locked and undisturbed, but my gut feeling told me I was missing something.

My parents were beside themselves with worry, and I knew Cadence would never put them through such turmoil for nothing.

There had to be more to it.

My boots hit the wooden steps that led into my house, and I stomped on the landing, ridding myself of the dirt packed into the crevices.

Cadence was always on my case about things like that.

Pain lanced my chest, and I moved my hand to rub at the unseen wound. My gaze roamed over the forest that surrounded my home, and I wondered if I had time for one last foray into the woods before night descended.

A loud clap of thunder answered me. With a heavy sigh, I pushed open the door and marched inside.

A small pile of letters sat on my mat, and I crouched down to retrieve them. I thumbed through them as I moved toward the kitchen, and my footsteps faltered as my eyes landed on a familiar script.

Cadence.

The other letters fluttered to the ground as I ripped the envelope open and pulled out the parchment. I devoured every word, but I felt even more confused than before.

I strode to my desk, pulled out my chair, and settled in to read Cadence's words once more.

To my dearest Callum,

As always, I hope this letter finds you well.

Kindly check on the apothecary for me.

She disappeared without a trace and the first thing she says isn't — *I'm alive, no need to fret* — but check on my fucking apothecary!

What the fuck, Cadence!

Even though our neighbors have the utmost integrity, I worry about the store being left unattended for too long.

Utmost integrity, my ass. Those bastards would rob her blind if they weren't so concerned she'd poison them for their efforts.

Never take anything for granted, as you always say.

In all my years, I'd never shared such a sentiment. I took most things for granted, threw caution to the wind, and lived recklessly.

And Cadence damn well knew that.

By the way, I hope you followed up on the opportunity with Teal.

You deserve to be happy whoever you choose.

Understandably, Roark may require some convincing, but I have faith in you.

If I recalled our conversation accurately, she'd chewed me out for it and even predicted Roark would kill me.

"You're so full of shit, Cadence!"

Now, as to the purpose of my letter.

See, I always wanted to explore more of the kingdom, but I have never had the time with all my responsibilities at home.

Eventually, my time will end, and I fear I will never see what's out there waiting for me.

Exploration, adventure, and possibly finding my mate — now is the moment for me to chase it all.

Love has never been important to me, but I'm starting to think I should have made it a priority long ago.

Her words made even less sense as I reread them. I practically had to drag her, kicking and screaming, to the tavern just to get her to leave her apartment.

Cadence was many things, but adventurous wasn't one of them.

As for finding a mate, the woman practically flayed me with her eyes for daring to suggest such an atrocity. There was no way I'd ever believe she left her home and our parents to find a mate.

None.

I know this may seem like it's all come out of nowhere, but trust me, Callum, this is what I want.

You don't fucking say!

Everything is as it should be.

Please try to understand.

Right now, I am choosing to focus on myself.

I am excited for the first time in a long while.

I winced.

Reading those words for the second time hadn't been any easier. Was her life so unfulfilling, so dull, that she felt the need to leave without a word just to escape the tedium?

I didn't want to believe it, but there was a part of me that wouldn't blame her if she did. She carried the load when it came to our parents, and I had unfairly allowed her to do so. The demands of her job were also all-consuming, and I had to believe that the monotony grew tiresome.

Now, I know Mama and Papa will worry, but they don't need to.

Could you please try to reassure them that I will be all right?

Eternally yours, Cadence.

Yeah, there was little chance of that, and I doubt her letter would ease their worries.

I leaned back in my chair, running my hand through my hair as I considered her words.

There was something not quite right.

Cadence had spoken with a formality that was devoid of her usual playfulness, and she never missed a chance to tease me.

Then there was the way she had written her sentences. They felt overly constructed — as if she were weaving an intricate knot, and all I had to do was pull the string taut for everything to fall into place.

Unease settled in my chest as I fought to make sense of it.

I placed the letter on my desk and drew a deep breath as I struggled to settle my spiraling thoughts.

Glancing around me, I took in the disheveled state of my home and tried to remember the last time I had tidied it.

My eyes snagged on the tiny wooden horse Cadence had made for me when we were children, and nostalgia mixed with anguish at the memory. It was a ghastly thing, and the only way to tell it was a horse was to squint so much you could hardly see it.

But Cadence had been so proud. She mentioned it countless times in our letters over the years.

Our letters.

"Shit!"

I tossed everything off my desk and scrambled to find a blank piece of parchment and some ink.

My pulse quickened as I recalled the way we used to hide messages in our letters as children. The first letter of each paragraph spelled out the hidden words. It was a simple trick, but it worked.

TAKENBYUNSEELIEPRINCE

Taken by Unseelie Prince.

The quill slipped from my fingers and clattered against my desk as I stared down at her message.

Cadence hadn't left. She was taken.

What could the Prince of the Unseelie possibly need with Cadence?

Unless he found out her secret.

Fear twisted my gut as a tremor wracked my body.

He couldn't have, could he?

I surged to my feet and grabbed my empty pack, stuffing it with anything I could reach.

Despite the lack of a plan, I knew one thing for certain.

I would find Cadence, and I would bring her home.

Acknowledgments

First and foremost, to my readers — thank you!

Thank you for taking a chance on Bonded Chaos and sharing Cadence and Ryker's journey with me. Your support and enthusiasm for my books means everything to me. Whether this is your first book of mine or one of many, I am truly grateful.

To my incredible beta readers — Sherrin, Alexa, Bec, and Brandi, your feedback, insights, and encouragement helped shape this book into what it is today. Your willingness to dive into an early draft and share your thoughts made all the difference. Thank you for your time, honesty, and support.

To my ARC readers — whether you loved it, hated it or found yourself somewhere in between, I appreciate the time dedicated to sharing your honest thoughts and feelings. Thank you!

To my family — thankyou for believing in me, even on the days when I doubted myself. Your unwavering encouragement, patience, and love have been my foundation. This book exists because of you.

Writing may be a solitary process, but I have never been alone in this. Thank you all for being part of this journey.

Much love,
K.J. Johnson
xx

About the author

K.J. Johnson is a fantasy and romance indie author who writes about headstrong heroines and morally grey men.

K.J. Johnson's debut novel, A Heart of Fire and Flame, is book one of the Fire and Flame series.

After a lifelong obsession with reading and escaping into different worlds where anything is possible, she decided to let her imagination run wild and penned her debut novel - A Heart of Fire and Flame.

K.J. Johnson enjoys writing romance of the darker persuasion, and you can expect plenty of spice, but check your morality at the door because it won't survive the ride.

Also by K. J. Johnson

In the realm of Aetherian, not everything is as it seems.

Dive into an adventure where dragons soar, hidden magic is awakened, and deadly secrets lurk in the shadows, in this dark Rumpelstiltskin retelling.

Turn the page for a sneak peek at the gripping first book, *A Heart of Fire and Flame*, book one in the *Fire & Flame series*!

A Heart of Fire and Flame

PROLOGUE

The heavy wooden door was slightly ajar, allowing the light from the lantern to spill into the hallway, illuminating the figures within. Their shadows reached high on the stone walls, making them appear ominous and imposing.

"The coin covered the first infantry, the maps the second. If you require further aid, you know my price," a crisp, deep voice announced from within the room.

I froze where I stood on the precipice of the threshold. I knew that voice. That voice always sent a shiver of fear racing down my spine.

"You're asking too much," the other man hissed.

My husband.

I inhaled a sharp breath and stepped closer, peering into the room. My Husband had his back to me, so I could see his broad shoulders heaving with the effort to contain his emotions. His long, copper hair hung in waves down his back, swaying as he shook his head in anger.

A pair of striking blue eyes met and locked with mine over his shoulder. "That is my price," he said coolly, without releasing me from his gaze. Tattoos snaked up his throat, disappearing into his shoulder-length, snow-colored hair. His face was a work of fine artistry, with his chiseled jaw and light stubble, a straight, symmetrical nose, and eyes so captivating you could lose yourself in their blue depths. When I looked into those eyes, however, I saw the blackened soul beneath. The promise of cruelty and suffering.

My husband curled his hands into fists at his side as he weighed his options. After a long pause, my husband exhaled a shaky breath and replied, "As you say." His shoulders slumped with his words, defeat evident in his tone.

Those blue eyes remained locked on me as they sparkled with victory, and a small smirk tipped up the corner of his mouth. Shadows began to swirl in the space between the men, and then, just like a whisper in the wind, he was gone, disappearing in the darkness. Dread settled in my stomach and the air in the room seemed suddenly stifling.

I rushed forward, grabbing my husband's arm and turning him to face me. His emerald green eyes widened in surprise and then narrowed in suspicion.

"Eavesdropping on your King are you, wife," he bit out in annoyance.

He scratched at his short beard, the same rich color as his hair, as he looked down at me. It was one of his tells, something he did often when trying to conceal his agitation. There was something else there, too. A weariness that crinkled the corner of his eyes and dipped his copper eyebrows. His head dropped, and my feeling of dread only intensified as it spread throughout my body.

"Atticus, what have you done?" I said in a strained whisper.

"What I had to," he replied, turning away from me, no longer willing to meet my gaze.

Dread turned to desperation as I shook his enormous frame and shouted, "Tell me!"

After a long pause, he looked back at me, his face reflecting his misery. I gasped, anticipating the blow he was about to deliver.

Atticus schooled his features, squared his shoulders, and took a steadying breath.

The King had returned.

"I have... arranged our daughter's betrothal, Clementine."

I felt the words like a physical blow, and I staggered back.

"Once she has come of age, Harlowe will wed the King of Netheran. In return, Kieran will continue to support our war effort, and through their union, we will achieve an unbreakable alliance between our kingdoms."

A strangled cry escaped my lips. I felt my stomach sinking, and my legs on the verge of collapsing.

Fear, grief, despair, and hopelessness slammed into me, overwhelming me all at once. My precious, tiny daughter. Only five days old and already I had failed to protect her. To keep her safe from harm.

He... he had promised my newborn daughter to that... to that monster.

Fury overtook me, and my hand darted out in front of me, slapping my husband across the face. Hard.

"HOW COULD YOU?" I roared.

My anger was a palpable energy as it filled the room. Before I registered he had even moved, Atticus had gripped both my hands in his and had pulled me flush against his broad, rigid chest.

"You want to strike me, Clementine? Go ahead. I understand you are upset, so hit me, scream at me, punish me if you must," he gritted out between clenched teeth. "But when you are done, it's over. We will not speak of this again. Some may seek to harm our daughter if they discover her role in the alliance."

We locked eyes, breathing heavily in the silence. Tears filled my vision and I let the sobs overtake me. His eyes softened, and he tucked me against his chest, patting my hair in a soothing gesture.

"I am King, Clementine," he whispered. "We cannot sustain an indefinite war on three fronts. It is what they are counting on. I bear the responsibility for every life in this kingdom. Kieran's alliance is crucial for our people's salvation."

I was unable to respond. Sobs continued to wrack my body. I had heard the stories about Kieran. Everyone had. He ruled his kingdom with an iron fist. Known to be cruel and abusive. Especially towards those who dared to share his bed.

I didn't want that life for my daughter.

Atticus continued speaking, but I heard none of it. My fear overpowered me; crippling me. As my sobs receded, he held me at arm's length to look me over. His brows furrowed for a moment and then smoothed. He gave a subtle nod as if acknowledging an unspoken question.

"You must not mention this to anyone, Clementine. Harlowe will not know she is betrothed. We will teach her what it means to be the heir to this kingdom. To be a ruler. With time, she will learn to prioritize her people's needs over her own. Only after that will we disclose to her what transpired tonight."

I was incapable of giving him the confirmation he was seeking, so I said nothing.

Sighing, Atticus straightened and turned towards the door.

"She will understand," he whispered to the silence enveloping the room as if begging it to whisper its agreement in return.

He turned and reached out his hand, saying, "Come, wife. Let us put this night behind us." Taking his hand, I let him lead me out of the room and down the darkened hallway.

Just as we rounded the corner, I peered back towards the open door, the light still glowing faintly from the lantern within. There would be no forgetting this night. Not for me. It would serve as a constant reminder that I failed in the one duty I swore to uphold above all others.

The duty of a mother.

Turning back towards my husband, I studied his profile in the small glimmer of moonlight sneaking in through the windows. He was deep in thought, his eyes strained as he battled his own thoughts within the confines of his mind.

No.

There would be no forgetting this night for either of us.

We were bound to this night and its consequences. The consequences that my precious infant daughter had been dammed pay in time.

Oh Harlowe, how will you ever forgive us?

Social Media

Connect with me on social media:

Instagram: @authork.j.johnson
TikTok: @authork.j.johnson
Facebook: Author K.J. Johnson

Or subscribe to my newsletter:
https://kjjohnsonbooks.com/newsletter

www.ingramcontent.com/pod-product-compliance
Lightning Source LLC
Chambersburg PA
CBHW070611310726
48982CB00001B/49